A Passage
Through Darkness

A Passage Through Darkness

Two Bestselling Novels Complete in One Volume

Berlin Encounter

Istanbul Express

T. DAVIS BUNN

Inspirational Press • New York

First Inspirational Press edition published in 1999.

Inspirational Press
A division of BBS Publishing Corporation
386 Park Avenue South
New York, NY 10016

Inspirational Press is a registered trademark of BBS Publishing Corporation.

Published by arrangement with Bethany House Publishers.

Library of Congress Catalog Card Number: 99-71879

ISBN: 0-88486-254-2

Printed in the United States of America.

Contents

I
Berlin Encounter

This book is dedicated to

Patricia Bunn

and

E. Lee Bunn

with love

And to

Jeff and Lisa Jarema

*With love and heartfelt
best wishes for a
joyful life together*

Chapter One

THE LEAD PLANE rocked its wings once, twice, but no voice cut through the radio static. There was too much risk of being overheard to speak unless there was an emergency. And if there was an emergency, they were all goners anyway.

The big Halifax bomber then lifted its wings toward the moonless night sky, and the pilot of Jake Burnes's glider jammed back the release catch. There was a loud *thunk* as the cable jolted from its hook, and a shudder ran through the glider as they caught the tow plane's parting downdraft. Then the bomber disappeared into the night sky, and the loudest noises were the glider's creaking frame and the wind.

Their glider was an enormous British Horsa, designed to transport either a full squad of heavily armed troops or a small tank. Jake glanced behind him, saw that the two trucks and their unmarked bundles were riding steady. Behind the load, all was empty shadows and rushing wind. He turned back to the glider's narrow windows, squinted out, saw nothing but gathering rain droplets. They were flying through clouds.

The glider jerked violently. Jake gripped his seat with white-knuckle panic. The plane seesawed, the wooden frame groaning with protest. But nothing gave.

Jake glanced at the pilot seated next to him. The man remained utterly unconcerned. But Jake took little comfort in the pilot's calm. He had already learned that glider pilots had their nerves surgically removed during training.

"Ten minutes," the man said, his voice a casual high-class British drawl. "Best strap in."

They escaped from the clouds, but the droplets only grew larger. This was what the powers that be had wanted, a rainy night with low-lying clouds. That way, though the tow plane's mighty engines would be heard, spotting would be impossible. Their exact landing point was relatively unimportant because no one would be there to meet them. All they needed was a flat and isolated field.

Jake squinted through the rain-blurred windscreen, tried hard not to let his fear take over. How the pilot was supposed to find a landing field in these conditions had never been fully explained.

The Horsa transport glider had been used in various World War II battles, including the D-Day invasion. That had been Jake's first thought when he heard how his mission was to begin, and the knowledge had stifled his protests a little. His younger brother, his last living relative, had died in the assault on Omaha Beach, and even that minimal connection left Jake feeling a little closer to the family he still sorely missed. The glider was canvas-covered wood with only the most rudimentary of controls, built as cheaply as possible. Which made perfect sense. Transport gliders were seldom used more than once.

Jake grimaced as another rain-swept gust buffeted their glider. He wished he had protested after all.

"Here we are," the pilot shouted over the wind. "Just the ticket."

Jake leaned forward and searched as hard as he could, saw only faint patches of shadows. "Shouldn't we check closer down and make sure?"

"Nonsense," the pilot retorted loudly, and nosed the giant glider downward. "That field is level as a cricket pitch. Couldn't ask for a more delightful spot."

Jake saw that further argument was useless. He gripped an overhead guide wire with one hand and his seat with the other, braced his feet, and sent a frantic prayer lofting upward.

An endless moment of rushing wind and drumming rain and jerking, jouncing downward flight, then shadows coalesced into tight squares that looked far too small to ever catch and safely hold a plane like theirs. Down farther, leveling and pulling back and nosing up and slowing more, and Jake had a sudden notion that he might actually live through this after all.

Then a tree appeared out of nowhere, reached out great shadow-limbs, and neatly tore off one wing.

The glider hit the ground almost level, then the remaining wing dug into the earth and wrenched off with the sound of screaming timber and ripping canvas. The plane went into a gentle sideways skid, held upright by the weight of its cargo. The Horsa dug a deep furrow in the boggy soil, as forward progress was gradually braked by whipping through a field of ripening wheat.

Then they stopped.

Jake looked over at the pilot, took his first full-sized breath since the nose had pointed downward, and laughed.

The pilot, a jaunty ace with sunburned cheeks and a sidewise grin, replied, "I think that went rather well."

Jake unclenched his death's grip. "At least we're alive."

"Precisely." The pilot snapped his belt, stood, stretched his back, said, "I suppose we'd best be moving along, then."

"Right behind you."

Even though it was early June, the rain that sluiced through the two great gaping holes in the fuselage was bitterly cold. Jake kept his flight jacket zipped up tight to his collar as he set his shoulder alongside the pilot's and strained to open the loading door. But their landing had knocked the portal off its hinges and jammed it tight. Jake heaved with all his might and strained until he felt he was about to blow a gasket, but the door did not budge.

Finally the pilot leaned back and took a gasping breath. "Rather a bother, that."

"What about—" Jake stopped, tensed, and listened. For a moment, all he heard was the sound of rain drumming on taut canvas. Then there it was again. Voices shouting from a distance.

The pilot hissed, "Is that German?"

"Can't tell." He strained, listened further, said, "Maybe. Maybe not. Could be Russian."

"Then it is time, as they say, to scarper." The pilot leaped for the rear truck. "Only one shot here," he said. "If your motor doesn't catch, you come in with me. I'll do likewise."

Jake nodded, climbing aboard the front truck. Just what he liked in a jam, to find his back watched by a man who knew how to think on his feet. He found the starter button, pumped the gas pedal, turned, and when the pilot gave him a thumbs up, he fired the engine.

The motor whirred, grumbled, and roared to life.

Even above the pair of racing engines, Jake could hear voices rising to shouts of alarm. He gave no time to thought, however. No time. He raced his engine once more, unsure what the pilot had in mind, but at this point ready for anything.

The pilot revved his motor to full bore, then jammed his truck into reverse and rammed it straight through the back of the plane.

Without a moment for caution, Jake followed suit.

There was a rending, scraping shriek, then a moment of sailing through air, then a squishy thud. Tires spun, engine roared, wheels found purchase and propelled the vehicle in a tight circle. In reverse. At a pace far too fast for driving through a field of wheat at two o'clock in the morning.

Jake braked, shouted at the gears when he could not find first, looked up in time to see the second great truck come barreling out of the night headed straight for his door. The pilot managed to spin his vehicle out of range at the very last moment, sent a cheery "Beg your pardon" across the distance, and disappeared into the field.

Jake revved his engine and followed suit.

Only to find himself plowing straight through a squad of soldiers.

He would have been hard put to say who was more startled, he at the sight of these armed men appearing out of nowhere, or they at the vision of a roaring truck parting the wheat and barreling down on them without lights. Rifles were tossed to the heavens as soldiers dived in every conceivable direction. Jake jammed the pedal to the floor and kept right on going.

The field gave way to a rutted road which he found and lost and found again, in the meantime dismantling the corner of what, given the squawks of protest his passage caused, he could only assume was a chicken coop. He did not stop to investigate.

It was only when he was a good hour down the road that Jake finally decided it was time to put on his lights, slow down, and try to find out exactly where he was.

Chapter Two

SIT DOWN, COLONEL. The hard-eyed gentleman with whom Jake met two weeks before his departure had worn civilian clothes with the ease of a courtier. "I understand you speak German."

Jake took the offered chair, knew immediately that he was dealing with one of the new types. Quentin Helmsley was a man who had not served in the war, who knew how to fire a gun because he had studied a book and practiced at a firing range. "Some."

"Records I have here say it's more than that."

"What records would those be?"

The man simply patted the closed folder under his hands. "Three and a half years of German at college before signing up, just one semester shy of a degree, isn't that right? Then your operations at the Badenburg garrison after the war's end showed near fluency. Quite impressive, I must say, your initiative to stop the cholera epidemic. Understand you're finally to receive a medal for that one. Rightly so."

If Jake's months of training had taught him anything, it was that these nonmilitary types treated information like jewels, to be treasured and displayed only at the right moment. "Showed fluency according to whom?"

The man ignored his question. "I take it you have been following the news lately, Colonel?"

"Some." Force fed, more like. Jake's recent training had been haphazard in many respects, but not in this one. Daily seminars, each led by masters in the field of international assessment, focused on teaching a select few to see the globe as a continually evolving entity. Political trends and economic interactions and military power flowed like the wind, sometimes quiet and stable, other times raging with hurricane force. Jake was being taught to read these earthly elements like a weatherman watched the sky, predicting where the next tempest would erupt, being there to observe and prepare. The greatest threat now facing them was of Soviet domination in Eastern Europe. The wartime alliance with Russia had collapsed into mutual suspicion, and the world's balance of power was shifting dramatically.

"You are one of the highest ranking officers we are bringing in at this point," the gentleman said, switching gears. It was another action Jake had observed, this desire to keep their quarry off balance at all times. It did not matter that he and Jake were on the same side. The nature of the business required reactions that were so ingrained as to be automatic. This was one of the things that bothered Jake most about his training. He liked his reflexes just the way they were.

"There is some debate as to whether our man in Paris made an error in offering you an administrative post. You see, we prefer to bring our top men up from within."

Administrative. Jake kept his face impassive, but grimaced internally. You chain me to a desk, bub, and I'm out of here.

"You were scheduled to return to Washington for six months of local, shall we say, orientation. We have been wondering if you might be willing to put this off for a bit of field duty." The man straightened, as though preparing for an argument. "Strictly off the record, Colonel, a successful stint in the field would improve your position considerably with the boys back home."

Jake hid his growing interest. "So what do they call the action I saw before you offered me this job?"

"*Independent* field action." His face showed a flicker of distaste. "Quite successful, such as it was. This has swayed many in your favor. But not all."

Including you, Jake thought, his feelings hardening to genuine dislike.

"A stint as a field operative under standard supervision would mean a great deal to the fence-sitters, I assure you."

"Sounds reasonable," Jake said, trying to put a reluctant note to his voice. In truth, the thought of spending six months playing trained seal for the bigwigs back in Washington held about as much appeal as brushing his teeth with battery acid.

They were seated in a grand country estate in the county of Surrey, some thirty miles outside London. Through the tall window behind the man's desk, Jake had a fine view of rolling countryside, the green broken only by a single church steeple poking through distant trees. During most of the war, the country estate had served as a U.S. command post. After D-Day it had been left more or less empty. Now it saw duty as a training-and-admin center for

Allied operatives engaged in the infant science of intelligence gathering. The manor house itself was huge, with two wings containing fifty bedrooms each, and a central portion longer than a football field. The Americans had been assigned two floors in the west wing and used hardly half the space.

Jake found it comforting to observe that work here seemed to proceed in the same haphazard way as it had in the army, making progress almost despite itself. NATO was now up and running, at least on paper, and as part of this show of unity, operatives were now being trained jointly. At least, that was what was supposed to be happening. In truth, Jake saw little of his counterparts from other nations except in class, and clearly some of them had been given strict orders to keep all other nationals at arm's length. They treated a simple hello as a threat to national security.

Jake did not mind keeping his distance. Although the majority of his fellow trainees were only a few years younger than he, most had missed the war. He found almost all of them, including the Americans, naive and overly serious. Their eager earnestness left him feeling like some crusty, battle-weary soldier. He had stopped wearing his uniform. The display of medals tended to halt traffic in the halls.

His teachers came from every country in western Europe; this was the primary reason that Jake relished his time here. They were older and had seen duty of one sort or another, many transferring from frontline service to intelligence and back again several times. They treated Jake as an equal and opened their vast stores of wisdom to him without reserve.

Idly Jake fingered the invitation in his pocket and allowed his mind to wander away from this frosty fellow and his maneuverings. The invitation had arrived that morning, engraved and embossed with a floral design, requesting the honor of his presence and that of his wife Sally at the Marseille wedding of Major Pierre Servais and Mademoiselle Jasmyn Coltrane. Jake already knew of the upcoming nuptials, of course, since he was to be best man. Sally had pasted stars around the date on their calendar at home, a not-too-subtle reminder that under no circumstances was Jake to let his new responsibilities come between him and his friends.

One excellent aspect of this new duty was being able to see his wife at work as well as at home. He and Sally had been married just over a year now, but a glimpse of her in the grand hallways still caused something to catch in his throat.

After heartrending months of separation, a breathless reunion, and a romantic engagement in Paris, they had returned to Karlsruhe—where Jake was commander of the U.S. garrison—for the wedding. From there they had expected a quick move to England for Jake's new intelligence position. But the transfer had not been as swift as planned, for the army had proved most reluctant to release him from his command. Jake had only caught faint wisps of the smoke, but it appeared that the battle had raged all the way back to the Pentagon before a final broadside from War Department level had cleared him for action.

Sally had found an excellent posting right there within NATO Intelligence headquarters, working for the top British administrator. A husband and wife working within the same operation was certainly not standard operating procedure, but Sally's top-secret clearance and her experience with general staff made her a prize beyond measure. They had rented a small country cottage five miles from the base and filled every nook and gable with the joy of their newfound love.

Jake's attention returned to the man behind the desk when he realized he was being asked a question. Quentin Helmsley had recently arrived from Washington. The senior staff either treated him with great respect or quiet disdain, depending on what they thought of the power he represented. He was asking, "By any chance, Colonel, have you traveled the region of Mecklenburg-Vorpommern?"

"Never set foot in it, so far as I know."

"A pity," Helmsley said. "We have had, ah, several setbacks in this area recently."

Jake searched his memory, located the German state as lying just east of Hamburg, the northernmost state in the Russian sector. "You mean you've lost your local men."

The fellow did not deny it. "Stalin's edicts have proven to be just as harsh in practice as they sound in rhetoric. This is causing no end of distress throughout the regions now under his control, especially Eastern Europe. Entire towns are being awakened in the middle of the night, herded into trucks, and driven off, never to be seen again."

Jake nodded. This he had already heard. Firsthand accounts of Stalin's mass resettlement operations were now filtering out to the West.

"These policies are now being applied in increasingly harsh measure to the Russian-controlled region of Germany," Helmsley went on, "and the Russians have been setting up puppet regimes. This process was formerly limited to the local level, which did not bother us very much. But it is now being extended to the establishment of regional and even a quasi-national administration. And all of the new officials, so far as we can tell, are German Communists who either fled Hitler's Germany and hid in Russia or spent the war years locked in concentration camps. The majority of these returning Communists see all the people under their control as having sold out to Hitler and thereby responsible for their own persecution. They *hate* their own countrymen, or many of them do, and use their new powers with truly brutal force."

This was news. Despite his recently acquired caution, Jake found himself growing interested.

Helmsley sensed this and gave a small smile of satisfaction. "It also appears that there is soon to be a resettlement of German scientists whom Russia finds useful. And this is what concerns us. There is a town in Mecklenburg-Vorpommern called Rostock, about thirty kilometers north of the capital, Schwerin. It was there that Hitler's scientists developed the most sophisticated rockets in the world."

Rockets. Jake gave a single small nod. Of course. It would have to be something big to risk going in where other men had already been lost.

"Several German scientists escaped from Rostock just before the war," Helmsley went on. "Through our contacts, we were able to get several messages to those who remained. As a result, we have managed to entice two of the remaining experts to join us."

"You want me to risk my neck," Jake said, "to rescue a couple of Nazi scientists?"

"One of them is a Nazi," Helmsley admitted with a wintry smile. "Former Nazi, in any case. And needing their minds does not mean that we must necessarily like them, Colonel."

The idea of going in to rescue an enemy, even a former enemy, unsettled him mightily. And this was a surprise. His work at Karlsruhe and before that at Badenburg had brought him in contact with more than one former Nazi, and he thought he had put the old feelings behind him. But now, abruptly, Jake found his Christian principles and his awareness of new political realities doing battle with a vision of his brother lying dead on the Normandy beaches. "And they really have information we don't have?"

"I assure you," Helmsley replied. "We would not go to all this trouble unless it were absolutely necessary. From what we have gathered, this group has managed to forge a full generation ahead of us in rocket research. All of London bears witness to the effectiveness of their flying bombs." Helmsley inspected him a long moment, then demanded, "We need these two men, Colonel. Will you go in?"

"Go in?" Despite the inner turmoil, he did not have to think it over. "Sure."

There was an instant of hesitation, as though Helmsley was finally forced to see Jake as something other than just a potential operative to be swayed to his purpose. "I was informed that your abilities were matched by a capacity to think on your feet."

Jake had difficulty keeping the surge of excitement from showing. No need to let the guy know he'd have paid a year's wages to work in the field again. "What can you tell me about the place where they're kept?"

"Operations will brief you on details. It appears, however, that we were never able to do this particular facility much damage with our bombing campaigns. Part of your objective will be to, shall we say, rattle the Russians' scientific cage a little." Helmsley tapped a nervous finger on the closed file, then went on, "I must tell you that having several of our men disappear has troubled us. We cannot be sure, but it appears that they were not apprehended as spies, simply picked up with the local population and carted off to goodness knows where. But we cannot wait for them to return, Colonel. We must bring the two key scientists out now. Time has become of the essence."

"You think the Russians might move them back into their own territory," Jake surmised.

"What your other supporters have said of you appears to be correct," he said, the look of respect deepening. "There is one other thing. I don't suppose you would mind carrying in a load of contraband, would you?"

"I guess not. What did you have in mind?"

The glimmer was replaced by cynical humor as he replied, "Bibles."

Chapter Three

*J*AKE WAS DRIVING slowly enough to spot the disused forest track and pull off in one smooth motion. He saw no other headlights on the lonely pre-dawn road, and he had not passed a house in ten minutes. Still, he pulled the truck into a tight nest formed by a dozen fir trees, then snaked back through the woods on foot. When he reached the road he squatted in the cold darkness, rain dropping from the hood of his poncho, and searched the shadows. He waited and watched, no reason to hurry except his own discomfort. The war had taught him that errors made in haste sometimes left no escape except death.

To keep him company as he waited in the wet woods, straining to ensure that none of the trees or bushes grew legs and approached, he thought of Sally. She had refused to see him off at the airfield, and he had not objected. He had no desire whatsoever to share their leave-taking with anyone, much less a bunch of gawking military types.

Jake's battle-trained reflexes had returned after almost two years of disuse, permitting him to reset his internal clock in anticipation of night action and to sleep the afternoon away. He had awakened toward dusk to find her stretched out on the pillow next to his, watching him with that calm, strong gaze which was hers and hers alone.

"I hate to see you go," were the first words he heard upon awakening. "Just thinking about it leaves me feeling like a part of me has gone missing. But I've come to see something as I've been lying here. Something really important."

Jake rolled over and faced her fully. He resisted the urge to touch her, knowing she did not want it. Not just then. "Tell me."

"Maybe I knew it already. Maybe I saw it when I was back in the States shepherding those generals around and you were back here. But it wasn't clear to me then. I just knew my life wasn't complete without you. Now, all of a sudden, I understand."

She propped her head up with one hand and said in a voice that was soft and yielding, yet utterly practical. "It had to be you, Jake. All my life I've been waiting to meet the man who rides the wind, the man who travels the paths that no one else even wants to find. The man filled with faith and mystery and strength and action." Her voice quivered, but she forced herself to finish, "And danger."

"Sally—"

"Wait, let me finish. I knew you had the strength and that special focus that is all your own. This is what appealed to me from the very beginning. But I've been lying here, waiting for you to wake up and hold me and then get up and walk through that door, and now I understand that this really is part of it. Now and for the rest of our lives." She shifted, made uncomfortable by the raw truth. "Oh, I don't know if you'll stay with this work. I don't really care, to tell you the truth. But I know that you'll always find something that requires more from you than most other people are willing to give.

Jake found himself unable to speak. He just lay and watched her and marveled at her ability to see to the very depths of him.

"This is who you are. Living life to the fullest for you means living beyond the borders, going into the places where others are afraid to walk, maybe even to see. Only now there are two of us, Jake." Her eyes welled up at this, and a single tear escaped to descend in gentle sorrow across her cheek. "You aren't alone anymore."

"I'll be careful," he whispered, and reached across to catch the tear. It rested on his finger, an incredible gift of her love.

"That's not enough, Jake. You were always careful. That's why you're still here. But now you need to remember that you carry two hearts with you everywhere you go." She reached for him then, pressing her entire length to him, melding to his form and holding him close. "Our two lives are woven together now, my beloved. Two destinies follow in each footstep you take. So you've got to take more than care. You must promise to return."

She drew back just a little, to meet his eyes again. "I will learn to let you go with love and confidence. But you must always return. Always."

That same evening, when Jake had returned to headquarters to complete his preparations, he had been approached by one of the senior administrators. Harry Grisholm was another American, whose misshapen body disguised a rapier-keen mind. He had started as a field operative, but a bad night-landing in

Holland had shattered hips and legs so badly that neither could be completely corrected. But instead of returning to a desk job and well-earned honors, Harry had seen out the rest of the war coordinating clandestine radio operations throughout northern Holland.

He walked with a rolling lurch, his oversized head bobbing like a poorly strung marionette. Months of agony had etched deep lines across his forehead and out from his eyes and mouth. Yet his cheerful demeanor had altered the creases into permanent smile lines. "What did you think of our Mister Helmsley?"

"Made me wonder if maybe I hadn't made a mistake taking this job," Jake replied.

"He and his kind are the wave of the future, Jake. Best you get used to them."

"This is supposed to cheer me up?"

"Listen, my friend. In our business, we must be the ultimate realists. Our very existence depends upon it." He fastened Jake with a piercing ice-blue gaze. "He has been shaped by his background just as you have been shaped by yours. Both have pluses and minuses, my level-headed friend. He would never make a field operative and would most certainly never handle men very well. His is the kind who would vastly prefer to fire every human being in the service and strive for ever more sophisticated electronic devices."

"So?"

"So a service such as our own will never survive and do its job when given over to people like this," Harry said patiently. "Field operatives are the service's infantry, often maligned but always needed. It is only through the eyes and ears of trusted men there on the spot that we shall ever truly understand what our electronic devices have gathered."

He reached up and thumped Jake's chest. "At the same time, my friend, you would never be happy doing our man Helmsley's job. Never. Not in a million years would you spend your days running from office to office, passing on just the right information to just the right ear, making sure that your budget remains intact, sitting through day after day of committee meetings, trying to advise presidents and their aides about international crises which have not yet happened and thus are not urgent in their eyes—"

"A nightmare," Jake declared. "I'd rather walk across a field of live coals in my bare feet."

"Precisely. What our man Helmsley fails to realize, just as it has escaped you up to now, is that you need each other. You *complement* each other." Harry stopped and waited, making sure his words were sinking in. "The world is made up of a myriad of peoples. You will do far better looking for those who share your objectives than trying to live only with those who see the world through your perspective. And once you learn that lesson, you will need to teach it to the equally stubborn Helmsley."

"That makes sense," Jake agreed.

"You're most welcome." Harry gave him a frosty smile which did not descend from his eyes. "Would you accept a further bit of advice?"

"From you? Always."

"Your orders and your instructions have been made extra complex, I am sorry to say, because a few of these fellows here feel threatened by your record, and would just as soon see you fail."

"I thought maybe something like that was going on." Jake snapped the catches on the leather satchel he had been packing. "Still, they all seemed to make good sense."

"They make good sense to you *here*." Harry's eyes were keen with the strength of hard-earned wisdom. "Take it from me, Jake. A successful field operative is one who has the sense to divert from orders when the situation merits it." He patted Jake's arm. "And a good field operative, my friend, is one who survives."

Twenty minutes of searching shadows to either side of the rain-drenched road satisfied Jake that the coast was as clear as it would ever get. Twice he had watched army convoys trundle by, but neither had appeared to be on alert. The woods had remained still and wet and empty. Jake returned to his truck just as dawn began to push away the grudgingly stubborn night. He felt chilled to the bone.

While water heated on a paraffin stove, Jake began the job of changing his own and the truck's identity.

First he stripped off the truck's green army-issue top, which proved not to be made of canvas at all, but rather of flimsy parachute silk. He then peeled off the green sidings, which were not wood and metal, but burlap stiffened with multiple layers of paint and nailed into place. The U.S. Army stars disappeared from the truck doors, as did the army license plates and stenciling across front and back. Finally the camouflaging was peeled off the hood and cabin top and the rear loading platform.

Despite the low-lying clouds, the argument had gone, there was still a chance that their landing would be observed. So both trucks were to depart from the landing site declaring to all the world that they were indeed standard army issue.

Jake pulled the shovel from the back of the truck, walked to a clearing beyond the trees, and began to dig. By the time the hole was deep enough, he was sweating and breathing hard. He returned to the truck, stripped off the sergeant's uniform in which he had traveled, and dressed from the clothes in his satchel. He then buried both the uniform and the truck's false covers. He strew pine needles and sticks over the fresh earth, then stepped back and surveyed the scene. It would not stand a close inspection, but it would probably do.

He returned to the truck and his breakfast, standard fare for that region—chicory coffee, hard cheese, day-old bread, a couple of wizened apples. As he ate, Jake inspected himself in the truck's cracked side mirror. What he saw made him grin with satisfaction.

The clothes matched the truck's new identity, that of a small-time trader. Jake's cheap black-leather jacket crinkled and squeaked with each movement. His black turtleneck and dark shapeless trousers were matched by his three-day growth and a haircut which had raised shrieks of dismay from Sally the day he had brought it home. He looked shrewd, hard, tired, and thoroughly dishonest.

The truck looked in wretched shape, at least unless someone did a careful inspection under the hood. The sides were scarred and weather-beaten, the canvas top so patched that it was hard to tell what the original color had been, the front end battered to a paintless pulp. It looked like a thousand other trucks trundling through Germany's war-ravaged landscape, dregs discarded by retreating armies, scarred by thousands of hard-fought miles.

But the muddy tires were the best that money could buy, the tank three times normal size, the suspension perfect. The gears meshed like a Swiss watch, and the well-muffled motor was tuned and tightened until it could easily push the truck to over a hundred miles an hour, even in four-wheel drive.

Not to mention the fact that spaced over the truck's frame were two secret compartments designed to escape even the most careful of inspections.

As Jake repacked his meager utensils, he gave a passing thought to the British pilot. The man had been ordered to round up four of their remaining operatives, people considered to be in the worst danger of being resettled and lost forever. He had more than nine hundred kilometers to cover behind Soviet lines, with the Russian army patrols constantly on the move. Jake did not envy him the challenge.

As he started the engine and pulled out the compass concealed beneath the dash, Jake had a fleeting image of the pilot thinking the same thing about Jake's assignment.

Chapter Four

THE JOURNEY TO Rostock went so well that Jake found himself mildly disappointed.

Their landing zone had turned out to be a thin strip of farmland separating the dangerously sandy Baltic shoreline from the hilly forests and industrial towns of inner Mecklenburg-Vorpommern. Jake trundled down an empty brick-and-mud country lane with a carefully battered road map in his lap. The rain had lessened with the dawn, and the wind had freshened to gusty squalls.

He drove slowly, looking for what should be the turnoff to Rostock. Jake squinted down at the map, felt the dismay of a lost traveler. He had a fleeting image of perhaps wandering along some uncharted road, the glider having been set free a thousand miles off course and depositing them in a land so far from where he was supposed to be that the map was utterly useless.

Then in the distance he spotted a great metal crane, the sort used for unloading ships, and suddenly the map came into focus. The road was identified, his target pinpointed. A few miles later he crossed a rise, and the port of Rostock spread out beneath him.

The harbor was a mere shadow of its former self. Four of the five giant loading cranes had been reduced to hulks of steel and slag. Of the dozen port buildings, none had their roofs intact, three had been totally destroyed, and another four were so pitted and scarred that he could watch men moving the pallets about inside. Roads and rails surrounding the port were studded with shell holes. The ships waiting patiently at dockside appeared to be in equally bad shape. Jake spent a long moment inspecting the scene, then gunned his motor and drove on.

His way took him down and around the city's western side, skirting the main roads and most activity. Still, what he saw depressed him. Little repair work appeared to be going on. Two and a half years after the war's end, and most of the damaged homes and factories still bore only the most basic reconstructions. The contrast with the frenetic activity surrounding every town and city in the western sectors was staggering.

Most bomb-splintered windows had been replaced with plywood or cardboard; Jake saw almost no glass. Crumbling walls had been propped up with uncured tree trunks still bearing leaves and limbs. Roads were pocked with shell holes filled with dirt and gravel or simply left in their dismal state. Wires and cables remained strewn everywhere, which more than likely meant that electricity had not been generally restored. Jake found this remarkable. The entire region around Karlsruhe, where he had served, had returned to full power within a year of the peace settlement. How else were the factories to run, giving people jobs and the economy a chance to get back on its feet?

It was hard to tell much from the people. They looked grim, but so did most Germans. Five hard years of war, followed by total defeat, had left scars which would not fade so swiftly. But he had the impression that there was more hunger here than in the western sectors, more hardship, more despair.

And less traffic. Jake's was one of the few vehicles he saw upon the road which did not bear military markings. He saw only an occasional car, and the few civilian trucks he spotted looked as bad as his. So did the scattering of trams and buses, all stuffed to the point that passengers hung from the stairs and outer railings and children crammed onto the back runners.

The closer he drew to the town, the more stares he drew. Some looked with hostility, others with outright envy. Here was a truck. Privately owned. A man wealthy enough to have both transport and fuel and some reason for both.

He arrived at the unmarked crossing with vast relief at having escaped those hostile eyes and at not having passed a checkpoint yet. The longer he could remain unchecked, Jake reasoned, the less chance there would be of his being connected to the mysterious arrival of a British glider bearing two trucks with U.S. Army markings.

Jake stowed the map back under his seat. It was of no use to him now. This road and all that was yet to come had been committed to memory before he had left England.

Jake drove two miles farther and reached the last farm before entering the woods. He checked his watch and pulled off. His instructions were to arrive at the installation's outer gates precisely at noon. If not that day, then the next, or the day after. But only at noon.

Jake did not need to see the people to know that eyes were watching him. He climbed down, stretched his back, proceeded to make and eat an early lunch. Calm, casual, easygoing, but watchful. A trader operating on his own had every reason these days to seek a solitary lay-by before stopping.

Twenty minutes later the farmer finally stepped from behind his ramshackle barn. He stood for a long moment before walking slowly over, using a sharpened pitchfork as a staff. Jake turned and watched him approach, but did not stop eating. He returned the farmer's suspicious greeting, decided he might as well give his story one trial run before hitting the big time.

"You a trader?" The farmer tried for nonchalance, but his squinty gaze continually flitted toward the back flap.

"Feed and seeds," Jake replied, his tone laconic. "Some tools. Pots and pans. Boots."

"Boots," the man said, and glanced down at his own feet. His shoes were bound to his ankles with twine. Newspaper poked from holes at the toe. The squinty gaze rose and leveled on Jake. "Where you from?"

"Everywhere," Jake said, knowing his accent was rough, but hoping the instructors had been correct when they said he did not sound like an American. Americans tended to mangle the tones of other languages, they had told him. Jake had a careful ear, holding the tones as correct as he could. He sounded foreign, but not from any particular place. Dutch, perhaps. Or Hungarian who had learned Swiss German. Or Danish, except his coloring was too dark. "I've spent my whole life traveling, buying and selling."

Envy flashed across the farmer's seamed features. "Been here all my life. Watched the world come and go, I have. Trouble and woe, only things that have remained."

Jake grunted, figuring that a man who made his living off small-time deals would not have much time for the troubles of others. He reached into the back, carefully shielding the payload from the farmer's prying eyes, and drew forward one of the two sacks bearing boots. Both the canvas sacks and the boots themselves had been brought to England from the western sector of Germany, as had all the other manmade products.

Jake unleashed the neck catch of one bag and drew out samples of recovering Germany's workmanship. Each segment of the boots had been cut from different-colored leather, the stitching was irregular, the eyelets were uneven, and the soles were made of tire rubber. But from the farmer's expression Jake realized they were far better than anything he had been offered recently.

"We don't have money for boots," a woman's voice announced sharply.

The farmer did not look around as he accepted one of the boots, handed Jake the pitchfork, and raised one foot to compare the sizes. "The trader's got pans."

The woman took an involuntary step forward. "Took all our pots, they did. All of them."

"Been cooking on a coal griddle and a shovel blade," the farmer said, giving the second shoe a careful inspection. "*Ach du lieber*, I grow mighty tired of fry-grease."

Jake's only reaction was to reach back inside and heave close the nearest crate. He lifted the first handle, unwrapped the burlap used to keep the pots from rattling, hefted the great cooking-pot and said as he had been instructed, "These come dear."

The woman was unable to conceal her desire. The farmer inspected his wife and sighed in defeat, "How much for the boots and the pan?"

"We don't have money," the woman warned. "It's gone."

"We sell to the commissar," the farmer said, his eyes pleading, though simple pride kept it from his voice. "Have to. They pay in scrip. Lets us buy supplies, if there are any, which isn't often."

"All the farm is listed," the woman said bitterly, grasping the handle from Jake and clasping the pot to her chest. "Everything we own, or what's left. Every cow, every chicken, every tool. Can't let you have an animal."

Jake bit back the urge to give them the goods, said simply, "What can you trade?"

Thirty minutes later he drove away, feeling for the first time that he just might make this whole thing work. His tank was topped off with twenty liters of fuel siphoned from the farmer's worn-out tractor. The truck was sweetly perfumed by a quarter ring of homemade cheese and half a loaf of fresh-baked bread. Two jars of honey nestled within straw in his glove box, and on the seat beside him rode two dozen newly laid eggs.

Which was why, when he approached the sentry guarding the derelict control station and did not see his contact, he leaned from his window and said as casually as he could muster, "Got any need for fresh food?"

Before the soldier's evident hunger could descend from his eyes to his tongue, a second man stepped from the sentry house. This one was dressed in the blue uniform of the political officer. "What's this, what's this?"

Jake watched the soldier stiffen to attention, saw the disappointment which could not be masked. He made mental note of this as he slid from the cab. If soldiers at key installations were going hungry, things must indeed be bad. "Farmer up the road said I might find a buyer for some fresh goods."

"All produce is to be sold directly to the commissary and given out according to passbook regulations," the officer snapped. He squinted at Jake. "What was the farmer's name?"

"Didn't say I bought anything from him. Just got directions, is all." He cocked a thumb at the open door. "You want the stuff or not?"

The political officer jerked his head around the door, and his eyes widened. "Eggs!"

"Two dozen, fresh as they come," Jake said, enjoying himself despite the risk. Maybe he had a knack for the world of high finance, if this present line of work gave out. "You take them all, I'll make you a good deal."

The officer raised himself up to full height, a shrewd glint appearing in his eyes. "These are legally licensed eggs?"

"They're mine," Jake replied, an edge creeping to his voice. "And they can be yours if you've got anything to offer besides—"

"You made it, good, good!" His contact scuttled through the sentry point. "Herr Thalle, this is the trader I mentioned, the one with the tools!"

The political officer saw his hopes fading. Greed turned to sullen anger. "Not to mention unlicensed eggs."

The scientist wore a white lab coat turned gray with age and hand washing. He gave a false little laugh. "Ah, but what are a few eggs among comrades?"

"I could have him thrown in jail for such a crime."

"Yes, but then where would we be? You know we've been waiting almost six months for these tools." Sweat beaded his upper lip as he turned to Jake and demanded, "You have them?"

"I might," Jake drawled, his eyes still on the political officer. The man was an officious little puppet, all spit and polish in his bright blue uniform with the silver buttons and the ribbons on his lapel. "Then again, I might have stashed them up the road a ways. Until I could see what kind of reception I was going to have here."

"An excellent reception!" The dark-haired scientist positively burst with nervous bonhomie. "We have been looking out for you now for over a month, haven't we, Herr Thalle?"

"Even so," the officer grumbled, "I still say we have no cause to deal with common criminals."

"Then I'll be on my way," Jake said, and turned back toward the truck.

"No, no, please, wait!" Frantically the scientist grabbed at his sleeve, his spectacles sliding down his nose in the process. He let go of Jake long enough to readjust the glasses, then slid between Jake and the cab. The smile was still there, but slipping around the edges. "Perhaps a small gift, a token, to the good Herr Thalle would ease our way through this misunderstanding, yes?"

A little smirk painted itself on the officer's face as he replied, "Perhaps."

"A bribe, you mean." Jake felt his hackles rise at giving this petty troublemaker anything. Still, he was blocking Jake's way inside. Reluctantly Jake turned to the cab and brought out four eggs. And as he placed them in the man's hands he brought his face in close and said with quiet menace, "I think that should be more than enough, don't you?"

Something in Jake's gaze caused the man to take a single step back before replying, "Sentry!"

"Sir."

"Take his papers for inspection." The officer then wheeled about and retreated to the sentry building with as much firmness as he could muster.

Jake reached back inside the cab, took another four eggs, reached to the sentry, and said quietly, "My papers."

In his haste to take the eggs, the sentry almost dropped his rifle.

The scientist said, "The tools are very heavy. We will need to draw the truck up alongside the second entrance." When the sentry nodded without looking up from his prize, Jake shoved the scientist inside the cab, slid in beside him, slammed the door, and drove on.

"That was awful," the scientist said. "Why were you so rough on Herr Thalle?"

"No small-time trader is going to be an easy mark for a worm like that," Jake replied. He glanced over at the heavily perspiring scientist. "You are Doctor Rolf Grunner?"

"Yes. And you?"

"Jake Burnes. Colonel, NATO Intelligence."

"What has taken you so long, Colonel?"

"Had to set things up, then wait for the weather," Jake said succinctly. "Where to?"

"There, beside those green doors. We have been waiting almost a month. Hans, Dr. Hechter, he almost gave up hope. Things have been increasingly difficult in the laboratories. The rumors have been constant. Again yesterday we heard that they were taking us to a new facility. One somewhere in Kazakhstan, I think they said." The scientist pointed and said, "Stop here."

At first glance Jake understood why wartime bombing of the facility had been so ineffectual. The great metal doors did not open into buildings at all, but rather into cliffs that protruded from a steep-sided hill like buttresses from a great sand and rock vessel. The only exposed points were the outbuildings, several of which were blackened hulks. The concrete launching strip was also pocked with hastily repaired holes. Jake eased up to the set of crumbling concrete stairs, cut the motor, and let the scientist slide out.

"Bring help," Jake said laconically, scouting the area.

The scientist paused. "What?"

"The tools weigh a lot," Jake said. "Get help. Like maybe the other scientist."

"Oh. Yes. Of course."

"And the money," Jake reminded him. "And calm down."

The scientist gave him a dazed look from behind his spectacles, then disappeared inside. Jake walked around to the back, let down the tailgate, started heaving out the four bulkiest sacks from his cargo.

In moving the sacks, he noticed the well-hidden lever which opened the first of the hidden bays. It was recessed into the side of the hold and looked like nothing more than an extension of one of the canvas top guide-poles. Only if it was twisted in a certain way and then pushed out rather than back would it pop open. The door itself was hidden beneath layers of oil and grime and burlap. As Jake eased the first of the heavy sacks to the earth, he found himself thinking of what lay inside the bay, and of the conversation he had with Harry Grisholm after learning what he would be carrying.

"Bibles," Jake had repeated. The more he had thought of it, the less he had liked it. "Helmsley threw it out like he was offering the good little doggie a bone."

"It was a mistake," Harry affirmed. Harry was the only other professed Christian among the staff, another reason Jake enjoyed working with him so much. "But then again, he is not used to working with a believer. I'm sure it leaves him feeling uncomfortable. Suddenly he's faced with something that doesn't fit comfortably into his perspective."

Jake eased back and grinned. "How am I supposed to stay mad when you're agreeing with me like that?"

"The fact that you and I must learn to work with such people does not mean that I necessarily care for the man and his ways," Harry replied.

"I hated the way he used my faith," Jake went on, but without animosity. "Like it was just another point to stick in my file and bring out whenever it suited him."

"Listen to me, Jake." Harry sat up as far as his diminutive stature would allow. "You are being confronted with one of the basic problems of intelligence work. It attracts people whose dispositions make them enjoy manipulating both people and information. In some cases, I am not sure that they actually see so great a difference between the two. This is not new, Jake. I am sure that when Moses sent the young men to spy out the tribes inhabiting the Promised Land, there were some who saw it as the opportunity of a lifetime—not to do God's work, but to possess this knowledge and parlay it into personal power and status."

Jake took a seat across from Harry's chair. His friend's stunted legs barely reached the floor. "How do you stand it, Harry?"

"First of all, because I happen to believe in what I am doing. There *are* enemies out there. There *is* a need to do our work, and to do it well." Harry had the remarkable capacity to smile more broadly with his eyes alone than most people could with their entire face. "I have the feeling that you think the same way, Jake."

Jake thought it over, nodded slowly. "Maybe so."

"Then should we allow the discomfort of working with such people keep us from the job? Should we leave *any* field to people who do not hold to our own ideals? If we feel ourselves called to this work, should we ever permit another to turn us away?"

An imperious voice behind him demanded in lofty German tones, "And just what excuse do you have for keeping us waiting so long?"

Jake stiffened, eased himself up slowly, found himself facing a tall man perhaps ten years older than he. His neatly cropped hair was so blond as to be almost white, his eyes pure Aryan blue, his jaw strong, his nose lifted high enough that he might look down upon Jake, his left cheek bearing a well-healed scar. It was, Jake knew, the result of a saber duel, the required mark of courage within upper-class Prussian families. "Doctor Hans Hechter?"

"*Professor* Doctor Hechter," the imperious voice corrected.

"Colonel Jake Burnes, U.S. Army. Currently operating with NATO Intelligence."

The man's chin raised another notch, granting him the angle to stare down his nose at Jake. "You have not answered my question."

Jake's eyes narrowed. The guy was already getting under his skin. "Preparations took a while. Then we had to wait for the weather to cooperate."

"I do not find that a reasonable response," the man snapped. "Do you have any idea how greatly you have inconvenienced me? No, of course you do not. Well, Colonel, it has been positively horrid."

"You cannot imagine," Jake responded dryly, "how this news affects me."

The dark-haired scientist stepped forward and said nervously, "Come, Hans, this is getting us nowhere."

"Quite right." The frosty visage nodded once, satisfied with the dressing down. "You are American?"

"I just said that."

"You don't sound American," he said suspiciously.

"Good." Jake inspected the man, wondered if he would be able to keep hold of his temper during the days to come. "Where is your beard and haircut?"

The lofty irritation returned. "Really, Colonel. Your people could not truly have expected a man of my standing to resort to such pettiness."

"This affects all our security," Jake said, tempted to leave the man behind.

"I have a hat he can wear," Dr. Grunner said with a nervous desire to ease the tension. "And his beard will grow swiftly."

Jake locked eyes and wills with the blond man and had a sudden impression of this man standing with a gun on the hills above the Normandy beaches, watching as Jake's brother struggled in futility to land and find safety. Not some fellow Nazi, not some soldier with similar features, *this man*. The rage which filled him was so great and came so swiftly it almost blinded him. But before the anger was transformed to action, the doors leading into the hillside creaked open once more.

"And what is this?" The voice was scarcely above the level of a whisper, yet it had the effect of shaking the arrogant Dr. Hechter as Jake could not. The ice-blue eyes faltered, the shoulders hunched slightly. Jake glanced up, and understood.

Like the official at the main gates, this man also wore the blue uniform of the People's Police, the puppet officials of the occupying Soviet forces. But this was no ineffectual marionette. Instead, he was lean to the point of perpetual emaciation. Years of suffering had pressed his lips to thin bloodless lines, stripped his features of all softness, and turned his eyes to slits of gray-marble. "Well? I am waiting for an answer."

Jake shifted his gaze back to the blond scientist and stated flatly, "I don't care who you parade out here. I am not dropping my price one pfennig."

There was a slight relaxing of the officer's tight features. "A trader? Two of my top scientists are out wasting time with a trader?"

"He has our tools," Grunner said, picking up the thread.

Jake saw the officer's reaction, knew the way this one would think. Life meant nothing to someone like him. Jake added swiftly, "Half of them. You want the others, you pay full for these. No talk, no threats. The price we agreed on."

"*I* agreed to nothing," the officer snapped. "And you, gypsy, you watch your tone or I'll call out the guard."

The blond scientist turned about and announced, "You know full well the condition of our machinery. It is vital that we receive these tools. *All* of them."

"I know that you are falling further and further behind schedule in your work," the officer snapped. "And when I see the way you waste your time, I can well understand why."

"You will address me as Herr Professor," the scientist responded icily. "Or you will not address me at all."

Dr. Grunner lifted a battered envelope from his coat pocket and brandished it between them. "We have the money," he cried. "Our tool budget has been approved for months. You yourself signed the requisition. But there have been no tools anywhere, for no price. And now he has come with exactly what we need."

The political officer radiated a viciously compacted disapproval. "Exactly? You are sure?"

"We would be," Dr. Hechter replied frostily, "if you would allow us to go about our business."

The disapproval focused into vengeful bile. "It may not be possible to shoot you as should happen to all Nazis, *Professor*. But punishment can be arranged if your attitude does not improve. You do not need both feet to perform your duties, for example. You would do well to remember that."

When the door had closed behind the officer, the blond scientist said quietly, "Former Nazi."

Rolf Grunner took a shaky breath, said to Jake, "You truly have the tools?"

"The ones you requested in the last message we received before our man disappeared," Jake answered, his eyes still on the door. "That was too close."

"That man should be taken out and shot," Dr. Hechter said from beside him.

Jake found his own unreasoning anger resurfacing. "That would be your answer to everything, would it?"

The scientist jerked as though slapped, but before he could respond his colleague was between them. "Gentlemen, please, I beg you, our very lives hang in the balance here."

Jake took a breath, nodded. "Let's unload."

When the bulky sacks were piled at the landing on top of the stairs, Grunner handed over the money. "This was the amount the last communique told us to have. Exactly."

"I need to count it in case someone's watching." Jake bent over the packet, lowered his voice, said, "There are two grenades in each of the sacks, one smoke and one frag. If you have to use them indoors, be sure to crouch and cover your ears."

"I've never used a grenade before," Grunner stammered.

"Let's hope you don't have to learn tonight. If you do, it helps to pull the pin before you throw." Jake scanned the empty field across from the laboratory. "How is security?"

"Poor," Grunner replied, certain for once. "The guards are as badly paid and poorly treated as we are."

"That makes our job easier. I will be by this door at two minutes to midnight. Get here early enough to check and see if it's locked. If so, I will blow it just before the diversion is set to go. Wait ten paces back, or around a corner, in a doorway, anything that will give you protection." Jake stuffed the bills into his jacket. "There is a path about a kilometer and a half before the main gate. I saw it on the way in. It looks like an old road, and runs straight as an arrow through the forest in this direction."

"I know it," Dr. Grunner said. "It comes out on the other side of the launch-pad. They used it when they were constructing these halls."

Jake made a pretense of opening one of the sacks, pulling out a gleaming tool, holding it as though for inspection. "If anything happens and you have to get out early, anything, head for where that path intersects the main road toward town." Jake thrust a tool back inside. He tied the neck of the sack, nerves over what was coming making his motions jerky. "There will be a diversion set for precisely five minutes after midnight. Whatever happens, if for any reason we don't rendezvous, don't be here when it goes off."

Grunner nodded nervously. "What sort of diversion?"

Jake turned back toward the truck. "Something loud."

"Just one minute, Colonel," Hechter said, stopping his progress toward the truck. The blond scientist stared at him, his lofty superiority back in force. "You really don't expect me to carry my own cases all the way through the forest."

"Your cases?" Jake shook his head in disbelief. "I don't expect you to carry them at all." Before the man could respond, he swung behind the wheel, started the engine, said through the open window, "Midnight. Be ready."

Chapter Five

SALLY HAD NEVER seen Harry Grisholm so angry.

She had been working at her desk when he arrived, trying to ignore her aching sense of loss. Adjusting to Jake's absence had been much harder than she expected. Before he had left, when she had thought about the mission at all, she had seen it as a shorter version of her own trip to America with the generals. But the reality had turned out far different from her expectations. Perhaps it was because Jake was the one who had done the leaving this time, perhaps because of the danger inherent in his mission, perhaps because she was more accepting of her own love. Whatever the reason, his absence was pure agony.

Being home was too much for her to bear alone. The lack of him was with her everywhere. So she had taken to spending more and more time in the office, surrounding herself both with work and with people who knew more about his mission than she did.

Jake had told her what he was going to do. That had been one of his departing gifts. If the intelligence forces themselves had granted her top-secret classification, he had reasoned, why on earth shouldn't he use it for something this important? She had listened and struggled to hide her anxiety, knowing that it had to be done, knowing that he was going, knowing that to weigh him down with her own worries would only increase the risk.

Her office was connected to one of the three administrators assigned to coordinate NATO Intelligence activities. Commander Randolf formerly led a British antisubmarine squadron. His demeanor was as rigid and unbending as his sparse frame. The sea-green eyes which peered out from beneath his bushy brows had the singular intensity of two minutely adjusted gun barrels.

Yet even his iron bearing had been shaken by that unexpected late afternoon meeting.

The commander had not wanted to go at all. There had been a visiting dignitary from Holland, a meeting with the Canadian ambassador, two majors arriving from U.S. Army Intelligence, a hundred urgent papers on his desk, and suddenly this call had come to drop everything and run to an urgent meeting for which Sally had been given no reason whatsoever.

The commander had stormed off, ready to give a solid broadside to whoever was responsible. But he had returned two hours later so troubled that his normal ruddy features had been positively ashen. Sally had risen in alarm at the sight, for some reason pierced by a brilliant shaft of fear. The commander had waved her back into her chair and wordlessly entered his office.

Harry Grisholm arrived thirty seconds later. He was not shaken. He was furious. He stormed through her antechamber without even seeing her, entered the commander's office, and shouted, "What an utter shambles!"

"Lower your voice," the commander rumbled.

"Six months in the making," Grisholm went on, only barely quieter than before. "Delete that. Six months of maneuvering before even the first step could be taken. Then what happens, but we find ourselves faced with the loss of every single American agent NATO Intelligence had in the Soviet sector. But did we suspect something? Of course not. How on earth could we? We're all so naive as to think that those seven villages just happened to have been chosen for relocation. All within twelve weeks of each other."

As quietly as she could manage, Sally scooted her chair into the corner of her office. She was certain that if they realized she was still there they would close the door and close her out. And this she wanted to hear.

"So we send our most senior American operative," Harry went on in barely controlled fury, "the man slated to rise into commanding position, over to pick up two defecting German scientists. A trial run, we call it. A chance to pick up some field experience."

There was the sound of Harry's chair being shoved back so hard it slammed up against the wall near her head. Then the little man began his rapid limping pace. Back and forth, back and forth, the words a furious torrent. "And what do we learn now? That the agents in place were identified and picked up because they were *known* to be agents. Why? Because we, the supposed crown jewel of NATO operations, have been infiltrated by Stalin's henchmen."

Sally heard a faint scratching below her. She glanced down, realized it was the sound of her own fingernails digging through the fabric of her chair, the knuckles white with the strain of not screaming out her fear.

"I feel as though I've taken a direct hit amidships," the commander mumbled.

"And well you should. We all have. Every one of us. Especially that poor fellow we've just sent out without the first hint of warning."

"You think the Soviets know what his mission is?"

"I dare not." The pacing became even swifter. "They must have the same communication delays as us with their agents in the field. They *must*. It would take a certain amount of time to first receive the information, and then act on it, especially as far away from Moscow as Rostock."

Rostock. There was no longer any doubt, despite her every desire to refuse to imagine it really was Jake. Jake. Her Jake was in terrible, terrible danger. Sally sat there, her body stiff with terror, her head slowly shaking back and forth, unable to even draw breath.

The commander sighed. "So what do we do now?"

"There is nothing we *can* do. Not until we are certain where the leak is located."

"I suppose I could go," the commander offered.

"Oh, don't be a total fool," Harry barked. "You're far too well known. As is every other senior officer here, including myself. That's why we're here and not still in the field."

"You're correct, of course," the commander admitted. "But we must do something."

"We can do *nothing* until the leak is isolated," Harry countered. "You know that as well as I."

"Quite right," the commander murmured. "No sense sending even more men out to their doom."

Doom. The word echoed through her being like the tolling of a funeral bell. Her own. For without Jake her life was over. Finished. No longer a life at all.

"Not to mention the fact that we might be sending word to the enemy that we know of their infiltration. If they hear that, they will speed things up, make every effort to seal off his escape." The pacing slowed, halted, the angry voice lowered to a worried mutter. "If he can still escape at all."

Chapter Six

*I*T WAS THE LONGEST afternoon of Sally's life.

She remained brisk and busy, forced herself to stay cheerful and show nothing was wrong as far as she knew, even though inside she died a little with every passing second.

To make matters worse, much worse indeed, she knew she could not give in to panic and desperation and worry. She had to *think*.

The first time the commander happened to leave the office, she called her colleague on the floor above. "Rose? It's Sally." She paused impatiently while the phone chattered in her ear. "Yes, I know. The commander's in a major tizzy down here, too. No, no idea. Listen, I need you to cut me a set of travel documents. No, leave out the name, I haven't heard anything about who yet. Flight tonight to Berlin. Yes, that's right. Tonight. Official pass into the Soviet sector. Leave the names blank, I'll type them in as soon as it's cleared up, then call you back. You're a dear. Thanks. Bye."

When she set down the phone, Sally found that the strain of keeping her tone light and easy had caused her knuckles to squeeze the receiver so hard they had difficulty unlocking.

Another hour of agony, then the commander left a second time. She was up and out of her chair as soon as the outer door closed behind him. Sally bundled up a pile of papers and her shorthand pad, shook her head violently enough to unpin her hair, took a deep breath, and left the room.

She raced up the stairs, arriving on the third floor out of breath and flushed, just as she intended. She tripped down the hallway, casting out hurried smiles and hellos to everyone she passed, knocked on the door, and breezed in immediately, saying, "What a day, what a day, what a day."

The heavyset bespectacled man looked up and drawled in best New England nasal boredom, "Why, Sally, dear. You look positively frazzled."

"Something big is going on, I can feel it." She leaned across the wooden barrier, asked with the gaiety of just another office snoop, "Heard anything?"

"Even if I had, do you think I would tell you?" His head dropped back to the document under his oversized magnifying glass. "You'd just hop back down to the power station and tell some bigwig on me."

"Wendell, dear, you know I'd never do such a thing. Not to you." Wendell Cooper was the operation's forger, his work so good it passed inspection by top experts. Which was the only reason he was tolerated. Those occupying the power station, the name given to the offices on the ground floor, thought him overly effeminate and slightly balmy besides. They avoided him at all costs.

Sally knew Wendell to be both truly lonely and a genuine lover of gossip. He fed voraciously on the little tidbits Sally passed him from time to time and responded with his own brand of friendship. Sally went on in her most excitable manner, "I'm sure something big is going on. I can feel it in my toes."

"You don't say." Wendell pretended boredom. "Well, you'll be sure and tell me what you hear. It helps to pass the hours. Speaking of which, how's the gallant colonel?"

"Off having loads of thrills and adventures," she said brightly, though it cost her dearly to force the words around the lump in her throat. "The lucky stiff."

"Good time to be away, if you ask me. There's the feeling around here that heads may roll."

"Speaking of being away," Sally said, unable to stand it any longer. "I need a passport, please. It's urgent."

Wendell sniffed. "It always is, dear. You'll learn that with time. Getting everybody into a whirlwind gives them a sense of power."

"Maybe so, but I was sent up here by rocket."

Wendell had still not looked up from his work. "Nationality?"

"Swiss."

"A neutral. Hmmm. Must be something very big not to be going with one of our own. Where is he headed?"

"She. I'm not supposed to say," Sally poised delicately, then added the spice. "But I was ordered to have documents prepared for a crossing into eastern Germany."

He looked up at that. "They are sending a woman into the Soviet sector?"

"Strange, isn't it?" She leaned farther across, kicked up one heel as though nothing mattered more than a little gossip. "Wish it could be me."

"No you don't. Not if you want to ever wake up in your own bed again. Those Russkies play for keeps." Wendell sighed, pushed his work to one side, opened a drawer, sorted through a pile, and plucked out a red passbook emblazoned with a gold seal. He carefully folded it open on his desk and slid it under the heavy glass ring, said, "Name?"

Sally gripped the papers to keep her hands from trembling, pretended to inspect her pad, replied, "Stella Frank."

A long moment of silence, interrupted only by Wendell's quiet scratching. "Residence?"

"Parc des Eaux Vives, Geneva."

"Best let me see that, dear, I don't speak a word of the Frog language."

"What, and try to decipher my chicken-scratch?" She spelled it out for him, then gave her birthdate and birthplace.

"We'll give her the standard travel stamps," Wendell said, choosing several from the revolving trays on his desk, knowing by rote whether blue or red or green or black ink was required. "Ready with the darling's photo?"

"Not yet." Sally shrugged at his look of irritation. "Don't get mad at me. I just salute and serve."

Wendell looked at his clock. Almost five o'clock. His anger became genuine. "Surely they don't expect me to sit here all night until the lab is finally ready to wake up."

Sally pretended concern. "Just let me have the stamp. I'll glue it in myself, bring everything back tomorrow."

"Thanks ever," he said, clearly relieved. "I wouldn't mind, but I've already made plans." He handed her the passport, a circular stamp, and the inkpad. "Top left-hand corner of the photo."

"You're a dear." Sally gathered everything to her breast and gave him a brilliant smile. "Whatever it is you're up to tonight, I hope it's fun." Then she fled.

The travel documents were on her desk when she returned, which almost stopped her heart until she realized that the commander had already left for the day. Sally slid them into the typewriter and filled out the requisite information before her nerves could give out. Her flight was not until eleven-thirty that night. Plenty of time. She sat and pretended to work as the clock crawled through two complete revolutions, the amount she had already decided was the minimum she could risk.

At seven o'clock she grabbed up a few interoffice memos and letters. They would normally be delivered the next morning by the office boy, but they gave her at least a flimsy excuse to do what was clearly the riskiest part of her preparations. She took a deep breath, willed herself to act both calm and tired, just finishing up another long day. Then she stepped into the hall.

The corridors were silent, save for the occasional guard and janitor. Sally walked from office to office depositing the papers, greeting all she passed, slightly amazed they could not hear her pounding heart.

The door to Harry Grisholm's office was unlocked. She pushed in, crossed to his desk, and stopped, wondering now where to begin.

Then she saw it. There in his file basket. Covered by other papers, but one edge poking out, and on it the name of her beloved. Jake Burnes. His file. Sally's legs almost gave way at her good fortune.

Her fingers shaking uncontrollably, she switched on Harry Grisholm's desk lamp, opened the file, and read. Because she liked Harry, she had been immensely glad when she heard that he was to be Jake's handler on this case. But nowhere near as elated as now.

It was all there. The contacts, the itinerary, the addresses, the handover, everything. Sally wrote as fast as her quivering hand would permit, certain every moment that the door would open and she would be caught, captured, chained, kept from doing what she knew she had to. Only she. No one else to trust. No one.

She slapped the file shut, hugged it once to her chest, whispered to the dark ceiling, "I'm on my way, darling." Then she was out the door and gone.

The officer of the guard at the main gate did not think there was anything out of the ordinary in Harry Grisholm's nine o'clock return. The little man was well known among the staff for his odd hours. The guard saluted his car, ordered the barrier to be raised, and made a note in the book. He then looked up, only to find the little man waving him over to the car.

"You're Lieutenant Towers, do I have that right?"

"Sir, yes sir," the young man replied, astonished and immensely pleased to be remembered.

"Good, good. I was just wondering, Lieutenant, is anybody working late tonight?"

"Sir, not that I know of, but I could check the book for you."

"No, that won't be necessary. I was just wondering if anybody might still be around."

"I'm pretty sure they've all gone home, sir. Mrs. Burnes, she was around again late, but she left almost an hour ago."

"I see," he said slowly. "Mrs. Burnes has left, has she?"

"Signed her out myself. The guards are going about their rounds now, but they all know you, sir. I'm sure there won't be any trouble if you need to get back in."

"No, no, not if everyone has already left for the night. Would you mind if I used your phone for a moment?"

"Course not, sir. Right this way." The lieutenant watched the little man pry himself awkwardly from behind the wheel, then limp over to the guardhouse. He could not help but stare. Everybody knew how Harry Grisholm had received his wounds.

Harry picked up the receiver and dialed a number. "Commander Randolf, please." A moment's pause, then, "Edgar. Harry here. I'm in the guardhouse at the main gate. I'm afraid I can't do that memo we discussed after all. Wanted to call you immediately and just let you know it will have to wait until tomorrow. It appears that your diligent assistant has already called it a night. Yes, that's right. She left almost an hour ago, according to the lieutenant here. No, no problem, just thought you should know. Yes. All we can do is wait, I suppose. Until tomorrow then. Goodnight."

Harry Grisholm hung up the phone. "Thank you, Lieutenant. Very good of you."

"No problem, sir. Anything else I can do?"

Harry looked up at the young man and gave that gentle smile from the eyes that warmed the young man to the bone. "Thank you, Lieutenant. I shall remember your kind offer."

"Thank you, sir." The lieutenant held the car door, shut it, saluted smartly as the car turned and went back out into the night. He watched long after the lights had disappeared. This was one for the books. The young man shook his head. It wasn't every day that he had a chance to talk with a living legend.

Chapter Seven

*T*HE HOURS PASSED with the brutal slowness of waiting for war.

The night was dry and warm and clear, and filled with the music of a forest in full June concert. Jake leaned his back against a pine just outside the perimeter fence, his face and hands blackened, his clothes as dark as the surrounding night. He knew it was useless to try and doze. There had been many in his squads who could drop off at a moment's notice and wake instantly refreshed ten minutes later, alert for the smallest sound even when asleep. But not Jake. Five minutes or five hours, if he slept at all he woke groggy. And tired as he was now, if he managed to doze off he would probably sleep for hours.

But fatigue was a familiar companion, as was the waiting. War had forced him to come to know many such cronies. Liking them had nothing to do with it. To survive meant understanding their ways and using them for his own benefit.

Jake's mind continued to drift back over the war. He found himself thinking of his younger brother, the one who had not returned from the Normandy invasion. Jake had never seen Bobby again after his own departure; all Jake's memories were of the young man before leaving the U.S. Suddenly his brother's fresh and eager face became superimposed over the image of the blond scientist, tall and arrogant and cold and superior. A perfect Aryan Nazi. The enemy. Just like the ones responsible for blasting his last living relative to smithereens. Now here he was, risking his own neck to bring the man out. Jake shook himself like a dog emerging from the water and began refitting his packs. There was no future in thoughts like that.

Strange, though, how being here in this midnight terrain brought him closer to the war than he had been since leaving the Italian battlefields. Nothing in Badenburg or Karlsruhe had affected him like this. Here in the depths of darkness, surrounded by danger, he was beset by memories and sensations which he had thought gone forever, lost both by time and his own acceptance of faith. Yet now he sat and struggled with both the external dangers and the same internal forces of fury and vengeance that once had dominated his existence.

Jake loathed the fact that he was risking his life to save an enemy. And that was how he saw Hans Hechter. No matter that he was needed by Jake's government, that his mind and his knowledge was deemed essential. In the instant of facing the scientist, Jake knew he had come face-to-face with the foe.

Yet there was something more. Jake knew this for a fact, and yet could not come to grips with how he knew or why it bothered him so. He was faced with an internal struggle so deep he could not truly fathom what it was, one which left him feeling unsettled and angry. With Hechter, with himself, with life. Jake was a straightforward kind of person, not given to long introspective battles. This sort of hidden confusion left him very disturbed.

He checked his watch, found himself genuinely glad to be able to focus on something else, even something so dangerous as his present mission. He tightened the straps to his two packs, one gripping his chest and the other his back. He slid the wire cutters from his leg pouch and started forward.

The wire gave him no problem at all. The strands were rusted almost through, the ground unkempt and so weed-infested he could almost have stood upright and remained hidden. Clearly the guards had wasted little concern on keeping up security since the war. Jake folded the two sides of the fence back to form an opening in the shape of an inverted V. As he slipped through, he had the fleeting impression that the wire had been left there more to keep the scientists in than the enemy out.

There were no dogs, only one pair of guards who gave the terrain a haphazard circuit every half hour. Jake had watched and timed and was certain enough of his relative safety to risk a run straight across the concrete launch-pad. The entire perimeter, both of the pad and the complex itself, was ringed with tall poles sprouting lights like multiple steel branches. Yet only a handful still worked, and these flickered and popped so much that they generated more shadows than light.

Jake reached the first set of steel doors, sidled around to where the cliffside was covered with a pelt of uncut grass, and began to climb. The cloudless night was so bright as to faintly wash the cliff and the doors and the fields and distant trees to colorless silver. When he was directly above the doors, he reached into the chest pack and drew out the first bomb.

The bombs he had brought were bulky, heavy, and made to be used by someone who had no knowledge whatsoever of explosives. Anticipating that he would be up against some form of reinforced subterranean compound, the bomb's designers had delicately balanced power with directive force. The intention was to focus the bomb's force inward to where it would hopefully inflict structural damage. The result was a squarish charge fastened to what looked like a heavy metal pie plate, with the timer a sort of afterthought dangling from one end. Jake gave the timer a final check, dug the hole, set the bomb. Then he scrambled down and moved on to the next door.

He set the four bombs, all he could carry, above the four doors closest to the entrance where the scientists were scheduled to be waiting. He scrambled down to ground level, crouched in the shadows of a concrete entrance platform, waited for the guards to pass. The single team talked loudly as they walked, keeping themselves company.

Carefully he skirted around the illuminated islands created by three working light posts. He checked a final time, then climbed the entrance stairs where Hechter and Grunner were to be waiting. The doors were locked. Jake made a swift inspection. Definitely a holdover from the former proprietors. Solid steel construction, bolted directly into the stone framework. Jake extracted his remaining three charges, all much smaller and less powerful than the ones dug into the hillside. He set them as he had been instructed, taping one to the top of the seam made between the two doors, the second at the base of the seam, the third directly over the central lock. He stepped back, desperately hoping he had it right. Otherwise Colonel Jake Burnes, spymaster extraordinaire, would be left standing there behind enemy lines with not even a butter knife to get the doors open.

Jake did a quick swivel-check of the surroundings and satisfied himself that his work had gone unnoticed. He slid off the platform, crouched down far enough that the concrete landing would act as a buffer, fitted in his earplugs, checked his watch, and prepared to wait.

It was strange how, surrounded on all sides by the night and by danger, his thoughts would turn to Sally. Jake settled into a more comfortable position and decided maybe it wasn't so strange after all.

Theirs was more than a loving relationship, he realized. She had *restored* him. The void caused by the loss of his own family had been filled by his marriage to Sally.

His marriage. The wedding had been a simple affair, held in the Karlsruhe military chapel now run by Chaplain Fox, their friend from the Badenburg relief center. Jake had called in all his chips and wrangled military transport to bring over Sally's parents. Pierre and Jasmyn had been there, along with Lilliana Goss and Kurt and a few military pals. The meager crowd had been vastly augmented by Jake's unbounded joy, so strong that he felt the chapel would burst from trying to hold it all.

Sally had worn a cream-colored wool suit with a pleated skirt and fitted jacket over a white silk blouse. Her hat had been trimmed with a half-veil of lace, as simple and beautiful as her bouquet of roses and wildflowers. Jake had often heard that grooms remember nothing of the ceremony. But not him.

The memory of Sally's luminous beauty, and the love which had shone from her eyes, was etched upon his heart for all days.

With his mind so far away, the explosions coming so loud and so close almost stopped his heart.

The three blasts of the door-charges, going off within a heartbeat of each other, sounded like a mad giant hammering a massive anvil and ripping it to shreds in the process.

Jake raised his head above the level of the platform. He was immensely pleased to find the frame and the supporting rocks shattered, the doors bent and smoldering and barely upright.

Then the night was shattered a second time. Sirens shrieked. Voices shouted. A single spotlight switched on, too far around the corner of the cliff to shine upon Jake as he vaulted onto the platform and wrenched open the door, using one of the bomb packs to protect his hands. He searched through the acrid smoke for the two scientists, saw nothing, was momentarily panicked by the fear that he had blasted the wrong door.

Then two familiar faces peeked through the smoke. Jake hissed and motioned frantically for them to move. Together the scientists stepped through the frame.

Jake pointed down into the shadows, opened his mouth to tell them to hide, when an icy voice howled, "Stop! I have you covered! Guards, guards, over here!"

The scientists froze to the spot. Jake hid behind the door, heard footsteps race down the hall, judged the moment the best he could. Then powered by the gallon of adrenaline coursing through his veins, he slammed the door home. It met the oncoming person with a resounding thud. Jake unholstered his gun, jerked the door back open, saw it was the cadaverous political officer who had challenged him earlier. The man was out cold.

"They're coming," hissed Grunner.

Jake pushed the two scientists off the platform and into the neighboring darkness. Pleaded silently with the charges to go off on time. Heard the footsteps and the shouts approach and held his own gun at the ready, wondering what good it would do against such odds, ready to try just the same.

The charge set farthest away blasted with light and thunder and a booming, rocking force that caused the earth to shiver and sent a dust cloud rocketing skyward. The footsteps and shouts abruptly veered off.

Then a closer charge blew. Before the dust began raining back to earth, while the spotlight's glare was dimmed to a frustrated grayish tinge, Jake lifted the two scientists and urged them forward with a shouted, "Run!"

Chapter Eight

*H*ER PLANE WAS delayed almost six hours.

Sally slept in fits and snatches on a hard wooden bench under a broken window. The hangar smelled of oil and diesel fumes and sweat and old cigarette smoke, so Sally was grateful for the fresh air, even if it bore an early summer chill. Occasionally she would start awake. Sometimes it was the laughter and shouts of men playing poker at the hangar's other end. Sometimes it was her nerves playing tricks with her dreams, imagining a hand reaching out, grabbing her, shaking her roughly, telling her it was time to give up, come back, face charges, go before the tribunal and be sent to women's pris—

"Mrs. Burnes? Ma'am?"

Sally jerked upright with a squeak. "No! I have to go!"

"Yes, ma'am." The mechanic wore dirty coveralls and had a cigarette tucked behind one ear. "That's why I'm waking you. The plane's ready. We fixed the engine."

Sally rubbed her face, heard the drumming sound of revving motors, tried to put her mind in order.

"Fixed it so it will stay fixed all the way to Berlin, I hope."

"You bet, ma'am." The mechanic boasted a smile brighter than the dawn. "When the army does something, it does her good."

"You better be right, soldier." She slipped on low heels and used his arm for support as she stood. "I didn't wait this long just to take my morning bath in the North Sea."

"Not a chance, ma'am. More than my life's worth. This plane's got more brass on board than the Pentagon. Something big must be going down in Berlin." He glanced over his shoulder and so missed Sally's fleeting look of alarm. "See the one with all the braid and the stars? He's been giving you the eye. Looks like you're the only dame, I mean lady, on board."

A flash of irritation ignited her heart and lifted it to cruising speed. She managed a genuine smile for that little gift. "Thanks, soldier. I've got a little experience handling guys with more brass than brains."

The mechanic's grin lit up the hangar. "Bet you don't even leave the bones, ma'am. Have a good flight."

Sally stood, checked herself in a window turned into a dark mirror by the predawn gloom. Sensible but smart—that was how she had chosen her clothes, not the way she felt about what she was doing. She was trying to act smart, maybe, but certainly not sensible. Beige silk blouse, cotton skirt one shade darker, light-brown pumps, a single strand of charcoal gray pearls, her only splash of color a bright silk scarf knotted at her neck and draped over one shoulder. Sally patted her hair into place, picked up her brown raincoat and bag, and walked toward the officers milling about the hangar exit.

True to the mechanic's warning, as soon as Sally started forward a light colonel broke off from the general's band and started toward her. He was a picture-book exec, his uniform tailored and hair freshly cut. Sally was certain he had earned all his ribbons driving a desk.

He touched his forehead with a casual smirk of a salute, said, "General Hastings was wondering if you might enjoy a little company on the flight."

"Why don't you ask the general to come on over here himself," Sally replied crisply, continuing to walk toward the exit, "so I can tell him no personally."

The colonel started at her response but recovered quickly. "Now, ma'am," he drawled. "A man like the general could do your husband, whoever he is, a world of good come appointment time. All he's asking is for you to be a little friendly."

"And all I'm asking," Sally retorted, stopping and facing him square on, "is to be left alone. And for your information, Colonel, my husband happens to be a *man*, not a nursemaid to a general's ego." She turned away. "Now, if you'll excuse me, I have a plane to catch."

As she stood in line waiting to board the plane, a voice behind her said, "That's sure telling him."

Sally wheeled about, ready to give someone else the remnants of her anger. But she was met by a rugged face, a cheerful grin, and two outstretched palms.

"Easy, ma'am. I was just offering my congratulations. Never did think much of an officer who used his brass as a battering ram."

She inspected his face and found only genuine friendliness. "I'll probably regret what I just did in the morning, Major. A lot."

"Don't," he assured her. He then pointed at a band of gold encircling his fourth finger. "Now, if you're looking for a traveling companion who's not going to offer you any trouble, I'm about as happily married as you'll ever meet in this crazy world."

"Sounds like the best offer I'm going to hear in what's left of tonight," Sally replied, deciding that here was a fellow she could trust. "Thanks."

It was only when she was inside and searching for a seat that she realized she had forgotten to worry. Sally walked down the crowded aisle, nodded when the major offered her the window, slid into her seat with a sigh. Almost airborne.

The major waited until they were both settled and the motors had begun their takeoff revving to offer her his hand. "Theo Travers."

"Sally Burnes."

"Burnes, Burnes," he rubbed his chin. "I know that name."

"My husband is Colonel Jake Burnes."

The major brightened. "Sure! The Karlsruhe garrison commander, or was. My last posting was in Stuttgart. Hey, is it true what they say about him and the desert crossing and all that Sheik of Araby stuff?"

"I wasn't there," Sally replied, "but he did receive the Croix de Guerre directly from the president of France for what happened."

"Wow." The major shook his head. "Adventures in the back of beyond, then he comes home and gets the girl. How come it only happens to the other guy?"

The plane was old, the soundproofing feeble. The great rumbling engines offered them an island of privacy. "What about you," Sally asked. "What takes you to Berlin?"

"Beats me. I was packing up ready to be shipped home, demob papers tight in my sweaty little grip. Then what happens but I get these urgent orders to strap on my gun and make tracks for Berlin." He rubbed a stubbled chin. "Been traveling almost twelve hours on a truck older than I am, and let me tell you, I could truly use a bed."

Sally kept her smile politely interested. "What do you do?"

"Construction. Real life, too, or I hope so. Been in since forty-three. Specialized in battlements and fortifications through the war, then demolition for the past couple of years. Which makes all this passing strange. I mean, Berlin is about seventy percent destroyed already, so demolition is out, and what do they need fortifications for since the war's over?"

"I'm not sure," Sally said, and dropped her eyes.

When the major did not respond, she raised her head to find him watching her. All humor was gone from his voice and gaze as he said, "You know something."

"I'm not sure," Sally repeated quietly, and studied the man beside her through the takeoff. His was a comfortable, lived-in sort of face, full of strength and integrity, lined with furrows that gathered comfortably into well-practiced lines when he smiled. "Tell me about your wife, Major."

"Call me Theo. I break out in hives when a pretty woman uses my title, especially when I'm this close to being a civilian again."

"Theo, then." Sally found herself liking the man. He had the look of someone who had come to grips with the good and the bad within himself, who was content with both his station and his direction. "Tell me about her."

"Oh, she's a gem." He leaned his head back on the seat. "Three kids, youngest only two when I was called up. Didn't bat an eye—well, no, that's an exaggeration. But she's done well by us, kept me alive in their minds, a tough thing to do when Daddy's gone for two long years. Only visited them once, and when I was back, gosh, I wish you could have seen how she treated me. Not like I was some visitor. No, like the time I was gone didn't matter now that I was back."

"Sounds like a wonderful person," Sally murmured, liking the way his face lit up as he spoke of her.

"Yeah, too good for me, that's for sure." His smile was directed toward someone only he could see. "She must've found it tough, taking up the reins while I was gone and then passing them back, but you'd never know by listening to her."

"What does she do?"

"Teaches high school math. Got a great mind, handles those kids like they're genuine people and not freaks that ought to be locked up until they hit eighteen." He switched his grin over her way. "Sorry to run off at the mouth like that, ma'am. But you got me onto my favorite subject."

"Call me Sally, please."

"Okay, Sally, so what brings you to Berlin?"

Sally liked him and trusted him. It was a decision at heart level, but she genuinely felt that their meeting was a gift. And she needed a friend. Desperately. She sent a prayer winging upward, then let her worry show through. "I have a problem, Theo. A big one."

"Those are the only ones worth talking about."

"And secret," Sally added. "So secret I could get us both shot just talking about it. Really."

He searched her face, asked, "Your husband?"

She nodded slowly. "He's in trouble."

"With the brass?"

"No, that's my department. Jake is, well . . ." She shook her head. "I don't even know where to begin."

"Try the beginning. Always like to set my buildings and my stories on a solid foundation." He glanced at his watch. "Besides, what else have we got to do with the next five hours?"

Chapter Nine

THE MARCH OF BRANDENBURG, as the region surrounding Berlin was known, contained more lakes than all the rest of eastern Germany combined. They were mostly small, set in shallow valleys between rolling hills, bordered by scrub and pine, and lined by some of the worst roads Jake had ever traveled. Many of these country lanes had been constructed of sandy shale to begin with, then blown to oblivion by off-target bombs. The larger roads were segmented muddy bogs, the multitude of bomb holes filled by recent rains. Their remaining surfaces were often ground to gravel by the invading Russian tanks and heavy weaponry. In the worst stretches, recent traffic had bypassed the roads entirely, creating parallel tracks over dunes and bushes that Jake negotiated at a crawl.

Dr. Hans Hechter sat beside him, sullen and silent, his well-trimmed blond head hidden beneath an ancient sweat-stained homburg. Dr. Rolf Grunner had been relegated to the back. The lid to the second under-compartment, now emptied of the satchel bombs, remained propped open, the interior padded with blankets and burlap. If there was a risk of discovery, Grunner could swiftly slide in and close the top. There was far less risk of discovery if inspectors found merely a trader and his helper.

The arrogant blond scientist's presence would have been much harder to bear had Jake not been so worried by what he had seen thus far that morning. Their way had crossed a major thoroughfare a little distance back, and despite its bomb-blasted surface, the larger road had been filled with a military convoy. A Soviet convoy.

And it was the contents of the convoy that troubled Jake.

For the second time their road approached a juncture with the thoroughfare. Jake stopped the truck and climbed to the top of the highest hillock in view. He crouched and looked down on what once had been the famous Berlin autobahn. Hitler had built these incredible four-lane highways—roads fit to carry the emperor of what he expected would someday be called the new Rome. Jake scanned the bombed and tankscarred surface, remembering Harry Grisholm's lessons as he did.

The two weeks he had been given for preparation and briefing had been too full and too short. Jake's two anchors throughout it all had been Harry Grisholm and Sally. At every turn, with every question, Harry had been there, available and ready with the answers. Even to the questions Jake did not know enough to ask.

"Observe," Harry repeated endlessly. "Do not try and sort at first. Nothing will make sense. Everything will seem either too mundane to be noticed or too bizarre to group together. This is inevitable, and although it will improve as you gain more field experience with us, still your first few days on every new assignment will seem a jumble of conflicting impressions."

"So what do I do?"

"Just watch and listen. You are both intelligent and perceptive. People often think one goes automatically with the other, but that is nonsense. The most intelligent people are often the ones who allow themselves to notice only what is in line with their opinions. So go in with no opinions at all. And block nothing out. Prearranged judgments are comfortable barriers, but they are death to genuine learning." Harry gave his patented smile, the one which touched nothing except his eyes. "Also good advice for people seeking to delve honestly into faith, yes?"

Jake nodded, unwilling to let the point go just yet. "But I need something to hold on to."

"All right," Harry conceded. "Most times, there will be concerns beyond your own specific assignment. Your superiors may even be afraid to tell you what they are, because they often battle among themselves over these very same points. Very little in this game is certain, Jake, especially for people who do not go across the line themselves."

This *game*. "Like what sort of questions?"

"Well, we know for certain that Russians are mobilizing large shipments of both men and equipment throughout much of Eastern Europe."

"I've heard about this."

"Of course you have. And you've also heard how some of our high and mighty decision makers think it is exactly as the Russians claim, that they are simply shifting things around, picking up squads and garrisons stranded since the war and consolidating their hold. Others, however, disagree."

Jake inspected his friend's face. "And you're one of them."

"I am concerned," Harry admitted. "Very concerned. Too much is happening at once. There are noises about the Russians wanting to take over all of Berlin. They positively loathe the idea that the Western allies maintain this hold right in the middle of their territory."

"I haven't heard anything about this."

"You will," Harry predicted grimly. "These politicians who think the problem is going to go away merely by talking are laying us open to very grave dangers."

"What sort of dangers?"

"That's what I want you to find out." Harry's gaze had a piercing quality. "Don't go looking for trouble, mind you. But if you can, find out what the Russians are up to. Have a look at things from the other side. See where these men are headed, what kind of equipment they are carting around. Observe. Seek the unexpected. Strive to fit the puzzle together. And above all, take care. You will be utterly alone out there, Jake. As alone as anyone can be in this day and age—surrounded by millions of people, none of whom you can trust."

Jake picked his way back down the steep hillside, only to find Hans Hechter waiting for him with both hands planted firmly on his hips. "Really, Colonel, this is too much. You know perfectly well that your primary objective is to deliver us safely and *swiftly* to the American sector. I order you to end these ridiculous excursions and get on with the business at hand."

Jake stopped in midstride, too dumbfounded to be angry. "You what?"

"You heard me," the scientist snapped. "I command you to forget this nonsense and drive!"

Jake opened his mouth a couple of times, caught between fury and laughter. He settled on, "Get in the truck."

Dr. Hechter started to speak, but something in Jake's eye snagged his attention. With a stifled oath he wheeled about and stomped to his door.

Jake climbed in his side with a long-suffering sigh. It had been like this since they had emerged from the woods the night before. Dr. Grunner was silent and servile and afraid. Dr. Hechter remained a consistent pain in the neck. He had vehemently refused to climb into the secret compartment, claiming it was beneath his station to travel under such conditions. Grunner had defused the situation by offering to remain there throughout the journey.

Jake continued to regret that offer, both because it left him seated next to the former Nazi, and because the atmosphere would probably have been improved had there been a confrontation in that first moment. But because they were less than a half-mile from the guard station, and because Grunner had already climbed into the truck, Jake had let matters lie.

They had driven through the night, or rather Jake had, going east rather than west, headed back toward Berlin. The powers that be had reasoned that the alarm would be sounded for defectors headed directly toward the western sectors. Jake had followed their pointers tracing a line on the wall-sized map and had not objected at the time; why should he, when he had never been there, had no idea what the roads would be like, and had never experienced what it meant to be behind enemy lines, heading farther and farther into unfriendly territory.

He pushed aside his fears and frustrations, and drove on. His mind was gritty from fatigue and strain, his concentration focused more on what he had seen from the hilltop than on the road or his compass. The military markings on the convey had been clearly visible, the contents of the trucks very disturbing. The trucks headed eastward were not laden with troops, as Stalin was claiming in the newspapers. Jake had seen no evidence that there was a withdrawal underway. The eastbound trucks had not carried men at all. They had been loaded to the gills with loot.

Some of the trucks had covers strapped over their bulky burdens. But not others. Jake had seen everything under the sun being carried eastward—great cheese rings stacked with straw for cushioning and insulation, clattering piles of pots and pans beneath a webbing of rope, tools, bleating animals, possessions of every imaginable description. Two trucks had trundled by while Jake watched, each bearing a trio of great chandeliers strung from an overhead bar, thousands of crystals tinkling and shooting rainbows in every direction.

There was no question in Jake's mind whatsoever. The eastern sector of Germany was being systematically looted, stripped to the very bone. Yet he knew from his own experience how desperate was the plight of the German people. How were they to survive the coming winter, much less begin rebuilding, if even more were taken from them?

His musings and his fatigue kept him from spotting the checkpoint until they were almost upon it.

"Into the compartment," Jake hissed. "Quick!"

As he heard the compartment lid click shut, he braked to a halt, trapped on one side by an armored half-track and on the other by a bomb crater so deep the bottom was lost in shadows. Ahead the road curved around the diminishing hill and joined with two other roads—the autobahn, and a second lane packed with refugees.

The sight of refugees struggling along on foot was a familiar sight, but one which he could never grow accustomed to witnessing. Here too was an element of unsettling surprise. He had thought that the flood of refugees had been almost stopped. The camps were established and well run, papers were being organized, food was relatively plentiful. At least, that was the situation as he knew it in the west. Jake stared through the windshield, drawn to the tragedy in front of him despite his own danger, and found himself transported back to the first bleak months following the war's end.

The refugees' faces were drawn taut with exhaustion and hunger. Men, women, and children walked on worn-out shoes, pushing cycles or barrows piled with their earthly belongings, or carrying everything on their backs. Their eyes were nightmarish caverns, blank and empty of hope. They walked, on and on and on, pushed by forces so far beyond their control that their pleas were silenced.

Jake watched a group of Russian soldiers pawing through a family's belongings, fighting over a shawl and laughing uproariously as the old mother clawed at them and begged for its return.

Jake forced his attention back to matters at hand as two men approached his side of the truck. One was dressed in the scratchy brown wool of a Soviet noncom. The other wore a new uniform of Prussian blue, another of the so-called People's Police. This organization, he knew, was in truth becoming a catchall for the ranks of political officers and assistants to their Soviet masters.

Jake nodded a greeting and handed over his greasy papers without waiting to be asked. As nonchalantly as he could, he motioned toward the refugees and inquired, "Where is this lot coming from?"

"Who knows," the political officer sniffed. "All over. Most recently from the station south of Berlin. There's been another outbreak of cholera."

Jake swallowed his bile and with it the retort that if there was cholera, the last thing they needed to be doing was walking.

"What about you, gypsy?" the officer demanded, his voice a permanent sniff. "Where are you coming from?"

"All over as well," Jake replied, his voice as bored as he could make it. The political officer was not a problem. But the Soviet sergeant was another matter entirely. He was dark, with the leathery skin and high cheekbones of a Mongol. His eyes showed a merciless battle-hardened squint, and he watched Jake like a hawk watched its prey. Jake shifted his gaze back to the refugees and intoned, "My life is that of a traveler."

The officer stood on his toes and eyed Jake's assistant, who sat with eyes straight ahead. He compared the picture on the second set of papers with that of the blond man. "You took an unemployed engineer as your assistant?"

"Is that what he was?" Jake tried for mild humor. "I wondered how he learned the fancy words."

"Was he a Nazi?"

"I don't care about the man's politics," Jake replied laconically. "Just whether he can work."

A wail arose from another group of refugees whose paltry belongings were being tossed to the four winds. The officer looked over, snorted his disgust, then handed back Jake's papers. "Let me see what you have."

Jake stepped from the truck, knowing his papers were supposed to keep him from being looted, yet aware that the sergeant with his unwavering gaze was an unknown force. The Russian stood behind the political officer, one hand continually massaging the stock of his rifle.

The political officer's attention remained distracted by the growing uproar from the refugees. He gave the truck's interior a cursory inspection and was about ready to wave Jake onward when the sergeant spoke for the first time. His guttural voice was barely audible over the din, but the officer stiffened, turned toward the other man, started to retort, then changed his mind. "Unload," he ordered Jake.

He could not help but gape. "All of it?"

"Everything." He was clearly as irritated by the order as Jake.

"But that could take an hour," Jake protested. "More. And we have a delivery to make in Berlin. You saw my papers. They—"

"Don't question my orders," the officer snapped. "Get started."

Resigned, Jake kept his eyes from the watchful sergeant and the itchy trigger finger as he walked to the open window and told the blond scientist, "Start unloading the truck."

But before Jake could walk back and lower the rear gate, Hechter had stormed around the truck, stiff and upright angry in his superiority. He raised his chin, looked down at Jake, and snapped, "Now see here, Co—"

Suddenly all the rage and the tension and the fatigue bundled together in his gut, raging through him like a freak ball of static energy. In one continuous motion Jake swept around and landed a single backhanded blow to the side of the blond man's head. The blast was strong enough to lift Hechter up and spin him around and slam him into the side of the truck. He clutched feebly at the canvas as he sank slowly to his knees.

Jake stood over him, his chest heaving, the rage flowing through him like waves. *Colonel.* There they were, surrounded by danger and foes on every side. And still the fool had almost said the word. "Don't you ever question another of my orders," Jake rasped, his voice alien to his own ears. "The war is over. You and your kind lost, engineer. If you want to live, you work. You speak when I tell you to speak. Otherwise you stay silent, and you *obey.*"

Jake waited, aching to have the man stand and try to give him more of that cold superior lip, just try. But the scientist dragged the back of one trembling hand across his face, inspected the blood, and stayed there on his knees.

The rage still roaring in his ears, Jake bent over and with one hand lifted the man as though he were a puppet. His other fist cocked back for a final blow. Hechter cowered, his bloody hand raised in abject defense.

Seeing the man crouch like that drained the fight from Jake. He unclenched his fist, stepped back, and rasped, "Now go unload the truck."

Jake turned around, only to find the sergeant grinning openly. Approval shone from those dark hard eyes. This was something the soldier could understand. Another man who maintained discipline with his fists. The guard nodded once, then stopped Hechter's shaky progress toward the truck's back with the gun barrel. He spoke more of those guttural words, then turned away.

"You may go," the political officer muttered, his own gaze full of cautious confusion.

Jake looked from one to the other, then motioned with his head for Hechter to climb back on board. He then walked to the back of the truck, pulled one of the grain sacks toward him, opened the neck, and stuck one hand inside up to the elbow. He fished out two hidden bottles, retied the neck, then walked over to the soldier.

He held them out, one in each hand, and met the fathomless gaze straight on.

The gap-toothed grin reappeared. "Wodka?"

"The best money can buy," Jake confirmed in German.

The sergeant shouldered his gun and took the bottles, his unshaven face split almost in two. *"Da, da, na zadrovie."*

"Anytime, mate," Jake replied, and started to turn away. But a hand on his arm stopped him. The sergeant shouted to the officer. The officer replied in what was clearly very rusty Russian, but the sergeant was having none of it. He gesticulated angrily with the bottles and roared a command so loud that activity among the refugees temporarily halted. Then his soldiers saw that the man's ire was directed elsewhere, and they returned to their looting.

The political officer pulled a sheet of paper from his pocket, looked at Jake's vehicle tag, scribbled something on it, reached and handed it to Jake, all without meeting his eyes.

Jake looked dumbly at the paper, then up at the grinning sergeant. "What is this?"

It took another bark from the sergeant for the officer to reply, "A Soviet travel permit. Show it to the other checkpoints between here and Berlin."

Jake nodded his dumbfounded thanks at the sergeant, who toasted Jake with the bottles. He then turned and bellowed at his soldiers, who left their sorting and began making a way through the flood of refugees. Jake clambered aboard, started his engine, and drove forward with a final wave to the grinning sergeant.

There was one brief moment when their truck was completely surrounded by refugees, a slow-moving river which blocked them from view. One of the men lifted himself from the morass and approached Jake's window. Jake recognized him as the husband of the woman who had lost her shawl. The woman stood beside him, two children clutching her ragged skirt, her eyes unable to shed any more tears.

Jake intentionally flooded the engine, then turned to the subdued Hechter and hissed, "Grind the starter. Do it!"

As the scientist reached across and pulled at the starter, Jake flipped the back canvas curtain aside, reached and grabbed and came out with four pairs of boots. He tossed them to the startled man, signaled hastily to wait. He turned back, came up with all the remaining eggs and bread and cheese. He handed these down, then opened the glove compartment and pulled out one jar of honey. Dumbfounded, the man looked down at the treasures that had appeared from nowhere to fill his arms, then brought his eyes back up to Jake. Jake saw the miles and the misery in the man's face, nodded once, said quietly, "Go with God." He pumped the choke, the truck motor started and caught, and he drove on, the man's gaze etched onto the surface of his heart.

Chapter Ten

AS FAR AS SALLY was concerned, postwar Berlin was a driver's worst nightmare, and the lighting only made things worse.

Major Theo Travers had picked her up just before dawn, and they had immediately proceeded to get totally turned around. There were few direction markers save on the thoroughfares used for military traffic, and those they wanted to avoid at all cost, since their desire was to go and return without being noticed any more than necessary.

It had taken Travers the previous day and much of the night to arrange things, and to do so without making the kind of waves that would draw unwelcome attention his way. Sally had stayed put in a run-down civilian hostel in the American sector, the best she could manage given her false Swiss passport.

The first thing Theo said when he picked her up was, "Why Swiss?"

"I wanted a reason for the accent they're going to hear with my first word of German, and Switzerland is filled with all kinds of foreigners," she replied, surveying their transport. "Why a dump truck?"

"I've been thinking," he said, climbing aboard. "A lot, as a matter of fact. Been quite an experience, hearing those rusty gears grind around."

"Speaking of which," Sally said, wincing as Theo fought the lever into first and lurched away, "I hope this thing gets us where we need to go."

"Get us there and back," Theo assured her. "What's more, it'll supply us with the best alibi I could come up with on short notice." He reached under his seat, came up with a sheaf of papers. "Blank order forms. I need a whale of a lot of sand for making cement. Need myself about, oh, four hundred truckloads. So happens there's two disused pits over in the Soviet sector. You're coming along as my interpreter."

"Smart," Sally agreed. Her glimmer of hope was mirrored by the first faint light of dawn. "Four hundred truckloads?"

"You heard right. But there's no need to be telling them that straight off. Leave a little room for bargaining when it comes down to price. Because we really will be needing the stuff." Theo stopped at a blank intersection rimmed by bombed-out buildings, pulled a compass from his pocket, took a sharp left. "You wouldn't believe what they want built here. A full-size garrison town, and that's just for the American troops. Nothing short-term about this baby. They're in for the duration, and the same goes for the other nationals, far as I've been able to make out."

"But why?"

"Seems Stalin's been making some noises that have the other nations pretty riled up. Uncle Joe's basically come right out and told them that he considers Berlin to be his exclusive bailiwick."

"But that's ridiculous. It goes directly against the terms of the UN agreement."

"Maybe so," Theo agreed. "But a measly piece of paper doesn't appear to mean much to that man. One thing I heard yesterday, over in the Soviet sector they're putting up these big old billboards. Imagine, the whole city's in ruins, especially their part, where there hasn't been much reconstruction going on. Anyway, the only thing they're painting are these wall-sized sheets of propaganda. The billboards are in Russian on top, then German underneath. The German says, 'The Soviet Union Wants Peace.' So does the Russian, only the word they use is *mir*, which means both 'peace' and 'the world'." Theo shook his head. "Gotta hand it to the guy, that's a tricky way to get his point across."

Sally took the opportunity of a stop at another intersection to settle her hand upon Theo's arm and say with all the sincerity she could muster, "You are a genuine godsend."

"Never been called that before, especially not by a pretty lady in distress."

"Well, you certainly have earned the title now. A godsend."

"Shoot." Theo Travers rewarded her with a grand smile. "This is the closest I've ever come to a genuine real-life adventure."

"I don't believe that," Sally said. "Not for an instant. I saw the ribbons on your uniform."

"Aw, in the Corps of Engineers they give those things out to anybody who can pick up the right end of a shovel." He pulled up to another intersection, as grim as the others, and declared, "Okay. The vote's in and the word's definite. We're lost."

"Don't look at me." Sally glanced around, saw nothing but rubble and war-torn remnants of buildings making stark shadows in the growing dawn. "This is as close to battle as I ever want to come."

"The American sector is in the south, from Zehlendorf and Dahlem over to Neukölln," Theo mused aloud. "The British sector runs in the middle of the western side, from Spandau to the Brandenburg Gate. The French are up north, and that address you gave me yesterday is directly across from the Froggies. I had planned on going up through the three western sectors, then jumping over at the last moment."

"Sounds good to me."

"Maybe." Another squint at the compass. "The only problem is, every doggone road I find that's not clogged with rubble is leading us right toward the dividing line."

Sally searched the gloomy bombed-out rubble and found no inspiration, only a growing impatience. "I say let's just go ahead and chance it, then."

"Right." He slammed the truck back into gear and started off. "Nothing like meeting trouble head on."

They drove in silence for another half hour, as the tattered city gradually struggled to awaken to another grim day. Lines appeared outside kitchens and bakeries and swiftly grew to incredible lengths. The people looked as gray and tired and used-up as their clothes.

"Horrible," Sally declared quietly.

"You're not kidding. And this is still the American sector. I hear it's a whole lot worse over on the other side." Theo popped the brakes, then continued forward. "Heads up. There's trouble ahead."

Sally searched the lessening gloom, saw the road-block and stiffened. As they approached, she forced herself to relax, sit back, unclench her purse. She had every right to be there.

Theo pulled up until he was surrounded on three sides by soldiers, all eying him with the sullen wariness of guards pulling long hours at boring duty. He rolled down the window as two men approached, one wearing a spanking new uniform of Prussian blue, the other well-worn fatigues bearing the red Russian star.

The blue-clad soldier saluted smartly and barked out a command. The Russian eyed Theo with eyes narrowed to slits. The major was dressed in a military windbreaker bearing his rank and insignia. He grinned down at the men. "Don't guess either of you fellows speaks Yank."

"Give me your pass," Sally said. When Theo handed it over, she opened her door, stepped down and walked around to the pair. She handed her passport and Theo's military ID over without being asked and said, "The major is head of a large construction project. He needs to buy materials."

The news was so startling that even the Russian soldier blinked, telling the world that he understood German. But it was the other officer who scoffed, "Americans want to buy materials from the Russian sector? Impossible."

"Sand," Sally replied, locking her legs to keep her knees from shaking. "And he'll pay in dollars. American. Cash."

That brought another shock wave. "Sand we have," the officer admitted reluctantly. "How much?"

"Fifty truckloads to begin with," Sally said, "if the price and quality are right."

"Fifty truckloads of sand?"

"To begin with. More later. A lot more."

The officer looked to the Russian, who jerked his head back toward the guardhouse. The officer barked, "Stay here," and scuttled away with their passes.

Sally turned back to the truck. "Now we wait."

"Waiting's fine." Theo propped his feet up on the dash, as relaxed-looking as a cat sunning itself, not a care in the world. "If the army taught me one thing, it was how to wait."

But it was tougher on Sally. She paced until the guards' silent eyes drove her back into the truck. There she sat, consumed with worries and fears and impatience, until the warming day and the scene's utter boredom finally drove her to sleep.

The next thing she knew was a gentle shake of her shoulder and the words, "Rise and shine, missie. The world's a-turning, and the brass've done arrived."

Sally clambered upright from her drowsy slump, rubbed at a sudden catch in her neck, and ungummed her tongue from the roof of her mouth. "What time is it?"

"Just gone noon. You've had yourself quite a nap. Must be feeling chipper and ready to take on the world."

Sally opened her door and slipped down to the earth. She did not feel chipper. She felt decidedly worse than she had when she had fallen asleep. She repinned her russet locks and straightened the scarf over them, pulled the lightweight overcoat straight along the hem, and walked around to where the little group of uniformed men stood waiting. As she approached, she had the sudden impression of her mind working only on one cylinder. Her German was suddenly a distant memory. So she made do with a jerky little nod.

A tall man with the face of an undertaker, white and cold and cavernous, gave a thin-lipped smile. "Nothing in my experience has ever suggested that a spy would fall asleep at a guard station."

"That's what you think we are?" Sally asked, finding her tongue at last. There was one nice thing about her nap. It had left her nerves so numb that her whole body could just as well have been dosed with Novocaine. "Spies in military uniform and driving a dump truck?"

"I admit it does sound a bit preposterous," the tall man agreed.

"More than a bit."

"So tell me, what does an American soldier find interesting about Soviet-held sand?"

"You have two unworked pits in your sector," Sally replied, rubbing at the crick in her neck. "We don't."

"We?"

She waved an impatient hand behind her. Her neck was throbbing. "The Americans. My employers."

The man examined her a moment longer, then consulted with one of the others, who first shrugged, then nodded. The tall man turned back to her. "It is indeed true what you say. And the sand is certainly better here in the east. So tell me, Madame Translator. What is it the Americans intend to build?"

She turned back, to where Theo sat looking down on the scene. "They want to know what it is you're building."

"How much did you say we needed?"

"Fifty truckloads." With her back to the group she motioned with her thumb toward the tall man, meaning, he probably speaks English.

Theo gave a single nod in response and replied, "We need to start reconstruction at several sites. From the ground up."

When Sally had translated this, the man responded immediately, as though already granted time to consider and prepare his answer. "Each truck will come and pay in cash. Each will be escorted by my men for safety, and for this you will also pay."

"Safety," Theo snorted at the response. "Tell the gent he can arrange a brass band for escort so long as the *total* price stays in budget. And my budget is seventy bucks a load. As far as payment is of concern, he can get it from the drivers or by carrier pigeon, it's all the same to me."

"He is unsure that his budget will support such escorts," Sally translated. "But he agrees to pay in cash per load."

But the tall man was already flushed with irritation before she spoke. He turned and signaled to where a trio of soldiers on motorcycles stood waiting. He then handed Sally a card and snapped, "You and the officer are to come to my quarters when you have inspected the pits."

"Nothing doing," the major drawled after Sally had translated, still calm and casual. "Site inspection is gonna take us through today, and tomorrow we've got to dig the samples. If the gent wants to get himself involved, he can come meet us out at the pits."

Sally turned to translate, but the tall man had already wheeled about and started back toward his waiting automobile. From behind her a cheerful voice asked, "Did I say something wrong?"

Sally returned a nod for the motorcyclist's salute, walked around to climb back into the truck, said, "I need a transfusion of coffee. Straight to the vein. Forget messing around with the mouth and stomach and all that nonsense."

Theo grinned at her and revved the motor. "Would you just look at the lady. Deals with some high muckety-muck, got the power to shoot us right out of the sky. Is she worried? Not a bit. Cool as a cucumber, this one. A real pro."

"Just let me wake up," Sally replied, settling back into her seat. "Then you'll have the pleasure of watching me shriek and climb the walls."

Chapter Eleven

*H*ANS IS ALIVE only because of good luck and two very important factors," the dark-haired scientist was saying quietly. He had told Jake to call him Rolf. With the journey and fatigue his nervousness had gradually worn away. "First, he resigned the Nazi Party the day after Hitler invaded Russia. He did so quietly, and with relative safety because of the project's importance. His actions meant he would never rise to a position of running the project as he should. But Hans is one of those people who are so sure of their own importance that they feel little need of receiving status from others."

They stood at the truck's tailgate, parked in a rubble-strewn lot. The region had once been a middle-class suburb skirting eastern Berlin's outer border. The lot was now a gathering place for black marketeers. There were perhaps three dozen trucks, another dozen or so horse-drawn farm wagons, and twenty or thirty people displaying paltry wares on threadbare carpets or wheelbarrows or from boxes attached to bicycles. The atmosphere was very subdued. Jake was parked to one side, slightly removed from the others. His display of pots and pans and boots brought many stares, but few who even bothered to ask the prices. They seemed to simply accept that such things were beyond their reach.

"Hans resigned in protest of what he called a tragic repeat of Napoleon's mistake," Rolf went on. "But he did not say this openly. So the Russians were able to view this as an endorsement of their Communist cause. Which of course was nothing more than a means of hiding their true reason for letting him live."

Jake found it difficult to watch the faces. They looked so tired, so resigned. This was far worse than anything he had seen in the days leading up to his Karlsruhe departure, and that had been a good half-year before. Unlike the constant banging and working and clearing and rebuilding which turned every city in the American sector into a unending din, here there was silence. Everywhere Jake looked, he saw the war's remnants standing untouched by any sign of reconstruction. The people mirrored this strange vacuum. They did not even bother to meet his eyes. There appeared to be no room for hope, for bargaining, for anything save a tired envy at the wealth he had on display.

He glanced over at Rolf. The neat, nervous scientist was gone, replaced by a hollow-cheeked trader in denim and tattered sweater, his ratty beard flecked with traces of silver. Jake asked, "And what was their real reason?"

"That Hans was truly the brains behind the project's success," Rolf answered. "Not the name, you understand. Not the senior man who wore the medals and met with Hitler and was pictured in the press. The brains. Your people are right to want him."

Despite Jake's best driving and the newly acquired Soviet pass, they had almost not made it to the contact point on time. Driving in and around eastern Berlin had proved more difficult than Jake had thought possible, with numerous streets still blocked by collapsed buildings and a total lack of road signs. He had finally bribed a teenager with a pair of boots, and the youth had sat on the hood of their truck and directed them with hand signals. They had arrived at the market precisely five minutes before the prearranged contact time elapsed.

There was only a one-hour window each afternoon, a condition of working with local contacts from the British secret service. It had been necessary to go outside normal channels, since all their own men had vanished. The British had refused to give details—names, addresses, descriptions—much to Harry Grisholm's chagrin. They had simply stated that if Jake were to appear at such and such a time and place, they would try and make contact. Try. No guarantees.

Jake had parked the truck, gone around to the back, and swiftly built a little barrier of bundles while Rolf had stood guard. He had then opened the compartment's lid, watched as Hans Hechter blinked in the sudden light, and said quietly, "Five minutes. Stretch your legs, but don't raise yourself up too far. If you hear a knocking, lie flat and pull the lid back down."

Hechter had not replied, just lain there rubbing his eyes. His face was bloodied and swollen where Jake had hit him. Jake walked around to the side cannisters, poured water over his handkerchief, and then filled a cup. He brought both back, said, "I'm sorry for having hit you. But you were about to call me colonel and drop us all off the deep end."

Hechter met his eye for the first time since the confrontation. "You are apologizing? To me?"

Jake looked down at the man, found his deflation unsettling. "Five minutes. No more. Then we'll have to set up shop."

Now Jake looked into the truck's shadowy depths and satisfied himself that Hechter was both hidden and silent. "What about you, Rolf?"

"Ignition and fuel, those are my specialties," he replied quietly, his eyes also scanning the crowd. "Important, but not crucial. I am the equivalent of a five years' advantage, if you see what I mean. Hans, though, he represents a lifetime. A full generation's difference in rocket technology to whoever controls that remarkable brain."

Jake looked out over the crowd, glanced at his watch, resigned himself to a night in the open and another day of waiting and hoping. "So why didn't he stay?"

"Resigning the party does not erase the reason for his having joined in the first place," Rolf answered. "The Communists who were put in control of our project need him, but they loathe him as well. Given half a chance, they would execute him on the spot. To make matters worse, we were told in no uncertain terms that we were soon to be relocated to the wilds of Siberia."

Their conversation was cut short as a pair of heavy, bearded men lumbered over, Jake straightened from his slouch and stepped one pace from the truck. Granting himself a little extra room in case the swinging started. Their presence shouted danger.

The taller of the two had one eye turned milky. He had allowed his beard to grow up and cover most of that cheek in a vague attempt to hide a ferocious scar. He reached forward and picked up one of the pans. "Nice wares. From the West?"

"Let's see your money," Jake said, "and I'll tell you all the stories you've got time to hear."

"No, stranger, let's see *yours*," the man said, hefting the pan like a weapon while his shorter companion, a barrel-chested man with the battered face of a barroom brawler, took a step toward Rolf. "There's a charge for displaying your wares here. We're the collection committee."

Jake stood his ground and replied in German, "You can try to make me pay. But it'll probably cost you your other eye."

The tension crackling between the two men was enough to push the crowd of would-be shoppers far away. All eyes were suddenly elsewhere, all attention focused on something safe. The taller man glanced about, then cast the pan back on the tailgate and said quietly, "You do that well for a Yank. Maybe you should consider a different profession."

Jake had difficulty shifting from one danger to the other. "What?"

"Hand me some bills. There are eyes on us. Did you know you were being observed?"

Jake fumbled in his pocket, came up with a handful, passed it over unseen. "No."

"The Soviet minions are paid to check everything new. Yet it appears you two are attracting more than your share of attention." He stuffed the bills in his pocket, pointed with his head. "There is something else. Another stranger. This one's clearly from the West. Been hovering around the outskirts of the market for almost an hour, stopped twice by the police, checked, then let go. Red passport, probably Swiss. You expecting anybody?''

''Not that I was told,'' Jake said, totally confused by too much too fast.

The big man put a casual hand the size of a bear paw on Jake's shoulder, turned him about. ''Let's take a little stroll, I'll just be showing the new man around, pointing out where he's going to be setting up tomorrow.'' Together they walked down the lot, the crowd parting in fearful waves before them. The man pointed into an empty space between two other metal traders. Jake responded with a single nod. Then as they turned back, the man directed his eyes with pressure on his shoulder, said softly, ''There. Beside the curb with the two coppers eying her. In the scarf and macintosh.''

Jake felt a blow so strong it whooshed the breath from his lungs. He stumbled as the hand continued to turn him around, managed to whisper, ''That's my *wife*.''

By the time they had returned to the truck the big man had recovered sufficiently to say, ''Something is wrong.''

''I'll say.'' Jake still found it difficult to believe what his eyes had shown him. ''How—''

''No time,'' the man said, and signaled for his companion to join him with a jerk of his head. ''I cannot be seen to talk more with you than normal, not until I know what is happening. Traders camp here at night until their wares are sold. Join them. At the far end is the corner of a destroyed building. Back up close and you will be protected from whatever the night brings. Perhaps. There is a working faucet and public facilities two blocks north."

Jake felt as though all the world could see through his subterfuge. "Can we still make it work?"

"We must, though I know not how. The situation has become critical." The big man gave a casual glance over his territory, stretched and said without moving his lips, "My other contacts have vanished, and I have information. Something vital. You must carry it out. How we can accomplish this, with security and spies tightening the net around this place, I do not know. But we must try." He turned, signaled his companion, and stomped away.

Jake stood immersed in confusion and the sense that his carefully constructed world was unraveling. Sally. Here. Part of him wanted to rush to her side. The other part shrieked danger.

The silent clarion grew more strident as he spotted her drifting along with the crowd, allowing herself to be brought along with no sense of her own volition. At each stall she hesitated, picked up an item, set it down, then allowed the shoppers to herd her along. Jake inspected her face, still hardly able to believe it was her. She looked tired. And drawn. Taut to the point that her face held masklike tension. He realized he was staring, felt unseen eyes watching, did the only thing he could, although it tore at his heart to do so.

He turned away.

Jake busied himself with his wares, restacking the pans, pulling bundles about, feeling her draw closer. Then she was there. Standing beside him, close enough that he could smell her scent, feel her presence, and the aching fear and confusion threatened to engulf him.

Sally picked up a pan, inspected it with unseeing eyes. Jake opened a sack, felt inside as though the search occupied all his attention, realized she was holding the pan clenched so tightly her knuckles were white. With the faintest tremor she set the pan back down, and in doing so allowed a slip of paper to fall between the one she held and the one beneath.

She turned away, never having looked in his direction, and as she did so there came a whisper so soft it was almost lost among the crowd's murmuring and the shuffled steps and the gentle evening wind.

"Oh, my Jake."

Chapter Twelve

$\mathcal{F}$IRELIGHT SENT LINGERING fingers of light and shadow over their meager campsite. The ruins which formed three sides of their shelter came to life, weaving a silent warning against the debacle of war. Jake sat surrounded by his worries, the note from Sally dangling from his numb fingers, the words read so often that they danced and flickered in his mind.

The scrap of paper looked as though it had been hastily scrawled as she walked. It read simply, "Bären Sand Pits, end of Bärenstr, two km west, 9:00 tom am. Urgent."

Sally. She was here. Everything else paled before the confusion caused by this fact. Was their cover blown? Was that why the nameless one-eyed giant had said there were unwelcome eyes? Jake watched the fire's sparks rise to form glowing copies of the stars and decided that they were probably safe for the night. If the Soviets had wanted to pick them up, they would have done so already. So what to do?

He glanced at his two companions. Hechter had crawled down from the truck, eaten dinner, and now sat staring at the fire without saying a word. They were utterly sealed from the other traders, the truck pulled in close to form the roofless building's fourth wall. Rolf Grunner lay silent and still in his bedroll alongside the truck.

Hechter stirred and rose and slid another rotten plank onto the fire. "I was thinking about the Depression," he said quietly. "No, that is not entirely true. I was thinking of who I am, what I have done, and how the Depression helped to form me."

Jake watched the scientist sit back down. All he had to do was look in the man's direction to feel the hostility well back up. He disliked Hechter on a level far below thought. "Why are you telling me this?"

"Because you apologized," Hechter replied. His voice was as subdued as his eyes. "I have been thinking about that too, Colonel. I have been forced to realize things that I do not like to see, have not wanted to accept. Such as the fact that, for me, power and authority has always meant the right to do whatever I deemed correct. Apologies were not a part of this. I am sure this must seem a minor thing to you. But to me it represents the changes my world is undergoing. And I find myself being confronted with something I have always hated, change."

"So." Despite his hostile feelings, Jake found the conversation a welcome shift from the questions whirling about in his head. "You were saying about the Depression?"

"Nothing you Americans experienced could compare with what happened to Germany in the twenties and early thirties. I know you think I am exaggerating, but I promise you it is not so. Let me tell you just one, story, Colonel. My father was a professor of physics at the University of Leipzig, one of the finest schools in the country. I used to go and meet him on Friday afternoons. He would receive his pay, and we would stop by a little cafe where I would have an ice cream and he would sit and drink a real coffee and smoke his pipe. That pipe and his one coffee each week were his only indulgences. We would always take a table far from the windows, so that we did not have to watch the beggars parade back and forth on the street outside. There were beggars everywhere. The women and children were by far the worst, pleading for pennies and clutching at your clothes and screaming obscenities if you did not pay."

He sighed and leaned back against the wall alongside Jake, more than the flickering fire streaking his face with shadows. "For you to understand what I am saying, I must tell you that at the end of the First World War, Germany signed a treaty which forced us to pay money to the victorious nations, especially France. I am not going to argue right and wrong with you, Colonel. All I will tell you is that we were forced to pay money which we did not have. The result was not only a depression like you Americans knew in the thirties, but depression and inflation at the same time. Such inflation as you cannot fathom. So what I describe to you was not happening just in Leipzig, but all over Germany. And it was growing worse on a monthly basis, even weekly."

The call of a night bird brought Jake to his feet. He quietly stalked their perimeter, climbed over the truck, peered out into the shadows and listened carefully. Satisfied, he returned to his place by the fire. "Go ahead."

"Is this hard for you, Colonel?"

"Is what hard?"

"Does it trouble you to hear that the enemy might have had a reason for its actions?"

"There are no excuses for what you people did," Jake said, his voice grating. "None."

There was a long moment's silence, then he sighed, "No, despite my desire to argue and battle, I agree. There was no excuse."

There was a stirring from the bedroll across the fire. A dark tousled head rose to enquire, "Do my ears deceive me?"

"I have always prided myself on my intellect," Hechter replied. "I cannot continue to do so and yet ignore what lies all around me."

Rolf looked from Jake to Hechter and back again. "Wonder of wonders."

"The war was wrong," Hechter went on, his eyes hidden within shadows of two caves carved from years of banked-up exhaustion. "The camps . . . have you seen a camp, Colonel?"

"Survivors," Jake replied, remembering faces behind the wires of the Allied internment camp at Badenburg. "I never want to see any more."

"No, nor I. I have received a letter from a colleague, a man who was employed by the research division of a Bavarian company. He worked in a village called Dachau. He wrote to say that when the Americans arrived, they forced the entire village to walk through the concentration camp outside town. He told me that he did not think he would ever sleep well again. Not ever."

"You mean he didn't have any idea what was going on before?" Jake snorted his disbelief. "You've got to be kidding."

"Of course he knew," Hechter replied impatiently. "We all knew. We all had heard stories of places where in wintertime the sky would rain a white ash that would lay inches thick in the roads. But we all chose to turn away. Not to see. Not to believe that our beloved Fatherland had truly sunk to this level. Such things were unthinkable. They could not be. They could not. They . . ."

The man could not go on. He turned and stared out over the ruined building, the wall's jagged edge pointing like wounded fingers toward a star-studded sky. He searched the heavens in silent appeal. Then he lowered his face and sighed at the ground, shaking his head slowly, his eyes showing haunted depths.

Jake glanced across the fire to where Rolf now sat and took in the scene with silent caution. Jake found himself agreeing with the man's calculating watchfulness. This change in Hans Hechter was too startling to easily believe. But Jake did not want to let the moment pass. Not yet. "You were going to tell me a story."

Hechter started, as though drawn from a nightmare, and turned his way. "You truly want to hear this?"

Jake nodded, his eyes watchful, unable to commit himself more than that.

"Very well," Hechter said, and straightened his shoulders with visible effort. "I agree that the war was wrong. But it is hard to see where the first step of a new turning will take you. All we knew when the Nazis swept into power was that a firm hand was finally restoring us to a semblance of order. After ten years of growing chaos, this was a tremendous achievement. And remember, Colonel, I am speaking to you as one of the privileged classes. I cannot myself imagine how it must have been for those whose families were worse off."

"Horrible," Rolf said quietly. "My father was an electrician. There were weeks, months even, when we honestly did not know if we would survive. All I remember of two entire years is a constant, raging hunger. And anger."

"The whole nation was angry," Hechter said quietly. "Even to a child that mood was clear. We had been beaten to our knees, and then beaten again. I myself had not fought in the Great War, and neither had my father. Why was I being forced to pay and pay and pay? I hated all those who had done this to me. Americans and Frenchmen and Russians and all the others, they were just names to me, but names to hate."

"It was easy to hate then," Rolf admitted. "The Communists were the first to use that hatred. The Nazis came later and mixed fury with patriotism, a mixture which proved too heady for some." Rolf stopped, as though waiting for an explosion from his companion. When none came, he raised questioning eyebrows at Jake, but said only, "The Communists were specialists at weaving spells with the magic of rage. That is why I did not join them. I was tempted by their ideals, there was much that they said which I agreed with. But I was frightened by how everything was woven together, not with brotherhood as they said, but with hatred."

"But there were many who did join," Hechter said. "Many. And the anarchists were gathering together many others who hated even more than the Communists, who hated so much that they could not believe in any government. By my tenth year, I had learned never to walk along a main boulevard after school by myself, because several times a week they would be overrun by marches, and the marches always ended up in running street battles. Always."

"The Weimar government was a sham," Rolf offered from his place across the fire. "They had no response to any of the people's demands except the barrel of a gun. The streets of almost every city in the nation ran red with the blood of people who called themselves patriots and whom the government banned as dissidents or criminals or traitors. It was an evil time."

"Especially for a child," Hechter agreed. "I remember one Friday, I believe I was twelve by then. My father came out of the university office, and he was carrying two great sacks, one in each hand. I ran up to him and asked what he had. 'My salary,' he said, handing me one. 'Come, we must hurry.'

"The sack was not heavy, but it was very bulky. Inside were stacks and stacks of bills. I wanted to ask him about this, but he was rushing ahead. My father seldom hurried anywhere. To see him run like this troubled me more than the sacks of money.

"Soon I saw why we were hurrying. I stopped to pull up my socks and saw that behind us was a crowd of other people, all carrying sacks, and all running in the same direction as us. I raced to catch up with my father, truly frightened now.

"Just then we crossed the first main thoroughfare leading to the center of the city, and there was a riot. Policemen and soldiers were shooting at a great mob of people carrying banners for bread. I remember reading that one word, bread. My father always avoided these scenes, especially when I was there. That time he simply cried, 'Not this too! Why do they have to riot on Fridays?'

"He gripped my shoulder, and together we skirted the worst of the fighting, then ran across the street.

Only then did I realize we were headed for the market district. I glanced behind me and saw that all the others were racing along behind us. One man, somebody I knew vaguely because he worked in the same department as my father, was caught by a policeman's truncheon and went down hard. All the others, people he had worked with for years and years, simply raced over and around him.

"My father stopped in front of the butcher's, reached inside my sack, and transferred two great handfuls of notes to his own bag. Then he turned me around and shouted, 'Go to the baker. Buy all the bread you can with that. Don't come outside. Wait for me there. Now run!' I ran.

"There was already a line when I arrived, but not long. Beggars were working the lines as they always did, and I hugged the sack with both arms, ready to kick anyone who came close. But today their plea was different. I came to hear it a lot in the coming days, but this was the first time, and it gave me nightmares. 'A crust, a crust for my babies,' they cried. 'Remember me when you come out.' They did not want my money. They wanted *bread*.

"When it came to be my turn, I did not need to say anything. There was a sign above the counter, with a number bigger than I had ever seen, and just as I was to be served someone came rushing in the door. I was shoved to one side as the sweating baker and his helper started handing one great sack after another over the counter. I was very worried that perhaps they would run out of bread with such an order, but then I realized it was only money. The man shouted something to the baker, who took a thick pencil and

added another zero to the giant number on the plac-
ard. I realized then it was the price of bread, and it
had gone up by another *ten times* just while I was
standing in line.

"I bought my bread. It almost filled the sack the
money had been in. Then I stood at the far corner and
waited for my father to arrive. People were carrying
their money in almost everything—knapsacks, bulg-
ing briefcases, even a couple of wheelbarrows. Every
few minutes the runner would come back, collect
the money, and another zero or two would be added
to the price of bread."

"Hyperinflation," Rolf said quietly. "It is one thing
to hear the word and another thing entirely to try
and survive it. Toward the end, when inflation was
running at over a hundred percent an hour, my father
would insist on being paid before he started a job. My
mother would collect the money each morning and
race to the shops because by evening his pay was
worth half what it had been that morning."

"So you see, Colonel," Hechter said tiredly, "when
Hitler arrived and began establishing order, there
were many sane and intelligent people who thought
the Nazis were saviors, not villains. I was one of
them."

Jake stared at the scientist, wondering at all he had
heard. Wondering also why his own heart remained
so hardened. "And now?"

"Now. Yes, now." Hechter's body had gradually
collapsed in upon itself. "How hard it is to admit
that my entire life has been built around a lie. Does
that give you satisfaction, Colonel, to hear me admit
that I was wrong, that I have been wrong for fifteen
years, that my entire life has been wasted propping
up an evil lie?"

Chapter Thirteen

*T*HE NEXT MORNING found Jake making the hardest decision of his life.

"I can't go," he told the others quietly. "It is one thing to have an assistant who takes off for a while with a friend. If we're being watched, though, and they see me do something strange, they may stop me from coming back. And this marketplace is the only point of contact I have for the man who met us yesterday."

He looked from one to the other, willing them to object, to demand that he come with them. "You've seen her note. I don't know why she's there, or what she can do for us."

"She will be expecting you," Rolf said doubtfully.

"I know." Jake sighed into his coffee cup, watched a glorious dawn turn faded and dismal as it rose over the ruins of what had once been the national capital. From his position leaning on the side of the truck, Jake looked out over an endless display of destruction. Those buildings which remained intact showed sightless eyes to the rubbled streets, their windows boarded over, their doors often barricaded. Jake reached into his pocket and handed over a folded pa-

per. "I have written her a note. It explains that we are
supposed to meet our contact here today, that he had
something urgent to tell me. Something vital. Those
were his words."

"But what—"

"If she can take you through the border, go," Jake
said. "That was my first objective, getting you to
safety."

Rolf and Hans exchanged glances. "How will you
know if we get through?"

"I won't," Jake said grimly. "But that can't be
helped. If there's something *vital* that man with the
bad eye needs to tell me, then I have to wait. I have
no choice."

The smell of coffee and frying bread drifted from
one of the early morning stalls. Across the open
space came the sound of footsteps scuffling over the
rubble. Jake watched the first patrons scurry toward
the traders selling black-market food. "She said nine
o'clock. You need to get there early, hide yourselves
well. Make sure there is no one observing. If there is,
wait until she moves toward you, don't go to her."
He glanced back at them, nodded once, ached with
the desire to go with them. "Good luck."

Theo's first words to Sally when he stopped to pick
her up in front of her hostel that next morning were,
"Something's wrong."

She felt her stomach zoom down below street
level. "You can't go?"

"Of course I can go. Who said anything about not
going? I said something is wrong."

She reached up for the side railing and climbed on
board, then shut her door. "Theo Travers, you are

about to catch some of what has been called my bad side."

He grinned. "A kitten like you?"

She started to snap, then realized there was a worry there beneath his smile of greeting. "What's the matter?"

His smile disappeared. "Easier to show than tell. Let's get started."

Their way took them back along the Kurfurstendamm. Even in the early morning, she saw signs of the growing difference between the city's eastern and western sectors. There was activity here in the west. Makeshift signs decorated the few buildings still intact, advertising everything from clothing to cooking oil. Besides the trundling military carriers, a number of antiquated private cars and trucks puttered about, most loaded to the gills with wares of one kind or another. The people she saw looked tired, but they lacked the haggard hopelessness of those in the east. There was a sense of purpose to their step, an awareness of having somewhere to go.

"It all looks the same to me," she said.

"No it doesn't," Theo replied, and pointed through the windshield. "Up there. Tell me what you see."

She peered, decided, "A police jeep."

"Right. Only the Russkies aren't there anymore." Theo watched the jeep pass before continuing, "I'm quartered over near one of the border crossings. Only place they could put us on short notice. Last night all the Russkies just up and vanished. Not a word. Just weren't there."

Sally felt her nerves draw to humming tautness. "So?"

"So all military police, vehicles and borders and foot patrols, *all* of them are supposed to have one guy from each of the four sectors. That's part of the plan, see. Four sectors, one city. Only the Russkies have all disappeared."

A sense of foreboding tolled deep within her. "What does it mean?"

"I wish I knew." He rubbed the stubble on his chin. "From what I saw around HQ this morning, it's got some others worried. It's been bad ever since they started erecting their border checkpoints here in the city. That was strictly against regs. But this is something more. This morning the brass were scurrying around like somebody stepped on their anthill."

"Did they make problems about you going over?"

"Naw." The now-familiar grin returned. "Those guys, they know as much about construction as I do about brain surgery. I gave them a song and dance, got them eating out of my hand. Told them how this sand is tons better, which it is, and heaps cheaper, which it oughtta be if those political joes'd get their thumbs out. Never knew buying a few loads of sand could be so much trouble."

Their day yesterday at the site had been almost as frustrating as Sally's trip to the market. A long line of suspicious political officers and their Russian counterparts had come by, each insisting on beginning the negotiations over from the start. Theo had handled it with remarkable calm.

"Heads up," Theo said. "Border check."

Instead of being passed through the American side as was customary, the guard-sergeant stepped in front of the barrier and waved them to a halt. He walked around to Theo's window and saluted. "You Major Travers?"

"The one and only. What can I do for you?"

"Got a call from HQ. Told us to have a jeep escort you over."

"That won't be necessary, soldier."

"It wasn't a request, sir. Orders came straight from General Collins. If they aren't let through, you can't go, sir."

"Eating right out of your hand," Sally muttered. "Better watch out or they might decide to take a couple of fingers."

Theo ignored her, kept his head stuck out the window. "Are my eyes deceiving me, or have the Russkies moved their border station?"

"Yessir. Been at it almost all night. Pushed it back a coupla hundred feet or so."

Theo opened his door and stepped onto the running board. "That a tank?"

"Looks like one to me." The sergeant looked up at him. "You sure you need to be going over there this morning, sir?"

"I'm sure." Theo climbed back on board and shut his door. "Round up your men, sergeant. Let's go see what they're up to."

"If you say so, sir." The sergeant signaled to a waiting jeep, then turned back and said, "Just make sure my buddies all get back in one piece, will you, sir?"

"Right." Theo edged the big truck forward, muttered to Sally, "Stranger and stranger."

The Russian border post had been transformed. Barriers formed from rail cross-ties had been erected in a long forbidding line, with strands of barbed wire strung between them. The long, ominous snout of a tank poked out from a tent of camouflage netting. Armed men were everywhere.

Their arrival was met by a phalanx of stern-faced soldiers with guns at the ready. The same political officer as the morning before came around, saluted them nervously, demanded, "Why are you traveling with an armed escort?"

Sally leaned across and retorted, "Why did you move the guard station? And why the tank?"

The officer reddened. "I will ask the questions here!"

A hand signal from Travers caused Sally to back down. "We have no choice. The major's superior has commanded us either to travel with guards or not to travel at all." She saw the man hesitate, and she pleaded, "We are very interested in beginning these shipments this afternoon. The major has received authorization for immediate payment."

Once again, the offer of dollars softened the man's resolve. "Wait here," he snapped.

He was gone almost an hour before returning and announcing, "There has been a change of plans. The materials will be transported on our trucks. You will pay the costs, of course."

"Of course," Sally said, and turned to translate.

"Tell the guy he can bring it to us by Chinese sampan if the price is right," Travers responded. "But I still need to go collect those samples and talk to the guy responsible for the dig. So how about letting us get out from under the eye of that big gun."

They were eventually let through, but only after they were joined by two Soviet jeeps. Their extended convoy made its way through streets void of life. Sally watched as one boulevard after another appeared, devoid of even the first glimmers of activity. "Something's really wrong."

Travers looked over at her. "We got a squad of Russkies in front and behind us, we've spent the best part of an hour staring down the business end of a tank barrel, and you're just figuring that out?"

Sally met his gaze straight on. "Why didn't you tell me you spoke German?" She watched his double take give swiftly over to a denial, but she cut him off with, "Don't even try, Theo. You knew what I had said to that turkey in blue, and I never even got around to translating."

Travers eased off and grinned ruefully. "Harry told me you were a fast one. Guess I just didn't understand how fast."

It was her turn to play dumb. "Harry? You know Harry Grisholm?"

"Old buddies," Theo affirmed. "Somehow he heard I was coming over. Asked me to keep an eye on you."

"But how—" Sally stopped, the bits and pieces clicking into place. "They left the door to their office open on purpose." And the file. No confidential file would have been left out for the evening, especially not if there was the possibility of a leak. "I've been played for a fool."

"Don't think that even for a minute," Theo retorted. "You were Harry's only hope. Of course, that's all unofficial. Officially, he's hopping mad over you disappearing without a by-your-leave." Theo eyed her with mock seriousness. "Not to mention something about a false passport and illegal travel documents."

"So he told you everything?"

"Not me," Theo assured her. "That's basically all Harry said when we talked, and I got the impression I couldn't ask anything more than that. Which was why I didn't have to play interested when you spilled the beans in the plane."

She looked at him with suspicion. "Are you a spy?"

"Not a chance," Theo replied cheerfully. "Just watched from the sidelines, is all. Which I guess is why Harry felt like he could trust me."

Sally turned her attention back to the window, her mind churning. The morning was strong and clear, the sky pristine blue. But nothing was stirring. No cars, no people, nothing. "I don't like this."

"Too quiet," he agreed. "Like the calm before the storm. A big one."

The atmosphere of buried tension and fear stayed with them throughout the remainder of their trip. The sand pits were at the end of a lower-class neighborhood whose low-slung apartment buildings extended almost to the company's rusted gates. They drove past the derelict office building, its myriad of broken windows staring down on them like sightless eyes. Two giant mixing towers had escaped the bombings, two others looked as though a giant's hand had crumpled them.

Beneath the last of the towers clustered a group of men who made no move as the convoy pulled up. Beside them waited a long, low sedan painted army brown with a single red star on its portal. As Theo and Sally's convoy halted by the first dig, a soldier opened the car's rear door. A Soviet officer emerged, straightened his tunic, and walked toward them.

"Stranger and stranger," Theo muttered. "What's a Russian officer want with somebody buying a load of sand?"

Sally opened her door and stepped forward to greet the officer, but he ignored her and walked directly to Theo's side of the truck. In heavily accented but understandable English he said, "You are Major . . ."

He paused to inspect a card in his palm. "Major Travers?"

"That's me." Theo opened his door and slipped down. "What can I do for you?"

The officer's eyes were as glacial as his voice. "Your papers."

"Sure." His cool unruffled by the officer, Theo handed over his military ID. "Mind telling me what gives?"

Instead of replying, the officer gave Theo's pass a minute inspection, then turned and snapped his fingers once in the direction of the waiting group. Instantly one older man doffed his cap and came scurrying over. "Ja, Herr Oberst?"

The officer acknowledged Sally's existence for the first time. "You will tell this man that he is to execute the major's instructions, so long as they are restricted to digging in the pits here within the compound perimeter. You will tell him that the major is to pay for his services. Is that not correct, Major?"

"Anything you say," Theo replied with false ease.

"Trucks will begin making delivery in four days, unless there are . . . delays." A hint of a smile appeared, then vanished without a trace. "You will pay seventy dollars for each load. Cash. No negotiations."

"Seventy it is," Theo agreed.

The officer glanced at his watch. "I was informed that you require samples."

Theo gestured toward the truck. "Got the shovels and the sacks in the back."

"You are to gather your samples and depart before twelve noon." He fastened his full attention upon the major. "You will not be permitted to delay your departure one minute beyond twelve. Is that clear?"

"Twelve sounds good to me."

"I don't care how it sounds, Major," the officer snapped. "I am telling you what you will do. You will treat these as orders, and you will obey. Now is that clear?"

Instead of anger, there was merely a deepening to Travers' gaze. Even from where Sally stood, she could see the depth and strength beneath the major's calm veneer. All he said was, "Perfectly."

Without another word, the officer wheeled about and stomped away. He stopped to give crisp orders to the two jeeps, then walked back to his car. The driver closed the door behind him, climbed in and shut his own door, then drove off.

Travers watched them depart in thoughtful silence. Then he turned to examine the old man who stood waiting to one side, his hands crumpling the brim to his battered hat. "Ask the fellow here what's planned for this afternoon. And why the streets here have about as much life to them today as a tomb."

When Sally had finished translating, the man nervously replied, "I know nothing, madam. Nothing at all. I am a simple laborer. My family is hungry. I will work hard. Please, tell us what it is we are to do."

"It's like trying to get an answer out of a rabbit," Sally told the major.

"Well, he's had a lot of experience in learning how to survive." He raised his hand toward the old man, motioning for him to stay where he was, then grasped her arm and led her toward the first sand pit. More quietly he asked, "See the good Colonel Burnes around here anywhere?"

"No." She squinted in the growing sunlight, searched the empty grounds, willed him to appear before her eyes, for them to get back in the truck and leave and have all this behind them for good. "Not a sign."

"With our minders over there, I'm not surprised." Theo motioned toward the bottom of the pit. "Okay, then let's make a little circuit, just the two of us. I'll point out places and afterwards you go back and tell them where they're supposed to dig. A sack from each. Got that?"

"Yes." They were so close. If he got her message. If he wasn't picked up. If, if, if. Her legs suddenly felt weak as water.

"Steady, now." They made a slow circuit of the first pit, started over the uneven ground toward the second hole. Beyond was a pile of dirt excavated and mixed and ready for shipment. It had rested there long enough to sprout a meager crop of weeds. Beyond it rose a motley-colored sand dune with a giant hunk bitten from the nearest face. Theo led her slowly but steadily in that direction, pointing every once in a while, Sally nodding with one hand pressed to her chest, certain that if she did not keep a solid grip her heart would leap from her body.

"Maybe he's worried about me," Theo muttered. "Guy doesn't know me from Adam. Okay, let's split up here, you walk over that way, keep your eye on me. I'll make little motions, you mark spots with your foot."

Sally moved off and headed toward the hillside. And even though she was waiting for it, eager for it, hoping with all her heart for it, when the hiss came from the little channel she was about to cross, she almost collapsed with fright. She recovered quickly enough to make it look like a stumble, returned Theo's signal, stood and looked across the pit toward the major, and whispered, "Jake?"

Chapter Fourteen

*T*HE PAN HE WAS just about to stack slipped from his hand, rattled on the tailgate, then clanged on the rocks below when the voice announced, "Your wife is a very beautiful woman."

Jake did not need to look to know it was Hans Hechter. "Where is Rolf?"

"Gone." He kept his voice low as he bent over, picked up the pan, and wiped it with his grimy handkerchief. "She is intelligent as well. Not to mention courageous."

"Gone where?"

"To the American base. Disguised as a sack of sand, riding in the back of a dump truck, escorted by two jeeploads of Soviet troops."

Jake accepted the pan, set it in place at the top of the stack, turned back and leaned nonchalantly upon the tailgate. The morning customers for coffee and husks were gone. Now the market was almost empty. A few stragglers stepped hesitantly over the rough ground, picking at the paltry items on offer.

Jake was stationed as he had been instructed, between two other trucks also bearing hardware and household goods. Their vehicle's front bumper rested

close to the single remaining wall of an office building; above their heads were the ghosts of a few plac-
ards proclaiming the proprietor who had lost all in
the war. Crumbling relics of walls extended to either
side, forming a mini-tunnel into which he had nosed
his truck. This position offered them a semblance of
privacy and distance from their neighbors.

Jake kept his face immobile as Hechter swiftly
sketched out their journey and the contact, his eyes
flickering in bored fashion over the few would-be
shoppers. If there were watchers, Jake could not identify them. Even their neighbors gave them little
mind. They had paid their dues like all the others
and been assigned a spot and merited little further
concern.

Hechter reached the point where they had spoken
from the ditch and said, "Your wife was most concerned that you had not accompanied us."

"I can imagine."

"More than concerned. She was distraught. It took
the major quite a time to calm her enough to make
plans."

"What major?"

A trace of humor came and went within the depths
of Hechter's clear blue eyes. "He said that you would
probably ask that very same question."

In a voice so low that it scarcely carried to Jake,
much less to the people around them, Hechter related the little that he had gathered from the pair
while remaining hidden in the ditch. How there had
been a leak, probably a spy, within NATO intelligence. How their local operatives had not been simply sent elsewhere, but rather eliminated. How Jake
himself might already be compromised. And how the

Russian officer had ordered Sally and the major to leave by noon and not return.

"I have to tell you," Hechter finished. "Your wife was less than impressed with your reason for not coming."

"No," Jake agreed quietly. "She wouldn't have been."

"She told me to remind you of the promise you made to her before your departure. She said that several times."

"I remember," Jake murmured, his heart aching. "One thing I don't understand, though. Why couldn't they take you, too?"

Hechter shifted his gaze. "They could."

"So?"

"I decided," Hechter said slowly, "that I owed you a message."

Jake inspected the scientist, wondered at his own inability to overcome his aversion and offer the man a simple thanks. But in that single glance toward Hechter's proud features, Jake found himself again confronted by the specter of the past and what he had lost. The anger simply would not let him be.

A querulous voice startled him by demanding, "Well? Are you open for business, or is this gossip of yours going to continue on all day?"

Jake swung around, then lowered his eyes to meet the impatient gaze of a woman as broad as she was high. Two beefy arms rested propped upon her ample hips. A pair of legs thicker than his waist were planted in the rocky soil. Jake started to comment about her not appearing to have suffered overmuch from a lack of food, then changed his mind. The woman looked like she packed quite a wallop. "What can I do for you, mother?"

"Mother, is it now? You'll not be garnering a higher price from me with those fancy words of yours, gypsy. That I can promise you for sure." She stepped forward, shouldered Hechter to one side, and went on loud enough for the neighboring trucks to hear, "I've a need for a skillet. One large enough to cook for a hungry man and six children determined to eat everything the cursed war has not destroyed."

"Then you'll be after this one," Jake said, shifting the pile around and hefting a cast-iron pan fully two feet across. "The finest you'll find anywhere."

She accepted the long handle, grunted noncommittally, and demanded, "So how much do you want to steal from a defenseless old mother, then?"

"You're the one who'll be doing the stealing," Jake replied, taking in the steel-gray bun, the hands so chapped they had swollen to almost twice their normal size, the determined set to her chin. "You'll not find a lower price anywhere."

"If that's the case, then perhaps I could find means to buy more than one." Her back to the market, she leaned over, rattled the pile of pots, asked quietly, "Do you have the Bibles?"

Jake faltered for a second time that morning. "What?"

"The Bibles, man, the Bibles." Her voice carried the continual hiss of a scalding teapot. "Don't you dare tell me that blind bear of a man sent me to the wrong truck."

"No, no," Jake muttered, collecting himself. "I have them."

"Then listen. Set them in the space between the front of your truck and the wall."

"But how—"

"Just do it, and if you want to save your own worthless hide, you'll take your lunch in the same spot." She wheeled about, said more loudly, "You're as big a thief as the rest of them."

"Take it or leave it," Jake said flatly, his voice as loud as hers.

"Aye, there it is," the huge woman said bitterly, handing him a tightly folded bundle of notes. "No choice at all for the likes of me, is there."

Jake made a pretense of counting the bills, shoved them in his pocket, hefted two of the larger pans, recognized genuine avarice in her gaze when he passed them over. There was need here, as well as subterfuge. "Wait," he said.

He scrambled into the truck and came out with three pairs of children's boots. He piled them on top of the pots in her arms, was pleased to see her eyes open larger and her voice say softly, "Shoes."

"A gift," he declared loudly. "All I ask is that you tell your friends, those with money, that here stands an honest trader."

"Huh!" she snorted. "And how many would a woman of my means know who have money? Saved all winter for these pots, I have." Then she pretended to shift the pots for a better grip, making a racket in the process, and saying swiftly, "All the shoes up with the Bibles. But none of the pans. Too much noise."

Jake nodded, pretended to help her organize her load, asked, "What's happening this afternoon?"

"Questions for later." She took a step back, stopped to eye him up and down. "It's not often I have to make a second judgment, especially of a gypsy and a man of the road. But I'll say to all who ask, it's a pity we don't have more like yourself."

"Good day to you, good woman," Jake called after her, conscious of the eyes. He then made a pretense of inspecting the almost empty market lot before turning to Hechter and proclaiming loudly, "Is that to be our only customer of the day? I've seen more activity in a morgue."

He motioned for Hechter to climb on board. "Get up there and start handing me down things. We might as well clean the truck as stand around here looking miserable."

Attention soon turned elsewhere, as Jake piled the pots and pans about his feet, then began accepting the bales of shoes and feed and taking them up front. With swift motions he shifted the secret handle, then started pulling out the burlap sacks of Bibles. There was nothing on the outside to differentiate these sacks from those holding the shoes.

By the time the compartment was empty and resealed, both men were puffing hard. Jake handed him a rag and said quietly, "Just move the dirt around as you wipe. Best to keep the doors hidden even if they are empty."

Hechter nodded and set to work, all his former bluster silenced. Jake watched him work and wondered again at his own lingering resentment. The man had clearly apologized as best as he was able. He had even returned to tell him of the contact with Sally, when all reason and self-interest would have urged him to escape. Yet here Jake stood, trapped within emotions which both reason and his own faith told him were not only wrong, but also unworthy. But telling himself these things did nothing to free him from what he felt, nor dim this flame of anger whenever he looked in Hechter's direction.

Jake waited until Hechter had settled down beside him, then asked quietly, "What was the real reason you came back?"

Hechter started to reply, then caught himself, looked beyond Jake, and his eyes grew wide. Before Jake could turn around, a tremulous woman's voice replied, "Because I begged him to."

Chapter Fifteen

*D*ON'T BE MAD with me. Please. I couldn't stand it just now."

"I'm not mad," Jake replied, and continued to hustle her up front. But when they approached the wall, Jake stopped cold, looked about, asked, "What is going on around here?"

"I couldn't go back without you. I just couldn't." Sally's features played halfway between stubborn defiance and a teary-eyed plea. "So I staged a fight with Theo, that's the major—well, only half staged, because he said I was being a total fool and might jeopardize your safety, but I didn't care, I don't care, I couldn't leave you here with goodness knows what's about to happen."

Jake walked around the space in front of the truck where he had left the sacks of shoes and Bibles. The space was completely empty. He inspected the wall, found it as rock solid and unyielding as before. "I don't understand any of this."

"I just walked off. The Russians didn't try to stop me. Their orders must have been about Theo and the truck, or maybe they were just worried because it was getting toward eleven-thirty and we had to be back by noon. The roads coming here were empty. Totally, completely empty. I wasn't stopped once. I came straight here. There aren't even any policemen down on the street in front of the market. Nobody." She reached over, stopped Jake's baffled gaze about the space in front of their truck, said, "Tell me you're not mad."

Hans stepped up beside them. "It's just gone noon." He looked around the area, demanded, "Where are the goods?"

"I was hoping you could tell me that," Jake replied.

"Jake, please, would you look at me and—" Sally stopped with a little squeak. She hopped back a step and sat on the hood of the truck. "The ground just moved."

A section of the dusty earth came up, pushed aside, and revealed the scraggly dark beard of the one-eyed man. He nodded at Jake, jerked at the sight of Sally, demanded quietly, "What is she doing here?"

"Long story."

"No time. Come, quickly, all of you. And watch your step. There are rats."

"Berlin has become a microcosm of all Europe," the burly man was saying. "This was Stalin's decision. What happens here will determine what will happen first in Germany, then France, then Italy. Then, my friend, it will be too late."

"Too late for what?" Jake still had difficulty fitting together the jumbled pieces confronting him. This one-eyed man and his precise speech. The surroundings, the atmosphere, the urgency with which this man spoke.

"Too late to do what must be done," he replied.

Before he could continue, Sally interrupted him with, "Where is everybody?"

He looked at her. Clearly he was unsure what to think of this woman and resented her presence. "We have sent everyone home until the emergency has stabilized. It is safer."

"What emergency?"

"All in good time." The man returned his attention to Jake. "You hold to the same error as most of your countrymen. I saw this coming, as did others. In order to fight the war with Stalin's Russia on your side, you chose to overlook the kind of man with whom you dealt. Now it is hard for you to accept the truth."

"And that is?"

"That this man is your enemy. And not just yours. He is the enemy of all freedom. And all faith."

A bear, Jake decided. That was what this Karl Schreiner most resembled. A big hairy bear, scarred from countless battles and carrying the burden of things which Jake could only imagine. He ventured a guess, "You were on the Russian front?"

"I was. And walked home when it was over, seven months on the road through ice and snow and mud and rain, with hunger and pain as my only companions." Karl started to scratch at his blind eye, caught himself and lowered his hand. "You think this is what has caused me to think the way I do? Listen, my friend. Stalin's world has no room for faith in anything but Stalin. He may dress his lie up in other words, like brotherhood or Communism or Mother Russia. But in truth Stalin is the new Caesar, setting himself up to be worshiped and made a god on earth."

Faith. This was the most jarring fragment of all. The man claimed to be not just a believer, but a lay minister as well. They sat together in a stone-lined office. Beyond the stout open door was what had become a meeting hall and before had been the wine cellar of a gracious manor. The manor was gone, the wine racks now stacked with Jake's Bibles, as well as clothes and shoes and medicines and children's toys.

Sally interrupted them again. Her voice was soft and tired, yet somehow stronger because of the effort it took to speak. "Jake and I are believers."

Surprise registered on the broad-bearded features. Karl looked from one to the other. "This is truth?"

"It is," Jake confirmed. Proud of her. So glad to be with her that for the moment, for this tiny sliver of time and safety and comfort, there was no room for worry or condemnation. She was here. It was enough.

Narrow windows lined one wall of both the office and the meeting hall, permitting in meager afternoon light. The ceiling in the hall was high and vaulted, rising in great stone arches which intersected before descending to sturdy pillars. The benches were hard and wooden and still bore the marks of vineyards which had supplied the crates from which they were made. The room was unadorned save for a single large cross, the timbers taken from the derelict manor, rough and scarred by war and bombs. Jake found his gaze repeatedly drawn through the office doorway and out to that war-scarred cross, as though there were a message being whispered to his heart, something he either could not hear or was frightened to accept.

Karl gathered himself and went on, "The West sits at the table and argues about border disputes and the fact that they can no longer move easily through the eastern sector of Berlin. But this is just a smoke-screen. It is intended to keep you occupied while other, greater operations go unnoticed."

"What operations?"

"This is what I shall have to show you." He rose to his feet. "We leave in fifteen minutes."

Sally waited until Karl had moved off before asking, "What do you think?"

"I don't know." Jake looked at her. She had not released his hand since descending into the sewer and watching the burly man and his assistant slide the segment of false flooring back into place. "How are you feeling?"

"Tired," she said, and showed it. Her face bore the finely etched lines of extreme fatigue and tension. "I don't think I've really slept since this started."

"Do you want to rest?"

"Later." Her eyes rested calmly on Jake as she declared, "I trust him."

He nodded, accepted the information, said, "You've changed since we've gotten here."

"What do you mean?"

"You were a frightened little mouse back at the truck," he replied.

"I was afraid you were going to try and send me away," she said, her fingers linking themselves more tightly with his. "I didn't want to fight with you."

He freed one hand to trace a feather-touch down the side of the frame made by her tousled hair. "I'm glad you came."

The haunted look returned, flitting across her features like clouds across a windswept sky. "After you left England, I found myself lying there awake at night, facing changes. Some nights I felt like it was the only thing that kept me intact, feeling like I needed to use this time to make these realizations and build for the future. A future together. Otherwise I might have drowned in my fears that you wouldn't . . .''

He stilled her words with a finger to her lips, or tried to, but she shook her head. Whatever it was, it needed to be said. Jake settled back, filled to bursting with the wonder of being so loved.

''I've always been independent, determined to go my own way and be my own person. I never thought being married would change this. But it has. Before, I thought it was going to be just fine, you'd go off on your own little adventures, and it would give me the space to be myself. But it won't work, Jake. I'm too much a part of you.'' Sally leaned over far enough to place her head on his shoulder. ''We have to do something about this, Jake. I'm not asking you to change. I'm only asking for you to make it so whatever it is you need to do, I can do it with you.''

''I understand,'' he murmured. He did.

A sharp knock sounded on the door. Karl pushed through, every action fueled by his impatient strength. He looked at Sally, said, ''You and your husband may take my quarters. They lie beyond the kitchen and the dorm where your Hans Hechter has bunked down. I suggest you go rest.'' His attention swiveled to Jake. ''Time to move.''

''Anyone who lives by faith in the coming days will have to be a fighter.''

They were crouched in the same rabbit warren of sewer tunnels that had carried them from the market to the manor's bombed-out hulk. Overhead rumbled a seemingly endless train of vehicles so heavy they caused the walls around Jake to tremble. The only light came from a kerosene lantern in Karl's massive grip. The smell of burning oil helped to stave off the worst of the sewer's stench.

"That's what you were thinking, wasn't it?" the burly man pressed. "How one of Hitler's soldiers came to be sitting here beside you, a spy for the West and a soldier for God."

"There is a lot about this whole business," Jake replied, "which I do not begin to understand."

"God speaks to a man when he is ready and able to listen. For me, it happened on an icy field in the middle of nowhere, when death was as real to me as the cold that blistered my feet. He spoke to me then. I heard His voice, and I knew that I was to be saved." He thumped his barrel chest. "Not saved in the sense of living longer in this pitiful body. For an instant of clarity I realized that if I lived or died, it was *His* choice, and I was going to be content with the decision."

"I understand," Jake said quietly.

"He called me back here," the deep voice rumbled on. "Back to a city and a country as ruined by war as I was myself. Filled with needs which no human hand could answer. Desperate with hunger for the truth I had found and brought back with me." The single dark eye glimmered in the lantern light. "But it will take a fighter to be a Christian in these coming times. Make no mistake. Stalin's world has less room for true Christian faith than the Nazis did. Already the NKVD, the secret police, and their German minions called the People's Police have started their sorties. Invading houses of worship, stripping them bare. One Bible per church."

"What about the ones we brought?"

"We will not keep them long." He pointed toward the gradually diminishing noise overhead. "As soon as this moment of crisis has passed, we will distribute them to those who have lost everything. There are many such among us. It is the struggle that keeps me busy, seeing to their needs." Karl paused, squinted as he examined Jake, then went on, "At least, the external struggle. My internal struggle is far different."

"So is mine," Jake said quietly, the words coming out before he had realized he had spoken, as though the burly man's own confession was an invitation he had been waiting for. Jake found the growing silence overhead pushing at him. Urging him to open doors that he vastly preferred to keep shut. He found himself struggling to speak, and at the same time to keep still, unwilling to discuss personal matters with this man who had once been his enemy. And then he could not remain silent any longer. "I feel like I'm going back over the same problems again and again inside myself."

"I have sensed this struggle within you." The burly man did not seem the least bit surprised to hear such things, seated there in the dank putrid darkness of a Berlin sewer. "Yours is a common trait among believers."

"I thought I had left all this behind me," Jake went on. "But here it still is, worse than before."

"Not worse," the man corrected. "Seen in the fullness of its proper time." He set the lantern on the stone ledge beside him and rubbed two tired hands down the sides of his face. "Four months after I set up the *Evangelische Keller*, that is what we call our cellar church, I was approached by a group of neighbors. The rubble lot where once three blocks of apartments and an office building had stood was being taken over by black marketeers. There was liquor and fights and growing evil. Yet the people did not want the black marketeers to leave. They needed the goods. What they wanted was for me to control them. They knew I was a fighter, a former soldier, and most of those who remained were either women with children or too old or too infirm to do it themselves."

Karl's deep voice echoed gently up and down the concrete way. "I was terrified that I would revert to what I had been before. After all, I had only been a Christian for not even two years, and I had been a soldier three times that long. The only reason I ran the Keller at all was that none of the priests who had been carted off by the Nazis had returned from the concentration camps. None. Our little region of Berlin was without either church or minister. But my neighbors did not see me as a preacher. They saw me as a *man*. Someone who could be called on in their hour of need. My fears meant nothing to them. So what if I returned to my angry ways and fought and struggled and even perhaps killed again? They trusted me because I was a Christian, but they needed me because I was strong."

The stare was inward directed, the coarse features twisted with the power of his struggle. "I did the only thing that made sense. I prayed. I prayed and I waited, and as I waited I watched the situation worsen. Prostitutes began collecting around the market area, drawing in more of the war's refuse. So with my former comrade whom you have met, a man who has also now committed his life to the Lord, together we did what was needed. We cleared out the worst of the criminals and set out to control the others. We paid the bribes demanded by the Soviet soldiers and the German bureaucrats. We fought when we had to. We collected payments from all the traders, and with this money we financed the church. The only working church now in all this segment of Berlin."

"You did right," Jake said quietly.

"Yes? You are sure of this?" The fierce gaze turned outward again. "But what of the anger that is drawn out of me? What of this pleasure I feel for the battle and the struggle and the power in controlling this market?" When Jake did not answer, the gaze returned inward. "Then through church channels, through *church* channels, I was asked to send my assessment of the Communists' attitude toward the faithful. This led to other questions, about the rebuilding, the economy, the attitude of the people, the police, the effects of the Soviets. And then to helping directly with problems such as yours. I did not hesitate to respond. Yet I knew great reluctance. Not about the actions, about *myself*. All these activities were drawing out things within myself which I did not wish to see. I was confronted time and again with my own anger, with my own unsolved problems, with battles that still raged far below the surface."

Jake nodded slowly, his entire being rocking back and forth in time to the man's words. His words and experiences were different, but the struggle was the same. He felt that in his bones.

"How could this be? I was a Christian, I felt in the very marrow of my being that I was saved. Then how could I still harbor all these vestiges of who I had been before? Had I not accepted the call to repentance? Had I not dedicated my life to the Master? Did I not feel that sense of solid rightness to my deeds?

Then why was I still so plagued by all of these storms in my mind and heart and soul?"

"You're not just talking about yourself," Jake confessed. "You're talking about me as well."

"Listen to me. I am talking about *every* believer. I do not have all the reasons, my friend. And those I have found may be valid only for me. But one thing I will tell you now, for I have seen the same storm in your eyes that has raged in mine. There is a purpose to it all. In the moment of greatest confusion, when the gale hurtles you about and all your questions are riddles without answers, remember the One who walks upon the waters. He calls to you to join Him, to do the impossible. He reminds you that in His gracious hands lies the power to calm all tempests and bring light to the deepest dark."

Karl picked up his lantern, lifted the glass face, and blew out the light. In the sudden darkness there was a grating overhead, followed by a sliver of light so brilliant that Jake had to shield his eyes. Karl waited for his own vision to clear, then poked his head up, inspected in both directions. "Come," he said. "It is time for you to see the new foe at work."

Chapter Sixteen

"*E*VERYTHING IS SO QUIET," Jake said. His voice was barely above a whisper, but still the sound rang loud in his ears.

"These people have long since learned when it is best to disappear," Karl muttered, his basso rumble kept low. "Even so, we must be grateful. It covers your presence in the chapel, which is a risk to all. We must find a way to send you on before people return to the streets and the sanctuary. Informers are everywhere."

They rode bicycles taken from a tumbledown storage shed set beside their exit from the underground passage. They rode down narrow ways, moving ever farther from the city. The condensed feel of a bombed suburb had been left behind. Their way was now lined by garden walls and stone cottages and occasional glimpses of open countryside. Their tires scraped loud over the gritty surface. They had seen no one since emerging from the sewer.

Jake was hard pressed to keep up with Karl. Despite his bulk, the man cycled along at a surprising pace. "What exactly is going on?"

"Exactly," the big man puffed. "Exactly, this after-noon Stalin sealed off Berlin."

Jake faltered, stopped, then had to race to catch up. "What?"

"They have created an island," the big man contin-ued without slowing. "The western sector of Berlin is now surrounded by Soviet forces and is totally iso-lated. Cut off from all aid. Stalin has given the world an ultimatum. Relinquish Berlin, or face the conse-quences."

The late afternoon sky was blue and cloud flecked and preparing for a glorious sunset. Jake caught the faintest hint of noise. Familiar, yet strange. The noise drifted away as a puff of wind slipped between two cottages, then returned, louder now. "What is that?"

"The sound of doom, if you are not careful. What you in the West do not understand," Karl went on, the words punching out in time to his impatient strokes, "is that Stalin plays with men and power as others play with chess pieces. Berlin is nothing more than a pawn's gambit, a test of your resolve and strength."

The sound was now strong enough to raise the hair on the nape of Jake's neck. He felt the sweat trickling down his spine coalesce and chill.

"Berlin is meant to occupy the West's attention while Stalin prepares the bigger operation. It is in-tended to blind you, and it is succeeding." Karl halted at the base of a tall hill, slipped to his feet, and started pushing his bicycle by foot. "Hurry."

Jake jogged alongside him up a heavily overgrown trail which paralleled the hillside. There was no longer any need for quiet caution. The rumbling was as loud as thunder. "But what does he want?"

Impatiently Karl dumped his bicycle into a bush and started scrambling up the slope. Over his shoulder he tossed back the single word, "Everything."

The rise was steep, the ground loose. Jake grabbed handholds of grass and struggled to keep his footing. His breath came in punching gasps by the time he made the summit and collapsed beside Karl. Together they scrambled forward on hands and knees. Keeping his head low, Jake pushed through the final growth and saw a sight he had hoped was lost and gone forever.

This was not a convoy. This was an army. A continuous line of vehicles stretched out in both directions as far as Jake could see. The trucks were full. With troops. And munitions. And they pulled heavy guns. And tanks. Hundreds of them.

All headed west.

He had seen enough military convoys to know what he was witnessing. The troops were dirty and battle weary, but they sat upright and held their guns calmly, like seasoned troops headed into battle. The tanks and big guns were blackened with powder and dust, but all were clearly in working order. And all rolling inexorably toward the West.

But who was the enemy? And where was the war?

A second line of trucks was pouring eastward, but these held a different cargo entirely. They were filled to the brim with loot. Cattle trucks piled with so much furniture they could scarcely move. Paintings stacked like plywood. Bathtubs and sinks and toilets and kitchen stoves jammed together so haphazardly that most or all would be destroyed long before they arrived. Jake saw three trucks loaded to the gills with radios.

"The eastern sector of Berlin is being systematically emptied," Karl murmured, following Jake's gaze. "Telephones are loaded onto trucks with pitchforks. Away from prying Western eyes, Soviet soldiers wear watches from their wrists to their elbows and drape women's jewelry around their neck. Some say their superiors accept it because it keeps them from having to find money for back pay. What the Soviets cannot take or have no use for, they burn. Our skies are often black with the smoke of burning books and archives. The Russians intend to wipe out every last vestige of our past, both good and bad, and replace it with their own version."

A series of perhaps two dozen trucks paraded by below them, carrying what appeared to be an entire factory—machines, spare parts, even doors and windows. Behind them trundled a series of troop carriers, but these were filled with civilians. Karl went on, "Thousands of our most skilled workers are being swallowed by the Soviet whale. Whole factories are disappearing overnight. Last week we watched them dismantle and load up one of Berlin's telephone exchanges."

Jake returned his attention to the westbound flow as a series of massive eighty-eights rolled by. Some were being pulled by bulldozers, others by tanks, one by a series of farm tractors chained into tandem. There was no question about it. He was witnessing an army on the move.

He slipped back until his head was covered, turned to the bearded man beside him, and demanded, "Where are they headed?"

Karl fastened him with his good eye and replied, "That you and your Western allies must decide for yourselves."

* * *

Jake waited until they were back and preparing a meager supper before asking, "How do we get out?"

He and Karl Schreiner were standing to one side of the main hall, which saw duty as dining room, meeting point, distribution center, and place of worship. The place remained empty, however. Only Karl's stocky assistant and the heavyset woman, who also worked as chief cook, were present that evening. "I don't know. All my normal channels are now closed. We will have to wait and see what develops." The beard parted in a rare smile. "As you can imagine, we are learning to deal in impossibles. It is a part of working and living here in the east."

"That's exactly how I would describe this situation," Jake replied, looking around the stone-lined chamber. "Impossible."

"Hopeless," Karl agreed. "Incapable of being dealt with. By us, that is."

Jake examined this immense man with his vastly disfigured face, wishing he could understand such a strength of faith. "I could not do it," he said flatly. "Stay here and endure what you are open to."

Karl turned his good eye onto Jake and pinned him to the spot. "You could," he rumbled softly, "if this was what God had called you to do."

Jake's attention was caught by a block of wood nailed to the wall. The timber had been shattered by some awful force which had left one end splintered and the other charred black. A bomb, Jake guessed, destroying what probably had been the cross-tie to a roof of someone's home. Upon the timber the following words had not been carved, but rather branded,

"Behold, I am the Lord, the God of all flesh. Is anything too difficult for me?"

"We are not a majority among believers," Karl was saying. "We are a select few. We have chosen to accept the call, to embrace the injustice of this worldly fate. To face the impossibility of living as evangelists in a world where evangelism is a crime. To be there and share the darkness with those who remain trapped by the world."

Jake glanced at the chamber's stone-lined windows. Carved in a continuous ring around one frame were the words: "For nothing will be impossible with God." Around the other frame was another inscription: "Jesus said, the things which are impossible with men· are possible with God." Jake looked back to the hulking man, feeling the words' silent impact resound deep within him.

"God's power is unlimited," Karl went on, his voice too solid with confidence to brook doubt. "Let me tell you something about unlimited power. It means that whatever situation I face, I can do nothing better than to face it in utter emptiness."

Emptiness. Jake recalled his time in the Sahara, felt something of the same sense of strength he had felt in the desert. Yet there was something else. A whisper of distress disturbed the surface of his peace, like a wind blinding his vision with bitter desert sand. He confessed, "I have been thinking about the war. Not only that." He struggled to make sense of the disturbed vision in his mind and heart. "I'm still angry about it."

Karl's eyes searched out where Hans Hechter sat at the corner table, his hands cupped around a steaming mug, his shoulders sunk in what had come to be perpetual despair. The effects of Jake's blow had healed to a plum-colored swelling under one eye. "You did that?"

Jake nodded. Ashamed and yet defiant. Ready with a thousand arguments as to why it was right to have struck the man, yet filled with remorse. Not only for Hans Hechter. For something else.

Karl's gaze turned back to him. "You still carry the war in your heart."

Suddenly Jake had no wish to deny what he felt. "I thought I had left it behind, that I had prayed through it and found peace. But I guess I haven't."

The single eye probed with surgical precision. "Have you ever thought that this has come upon you for a purpose?"

Jake searched the massive bearded face. "No."

"Perhaps only you can reach that man over there. Perhaps your anger was returned to you as a means of carrying out God's call." He shrugged. "I do not profess to have all the answers. But I have often found that the Lord not only replaces the years the locusts have eaten, but also grants us opportunities to make gold from the lead of our lives. Do you understand what I am saying?"

"I'm not sure."

"Why not go and tell that man what is deepest in your heart," Karl suggested.

Jake took an involuntary step back. "Hans?"

"Is that his name? For a moment I forgot." The glittering eye gently mocked him. "For a moment I saw only another sinner who needed help to find his way."

Karl started to turn away, then stopped. "But of course, it would be impossible for you to give such help to a man like this. A *sinner* like this. An *enemy* like this. Of course. Think of all the horror this man and his kind have done to the world. Just think. How could anyone come to help one like this, much less confess their own deepest failings and weaknesses as a way to show that they too are human and in constant need of help?"

Jake wondered if the burly man could see how much his words had rocked him. "You don't ask much, do you?"

"Only the impossible," Karl replied softly. "Only the completely and utterly impossible."

Chapter Seventeen

JAKE STIRRED IN the night, eased his position on the lumpy straw mattress. Sally was instantly alert and looking at him. "What's the matter?"

"I can't sleep," he whispered.

"I know you can't sleep." She shifted to her side, raised her head up so that she could look down on his face. "Your not sleeping has kept me awake all night."

He heard her words as an invitation, a gift. "I feel like I'm being torn in two," he confessed.

"Why?"

Jake looked at his wife. Sally's eyes were luminous mirrors in the soft light, showing him his soul's recesses, secrets which had remained invisible throughout the days and the struggles. "Something inside of me keeps saying I need to talk to Hans Hechter. Not just talk. Share with him. Tell him about faith."

"Then you should." Quiet. Definite.

"It's not that simple."

"Yes it is."

Jake shook his head, tried to put concrete form to his tumultuous thoughts. "I keep thinking about my brother. How he died fighting everything this man stands for."

"Stood for," Sally corrected him quietly.

"I wonder," Jake said. "I really do. I mean, just look at the guy. Tell me you don't see a Nazi."

Sally kept her eyes fastened upon him, her gaze softly penetrating. "You know what I see? A man who holds to the past because he hasn't been offered anything to take its place. Yet."

The truth of her words raked across Jake's soul, exposing much that he would have preferred to keep hidden. Even from himself. He sighed, his eyes closed, trying to hold back the tide of awareness that came flooding in.

But Sally was not finished. "You know what else I see?"

"What?" he said, the word a sigh without beginning or end. An admission that he needed to hear what she said, no matter that it stripped him bare.

"I see a very great man given a very great gift." She paused long enough to gentle his protest with a kiss. "I see you being granted an opportunity to work through something really important. I don't know what it is that's holding you back from sharing your faith with him, but I know in my heart it's important. Not for him, Jake. Important for you. Something that is just begging to come out."

The power rose within him like a ball of flame, searing his very being as it lifted from the depths of his mind and heart, entering his mouth, ready to come out. Finally.

But she stopped him with a finger to his lips. "Not to me," she said, her words feather light. "I'm not the one who needs to hear this. Talk to Hans. Show him that you are human. That you have failings. But that something has come into your life that gives you the power and the wisdom to rise above them. And to heal."

Jake found Hechter in the same corner as before he had gone to bed. "Can't sleep?"

The man raised his eyes from the empty cup in his hands, his gaze a blue-clad void. "I have slept enough," he replied slowly. "I feel as though I have slept through my entire life, building dream upon dream."

Jake walked over and sat down across the rough-hewn table from the blond scientist, wondered what he should say, how he should begin.

"I feel," Hechter said, then dropped his head in defeat. "I don't know what I feel. My mind runs in circles, and it returns over and over to the war."

"I've been thinking about the war too," Jake confessed. "A lot."

"Colonel Jake Burnes," Hans said, the words taking a slow bitter cadence. "The hero. The victor."

Jake closed his eyes to the sudden rush of irritation, and in doing so had the wrenching sense of a turning. A small repentance. The words came to him as suddenly as the flood of peace, as though they had both been waiting, hovering just beyond reach, ready for him to make the turning. Away from anger, away from the past, away from all that was old and dead and dust. Repentance.

"I never felt so alive as I did during the war," Jake said quietly.

The power of his admission broke through Hechter's self-absorption. His chin lifted with a jerk. "What?"

"War did that to me," Jake said, and felt a hot ballooning rush of emotion flood his chest. He knew
then that he was confessing not only to Hechter, not
only to himself, but to God. Giving voice to the un-
speakable. "I became a Christian about five months
after the war ended. Part of me looked for faith because of what I did in the war and what I needed to
release myself from. Memories, pains, burdens that I
did not want to carry for the rest of my life. Experiences that had branded me, warped my mind and my
heart and my spirit. Left me feeling crippled inside."

"This I understand," Hans said, his voice so soft
that the words were almost lost in the sputtering of
the lantern overhead.

"But another part," Jake said, and had to stop. So
much was filling his entire being that breath was
hard to come by. He looked out over the shadowy
hall to where the words had been inscribed around
the second window. Everything is possible with God.
The words flickered and danced in the lantern light,
taking on a joyful life of their own. *Everything.*

"Part of me was missing something," Jake went
on. "Not the war. But how the war made me feel.
More than alive. *Vital.* In those moments of combat,
there was something I never wanted to think about
because I knew it was wrong. But not thinking about
it did not make the feeling go away."

He stopped, his chest so tight he had to search the
chamber for breath. There was nothing else within
him except the need to see that part of himself for
what it was, and understand. "It was," he hesitated
long, his voice raw from the effort. "It was almost
ecstasy. Horrible, worse than death sometimes. But
totally overwhelming. Totally *now.*"

The silence lasted long enough to become a part of the night, like the shadows and the flickering lantern and the rough-hewn table and the burning pain of his confession. Finally Hechter strained against the night's hold and asked quietly, "This faith of yours, has it offered you the same ecstasy?"

"Not the same at all. So different it has been possible to pretend that the other never happened. But it did. And I see how some warriors come to think of battle and God together in their minds."

"But you don't?"

"They are opposites," Jake said, and stopped to swallow. His throat felt sandblasted. Hans offered him a cup, Jake accepted and drank without looking, without realizing he was drinking. He set down the cup, went on, "The presence of God has given me at times what the word ecstasy is *supposed* to mean. In such moments, it is not something outside myself that forces the world to disappear. It is the Spirit of God himself, granting me one small instance of knowing what it means to be truly selfless. Without self. Open and exposed not by life-threatening horrors, but by *life*. Pure, complete, eternal life."

Slowly Jake raised himself to his feet, surrounded by the emptiness of unburdening. His soul felt ripped asunder. "In those moments," he said quietly, his voice directed to the dark window, "everything seems so simple, and God feels so close. Then something like this happens, and God is a billion miles away, and I am trapped inside all my mistakes and my sins and my failings. And all I can do is try and remember that even though I am the most unworthy man who ever lived, still He has forgiven me and brought me back into the eternal fold."

Jake felt as though there were a hundred other things a better man could have said. But for him the time was over, his own weaknesses too overwhelming to continue. "Good-night," he said, and began shuffling away.

He was almost to the hallway entrance when a quiet voice behind him said, "Colonel."

Reluctantly Jake turned back, and met Hans Hechter's gaze for the first time since beginning his confession. The scientist watched him calmly, the blue eyes empty of both pride and shadows. He sat beneath the flickering lantern, nodded his head slowly, and said, "Thank you."

Chapter Eighteen

*I*T WAS A TOTALLY different Hans Hechter who woke him. A frantic, frightened Hans. Shaking him roughly, hissing softly, "Up, get up! We must flee!"

Sally was already out of bed and flinging clothes over her nightgown while Jake was still fighting off the fog of insufficient sleep. "What time—"

But hands were already jerking him up and onto his feet. "They have found me," an anxious voice whispered as Sally came around the bed and began tossing clothes at him.

"Who?" Jake's mind moved a half-step behind his fingers, which was why he buttoned his shirt up lop-sided and tried to fit feet into the wrong shoes.

Hans was bundling him toward the door when it exploded inward and the heavyset woman hurried in. Her nightshirt was as great as a sail, and it billowed out around her as she shouldered past. "Down the back," she whispered. "Through the closet, into the sewers, hurry." Then she slid into bed, pulled the covers up to her curlers, and commenced to wave them frantically out and away.

With Hans pulling and Sally pushing, Jake had little choice but go with the flow. His mind remained
sluggish, and his feet scuffled blindly until two steps
into the hallway he heard the ice-chilling voice. "I
asked you a simple question, Herr Schreiner. I suggest you not try my patience any further. Did you or
did you not speak with a certain trader at what the
locals call the chapel market?"

The cadaver. Jake came awake with electric sud-
denness, recognizing the voice of the rocket plant's
political officer.

"And I told you as clearly as I know how," the big
man rumbled back. His voice sounded bored and
sleepy and irritated with being disturbed. "I talk
with every trader who comes through. It is part of
my job of keeping order. Tall and dark hair and a
strong face could describe a dozen of them. More."

"Your job," the officer sneered. "All right, then. He
was traveling with one or both of these two men.
Look carefully, Herr Schreiner. Your very life depends upon it."

"Ah, why didn't you say you had photographs."
The bear's voice receded into the distance as together
they scurried down the hall, ducked into the dank
chamber used as a hold-all for medicines, lifted Sally
up and through the hole which opened into the
sewer. "Yes, this blond one. He looks familiar. But
I'm not exactly sure—"

"Search the place," snapped the officer, granting
Jake the adrenaline surge he needed to grab the lantern hanging on the wall, then lift himself one-
handed up and through the hole and follow Hans and
Sally down the dark concrete tunnel.

They stumbled around two turnings before stopping and lighting the lantern. Their faces looked

strained and hollowed from the fright. Hans looked at Jake and asked, "What do we do now?"

"I don't know," Jake whispered, his voice still shaky from the shock. "From what Karl said, the border is sealed tight as a drum."

"I have to go back," Sally said.

Jake shook his head. "We can't risk it. Not for us, not for Karl. He said there were informers in his congregation."

"I *have* to," Sally countered. "In the rush I left my passport. I don't have any papers."

Jake opened his mouth to criticize, then slapped his own pockets, and confessed, "Neither do I. Or money."

Back around the corner there was the faint sound of voices. Instantly Jake lowered the lantern's flame to a dull glow. The voices called back and forth in what was clearly Russian. Then there was the sound of grunting, the snick of metal on stone, the splash of foot-fall in water.

They turned and fled.

By midday they were running on empty. Stumbling in hunger and exhaustion, jerking at every sound, feeble with the fear that there was no escape.

There were checkpoints everywhere. Soviet military vehicles filled the streets not choked with rubble. Civilians went about their business with furtive haste, scurrying from place to place with heads bowed and eyes sweeping everywhere, jumping into shadows or doorways or ruins at the sound of approaching vehicles. In that, at least, Jake and Hans and Sally looked like all the others.

Twice they had circled back toward the ruined manor and Karl's cellar, but they had been stymied

by soldiers posted at corners and searching all buildings extending out from the chapel market.

Hunger gnawed at Jake's middle. They did not
have a cent between them. Passing food stalls, especially the ones grilling black-market meat, was agony. He could not look at Sally's drawn and haggard
face without feeling a rising panic. They had to do
something, and fast.

They crouched in the doorway of an apartment
building, hooded by makeshift repairs holding up the
crumbling facade. Jake looked from one spent face to
the other and felt his determination harden. "We've
got to make a run for it. They can't be watching every inch of the border area. There has to be some
place we can cross."

"Twilight," Hans said, his voice chalky with weariness. "At night they search with lights and dogs."

Jake looked at him. "You know Berlin?"

"Some. We are approaching the university. I have
lectured there from time to time. Beyond that is the
central city."

"How far to the western border?"

Hans closed his eyes, the strain of concentrating
tensing his features. "The closest point is about a
half kilometer to our left. Another half-kilometer beyond that, perhaps less, lies the Brandenburg Gate."

Jake gripped Sally's hand, willing his strength into
her. "Let's go."

They continued to skirt the main ways wherever
possible, but were drawn unwillingly onto the thoroughfares when smaller streets became impassable.
On one such instance, Jake caught sight of something that caused him to pause. Sally took it as another alarm, and started to draw into the closest

doorway. "It's okay," he murmured. Then to Hans, "What do you make of it?"

"I'm not sure," the scientist said uncertainly. "But they appear to be headed toward the western sector."

Jake continued to stare down the connecting street, watching as what appeared to be a continual stream of civilians headed down the thoroughfare paralleling theirs. All of them were headed west.

"Russians," Sally whispered.

They slipped around the corner, and continued holding to smaller ways. Another two blocks, however, and a caved-in office building left them with no choice but to return to the thoroughfare. This time they almost ran headlong into a Russian jeep. But they slipped back unnoticed. The jeep's four passengers were all watching one street over, where the tide of civilians was growing ever larger.

Jake waited for the jeep to pass, searched in both directions, then said, "Across the street, hurry."

"Where are we going?"

"Might be safety in numbers," Jake said. "At least as far as they're headed."

They crossed the thoroughfare, hastened down a narrow way, clambered over a hill of broken bricks and concrete, and stopped in the corner's shadows.

The stream of civilians had reached flood proportions. Hundreds and hundreds of people, most of them young, walked purposefully by. There was no talk, no banners, no anger or raised fists or clubs or pickets. Almost all the young men wore coats and ties, the women dresses and matching jackets.

Sally murmured, "What on earth?"

Jake shook his head, studied the determined young faces, saw how the political police and the Russian

soldiers lining the way watched but made no move
to stop them. He had no reply.

Then Hans pointed and said, "I know that man.
Come on!"

Before Jake could think of an objection, Hans had
already pulled him away from the shadow's safety
and out and into the stream. They worked their way
over toward an older bearded gentleman dressed in
tweeds and hat and starched shirt and tie. It was only
on closer inspection that Jake could see the coat's
multiple patches, the frayed collar edge, the caverns
that years of perpetual hunger had hollowed beneath
the neatly cropped beard. Still, the eyes were bright
and intelligent, the hands active as he punctuated his
discussion with the pair of students who walked
alongside him.

Then he caught sight of who approached and raised
up to full height. "Hans! What in heaven's name are
you doing here?"

"I should ask you the same thing," Hans replied,
falling in alongside the older man.

"We are leaving," he replied simply, his eyes upon
Jake.

"May I introduce," Hans said, and covered the hesitation by turning and placing a proprietorial arm
upon Jake's shoulder. Then his blue eyes glinted with
a faint trace of humor, and he went on, "Dr. Jakob
Burnes and Frau Burnes. Perhaps you are familiar
with his work on philosophy and metaphysics? He is
quite famous in some quarters. It did not save him
and his wife, however, from being rousted by our
new masters." Hans indicated the old man with a
nod of his head. "This is Dr. Ronald Hammer, head
of Berlin University's renowned physics department."

"Burnes, Burnes, no, I can't say . . ." The old man waved his hand. "No matter. You are most welcome, of course." He glanced at Hechter's rumpled and dirty form. "You are in trouble?"

"I am a wanted man," Hans confessed readily. "As is Dr. Burnes and his charming wife. Can you help us?"

"Perhaps, perhaps not. We are, as I said, leaving."

"Who?" Hans demanded, matching his step to the old man. "Leaving what?"

"All of us," Hammer replied simply. "The entire Berlin University. This very day. Students, professors, administration, even most of the janitors. Sixty thousand people, more or less. We see the hand of oppression tightening upon us once again, and we are departing."

"Will they let you out?"

The old man nodded ahead, toward the towering Brandenburg Gate. "That," he replied, "we shall see soon enough."

The gate was a mammoth affair, huge pillars rising to support a vast and ornately carved frieze. Upon the broad platform raced a divine chariot powered by mammoth winged beasts, the charioteer raising the crown of victory high toward the heavens. The closer they drew to the gate, the thicker the crowd became. Dr. Hammer was clearly well known and was permitted passage closer toward the front. Hans and Jake and Sally kept by his side and allowed themselves to be drawn further and further through the throng.

"The Free University of Berlin, it shall be called," Jake heard a voice ahead of him say. Despite the crowd's vast size, the people were so quiet that the words carried easily. "We shall found it in the western sector, if they will have us."

"That is the university chancellor," Hans said quietly. "A very brave man."

Dr. Hammer continued his gradual progress forward until Jake was able to make out a very erect old gentleman in university robes and a great mane of snow-white hair confronting a red-faced Russian officer. "You are gathered without permit," the officer rasped, his German carrying growling Russian overtones. "You are breaking the law."

"Then shoot us," the chancellor shouted back. "Show the entire world what your true colors are." He waved his arm beyond the three tanks and squads of Soviet soldiers to where the western correspondents stood massed. A pair of flatbed trucks had been backed up as close to the checkpoint as they could manage. At least a dozen cameramen stood crouched over their apparatuses, filming it all. "Either that," the chancellor cried, "or stand aside and let us go. For go or die we shall!"

With that he nodded once toward the massed assemblage, then turned and started for the checkpoint. As one, the crowd surged forward behind him. The Soviet officer raged a moment, raised his fist in threat, but as his soldiers raised their guns, the officer glanced over toward the cameramen. The officer dropped his hand, barked an order, and stepped back, defeated. The soldiers lowered their guns and moved out of the way.

In absolute silence, the gathering herded forward, carrying Jake and Sally and Hans along with them. Jake looked around as they passed under the great gate, passed the raised yellow barrier, passed the correspondents and the western soldiers. All in silence.

Not even the newspapermen dared break the power of that quiet moment.

Then they were past, and Jake's chest unlocked, and he could breathe again. Sally turned and swept into his arms. Hans deflated from his stiff posture, his shoulders slumping so far his chest went concave. They were through.

Jake motioned for Hans to follow them. Together they worked their way to the corner of the crowd, past the first line of soldiers, and into the guardhouse.

"I'm sorry, sir," the guard officer said, his voice still harboring awe from the scene. "You can't come in here."

"My name is Colonel Jake Burnes, NATO Intelligence." Suddenly Jake found himself so weak he had to lean on the wall for support. "I was told if I made it through to ask for an Uncle Charles."

The lieutenant's eyes popped wide open. "Yessir, I know about that one. Corporal, shut the door. Are these two people with you, Colonel?"

"They are indeed," Jake said, weakened even further with relief of being known and expected. And safe. Finally, finally safe. He felt Sally sway and held her close as he asked, "Could you find my wife a chair?"

"Your wife? I mean, yessir." The lieutenant snapped to action, lifted the chair from behind the corner desk. "Here, ma'am, you look all done in." Then to Jake, "The whole army's on the lookout for you, seems like, sir. Every guard detail here gets a call from some brass over at HQ, wanting to make sure we know what to do if you show up. I mean, when, sir."

"And what is that?" Jake asked, fatigue granting him patience.

"Call General Clay or Colonel Rayburn," the lieutenant snapped out, then realized what Jake meant. "Oh, right, sure. I'll do it now, sir."

"Excellent," Jake said. "And in the meantime, ask your corporal to find us something to eat."

"No problem, sir," the lieutenant said, motioning toward the door with his head. A soldier jumped to comply. As he dialed, the lieutenant glanced in Hans's direction and asked, "They'll want to know who it is accompanying you, sir."

Jake looked to where Hans stood propped in one corner, gray with exhaustion and hunger and confusion and released strain. And new fears. Jake waited until the scientist reluctantly met his gaze before speaking. "Tell them," Jake replied, "I travel with a friend."

Chapter Nineteen

*I*F BERLIN IS ABANDONED, half of Europe
will be in the Communist fold by next week." General Clay was a pepper pot of a man with a voice like
the bark of a bulldog. "Heard that from a journalist
this morning, and for once I agree with the press one
thousand percent."

They sat around the general's conference table, his
Berlin-based staff assembled and augmented by several other generals brought in for the meeting. The
confabulation was not on Jake's account; it had been
taking place almost continually since the Soviets
closed off the city.

The assembled brass were clearly unsure what to
think of Jake Burnes, dressed as he was in his dark
trader's outfit, not to mention dirt and a six-day
scruff. Sally's presence only added to the confusion.

"Tell me, ah, Colonel," one of the generals said, a
deskbound model with belly to match. "Just exactly
what makes you so sure that the convoy you saw was
not simply headed for some gathering point, from
which the return journey to Moscow could be commenced?"

"To begin with," Jake said, his voice grating with fatigue and growing impatience, "this was not just one convoy. More like a full army on the move. I personally saw several hundred troop carriers, half that number of tanks, the same of howitzers. And the line stretched out in both directions as far as I could see. Sir."

"Oh for heaven's sake, Phil," General Clay barked. "The Russkies have done everything but camp on your doorstep and stick a tank barrel down your kazoo." To Jake he went on, "You're the only one among us who's had a gander at the other side since this thing blew up in our faces, Colonel. I don't need to tell you that the situation is more than serious. The city is virtually without resources. Our western sectors will begin to starve in less than a week."

The thought of that was too much for the general to handle while seated. He popped to his feet and began pacing. "More than half my staff are pushing for us to assemble and force our way through. What do you think of that?"

Jake stared at the man. "By land?"

"That's the idea."

Jake recalled the massed force he had witnessed. "Sir, I guess there's a chance that the Soviets would back down. But it would go directly against whatever plan is behind their buildup. And if they don't give in—"

"Then we've got World War Three on our hands." The general stopped his pacing long enough to rake the table with his gaze. "A chance we cannot take, especially knowing about the massed armaments which you have described." He resumed his pacing, muttered to himself, "No, what we need is a show of force that is totally overwhelming, yet at the same time does not deliberately challenge them. Show them we mean business, but keep from having to fire the first shot."

A voice from across the table started, "Washington—"

General Clay cut him off with an impatient wave. "Forget them. They'll still be dithering when the city starts dining on shoe leather. No, what we need is a decision we can act on now, immediately, and then ask Washington's permission later." The sharp gaze returned to Jake. "Any ideas, Colonel?"

"Well," Jake said, struggling to bring his mind up to speed. "Air power was always their weak spot, and I haven't seen many planes at all the whole time I was over."

The entire room came to full alert. A voice across the table said, "I can confirm that, sir. They've been on our back constantly for sparc parts. Seems they can hardly keep a dozen planes in the air."

General Clay wheeled about. "Phil, how many bombers can you get off the ground?"

"Oh," the deskbound general shrugged. "Close to a hundred, I'd say."

"I want twice that number in Wiesbaden tomorrow." He stabbed his finger at another figure farther down the table. "Food, fuel, raw materials. Lots of them, George. Make up a list, but before you do, start organizing the first shipments. I want five hundred tons to arrive here tomorrow. Seven hundred by the day after. A thousand tons a day by the end of the week."

"But that's—"

"I'll tell you what that is," the general barked, and slammed his hand down on the table. "That's an order!"

Chapter Twenty

JAKE WALKED OVER to where Pierre Servais
stood on the garden's broad top veranda, playing host
and greeting late-arriving guests with the stiffness of
an honor guard. He stood resplendent in his dress
uniform and his momentary isolation. Jake asked
him, "Are you nervous? Exhausted? In shock?"

Pierre scanned the crowd below him and replied
somberly, "My friend, I am far too embarrassed for
any of that."

"Why, what's the matter?"

Pierre's features folded down like a stubborn bulldog. "You mean, besides the fact that more than half
our guests could not even get into the church for the
service, it was so full? Or the fact that my own wedding was taken from my hands, so that my mother
could combine forces with my fiancée and turn what
I thought would be a small chapel service for a few
good friends into a new village fête? Or the fact that
every woman within twenty kilometers has been
cooking for a week? Or that there are people here
today with whom my parents have not spoken since
before I was born?"

"Yes," Jake said, struggling to keep a straight face. "Besides that."

"Then you are right, my friend," Pierre replied. "I have no reason to complain about anything."

Jake took a step back as another tidal wave of relatives and friends and villagers whooshed through the house's back doors and enveloped his friend. Pierre composed his mobile features into proper lines, bowed, endured multiple lipstick stains, held his peace as he was crushed to one over-ample bosom after another. He nodded and murmured as the matrons in their ballooning dresses and unsteady hats and clinking jewelry fluttered about him like a flock of giant pigeons.

From the relative safety of the veranda's far corner, Jake looked out over the vast back garden. Pierre's entire family, down to the ninth cousin twice removed, had been enlisted into taming the former jungle. Now the acreage of grass was respectably cropped for the first time since the beginning of the war, and great trestle tables were spread out beneath the ancient fruit trees. From where Jake stood, it looked as though the region's entire population, from the oldest living inhabitant to the youngest squalling newborn, had turned out for Pierre and Jasmyn's wedding.

The house was decorated with flowers and plates of hors d'oeuvres. But the real action was there in the back garden. The tables literally groaned under their burden of food. Tiered trays loaded with steamed mussels and shrimp. Onion tarts big as tractor tires. Boat-sized tureens of bouillabaisse and potato casseroles that matched them in size. Mountains of home-baked bread. Garlic sausages thick as Jake's thigh. And three lambs roasting on spits by the back wall.

Not to mention two entire tables given over to desserts. And a bedroom stuffed with reserves, in case any of the guests began to feel peckish after the main dining was over and the dancing began.

Jake looked down to where Sally sat alongside Pierre's twin brother Patrique and across from Pierre's mother and father at the central table. Both of the old people looked bemused, tired, and glowing with unbelievable happiness. Two impossibles had come to life, two miracles blazed across the heavens, and everyone was here to share in their joy. One son, for whom the funeral service had long since been said, sat across from them, alive and smiling and growing stronger with each passing day. The other had returned from Africa with the woman both considered the daughter they had never had, the woman he had sworn was rejected from his life forever but today had taken as his wife.

Sally caught his eye, motioned toward the empty seat to her right. From her other side, Theo Travers gave a mighty grin as he toasted Jake with a brimming glass. Pierre's parents remained vague on exactly why Jake and Sally had arrived with this stranger in tow, but had latched on to the single word, hero, and used that as the introduction to all who were brought around.

Jake nodded toward them, raised one finger. Strange that he could find this moment of calm and isolation in the midst of such a celebration. He looked down at his wife with love and thanksgiving, knowing he was here today in large part because of her bravery. But he was not ready to give up his moment of quiet just yet.

The five days since their return to Berlin had swept by in a flurry. As soon as the scientists had been safely stowed aboard one of the departing planes, Jake and Sally had hopped on another. Theo Travers had insisted on using his connections at Wiesbaden, their arrival point in the American sector, to round up travel passes and train tickets. Jake had shown his gratitude by inviting him to the wedding.

Jake had no intention of hurrying back to England. He had nothing waiting for him there except the job of packing. He had forwarded his own resignation by military courier. The last thing he wanted was to give somebody a chance to involve him in the inevitable enquiry over Sally's actions. There was too great a risk that whoever tried to criticize her would find themselves dining on their own teeth.

"Jake." Jasmyn passed through the great French doors and floated over. Her ballet-length white silk dress was unadorned, save for a white lace mantilla pinned with pearls to her dark hair and a matching string of pearls doubled about her neck. She glowed with the calm, self-possessed beauty of a princess. "What are my two favorite men doing up here away from the celebration?"

"Waiting for you," Jake replied.

She smiled and shook her head. "This is one day when neither you nor Pierre will be permitted to remain apart and aloof and alone."

Before he could object, she placed a hand on his arm and said, "There is a man inside who wishes to speak with you away from the guests."

"Who is it?"

"He did not say. But whoever it is, you must promise not to remain away for too long. The place of the best man is beside the groom." She dimpled.

"Except, that is, when he is dancing with the bride."

Jake walked through the wide-open doors and had to stop to adjust to the sudden lack of sunlight. Then he tensed as a stumpy figure separated itself from an alcove and came limping toward him. "I suppose I should be quite angry with you for disappearing like that."

"Harry?"

"Having seen the bride, however," Harry Grisholm went on, "not to mention the food, I suppose you can be forgiven." He offered his hand. "How are you, Jake?"

"Surprised," Jake said numbly. "How did you find me?"

"What good is twenty years experience in the spy business if I can't track down a friend," Harry replied, grasping Jake's arm and leading him through an open doorway. "Let us see if we can find ourselves a relatively quiet corner. I have something I'd like to speak with you about."

They walked through the kitchen and entered the back alcove which Pierre's father used as his study. Before they were even seated, Jake warned, "If you're here to get us back before some review, forget it. I've already resigned my commission."

Harry tsk-tsked and replied, "That letter was unfortunately mislaid before anyone besides myself and Commander Randolf had an opportunity to read it."

"Then I'll send another," Jake responded stubbornly.

"You may wish to wait until after you've heard what I have to say." Harry gave Jake his patented smile, the one which did not need to descend from his eyes. "You have heard about the success of our operation in Berlin?"

Jake nodded. "I found a *Times* yesterday. Three days old, though."

"The Berlin Airlift, they're calling it," Harry went on. "Four thousand tons of supplies each and every day. The Americans are flying from Wiesbaden into Templehof airport. The Brits are using the Gatow airfield. Even the French are, managing to bring in a few supplies to Tegel and opening up their unused landing slots to us. All in all, a most satisfactory show of power and determination, all without firing a shot. The results are already evident, I am happy to say. Stalin has begun quietly pulling his troops back from the border."

"Say, that's good news."

"Indeed it is. What makes it even better is that General Clay has seen fit to include your name in virtually every dispatch he has sent back to Washington." The eyes twinkled merrily. "Which makes it most difficult for anyone else to condemn your actions."

Jake felt the first ray of hope. "What about Sally?"

"Ah. Well, as it so happens, both of our scientists were fulsome in their praise of the two of you. Again, the powers that be have decided that given the chaotic state of our organization, Sally's fast action might very well have saved our collective necks."

"You caught the spy?"

"Indeed we did," Harry proclaimed, the glint taking on a steely tone. "He happened to be Quentin Helmsley's very own number two. This unfortunately has left Helmsley himself in a rather precarious position, and unable to criticize anyone's actions at the moment."

Jake found he did not mind that news in the least. "The passport, the travel documents," he pressed. "Sally's absence without leave, what about all that?"

"I beg your pardon," came the merry reply. "What about all what?"

Jake studied the little man, observed, "You're not finished."

"With you? I should say not. I did not go to all this trouble, first to clear both your good names and then to track you down, just to enjoy a wedding feast." Harry's face grew somber. "Stalin's threat has not been ended, Jake. It has merely been deflected. Churchill gave a speech the other day. He told the world that an iron curtain had descended, blocking all of Eastern Europe from view."

An iron curtain. For some reason, the words brought a chill to Jake's mind.

"What is more, Stalin has begun pressing forward with aggression farther south. He wants an empire which runs from the Arctic Circle to the Indian Ocean, and it is only with diligence and fortitude that we shall be able to halt his onslaught. Are you with us?"

"I'll have to talk with Sally," Jake replied. He did not need to think it over. All such future steps would be taken together, or not at all.

"Of course you will. This involves you both." Harry leaned forward, his voice quieted. "I have been asked to take a field position, heading up a major new operation. I want you to come in as my number two. I will put you in as a senior diplomat, but your primary role will be to run operatives throughout the region and gather intelligence. This we will feed directly back to Washington, as well as to NATO headquarters. It may also interest you to know that Major

Servais is going to be offered a similar position, so that if you accept, you two might be able to work together once more."

Jake felt the prickle of excitement race through him. "Where will we be based?"

"Did I not say? Forgive me." The merry twinkle returned. "My dear Colonel Burnes, I would very much like for you to be my man in Istanbul."

II
Istanbul Express

TO AL AND EVAN STUART

With heartfelt thanks for
all that you have taught,
all that you have shared,
all that you are.

Chapter One

*B*Y THE FOURTH DAY, the glamour and the romance were wearing awfully thin.

Despite the wear and tear of war, the Orient Express remained a luxurious way to grow bored. The lounge and dining compartments were resplendent with leather, brass, and oil-stained wood. Jake and Sally's compartment offered fold-up beds, an accordion-style writing desk, high-back leather seats, and embroidered footrests. There were bells to call the waiter, wine steward, and porter. The nightstand was a model of rolling ingenuity, with the little crystal water goblet nestled in a suede-lined brass well, the pen with its capped inkwell and writing pad, and the locket-sized brass chest for chocolates—heaven forbid that they should wake up in the middle of the night faint with hunger. The daintily appointed bathroom had brought a squeal of delight from Sally. It reminded Jake of one of those expensive dollhouses, perfect to look at, and impossibly uncomfortable for anyone over nine inches tall.

Sally baffled him utterly. Since they had boarded the train in Paris, his normally sensible wife had stayed happily entertained on nothing. Whenever his pacing brought him within reach, she bestowed a delighted smile, then went back to her book or her perusal of the window or her happy chatter with another passenger. No matter that the passenger was about as interesting as a large rock and had the intellectual depth of a sparrow. No matter that the train was now more than two and a half days behind schedule. No matter that there was not a single book in the train's meager library with all its pages intact, or that it had rained continually since their departure.

Nor did it appear to matter that their best friends and companions for the trip had effectively abandoned them. The honeymooning couple, Jasmyn and Pierre, had emerged from their compartment only six times in four days, and in that period had spoken a grand total of nine words to anyone else. Nine. Jake had been counting. He had nothing else to do.

Their stop in Zagreb the morning of the fourth day was another excuse for more baffling enthusiasm from Sally. She rushed to him, grabbed his hand, pulled him out on the platform. "Look over there, do you see that woman?"

"Barely," he grunted, shielding his eyes from rain whipped sideways by the wind. "You really find this interesting?"

"Are you kidding? She's great. They're all great. It's like traveling inside a Victorian novel. The dowager empress, the English governess, the mysterious millionaire." She hugged Jake with excitement. "I never thought I would be doing anything quite like this."

"Me neither." Jake released a pent-up sigh. "Or for so long."

"Oh, you." She released him. "I wish there were some way I could make this last another couple of weeks."

Jake showed genuine alarm. "Don't even think about it."

She examined his face, then pulled him over so they were shielded by the train. "You're still worried about not having heard from Harry?"

"Among other things." Harry Grisholm was Jake's superior in his newfound field of international intelligence, and someone Jake admired tremendously. It was Harry who had followed Jake to Marseille and talked him into taking the Istanbul post. Harry was supposed to lead their project from the United States embassy in Ankara. After Jake had accepted the position, Harry had pressed upon them the urgency of the project, and stressed that there was not even time to return to England before beginning the new assignment. Every minute was required to bring Jake up to speed. Someone else would see to packing their belongings and shipping them to Turkey.

A scant three days later, with Jake's briefing barely started, Harry Grisholm had been called back to London. The command from headquarters had left the little man helplessly fuming. Furthermore, something in the tone of his orders had left him cautious about having Jake accompany him back. Instead, Harry had suggested they take a slower passage to Istanbul via the newly reopened Orient Express. Then he had departed, promising to make every possible haste to join them along the way and continue Jake's briefing.

Since then, there had been no sign of Harry, nor any word at all.

"He probably heard we were being delayed and went on by air," Sally offered. "He'll be there when we arrive."

"And if he isn't?" Jake's worries congealed in his gut. "I'm supposed to have so much money arriving I won't count it, just stick it on the scale and round it up to the nearest pound. And all I've been told so far is that I'm supposed to make careful note of how it's being spent."

"He told you more than that," Sally chided.

"Not all that much." Glumly Jake watched the platform vendors shout their way along the train's length, selling everything from espresso to fur hats. "And not nearly enough to get the job done."

"Well, there's nothing you can do about it now." At the sound of the train's whistle, Sally tugged him back up the steps. "Now promise me you'll try to have a good time, okay? We'll get there soon enough."

The lounge would have been his perfect hideaway, had not every other man in the train decided the same thing. And Jake was the only one who did not smoke. The puff of choice was either a cigar that brought to mind the word *pumpernickel* or pipe tobacco that smelled of a long-dead cherry orchard.

There were three distinct groups of passengers. In the majority were the men who wore tuxedos with starched high collars and white bow ties—at eleven o'clock in the morning. They held themselves as aloof as possible while being crammed together for days on end. They traveled with two hard-edged intentions; to return to a life of ease, and to restore their sense of position and status. To their minds, the recent war was an inconvenience, now best forgotten.

Next came the wealthy European business owners, in bright suits and nervous manners. Many were war profiteers, who quaffed back bucket-sized goblets of brandy and scotch as they gambled recklessly, and talked in voices that would have made foghorns shrivel with envy.

A third group, far smaller than the others, were professional travelers. These bore the hard-earned stamp of distant gazes and guarded reserve. Jake would have liked to meet them, but they came and went like the wind, holding themselves utterly aloof from the others. Sally had managed to briefly meet two, an English governess traveling to Damascus to take up a position with a sheik's family, and a Belgian missionary returning to his flock and family in Beirut. Travel still suffered from war-inflicted wounds, and for the time being all safe roads ran through Istanbul. Thus the Orient Express, such as it was, remained the best overland passage to the mysterious east.

Except for Sally, there were no gawking tourists on the train; postwar rationing saw to that. As for Pierre and Jasmyn, Jake did not bother to count them at all. For all he saw of his friends, they might as well not have been on the train.

Under Harry Grisholm's persistent urgings, the time following Pierre and Jasmyn's wedding had passed in such feverish preparation that the newlyweds had managed only a single day on a secluded Riviera estate. After a half-dozen urgent messages had brought the couple home early, Pierre had declared to Harry and everyone else within range that a one-day honeymoon was like being led to the wedding banquet and being granted a single bite of dry toast. Although clearly pleased to be assigned a post near his friend, Pierre had boarded the train intent upon making up for time lost.

The fifth morning dawned as gray and wet as the previous four. As was his habit, Jake rose at first light and made his way to the dining car. These solitary breakfasts were his only chance to be outside their compartment without being surrounded by smoke and noise. A sleepy waiter took his order and left him alone.

Sometime during the night, the train had pulled into yet another nameless Yugoslav village and stopped. Around the red-brick station spread a small hamlet of ancient cottages. The village was surrounded by fields of grain bowed under the weight of unending rain. Jake smiled his thanks when the waiter brought his coffee. He took a first sip, unbuttoned his shirt pocket, drew out his small New Testament, and was soon lost in his study.

"May I join you?"

Jake's head popped up. A rather sheepish Pierre stood waiting patiently beside his table. Jake motioned to the seat across from him. "By all means."

"What can you recommend?" The Frenchman slid into the leather-upholstered bench with a quiet sigh. "I regret to say that until now all my meals have been served in the compartment."

"I've noticed." His friend looked rested, but a little pale, and his voice sounded drained. "Everything is great."

"Then that is precisely what I shall have," Pierre said as the waiter approached. "A breakfast of everything."

"Very good, sir." The English waiter had the unshakable calm of one trained to handle the most difficult of passengers. "Eggs, bacon, sausage, tomato, mushrooms, kippers, beans, and fried bread?"

"Nix on the beans and kippers," Jake advised.

"As my friend suggests. And extra on whatever else you said," Pierre amended. "As well as a pot of that coffee."

"Right you are, sir." The waiter turned and left.

Pierre turned his attention to the window. Outside, a group of Slavic dancers entertained on the platform, though it was doubtful how many of the passengers were awake enough to enjoy the spectacle. Accordions and fiddles flew through ancient mountain melodies as the beribboned dancers gyrated and kicked their heels to incredible heights. Security was ominous and everywhere. The official police wore belted woolen overcoats with holstered pistols at their waists.

Pierre observed, "We are not moving."

"We've been doing a lot of that," Jake agreed.

Pierre rubbed the side of his face. "As I recall, we were supposed to arrive in Istanbul the night before last."

"Right again."

"Yet this does not look much like Istanbul to me."

"If it did," Jake replied, "then somebody's managed to move the city about four hundred miles."

"Ah." Pierre examined the plate of scrambled eggs and toast that the waiter set down in front of Jake. "That does not look very substantial."

Jake discarded the first comment that came to mind and made do with, "I don't have much appetite in the morning."

Pierre turned to the waiter. "Your chef understands that I wish to have a large portion of everything?"

"You will be digging for a week to find the plate, sir," the waiter replied calmly.

Pierre accepted the news with a grave nod. "That is what I like about the British," he said after the waiter had moved off. "They may mangle every other meal until you cannot tell whether you are dining on smoked salmon or roast beef, but their breakfasts almost make up for it."

"I think the food has been pretty good throughout the day," Jake replied.

"Then the day chef must be French." It was a statement of fact, not a proposition. Pierre turned back to the window. "Do you have any idea where we are?"

"Somewhere in Yugoslavia. The border guards came through, remember?"

"Ah, yes. Tito's new thugs." There was a brief furrowing of Pierre's expressive face, then, "That was yesterday, no?"

"That was two days ago," Jake replied gently.

"Of course. How time flies when you are standing still." A fleeting confusion swept across Pierre's mobile features. "Did not Harry Grisholm say that we were in a hurry?"

"Right again," Jake confirmed. "I guess it's the same as the army, hurry up and wait."

"Ah, here we are." Pierre's interest sparked as the waiter presented a plate arranged in neat layers. On the bottom was a liberal foundation of bacon, upon which nine or ten sausages had been set like pudgy logs. Surrounding these was an array of sliced tomatoes and wedges of fried bread. And laid gently on top was a blanket of six sunny-side-up eggs.

"Chef says that he will personally deliver seconds on anything," the waiter said, "free of charge."

"Please thank your maitre d'," Pierre replied solemnly. "I believe this shall do me quite well for the moment."

"If you eat all that," Jake declared, "we're going to carry you off this train feet first."

"If I eat all this," Pierre responded, grasping knife and fork with grim determination, "I shall hopefully survive the next four hundred miles."

"These delays are such a nuisance." The woman was dressed and coiffured from a bygone day, layer upon starchy neat layer, in a manner that told the world she traveled with a full-time maid. Her heavy jewels clinked and glistened with each grand movement. "I told the conductor again last night that I simply must get on to Istanbul. Do you know what he said? 'It is the war, madame.' As if the war hadn't been over for ages. I cannot imagine how one is expected to get on, what with the quality of service these days. If he had ever dared to offer my father such a quip, the man would have been sent packing in an instant, I can promise you that."

Sally hid her smile behind a discreet cough. For ten o'clock in the morning, her compartment was surprisingly crowded. Jasmyn sat beside her, her exotic features quietly radiant in the way of a happy bride, her dark eyes observing the scene from a contented distance. Across from Jasmyn, beside the rather obese English lady, sat the English governess, quiet and prim in her neat gray suit. Beside her sat a Swiss woman whom the governess had brought along; she had not spoken a word since her arrival.

Sally asked, "Do you have something urgent awaiting you in Istanbul?"

"Well, of course. You don't think I would make this beastly trip for my health?" Mrs. Fothering had the full-throated voice of a very large goose. "Phyllis Hollamby is having her annual gathering next Wednesday. You of course know Mrs. Hollamby."

"I'm afraid not," Sally replied.

"Oh, my dear, you simply must." As Mrs. Fothering played with the folds of her dress, her ring turned the rainy gray light into a cascading rainbow. The central diamond was as large as a robin's egg. "Why, Phyllis Hollamby is a pillar of Istanbul expatriate society."

Sally smiled and glanced contentedly around her cabin. The woodwork gleamed of oil and polish, the seats were heavy brocade with starched pillowcases over the headrests. When she and Jake were at dinner, the carriage butler arrived to fold down the beds, plump the eiderdown quilts, and set out a serving of hot chocolate. Sally found it all utterly delightful. "My husband and I are traveling there for the first time."

"Oh yes, I recall something now. An ambassadorial posting or some such, isn't that correct?"

She had to think a moment to recall the title Harry had discussed, the one intended to cover Jake's real purposes. "Jake has been appointed assistant consul."

"How perfectly fascinating, I'm sure." Mrs. Fothering gave the watch-pendant attached to her ample bosom a nearsighted inspection. "My goodness, just look at the time. I do hope my maid has managed to complete the pressing of my day dress. Well, if you will excuse me, I have a thousand things to see to. Good day, my dear. You must be sure and remember to look up Phyllis Hollamby."

"Cross my heart," Sally said, her smile breaking through.

Mrs. Fothering bestowed a ponderous nod upon the entire compartment. "Ladies."

As the compartment door slid shut behind her, the train's whistle gave a wheezing toot, the car jerked, and they began to move. The Swiss woman spoke for the first time. "Finally."

"It certainly is nice to be moving again," Sally agreed.

"I thought she would never stop," the governess told her acquaintance.

"Nor I." The Swiss woman was of late middle age and had the sun-dried complexion of someone who lived for the outdoors. Her clothes were expensive yet severe, and magnified the sharp lines of her chin and nose. Her eyes were gray and direct as they turned toward Sally. "My dear, your husband is in grave danger."

"What?" The word was a gasp torn from deep within her.

Instead of replying, the woman turned toward Jasmyn and continued, "Yours, too, I would assume, although his appointment came so swiftly it is hard to know who has been informed. Rest assured, however, that once his position is made clear, his life will also be in jeopardy."

"There is always danger," Jasmyn said, as tense and upright as Sally. "But Turkey is secure."

"I assure you it is not."

"Who are you?"

"That does not matter." She waited while the English governess rose and discreetly checked the hallway in both directions. "Listen, for that addle-headed woman has left us with little time. You are aware of the name Ataturk?"

"Of course," Sally replied, striving for calm, though it cost her dearly. Ataturk had led Turkey after World War One had ended the rule of the Ottoman caliphs. He had fought to draw Turkey closer to the West, and had severed ties with traditional allies and colonies in the Middle East and Africa. He had established alliances with Europe and America, granted women equal status as citizens for the first time in a modern Islamic state, and even changed the alphabet to Roman script. This much she had gained from the hurried tutoring given them prior to their departure.

"Ever since Ataturk's death, his followers have been attacked from all sides," the Swiss woman said. "Turkey's government is still openly sympathetic to the West, but its enemies are openly anti-Western. And the Communists are fomenting trouble wherever they can. They see your husband and the power he represents as a threat."

Sally glanced toward Jasmyn, saw that she was pale and tight-lipped. She placed one hand over the two clenched tightly in Jasmyn's lap and said as evenly as she could manage, "I asked who you were."

"You will be contacted upon your arrival," the woman replied, rising to her feet. "Someone will approach you and ask if you have happened to visit Topkapi, the sultans' summer palace. It was closed to visitors during the war and only reopened six months ago." She reached for the handle, halted. "This is most important. You must not forget the password."

"Topkapi, the sultans' summer palace," Sally repeated. "But how—"

"Do not try to contact either of us again. And be careful what you decide to tell your husbands." She slid the door open and stepped outside. The governess followed her.

"Whatever happens, wherever you might be, as soon as you hear those words, stop and follow. Your very lives may depend upon this."

Chapter Two

"*T*HAT'S ALL?" Jake looked from one woman to the other. "No idea of what we're heading toward?"

"Or whether we should go at all," Pierre added.

Sally examined the men's faces in turn. "Would you just get a load of you two."

Jasmyn clearly agreed. She rounded on her husband, said, "You don't have to appear so pleased."

Pierre's flexible features tried hard for wide-eyed innocence. "I am simply eager to arrive at the bottom of this, ma cherie."

But Jasmyn was not so easily convinced. She crossed her arms, huffed, "It is as though you are happy to see our honeymoon interrupted."

"Perish the thought," Pierre said, then made the mistake of glancing at his watch. "Although it has been quite a bit longer—"

"It seems like if those women were going to go to all the trouble of contacting us," Jake amended hastily, "they would have had some distinct purpose in mind." He found himself not minding the news at all, or the new tone to the voyage. But he did not like having Sally read him so easily.

"Something more definite than just passing on a general warning," Pierre agreed. "We already know the situation is dangerous."

Sally rounded on Jake. "Since when did you know?"

Jasmyn showed alarm. "Why was I not informed?"

"Nobody has said anything definite," Jake said soothingly. "But Stalin is dangerous, and it just stands to reason that any post this close to the bear's lair would have some risk attached."

Sally returned to perusing the gray scene outside her window. The rain had finally stopped, but no break had appeared in the heavy, brooding clouds. The train wound its way along a craggy hillside, the sense of speed increased by grinding wheels and shuddering cabins. No amount of plush comfort could disguise the fact that the track was in a dismal state of repair.

"I don't like it," she said finally.

"Well, what do you want us to do?" Jake grasped her hand, found the fingers cold as ice. "Turn around?"

"I want you to be careful," she said quietly.

"I always am. You know that."

"More than that," she said, turning back around her features creased with worry. "I want you to survive."

They crossed the Bulgarian border late in the night, the passage signaled by squealing brakes and heavy boots and rough-hewn voices. It seemed to Sally that all the world was asleep except for her. Above her head, Jake turned over, the bunk creaking softly at his movement. Her head rang with the words of warning spoken that morning, words that had transformed their train journey from an adventure to a prison.

The compartment door slid partway open, the curtains chinking gently to permit both light and a hulking form. She fended sleep as a flashlight scampered about the room, resting briefly upon her, then moving on. She cracked one eyelid, caught a fleeting image of a peaked cap, badge, broad shoulders, narrowed eyes. Then the curtain dropped, the door slid shut, and they were alone.

Instantly a shudder of fear ran through her, a fear not of unknown guards, but of being trapped. Nowhere to run, no way to protect what was most important to her.

There was the sound of movement, soft as a cat, as Jake slipped if from his bunk and crouched down beside her. Strong arms enveloped her, drawing her up and close and safe. She yielded to his strength and to her fears. "Oh, Jake."

"Shhh. I know." He slid into the bunk alongside her, never letting go of her for a moment. Giving her the comfort she craved. "It's going to be all right."

"How do you know?" Worries scampered about her mind. "What if—"

"Not now," he murmured, nestling into the space where shoulder joined neck. He took a long breath, something he often did when holding her like that, taking the scent of her down deep. The simple act consoled her far more than words. He was here and he was with her. He murmured, "Where is the strong and independent Sally I married?"

"She got left behind in Marseille," she said, trying for humor, but the smile beyond her grasp. "Sorry."

"Think we should go back for her?"

There it was, the invitation she had been hoping for, yearning to hear, the chance to turn around and leave behind all that had entered her life with the pair of women and their obscure message. But she felt Jake's arms about her, this man she loved with all her heart, a man who lived for life on the edge. "No," she sighed. "I guess not."

"That's my girl," he said, holding her tight, giving with his embrace what words could not, remaining there and close until sleep drew up and carried her away.

The train screeched around a sharp bend, and Sally awoke to another rainy morning. Jake was still there, one arm under his head and the other draped across her, the two of them somehow comfortable and cozy in the tiny bunk. She dimly recalled being awakened briefly around dawn, as the train rumbled into a station with squealing brakes and chuffing steam. There had been the sound of voices outside the window, strange after so much isolation, and she had lifted the edge of the window shade far enough to read the station sign overhead—Sofia. A shadow had flitted past her window, and she had let the shade drop back into place. Before long, the safety and comfort of Jake's slumbering closeness had drawn her back into sleep.

Jake stirred, on the edge of wakefulness. His arm tightened, searched, recalled the feel of her, all without reaching the shore of consciousness. She buried her nose into his hair, softly kissed his ear. He responded with a half-murmur. As smoothly as she could, she drew her arm up and around his neck, reveling in his strength and warmth. She nestled in, surrounded by her man, safe and isolated even here.

"Night before last I decided I would never be comfortable on this train," Jake said sleepily. "And that was trying to fit into my bunk all by my lonesome."

She raised up enough to watch his sleepy eyes open, the little boy there with the man. Such a wondrous moment of intimacy, each one the very first time. "And now look at you."

"I know what it is," he said. "This bunk is bigger. You've been keeping it a secret."

She kissed him softly. "Good morning, my hero."

His eyes softened, the light strengthened. "It really is you, isn't it?"

She nodded. "Right where I belong."

His arms tightened around her. "How did I ever come to deserve this?"

Suddenly the power of her love threatened to expand farther than her chest was able to hold. Breath came in a little catch, forcing itself about her swollen heart, the pressure pushing tears about her eyes. "Don't you ever change, Jake Burnes," she whispered, her arms holding him as close as she could possibly manage. "Not ever."

Beyond Sofia their world suddenly altered. Scarcely had they entered the dining car, seated themselves across from Pierre and Jasmyn, and exchanged smiles and comments about couples who did not eat breakfast until almost noon than the sun emerged. The sight was so startling and so wondrous after five days of unending gray that the entire car, waiters included, broke into a cheer.

Under the fresh sunlight, the train gleamed with seedy grandeur. The war years had left no funds for new paint, yet the ancient blue cars gleamed with recent polish. Not even eight hundred miles of hard travel could disguise the glorious bronzework.

Outside their window, the countryside was undergoing a drastic change. The clearing sky looked-down upon a landscape that was more accustomed to heat and dust than cold and rain Rocky clefts proved stubborn homes for gnarled pines and scraggly undergrowth. Hillsides grew steeper, the contrasts between green and rock starker. Goats and sheep bleated as they scampered in search of meager fodder, followed by young boys who whistled and waved as the train swept by.

"Colonel Burnes, I presume?"

Jake turned from the window, looked up at the urbane gentleman with his steady gaze. "Yes?"

The man clicked his heels and gave a stiff minuscule bow. "Dimitri Kolonov, at your service." He turned to the others and gave a lofty smile. "And this must be Major Pierre Servais, and these beautiful ladies Mrs. Servais and Mrs. Burnes. A great honor, I assure you."

"Forgive me, m'sieur," Pierre said, collecting himself first. "I do not recall hearing of you."

"Of course not." The man himself was in direct opposition to his dress and his manner. He had the hard-boiled look of a veteran fighter. His lips were two bloodless lines, his teeth sheered as though worn by years of clenched jaws. His eyes were as lifeless as marbles. Kolonov reached for his breast pocket and removed a slender yellow envelope. "Perhaps this will help clarify matters."

Jake accepted the flimsy envelope, read the words "Western Union" and then something beneath in Cyrillic. Instead of opening the envelope, Jake asked, "Are you Russian?"

"I do indeed have that honor." Kolonov motioned to the empty table across the narrow aisle from their own. "May I?"

"I do not recall seeing you on the train before," Pierre said.

"That is natural, as I only came aboard in Sofia," Kolonov replied, taking Pierre's remark as an invitation and seating himself. "Like yourselves, I have been pulled away from other duties at short notice."

Jake opened the envelope, noticed the last word. "It's from Harry," he told his companions. Jake read the telegram first silently, then again aloud:

HAVE BEEN UNAVOIDABLY DETAINED IN LONDON. YOU ARE TO PROCEED TO IS-TANBUL AND COMMENCE DUTIES WITH-OUT ME. BEARER OF THIS MESSAGE IS DI-MITRI KOLONOV FORMERLY OF NKVD AND NOW SECONDED TO SOVIET CON-SULATE IN ISTANBUL. I ASSURE YOU THAT YOU MAY TRUST HIM FULLY AND REMIND YOU OF ASSISTANCE GIVEN BY MR RASULI. REGARDS HARRY.

"I do hope this has explained the situation," Kolo-nov said.

"No doubt," Pierre murmured, his voice a quiet purr. "May I trouble you for the telegram, Jake?"

Jake handed over the yellow sheet, caught sight of a courtier's smile creasing Pierre's otherwise blank face. He turned back to Kolonov, willing himself to remain as composed as his friend, acutely aware of the telegram's double message. Sultan Al-Rasuli, as Harry Grisholm well knew, ruled a fiefdom in Mo-rocco's central highlands. He had held Pierre's brother, a former leader of the French Resistance, in his dungeons while offering to supply Patrique's head to the highest bidder.

"I don't see how much use I'm going to be to anyone," Jake said carefully to Kolonov. "Not only do I not have any training in diplomatic operations, but I'm not even fully briefed."

"Our departure was very hasty," Pierre added, maintaining his calm composure.

"Harry said it was imperative to get us into place," Jake finished. "He insisted that our training could be completed once we were settled. All I know is that the first batch of building funds were to arrive three weeks ago, and that someone needed to be in position to manage their dispersal."

That much had been clear from the news and from Harry's hasty summary. Relief funds had been pouring into Europe since the war, including some construction funds for Turkey. Not much, compared to what was being poured into Germany and Italy and France, but what was relatively small by international standards was a staggering amount in Jake's eyes.

"Then what happens, but you have been trapped upon this train for five days now," the Russian commiserated, oozing slick sympathy. "Never fear, my new friends. I have it on strictest record that we shall experience no further delays and shall arrive in Istanbul by daybreak tomorrow." He flashed another humorless smile. "I have personally spoken with the man at the controls, and assured him that otherwise the train will be forced to find itself another engineer."

All four joined him in a moment's tense laughter, and shared blank looks about their table. Jake then said, "NKVD. That's the initials of the Soviet secret service, am I right?"

"It has indeed been my honor to serve my country as you have served yours," Kolonov announced proudly. "Which shall grant us wonderful opportunities to exchange our stories and know-how, did I say that correctly, know-how?"

"Absolutely," Jake said.

"Your English is impeccable," Sally assured him, her tone as cool as her gaze.

"Thank you, Mrs. Burnes. And speaking as one professional to another, Colonel, I must tell you, your lack of training matters not a bit. Why, I myself have not the first iota of experience in such matters as the distribution of funds. And just look at yourselves. What in your military backgrounds has prepared you to handle so much money?"

"Not a lot."

"Precisely!" Kolonov thumped his open palm triumphantly upon the table. "So why have we been selected for these positions?"

"Search me."

"As figureheads!" Kolonov beamed at all and sundry. "We shall be paraded here and there, attend the openings and meet the government leaders, be seen at all the best functions. And why not, I ask you? We have served our countries through the hard times. Let the pencil pushers count the zeros and keep their books, that is what assistants are for. Is it not time that we should savor a little of the easy life?"

Before Jake could think up a response, Kolonov gave a quick glance up and down the almost-empty car, then leaned conspiratorially across the aisle. "Listen, my friend, I tell you, this posting will do wonders for our careers. Just think of the contacts we

shall make. And the businesses eager to win the contracts, why, two years of being wined and dined,
then—"

"Oh, the honeymooning couple, how absolutely
charming."

The overstuffed English woman, Mrs. Fothering,
bustled over to loom above their table. "I was so
looking forward to meeting the dashing French officer. And you must be the famous Colonel Burnes."

Jake caught Sally's silent flash of humor as he rose
to his feet. "I don't know about the famous part, but
the rest is right."

"Oh, stuff and nonsense. Medals were made to be
worn, not hidden in a drawer, that's my motto."

"Jake, this is Mrs. Fothering." Sally's voice had the
lilting charm of a carefully disguised smile. "She's
traveling to Istanbul for a party to be given by Phyllis
Hollamby."

"I don't know why I am surprised to find you were
paying attention, my dear. You most certainly have
the marks of a proper upbringing about you." She
offered Jake a yellow claw of a hand, surprisingly
parched and narrow given the ample size of the rest
of her. "How do you do."

"Charmed, I'm sure." Jake motioned to where
Pierre stood. "This is Major Pierre Servais and his
wife, Jasmyn."

"Yes, I have already had the pleasure of meeting
the lovely young bride." She extended her hand once
more, gave a subdued cluck of pleasure when Pierre
leaned over and kissed the air above her wrist, then
purred, "Major."

"Won't you join us?" Jake asked, with all the
sincerity he could muster, both because of Sally's
sudden smile and because the Russian was clearly

irritated by the interruption. Jake motioned toward him, said, "May I present Mr. Dimitri Kolonov, who has just joined the train in Sofia."

"How positively fascinating," she sniffed, and managed to avoid offering her hand by stumbling slightly as Jake held the back of her chair. "Oh, thank you—these blasted rails, they really should do something to smooth out this journey, don't you agree?"

"There has been a war on," Dimitri offered, resuming his seat.

"Just what the conductor told me," she said, her tone icy. "You and he must have a chat, I am sure you shall no doubt find positively hordes of things to discuss." She dredged up a smile for Pierre and Jasmyn and said, "Now then. You must tell me all about your ceremony. I positively adore weddings, particularly my own."

Pierre asked, "You are married?"

"Oh, my goodness, yes. Let me see now, is it three or four times? I never can remember. No, five, if you count the disastrous second try Alistair and I made. That was an utter mistake, I am sorry to say. But a positively beautiful wedding. Absolutely gorgeous. I had to forgive him for pressing me into giving it that second go since he let me fulfill my every wish with the wedding."

Kolonov rose to his feet, steadied himself as the train gave a squealing lurch, then bowed and said stiffly, "Perhaps we can speak further at another time."

"That'd be just swell," Jake said smoothly.

When the Russian had given the ladies a stiff bow and departed, Mrs. Fothering sniffed once more.

"What an utterly beastly man. However did you meet him?"

"He met us," Pierre replied.

"Yes, that is the problem with his sort, I'm afraid."

She rose to her feet, drawing them with her. "Well, I shan't keep you any longer."

"Oh, you mustn't rush off," Sally said.

Jake found himself liking the old dame, if for no other reason than that she had saved them from further time with the Russian. "Maybe you'd like to join us for dinner tonight?"

"What a positively gallant invitation. Alas, as I wish to be fresh for our arrival tomorrow, I shall most likely dine in my compartment." She reached across the table to take Sally's hand. "You must remember to look up Phyllis Hollamby when you arrive, my dear. And be sure to suggest that she show you Topkapi. No one knows the sultans' summer palace better than she."

Chapter Three

THEY ENTERED ISTANBUL at the breath-
less hush of first light. The train wound past a series
of dry-scrabble rises, farmland, and individual houses
gradually giving way to dusty streets and ancient ten-
ements. The buildings grew in size, the space between them lessened. Then they rounded the final
rise, and before them stretched the glittering waters
of the Bosphorus.

"This is perfect!" Sally flung her arms around
Jake's neck and planted a kiss with perfect accuracy.
"How ever did you arrange it all?"

Pierre covered his laughter with a discreet cough.
Jasmyn rewarded them with a warm smile. Jake
looked from one woman to the other and saw no
trace of worry, nothing but the excitement of new
beginnings. "What has come over you two?"

Jasmyn asked, "You are complaining?"

"Not at all."

"You just have us wondering," Pierre allowed, "after the long faces and worried voices of yesterday."

"Oh, hush, you two, and let's enjoy this." Sally's
face was pushed up close to the glass. Without turn-

217

ing away she found Jake's hand and drew it into her lap.

"This is the first glimpse of our new home. Aren't you the least little bit excited?"

"Absolutely," Jake agreed, then nodded to Pierre's shrug. Women.

The sun rose huge and smoldering into an empty sky. The light turned the entire world a ruddy orange. Cargo ships plied the fiery waters like vessels of old, their scarred and battered hulks transformed into ships of mirrored gold. Tiny fishing craft spun and darted about the behemoths, glittering fairy boats whose nets rose and fell like gossamer wings.

They followed a gradual curve around the water's edge. Then they ducked inland and were swallowed by the tall buildings of a great metropolis. Only this particular city was dotted with structures beyond time—crumbling aqueducts, remains of medieval walls, a city garden sprouting a forest of Roman columns. Everywhere rose the slender needles of minarets, the mosque towers from which the Muslim faithful were called to prayer.

Jake waited until Sally turned her beaming face back to the cabin to ask, "What's with the change this morning?"

"Oh, you," she smiled. "Isn't it enough just to sit here and be excited about everything that's up ahead?"

"You've been acting strange since yesterday," Jake persisted. "One minute you're as worried as I've ever seen, the next and you're like a little kid at Christmas."

"Not just Sally," Pierre added, watching his new wife.

"It's out in the open now," Sally said, refusing to release her excitement, her eyes stealing more glances out the window as the train wound through the slowly awakening city.

"What, the Russian?"

"He was a snake," Jasmyn said definitely. "But at least we can now see who it is we face."

"Dimitri Kolonov is supposed to be an ally," Pierre reminded them.

Sally joined Jasmyn in a double-barrelled glare. Pierre raised hands in mock defeat. "I just thought somebody should mention it."

"He is a snake," Jasmyn repeated. "But a visible one."

"It wasn't the threat that scared me so," Sally said, facing Jake. "It was the fact that I was hit when I felt protected."

"And from such an unexpected direction," Jasmyn added.

"Seeing that these are real people brings everything back into focus," Sally went on. "It shrinks the danger down to size."

"There are a lot of risks here besides Kolonov," Jake reminded her quietly.

"Of course there are." Her dimpled smile returned. "You wouldn't want it any other way, neither of you would. And you both know it."

"My friend," Pierre offered, "I think we should accept that we are surrounded by superior minds."

The train chose that moment to slide into dusty shadows and enter the station. The engine chuffed in noisy relief, the whistle gave a long satisfied toot, the brakes squealed tiredly, and the train shuddered to a halt.

The little group remained seated, looking from one to another, until Pierre said, "Something is missing here."

"We need to start this adventure off right," Sally agreed, reaching for Jasmyn's hand. "Jake, will you lead us in prayer?"

"Excellent, excellent. You arrived safe and sound." Dimitri Kolonov stepped up as they were unloading their bags, as cold and polished as an ice sculpture. "You do not have someone from your consulate here to help you with your cases? What a disgrace."

Jake accepted the larger satchel from Sally. "We're used to getting our hands dirty."

"Ah, but those days are behind you, Colonel," Kolonov responded, waving one gray-gloved finger. "Remember, that is what underlings are for, *nyet?*"

"Are you traveling with your wife and children, Mr. Kolonov?" Sally asked.

"Call me Dimitri, please. After all, we shall be seeing so much of each other."

"I can hardly wait," she said, smiling her thanks as Jake offered her a hand down from the train.

"Alas, my wife is unable to join me just yet." Kolonov gave a mock sigh. "The price one pays for an overseas assignment can be high."

"Colonel Burnes? Colonel Jake Burnes?"

Jake turned and called, "Over here."

A lean, sunburned young man hustled over. He started to salute, then realized he was in civilian clothes and forced his hand back down. "I'm Corporal Bailey, sir. The consulate sent me over to fetch you."

"You see, what did I tell you, my friends? A new life!" Kolonov beamed triumphantly. "Well, I simply must dash. You will all come and be my guests for dinner at the Soviet consulate, yes?"

"Soon as we're settled," Jake assured him, accepting the hand, then turning back to the young man. "This is my wife, Corporal."

"Ma'am." The young man waited impatiently for the Russian to shake Pierre's hand and bow a final time to the ladies before departing. His tone was insistent as he said, "We need to be shoving off, sir."

"Lead on, Corporal."

"Yessir. Is this, I mean, are you Major Servais?"

"I am."

"I have a message for you too, sir. The French consulate called to say you should check in immediately. I can drop you off, if you like. Then I'll take your wives and the gear over to your hotel." Not waiting for a response, he hefted as many valises as he could manage, and started for the exit.

Jake caught up with him. "What's the rush?"

"The whole consulate's all sixes and sevens, sir. You were supposed to get in a couple of days ago."

"Our train was delayed," Sally pointed out.

"I know, I mean, yes, ma'am. There's been radio traffic like you wouldn't believe about that as well."

Jake demanded, "As well as what?"

"I'm not supposed to say, sir," the corporal responded carefully. "My orders are to get you back to the consulate and do it on the bounce."

Scarcely had they all settled into the big consular sedan than the swarthy Turkish driver let in the clutch and squealed away. Jake leaned forward from his station in the backseat and demanded, "Why can't you tell me anything?"

"Leave him alone, Jake," Sally said quietly, her gaze on the scene zipping by outside their window. "He's just following orders."

The corporal shot her a grateful glance, then returned his attention to the front windshield in time to call, "Heads up," and grab for the top deck. The driver swung wide around an overloaded donkey cart, then swept back in front of the animal's nose and ducked down an alley.

Corporal Bailey turned around and said apologetically, "I'd yell at him, sir, but it wouldn't do any good."

Pierre nodded approvingly in the driver's direction, then announced brightly, "I do believe I am going to like it here."

The driver traveled with equal pressure on the gas pedal and the horn. The only one who seemed perturbed by their lightning dash through gradually thickening traffic was Jake. After they had come within a hairsbreadth of derailing a streetcar, Jake asked Jasmyn, "This doesn't bother you?"

"I was raised in Marseille," she reminded him.

"The French only wish they could drive like this," Pierre said in admiration. He turned to the corporal. "Where can I buy myself a car?"

"Here we are, sir," the corporal announced as the car swung through great iron gates and halted in a cobblestone courtyard. "I'll let them know the colonel's arrived, then be back to escort everyone else onward."

Jake slid from the car and turned a worried frown toward Sally, but she stopped him with a smile. "We'll be fine. You go see to business."

He followed the corporal across the plaza, taking in the central fountain and the porticoes and the sculpted trellises around tall upper-floor windows. "This is nice."

"It used to be some sultan's palace," the corporal said, bouncing up grand front steps to hold the door for Jake. "There's a lot of them around here."

The entrance hall was grand in a seedy and ancient fashion. The ceiling curved up a full two stories, and the ancient marble-tiled floor was ribbed where eons of feet had trod shallow channels. Just inside the second set of double doors stood a waist-high desk and behind it a uniformed Marine. Corporal Bailey announced, "This is the colonel."

"Thank the heavens above," the second young man announced. "I mean, welcome to Istanbul, sir. I'll just go and tell the chief you're here."

The young man trotted down the long formal hall, then took the sweeping staircase three steps at a time. Jake turned to the corporal and asked, "The chief?"

"Meester Jake!" The delighted cry turned them back around as a corpulent little man came rushing down the stairs. "Eeet ees so excellent to have you arrive, oh my, yes, so very excellent!"

"I'll just go and see to your wife and the major." The corporal began another salute, then stopped himself, started to offer his hand, decided that was too informal, finally settled on, "Good luck, sir."

Jake watched the round little man come bouncing down the hall. Too much too fast. "This the chief?" he asked the corporal.

"Chief? What chief?" Stubby legs carried the little man up and in front of Jake. "I am Ahmet," he announced proudly, as though that were all the explanation anyone needed.

"He's building superintendent, but unofficially sort of chief dogsbody," Corporal Bailey explained, sidling for the door. "Whatever you need, he's the guy. Does some of the local hiring as well. Handles official red tape."

"Exactly yes, is so!" Ahmet waved the corporal away without turning his dark eyes from Jake. "What you need, Ahmet finds. Even before you ask."

"Sounds like a quartermaster I once knew." Jake accepted the little man's hand, felt the damp fingers squeeze once and release.

Ahmet looked like a little balloon balanced on top of a bigger balloon, with almost no neck between head and body. A few remaining strands of hair had been allowed to grow long, then were greased and plastered in black pencil lines across his otherwise bald scalp. His mouth seemed permanently creased into a smile that did not reach his glittering black eyes.

"You will soon see, what Ahmet says is true." He waved his hand in the general direction of the consulate's interior. "I have office all ready, yes, with files and papers and desk and chair and even assistant."

Jake stared down at the little man. "You've hired personnel for me?"

"Mr. Burnes?" Jake turned to see a woman leading the uniformed Marine across the entrance chamber. "I am Mrs. Ecevit, assistant to the political officer. Welcome to Istanbul."

Jake straightened, forced down his ire at this Ahmet and the sensation of being railroaded. "Thank you."

"I hope you had a pleasant trip." The woman was as cool and official as her voice. Middle-aged, a strong face framed by dark hair disciplined into a tight bun. Dark suit, white shirt, no jewelry that he could see. Intelligent eyes. But distant. She gazed at him with calculating prudence.

"Not bad." Jake glanced back at Ahmet, saw he had frozen up in silent disapproval. The little man did not like Mrs. Ecevit, that much was clear. For this reason alone, Jake found himself drawn to the woman and her cold stare. "Sorry we were delayed."

"Yes, no one has been able to fathom why Mr. Grisholm suggested you travel by rail." Her words were overlaid with a slight accent, yet her English was precise as her manner. "Your late arrival has caused us all a tremendous amount of concern. Would you come with me, please?"

"Lead the way." He nodded in reply to the Marine's salute, followed her down the hall and up the carpeted stairs. Far overhead hung a chandelier of glittering crystal leaves. "This is some place."

"It belonged to the grand vizier of the last Ottoman sultan," she said, neither turning around nor taking any notice of her surroundings. "The Ataturk regime gave it to us as a consulate soon after the capital was moved to Ankara." She stopped before a great door whose frame was embellished with plaster carvings in an intricate Oriental design. She knocked, said to Jake, "In here, please."

"Mr. Burnes, thank goodness you've arrived." A gray-haired man ignored Jake's outstretched hand, grasped his upper arm, and guided him in. Jake twisted about to thank Mrs. Ecevit, but she was already closing the door. "I can't tell you what a crisis your delayed arrival has put us into."

"So everybody's been telling me."

"Take that seat, why don't you?" He directed Jake to the straight-backed chair placed front and center before his oversized desk. As an afterthought, he leaned across the desk and offered his hand. "Charles Fernwhistle, Consul General Knowles's Deputy Chief of Mission."

The man's handshake brought to mind a wet mop left overnight in a refrigerator. Jake made no move to sit. "Consul General who?"

"Knowles. Ah. You were expecting Gramble, I see. No, unfortunately he was recalled." Fernwhistle had the elongated neck of a crane, a bowtie, and a nervous manner. Each sentence was punctuated by a quick little tug of his tie, an adjustment of his glasses, a smoothing of his jacket. "A dispute with our Russian allies. Quite sudden."

Jake felt his sense of isolation growing. He remained standing. "The Russians are dictating the choice of our consul general?"

"Our *allies* have every right to request such changes, especially in such times of delicate negotiations. I happened to have served with Consul General Knowles in Mexico during the war."

"Mexico," Jake echoed.

"He was not consul general then, of course. Actually he held my position. Gramble, on the other hand, was, well, a military man, no real experience with this type of work. Still, it was quite a jolt to everyone when he was abruptly replaced."

"Yeah, you look all broken up over it," Jake remarked.

The nose tilted up one notch further. "Sit down, won't you." When Jake had eased himself into the seat, Fernwhistle said, "While military experience no doubt has its merits, unfortunately delicate negotiations require someone with a little more, well . . ."

Ability to cringe, Jake offered silently, and changed the subject with, "So I guess it's up to you to tell me what's going on."

"There is unfortunately no time for that." A glimmer of satisfaction surfaced in Fernwhistle's bland voice. "Perhaps if we had not seen these personnel changes foisted upon his, or if you had arrived on time, but as it is," he spread his hands and concluded, "I certainly do not have the time, nor does anyone else."

"You expect me to start handling my responsibilities without any briefing?"

"Quite an impossibility, I most certainly agree." This time the air of satisfaction was unmistakable. Fernwhistle opened the first of two files on his desk and slid across a paper. "The first allotments of funds have already arrived, you see. We are all under tremendous pressure to release this money and begin the building process."

Jake glanced at the sheet, did a double take. There was a dollar sign, followed by a nine, and then a string of zeros. The sum hit him with an electric shock. It was one thing to hear Harry Grisholm talk about overseeing expenditures, the task kept at arm's length by time and distance. It was another thing entirely to be confronted with the actual *amount* and the responsibility of disbursing it. He gave a dry-lipped whistle.

"Just yesterday I had the deputy prime minister and the mayor of Istanbul both in here together," Fernwhistle told him, "demanding to know when I was going to release the apportionment. I simply must have immediate access to these funds."

"And you will," Jake replied steadily, "just as soon as I've had a chance to get my feet on the ground."

"Absolutely out of the question," Fernwhistle snapped. "This entire situation is preposterous. You were intended to answer not to me, nor to the consul general, but rather directly to this Mr. Grisholm, whoever he is. A man nobody knows, stationed five hundred miles away in Ankara, given direct responsibility for a staff member of this consulate." Fernwhistle snorted his derision. "A ridiculous arrangement. Now this Grisholm character is not even in the country. And his associate arrives here with no idea whatsoever of the pressures we are facing, then insists that the consulate set aside a thousand urgent issues just to bring him up to speed."

"Not the consulate," Jake replied, grimly holding on to his temper. "Just one person. If this is so allfired important, somebody is bound to be able to spare me a little time."

"It would not be a *little* anything. This situation is vastly complicated. I have been here almost a year now, and I am just beginning to unravel the complexities." Again there was the faint glimmer of satisfaction. "I therefore insist that responsibility for these funds must pass from your hands to the consul general and from him to me."

"Insist anything you like," Jake replied evenly. "But until I hear something to the contrary from Harry Grisholm himself, things stand as they are."

"Out of the question! There is absolutely no way this absurd arrangement can be permitted to continue one moment longer. We simply must organize a proper chain of command." Fernwhistle opened the second folder and slid a typed document toward Jake. "Sign this, please."

Jake took in the embossed seal of the United States, read the heading, "Protocol of Authority," then looked up and asked, "What is this?"

"It simply confirms what I have been saying," Fernwhistle replied primly. "You are hereby granting me the authority to sign over whatever funds I deem are correct to the authorities in charge of the various projects."

Jake had to laugh. "You've sure got nerve, I'll grant you that."

Fernwhistle popped up like a marionette. "Now you look here, Burnes—"

"No." Jake heard the danger bells go off in his head. He rose to his feet, announced, "This meeting is over."

"The consul general will hear about this!"

"He sure will," Jake said, heading for the door.

"I assure you, Consul General Knowles will not look kindly upon your hindering this *crucial* work." Fernwhistle fairly danced out from behind his desk. He followed Jake toward the door with arms flapping, looking like an overgrown crane in a tailored gray suit. "If you stand in the way of this work, you'll be sent packing as fast as Gramble was."

Jake turned back and said as mildly as his ire would permit, "Seems to me, bub, the only one standing in the way of getting things done is you." He opened the door, said as an afterthought, "Now, why don't you just pack up all those papers and go find somebody who can start clarifying the situation."

He slammed the door behind him, took a fuming pair of steps, found himself almost colliding with the roly-poly figure of Ahmet, who announced, "Is already found."

Jake squinted down at the fat little man. "Say what?"

"The assistant to help with matters and understandings," Ahmet said with a beam. "Is waiting in your office."

"I'll just bet," Jake said, motioning with his chin for Ahmet to lead the way.

They went down one flight of stairs, passed along a broad corridor, and stopped at a doorway set within a narrow alcove. Ahmet opened the door with a flourish. "Is young Selim, at your service."

Jake entered a windowless chamber hardly larger than a broom closet. He nodded at the young man standing in the center of the chamber, then took in the dingy walls, the metal desk and matching filing cabinet, the pair of wooden chairs with peeling varnish, the utter lack of decoration. "They spared no expense, I see."

"Oh, is only outer office. Your office is through here." Ahmet bustled forward, opened the inner portal, motioned Jake through. "Please, please."

"The excitement can wait awhile," Jake decided, turning back to the young man. "Your name is Selim. Do I have that right?"

"Is Selim, yes, sir." He was as slender as Ahmet was rotund, with delicate olive features and expressive dark eyes. He stood confidently in an oversized suit jacket, mismatched trousers, and a white shirt without a tie.

Jake eased onto the corner of the desk and motioned Selim toward the nearest chair. "Take a seat, why don't you?"

"Is most kind." Selim slouched down, extended his legs, reached into his coat pocket, drew out a cigarette and lit it. "Can start with work tomorrow," he announced with the smoke.

Jake propped one arm across his chest, placed the other up at his chin and tugged down the corners of his mouth. "Is that so?"

"Indeed, yes." Another puff, then, "Have made much sacrifice to present self at proper appointed time."

"I should be eternally grateful," Jake managed. "Maybe even offer you a couple of free days straight off so you can get yourself settled."

The dark head nodded thoughtfully. "With pay, of course."

Jake coughed discreetly. The shirkers he had known in the army had nothing on this guy. "So how much accounting do you know?"

The delicate brow furrowed. "Please?"

"You know, like how to balance books."

The hand and cigarette waved carelessly. "Books weigh different amounts, yes? Is need to balance?"

"You've got a point," Jake agreed thoughtfully. "Typing, shorthand?"

"Oh no," Selim replied, extending his arms proudly. "Hands very long."

"Perfect." Jake slid from his desk. "I'm sorry my wife wasn't here to meet you, Selim."

"Perhaps with time," the young man replied, rising languidly.

"You bet." Jake motioned toward the outer door. "Wait outside for a second, will you? I want to have a word with Ahmet here." When the door had closed behind the young man, Jake demanded, "Whose idea was this, anyway?"

"Fernwhistle, he say find you assistant," Ahmet declared proudly. "I find."

"Figures. You don't happen to know when the consul general is due back, do you?"

"Day after tomorrow," Ahmet replied promptly. "Selim is good boy, yes?"

"A great kid," Jake affirmed. "But he's not going to cut the mustard in this office."

The round forehead grew creases. "Please?"

"I want you to find me some alternatives," Jake said. "Put an ad in the paper, run a flyer, whatever you do around here. I want an assistant, male or female, who speaks fluent English, types, and has an accounting background. Shorthand is optional."

The creases deepened. "You no like Selim?"

Jake let a little of the edge he had been hiding come to the surface. "Did you get what I just said?"

"English, type, accounts," Ahmet replied, his traditional smile slipping a notch. "Will be most difficult, Meester Jake."

"Just put the word out, will you?" Jake said, turning for the door. "I'm going to see if I can find what they've done with my wife."

Chapter Four

*T*HEY HAD BEEN put up at the Pera Palace, a grand European-styled structure whose central lobby rose all the way to the six-story roof. Hand-wrought iron balustrades lined each of the inner halls, with carpets and matching drapes to muffle sound and add to the ancient feel. The creaking mahogany elevator was open and clanking and slow as molasses.

Jake scarcely had time to enter the room, hug Sally, and take in the lofty ceiling and overstuffed furniture and grand four-poster bed before there was a knock on the door. He opened it and took a step back at the sight of Jasmyn in an evening gown, her green eyes unreadable. Behind her, Pierre stood in formal dress whites, his features folded into an enormous scowl. Sally stepped up beside Jake. "What on earth?"

Pierre asked, "Can we interest you in attending a formal reception? It is being hosted here in the hotel by the Norwegian consulate."

"Swedish," Jasmyn corrected.

"Norway, Sweden, what difference could it make?"

"You've got to be kidding," Jake said, ushering them in.

"I wish that I was." Pierre stepped into the room, said, "You are now looking at the new deputy military attaché to the French consulate."

"I thought you were supposed to be working with me."

"It appears the consul general had other ideas," Pierre replied.

"They had an argument," Jasmyn announced.

Sally asked, "You were there?"

Jasmyn shook her head. "I was waiting in Pierre's office."

"Which was on another floor," Pierre added, "at the opposite end of the building."

"Well, that beats my tale," Jake said. "I didn't have the guts to lose my temper."

Pierre eyed his friend. "You, too?"

Jake nodded. "You get the impression we're being railroaded?"

"All I can say for certain," Pierre said carefully, "is that the consular staff seem extremely concerned to keep me as busy doing nothing as they possibly can. Already I am assigned to attend conferences and receptions every day this week and the next."

Before Jake could respond, there was another knock at the door. Sally walked over, opened it, said, "Yes?"

A rich voice said, "I was wondering if a Colonel Burnes might be available."

"We need to be going," Pierre said.

"Stick around," Jake pleaded. "This may be my chance to make up for my poor showing back at the consulate."

An older gentleman entered the room. His appearance was grandfatherly, his gaze keen. "Colonel Burnes? I'm Tom Knowles."

Jake stiffened. "The consul general?"

"That's right." He motioned behind him and was joined by a tall corpulent man in a rumpled suit. "This is Barry Edders, my political analyst."

"I thought you weren't back until the day after tomorrow."

"We're not," Edders agreed cheerfully. "He's not here, and we haven't met."

"I needed to get to you before attention turned your way and the avenues were closed off." He turned his steel-gray eyes toward Pierre. "You must be Major Servais."

"At your service, m'sieur." He motioned to Jasmyn. "My wife."

"And this is Sally Burnes," Jake added.

"Pleased to meet you." The consul general gave a swift but cordial nod before returning his attention to Jake. "It's good I caught you both together. This may be our only chance to speak freely, at least for a while." He glanced at his watch. "I'm afraid we don't have much time."

"We don't have any time at all," Edders agreed, his cheerfulness untouched by the consul general's serious tone. "Which doesn't matter, of course, since we're not really here."

"Won't you gentlemen sit down?" Sally offered.

"Thank you. As Barry has just said, this meeting is not taking place. It is imperative that we seem to be at odds with you both, but I really must speak with you openly. So I have decided to risk using the Swedish consular reception downstairs as a smoke screen and come here. This may be our only chance."

Jake motioned for everyone to find chairs, seated himself beside Sally on the sofa, and demanded, "Because we're not going to be around that long?"

"That may well be the case," Knowles admitted. "Hard to say at this point, however. For the time being, you are here, and faced with a situation that is growing more difficult with every passing day. You are aware that the funds have begun to arrive from Washington?"

"I saw the transcript upstairs in Mr. Fernwhistle's office."

"That was actually the third transfer. Ah, I see he failed to tell you that. No wonder. Yes, the first two arrived after the former consul general departed and prior to my own arrival. Acting on authority passed down by a very harried DCM in Ankara, Fernwhistle took it upon himself to dispense the initial funds."

"DCM stands for Deputy Chief of Mission in diplomatese," Barry explained easily, slouched far down in his chair. He seemed content to sit and chat all night. Whatever tension, the others might be feeling did not faze him in the least. "He's number two at the embassy in Ankara. Whenever the ambassador is away, the DCM rules the roost."

"Precisely," Knowles agreed. "But with this initial disbursement, Fernwhistle found himself possessing power and influence on a breathtaking scale, something rarely experienced by a diplomat at his level."

Pierre demanded, "What about bribes, kickbacks?"

"Not Fernwhistle," the consul general replied definitely. "I've worked with him before, and I know him to be an honest diplomat, quite diligent in his own somewhat limited way."

"Not enough imagination," Barry agreed easily. "He's so clean he squeaks. Now if it were me in that situation—"

"Which it is not and never will be," Knowles responded, his eyes never leaving Jake. "But there is more to this than just some second-tier Foreign Service official out for his own taste of glory."

"I sort of figured that," Jake said quietly.

"Of course you did. There are actually two battles going on. Fernwhistle is the tip of one iceberg, which is the struggle over who is going to control this outlay of funds. State Department wants it, as does the Pentagon, not to mention the fact that numerous White House officials are weighing in personally. You are simply facing the field skirmish in a vicious turf war back in Washington." He glanced at Pierre, added, "I fear you shall face much the same difficulty from your own officials, Major."

"I already have," Pierre replied.

"Sorry to hear that." He turned back to Jake. "For the moment, because of the Soviet Union's interest in Turkey, the military has been assigned equal status, which of course is why you are here. And which brings up the second battle." Knowles leaned back, lines of weariness suddenly appearing about his mouth and eyes. "Why don't you take over, Barry."

"Right." The political officer made a futile attempt at straightening the lapels of his jacket and began, "You're aware of the struggle to get the United Nations up and running?"

"As much as the next guy, I guess."

"In that crisis you can see a concentration of everything we're facing here. On the other hand, we're trying to deal with the Russians as allies and let them have a hand in the UN and everything else that has resulted from our victory. On the other, we're being forced to accept that Stalin's Russia is just about the biggest threat our nation has ever faced. And Russia's been trying to get its hands on Turkey for centuries." Despite the bleakness of his news, the buoyant attitude never slipped a notch. "I guarantee you, Colonel, you'll never come across a more confounded mess in all your born days."

"Call me Jake."

"Right. There's no clear-cut agreement on this problem, not by the boyos sitting in their comfy offices back in Washington. Of course, everybody who's been up close to the front lines agrees that the Soviets are a menace and that they're on the march. But actual evidence is hard to come by. On the surface, these Russkies are all bonhomie and back-slapping."

"I've just experienced a little of that firsthand," Jake said and described their meeting with Dimitri Kolonov.

"Yeah, that Dimitri is a piece of work. I've already gotten the word on him from a buddy back in Sofia. You'll find a lot of them like that, so slick you can't keep a grip on them with pliers and a noose. But mark my words, they're up to no good."

"You think," Knowles corrected.

"I know," Barry insisted comfortably. "I just haven't managed to get my hands on the evidence to convince the rubber stampers back in Washington."

"Those are our superiors you are referring to," Knowles chided, but there was no condemnation to his tone.

"Yeah, well, this meeting didn't ever take place, so I guess it really doesn't matter what I don't say."

"Then what you need from me," Jake said, "is help finding something to pin the Russians down with."

"I heard about your escapade up in Berlin," Barry acknowledged. "Sounded like quite a time was had by all. I told Tom here about it, and he decided to risk this meeting."

"Officially we will have to be on opposite sides of the fence," Knowles reiterated gravely. "At least unless or until State and Defense can iron out their differences."

"Or until I'm replaced," Jake interjected.

"Let us hope that does not happen, Colonel. I feel certain we would work well together." Knowles rose to his feet. "Unofficially, if there is anything you need, anything at all, I want you to discuss it with Barry. He will bring it up with me."

"We're not allowed to talk with you," Barry explained. "But everybody's sort of given me up as a lost cause. So long as you keep your visits down to a few minutes at a time and not too frequent, I can run interference for you."

"Thanks, I guess."

Knowles extended his hand. "Make no mistake, Colonel. Your work is absolutely vital to America's future interests in this part of the world. But sorting out the conflicts between politicians who still see the Russians as friends and those who see them as our single greatest enemy will take some time and a good deal more hard evidence. Remember, any number of senior officials back in Washington have built their careers upon the fact that Russia has been an important ally throughout the war. We must be patient and work together to convince them that times have changed, and changed drastically."

Knowles's grip was as steady and strong as his gaze. "Mark my words. The confrontation in Berlin was not some isolated incident, but the herald of things to come."

Chapter Five

*T*HE NEXT DAY, Jake entered the consulate grounds to find a courtyard flooded with people. Ahmet greeted him at the door and announced with his great, beaming smile, "Is people wishing to apply for position of assistant, Meester Jake."

Jake turned and looked back over the assembled throng. "All of them?"

"Ahmet do just what you say, Meester Jake, look high and low for good assistant."

He looked doubtfully at the little man. "All of them have been vetted? They are all qualified?"

"Oh, most certainly yes, Meester Jake." He took in the courtyard with a proud sweep of his arm. "These the best you find." He dropped his arm, stepped closer, said more quietly, "Unless, of course, you are accepting Selim as assistant."

"Out of the question," Jake said, turning for the door. "I'll see them in my office. Have them come up one at a time."

The line of applicants seemed endless. All had dark complexions and finely sculpted features, male and female alike. All spoke English in varying shades and disguises. Some used a grammar so convoluted Jake

241

was positive they had learned it from an outdated book, without aid of a teacher. These applicants he treated with great respect, for there are few endeavors more difficult, or more indicative of determination and intelligence, than learning a new language alone. Yet none of them had any experience with accounting, and few could even type.

Some applicants had an accent so heavy they might as well have been speaking another tongue. Jake smiled his way through these interviews, asking a few polite questions, explaining carefully that he was under pressure to get up and running and so needed someone with an absolute and total grasp of English. He was not sure they understood him any better than he did them.

Throughout the entire day, Ahmet remained in Jake's outer office. The obsequious man smoked so many of his foul cigarettes that every time Jake opened his door he was struck by a billowing cloud.

Halfway through the afternoon, the phone in Jake's office rang for the first time, startling him almost out of his seat. Tentatively he lifted the antiquated receiver, heard a series of pops and hisses and static squeals, said repeated hellos with increasing volume.

Suddenly through the static came a familiar voice. "Jake, is that you?"

"Harry?" He made frantic hand motions for Ahmet to usher out the next incoming applicant and to close the door. "Where are you?"

"London. Good grief, this line is awful. Can you hear me?"

"Barely."

"Well, it will have to do. I've been trying to get through since yesterday. And that, mind you, with every ounce of political pressure I could bring to bear."

Jake raised his voice, shouted, "When do you arrive?"

"That's the problem. I still don't know. I would swear that there are unseen forces at work here."

Jake looked over at his now-closed door, said, "I can imagine."

"Eh, what was that? You'll have to speak up, man."

"There have been developments here too," Jake said.

"No doubt. Kolonov has introduced himself?"

"In a manner of speaking."

"You got my message then. Good. I assume I do not need to discuss with you the matter of security."

"Or trust."

"Exactly. You may assume that every wall has ears, and there are a dozen listeners to every spoken word."

Including the present conversation, Jake understood. "I sure could use a friend close at hand."

"I shall arrive at the soonest possible opportunity, I assure you. In the meantime, there is always the chance of our turning this situation to our advantage and learning what we can."

"I'm afraid I'm in over my head," Jake confessed, this time not caring who heard.

"Nonsense." Harry Grisholm's confidence managed to pass over the crackling line. "There is no one else I would rather have watching out for our interests, Jake."

"Shows how misguided even the experts can be," Jake said, but found himself smiling in spite of himself.

"Look for allies in unexpected places, that's my advice. You always were one for landing on your feet. I count on you to do nothing less there in Istanbul."

"A few allies," Jake said, "would be a welcome addition."

"Go beyond the normal routine, then. Examine avenues which are overlooked by the ones wearing blinders."

"Hard to find those avenues," Jake replied, "when I can't even read the street signs."

"A joke. Good. I like that." The exuberance refused to be contained by the static-filled line. "Now as to the funds."

"The third allocation arrived yesterday," Jake said, glancing over to the closed folder. So many zeros. "It boggles the mind, Harry."

"Our job is to make sure it is money well spent. If you are not satisfied about anything, then wait. Delay payment. Demand better details. Ask questions. Inspect in person. We must be sure that these initial actions follow correct procedures."

"Easier said than done."

"You are experiencing pressure?"

"From all sides."

"And I am not there to protect your back." A somber briskness pressed on. "Well, it simply cannot be helped. You must be strong, my friend. And stubborn." The line faded away entirely, then came back with a shouted, "Jake? Are you there?"

"Still here," he yelled.

"I am losing you. Take care, my friend. I shall join you as soon as I can. And remember—" But the line chose that moment to go dead.

Slowly Jake replaced the receiver, feeling more isolated and distant from protected waters than at any
time since the war.

By six o'clock his head felt as if it were full of used
chewing gum, and he was no closer to finding an assistant. Wearily he smiled and shook another hand
and ushered another applicant out. He leaned on the
door-post and said, "I'm positive I asked for someone
with accounting expcrience."

"Was no good, Meester Jake?"

Jake looked down at Ahmet's beaming face and the
oily strands of hair plastered down tight over the
gleaming skull. "Mr. Burnes, Jake, Colonel, Colonel
Burnes. All of them are fine. This Meester Jake business has got to go."

Ahmet nodded, all smiles. "Was not the ideal candidate?"

"Ideal is somewhere on the other side of the moon.
I'm not searching for ideal. I just want someone who
can add, subtract, and tell me the result in an English
I can understand." Jake examined Ahmet and said for
the dozenth time that day, "I thought you said you
had vetted these candidates."

"Oh yes, most careful vetting," Ahmet agreed.
"This last lady, she was very pretty, no?"

"Grand. Just grand. Only I don't see how a background as a music teacher and two courses in French
prepare her to be my assistant."

Ahmet made grave eyes. "She was not mathemat-
ics teacher? She did not live in England?"

Jake had to laugh. "When I showcd her the rows of
numbers, she looked like they were going to reach
out and bite her. And I'm still not sure how it was we
communicated at all, since I don't speak any Turk-

ish, and I am pretty sure she's never been anywhere within shouting distance of an English dictionary, much less England."

"Oh, oh, oh." Ahmet gave his head a mournful shake. "Is so hard to find worthy employees in such times." He paused for a moment of sober reflection, then brightened. "Perhaps you should speak yet again with young Selim?"

"I believe I'm finally beginning to get the picture," Jake replied. "The mist is finally clearing before my eyes. Selim wouldn't happen to be a relative of yours, would he?"

"Oh no, Meester Jake. Not mine. Sister's husband's nephew." The patented beam returned. "Is very nice boy."

"Your very nice boy can't add, thinks subtraction is something to do with his fingers and toes, and wrestles with English almost as well as I do with alligators." Jake pushed himself erect. "Bring on the next candidate."

Ahmet opened pudgy palms toward the ceiling. "Is no more."

"That's all?" Jake had to smile at the man's audacity. "You've scoured the streets and filled my day with twenty-three people who don't know accounting from acrobatics, and you say that's the best you can do?"

"Is terrible, no?" The beam widened. "Perhaps you see Selim tomorrow after all."

"Highly unlikely." Jake found himself not minding in the least when a glint of exasperation showed on the little man's face. He reached for his coat, shut and locked his door, turned back to see Ahmet struggling to recapture his grin. "We'll start again tomorrow."

"But Meester Jake—"

"Accountants," Jake said, stopping him with a hand that pushed at the air between them so hard the little man squeaked back a step. "Accountants with English. Remember that. And don't waste any more of my time."

His anger and his fatigue powered him down the stairs and through the lobby so swiftly that he was already beside the Marine's desk before the oddity struck home. He turned for another glance, saw that there was indeed a thin, bearded man hunched in the corner of the corridor's only bench. It was very strange, for security measures forbade anyone inside the front door without an escort.

Jake leaned over the Marine's barrier and faced the young man who had brought them in from the train station the day before. For the life of him, his fatigue-addled brain could not come up with the soldier's name. "Who's he waiting to see, Corporal?"

"Why, you, sir."

Jake glanced from the tired, disheveled-looking man on the bench to the Marine and back again. "Say that again?"

"He was the first applicant to be passed through this morning." The young man was typical of the consular guard staff, spit-shined and erect and so fresh he made Jake feel ancient. "Mrs. Ecevit vetted him personally."

Jake searched his memory, came up with another vague recollection from the day before. "Let's see, she's aide to the political officer, do I have that right?"

"That's the one." The Marine hesitated, then said, "Sir, is it true what they say, that you were in the push through Italy and all?"

"That was a long time ago, soldier. Another life-time."

But the Marine wasn't finished. "And that story about you rescuing the French resistance officer and carrying him through the desert? And what about you getting behind the Russkie lines and sneaking out those scientists and helping to start up the Berlin airlift?"

Jake gaped at the young man. "Where on earth did you hear all that guff?"

"From the Frenchie, sir, I mean Major Servais. He talked about you the whole way to the hotel yester-day. Your wife too. The major stopped by here this morning, but when he saw the line of people waiting to see you, he hung around a little, talking with us here at the station, then took off."

The young man could no longer suppress his grin. "The stories are all true, aren't they, sir? Boy, wait until the other guys hear about this. The major said you won the Silver Star and the Croix de Guerre, had that one pinned on by DeGaulle himself, I guess that's true too, sir?"

Jake started to brush off the admiration, then found himself staring into those clear gray eyes and wondering if perhaps he had found himself an unex-pected ally. "Do you know this Mrs. Ecevit person-ally?"

"Oh yes, sir." The Marine bounced to full atten-tion at the chance to offer more than polite chitchat. "I've been here almost a year now. I guess I know everybody, at least enough to say hello."

"What can you tell me about her?"

"She's a real firecracker, sir." The grin was hard to keep trapped, even at attention. "Sharp as a tack, too. I've seen her lay into that Ahmet fellow right back there in the corridor, peel skin from bone better than my drill sergeant back on Parris Island."

"She did?" The woman's stock just shot up. "You know why?"

"No, but I can guess. She doesn't have time for pencil pushers and official sneaks, sir."

"She doesn't."

"Not a second." A glance around the empty hall, then, "A guy who keeps his eyes open can see a lot from here, sir. That Ahmet's always scampering around, sticking his nose where it doesn't belong, sucking up to the guys with perks and power."

"I've noticed."

"Sure, I mean, yessir. Anyway, I imagine he tried it once too often with the lady, and she proceeded to blister his hide." A flicker of movement out of the corner, and the Marine snapped to rigid alert, finished with a crisp, "Sir."

A deeper voice said, "Can I help you with anything, Colonel?"

Jake turned to face the guard sergeant, a stern-faced leatherneck with four rows of campaign ribbons. Jake nodded a greeting. "Just getting to know one of your men a little. Hope that's all right."

"Long as he sticks to his duty, I suppose it's okay, sir."

"Thank you," Jake said, playing at ease. "What's your name, Sergeant?"

"Adams, sir." A half-made salute, just enough in the gesture and the eyes to let Jake know he was not going to curry favor with anyone. He was far beyond either the need or the desire.

Jake decided it was worth meeting the man head on. He glanced down at the ribbons, found two he recognized. "You were at Anzio?"

"That's right." The gaze sharpened. "What about you?"

Jake shook his head. "Came ashore at Syracuse. Met some of your group outside Naples. Tough assignment."

"Yeah, ain't they all?" The rigid reserve relaxed a notch. "There's been a French officer around here this morning, you catch his name, Bailey?"

"Major Servais, sir." The young Marine officer bit off the words.

"That's the one. He had some pretty interesting tales to tell, Colonel. Any of 'em true?"

"Old war stories grow like fish caught yesterday," Jake replied. "They get bigger with each telling."

The measuring gaze granted him a hint of approval. "Now, ain't that the truth."

Jake decided it was time to plant a seed. He leaned over the guardpost barrier, said quietly, "You soldiers know what it means to be a duck out of water?"

Within the sergeant's steely gaze appeared a glinting blade of humor. "We're here, ain't we?"

"I've been pulled from garrison duty at Badenburg, given a grand total of three weeks' training," Jake said, stretching the truth a mite, "then thrown out here and told to do the impossible."

The sergeant glanced at the Marine. "Sounds just like the corps, don't it, Bailey?"

"Sure does, Sarge."

"What's your first name, Corporal?" Jake demanded.

"Samuel. Samuel Bailey, sir."

Jake nodded, as though taking the news in deep, giving it value. Then back to the sergeant. "I need use of your eyes and your ears, Sergeant. Yours and your men's."

Back to the measuring gaze. "This a formal requisition, Colonel?"

"If it is," Jake replied, "then no matter how tight I try to keep it, sooner or later it's going to become common knowledge. Two days here, and I'm already aware of that."

A single chop of a nod in agreement. "The political officer appears to be a guy who doesn't leave a paper trail."

"You want me to let somebody else know we've talked," Jake said, understanding him, and taking great comfort from the fact that he had suggested Barry Edders. "I don't have any trouble with that at all. Tomorrow I'll lay it out." He let a little of his fatigue and his desperation show through. "I've got to find some people I can trust, Sergeant. And fast. I'm not asking for anything in particular. Just to keep watch and let me know what's on the up and up."

"Help you find the bear traps and the land mines," the sergeant offered.

"That's it exactly."

The sergeant glanced at the soldier standing duty. "I don't see as how I've got a problem with that. What about you, Bailey?"

"It'd be an honor, sir. I'm sure I can speak for all the guys. A genuine honor."

Jake dropped his eyes in an attempt to mask the relief he felt. But he looked to find the sergeant's steady gaze looking deep and had to say, "You don't know what that means, finding somebody I can rely on. My back is truly to the wall."

The leatherneck broke the hardness of his face enough to offer a quick thin-lipped smile. "Any chance of some action, Colonel? This guard duty starts to weigh heavy after a while."

"I would say there is a good chance of that," Jake replied, and then was struck with an idea. "How'd you like me to see if the consul general would assign one of you fellows to travel up country with me? Could be dangerous, though."

That brought a reaction so strong Jake felt he was watching the sun appear from behind heavy cloud cover. "You just said the magic words, Colonel. Travel and danger."

"I'll speak with somebody first thing tomorrow morning," Jake promised. He nodded at their crisp salutes, the sergeant's now as snappy as the corporal's. Then he turned back to the corridor. "And thanks."

He walked over to where the bearded man sat slouched upon the bench. The eyes did not rise at Jake's approach. Jake slowed, took the time to inspect the man more closely. His black suit, shiny with age, hung limply upon his bony frame. The scraggly beard was laced with gray threads. A battered and dusty fedora rested in the man's lap.

Jake sat down on the bench, watched as the man emerged slowly from his stooped reverie and lifted hollowed cheeks and dark eyes to stare back. Then for a moment Jake found himself unable to speak. The sight of that ever-hungry gaze drew him back to another time, when he had stood outside a barbed-wire compound and watched the haggard faces of war stare back. He swallowed, managed, "They told me all the applicants had been seen."

The man continued to watch him for a moment, then replied in softly accented English, "It is the way of people such as your Mr. Ahmet. They will grant me entry, then leave me seated here for as long as I am willing to remain and endure the silent humiliation. Then, you see, they are able to claim that they have never practiced discrimination. It is a most Turkish of solutions.''

Jake nodded slowly, ''You are Jewish?''

''I am.'' The steady gaze faltered, and one pale hand lifted to cover his eyes. ''Forgive me. I should not have spoken as I did. But I have been waiting here . . .''

''Since early this morning. I just heard from the guard. I am sorry. That is unforgivable.''

''It is expected.'' The hand dropped tiredly. ''But I decided to try, nonetheless, even though it was known that all consulates are closed shops, with local employment controlled by one such as Ahmet.''

''He's obviously let one slip through his grasp. Mrs. Ecevit.''

''Indeed. A friend of my mother, the only reason I learned of your need for an assistant. She was hired by the political officer while Mr. Ahmet was out sick. She is a breach of his little empire which will not be permitted to last. Something will happen, some unforgivable accident or theft or loss of passage of information to the enemy. And it will be traced back to Mrs. Ecevit. There will be no question, none whatsoever, who is responsible.''

''Not,'' Jake replied grimly, ''if I have anything to do about it.''

The bearded man gave a tired, tolerant smile. ''You have entered a country with almost forty percent unemployment. The power to give someone a job is greater than that of having money. Your Mr. Ahmet will not be pried loose easily, Mr. . . .''

He offered his hand. ''Burnes. Jake Burnes.''

''Daniel Levy.''

The man's grip was cool and firm. Jake felt a sudden urging, said, "Levi. The tribe of priests. The ones granted no province of their own, but rather cities within all the other tribes' lands."

The veil of fatigue lifted from the man's gaze. "You have studied the Torah?"

"The Bible," Jake replied.

"Ah. You are Christian."

"Yes."

"I do not use the word as a description of your heritage."

"No," Jake agreed. "Nor I."

There was a slow nod, one which took hold of the man's entire upper body, back and forth in measured pace. "You are far from home, Mr. Burnes."

"Very far," Jake agreed. "Where did you learn your English?"

"Here and there," the man said, his offhand manner suggesting he was still caught by Jake's earlier admission.

"Do you speak other languages?"

A continuation of the same slow nod. "Turkish, of course. And Greek. My nanny spoke no other language. And my family spoke mostly French within the home. That and Ladino."

"Come again?"

A hesitant smile parted the strands of his beard. "Perhaps that is a story that should wait for another time."

"What work experience have you had?"

A hesitation, a strange sense of regret, then, "Until the last year of the war I was employed by a large local company as their accountant."

"You don't say." Jake felt the thrill of discovery. "And since then?"

The regret solidified into gaunt lines. "How long have you been in this country, Mr. Burnes?"

"A grand total," Jake replied, "of two days."

"I regret that to answer your question I must reveal one of my country's more shameful mistakes."

"A camp," Jake breathed. "They put you in a concentration camp."

Dark eyes inspected him closely. "You have seen the death camps?"

"Some of the survivors," Jake replied. "As close as I ever want to come."

"This was nothing so horrendous," Daniel Levy stated. "But bad enough, nonetheless. Turkey held grimly to its noncombatant status, as did Switzerland. But we are far larger than Switzerland, with eight times the population and even more land mass. Germany continued to push the Turkish government into declaring itself a Nazi ally. Two of the most strongly worded directives were to supply Germany with troops and to round up the Jewish population. Turkey made the first small step to obey just eleven months before the war finally ended, when Germany threatened to lose its patience and invade."

The consulate's cool marble entrance hall was no place for this pale gentleman and his quietly suffering voice and his story. Jake said, "You don't have to tell me this."

"The government issued a proclamation," Daniel Levy continued in his soft voice, speaking to the opposite wall. "Male Jews over the age of eighteen were rounded up and taken to camps. The soldiers who came for us were most polite and regretful. I remember that one sergeant even saluted me as I stepped into the truck. I also remember how the lieutenant driving our truck told us to take a good look, because if the Germans came any closer to our borders we would not see our homes again."

Jake took in the words, the pallid features, the waxy long-fingered hands, the unkempt beard, the lost gaze. "And still you call this your country."

"Some are now leaving, those with relatives elsewhere, especially in America. Others are speaking of new beginnings in Israel. But my family has lived in Istanbul for almost five hundred years. We have lived in our home for seven generations. I, my father, his father before him, and his before that, all were married in the same synagogue." Dark eyes turned with resigned sorrow to Jake. "Tell me, Mr. Burnes, if we were to leave, who would remain to keep our heritage alive?"

"I understand," Jake said. He planted his hands on his knees, asked, "Can you type?"

"Some." The man's gaze was questioning. "Why?"

Jake had heard enough. The emotion drawn from Daniel Levy's responses was too raw for him to do more than stand, offer his hand, and ask, "Can you start tomorrow?"

Chapter Six

"YOU DON'T WASTE time, do you?"
Jake slid into the seat opposite Barry Edders' cluttered desk. "I'm a little short of extra minutes."

"Yeah, I suppose that's so." Even first thing in the morning, the political officer's cheery manner was solidly in place. "So you want me to talk with the CG, let him know you'd like to enlist our marines to your little effort."

"Just borrow them from time to time, is all."

"Well, I don't have any problem with that. Don't guess the CG will, either." He shuffled through a haphazard pile of papers, came up with a relatively clean sheet, scribbled on one edge. "Anything else?"

"Yes, as a matter of fact." Jake had spent much of the previous night planning this discussion. Keeping their talks to a minimum meant getting as much from each one as possible.

"Figured there would be." Barry sighed contentedly as he propped his shoes upon the desk's corner. He sipped his coffee, waved the mug in Jake's general direction. "Sure I can't offer you some?"

"I'm fine, thanks. I need—"

"You'll learn soon enough never to pass up a chance for a decent cup," Barry said, sliding down a bit further in the chair, getting himself truly comfortable. "The local stuff tastes like wet sand."

"I've had Arabic coffee before." Jake cocked his head to one side. "Do you ever let anything bother you?"

"Used to." Another sip, taking it slow, breathing in the steam, sighing at the flavor. Savoring the moment. "You see any action, Jake?"

"You mean, in the war? Some."

"Me, too. Philippines, Okinawa, Tinian. Political science professor one day, captain of infantry the next." He took another contented sip, glancing back over his shoulder at the sunlight that streamed in through his floor-to-ceiling windows, said mildly, "There couldn't have been, oh, more than a couple dozen times when I scraped through by the skin of my teeth."

"I know the feeling," Jake said quietly. "All too well."

"Way I see it," Barry went on, turning back to the room, "every day's a gift. My job is to enjoy it as much as I can. I love my work, love being overseas, love serving my country. I just can't let any of the memories or any of the current pressures get between me and appreciating the gift of life." Another thoughtful sip. "Or between me and my God."

"Faith has helped me a lot," Jake said carefully. "But I'll never get to where you are. Not in a thousand years."

"Yeah, I thought maybe you and your wife were believers." He snatched up another sheet of paper, scribbled busily, then passed it over, all without shifting either shoes or cup. "Address of the church where a lot of the expatriate community worships. Good place. You'd be most welcome."

"Thanks," Jake said, and suddenly found it necessary to duck his head and hide how much the simple gesture meant to him just then.

"We're cut from two different stalks, you and I," Barry went on. "My way of dealing with the world suits who I am. Same with you."

"It doesn't mean," Jake said, lifting his gaze, "that I couldn't learn from you. A lot."

Barry eyed him thoughtfully over the rim of his mug, then said, "I hope the situation changes, Jake, and gives us the chance to become friends."

"Maybe we already are," Jake replied.

"Yeah, maybe you're right at that." The brisk cheerfulness returned. "So what else can I do for you this morning?"

"I need all the accounts and correspondence dealing with the first two outlays of funds."

"That ought to stick a feather up old Fernwhistle's nose." Barry grinned as he scribbled a note. "Consider it done. Anything else?"

"A car and driver. Available day and night, short notice, maybe no notice at all. Somebody competent, safe, and able to keep his trap shut."

"Competent and safe are words that don't exist on Turkish roads. Confidential isn't a problem, though. These guys are so grateful for a job they wouldn't dream of yapping." Another scribble. "Car will be placed at your disposal day and night, driver available days only unless you give prior notice. See Sergeant Adams for how the roster works. What else?"

"Keep Ahmet off my back."

Barry grinned. "Heard about your little escapade with the hiring process. Pretty neat the way you did the end run on him."

"Why do you put up with him?"

"I don't, personally. As to the others," Barry shrugged. "You got to remember, most of the Americans here have had years experience back in Washington learning how not to make waves. Most of them are so grateful for the chance to serve overseas they'd eat a yard of wet laundry to keep the job."

"That guy is a menace."

"Yeah, well, I could push my weight around, but if I do, I'd tip our hand. So I'm going to have to let you handle this one on your own."

"Thanks a million."

"Hey, what are pals for, right?" An easy grin across the desk, then, "Anything else?"

"Just one point. I'd like to meet with your assistant."

"You want to spend time with Mrs. Ecevit?" For once, Barry registered genuine surprise. "Why?"

"You're not supposed to be asking me that," Jake said. "You were the one who hired her."

"Oh, don't get me wrong. She's fantastic. But she's also fairly high up the hard-to-handle scale. My two staffers call her Mrs. Prickly Pear. Personally, I love her mind, but not her attitude." He waited, granting Jake a chance to opt out. When he did not, Barry continued to press the point home. "Even I prefer to keep her at arm's length and receive everything she has to say in writing."

But Jake had already made up his mind. "I'll take my chances, if it's all right with you."

"Be my guest. She's off doing some work for me just now, but she should be back after lunch." A grand smile creased his features as he turned away. "Just don't say I didn't warn you."

"Are you sure this is it?"

Sally glanced from the note in her hand to the brass plaque set upon the tall entrance gate. "Rosewood Bungalow. See for yourself."

Jasmyn peered doubtfully at the great stone edifice rising beyond the formal gardens. "This is a bungalow?"

"Somebody's idea of a joke, more likely." Sally started forward. "If it is, she's in for a nasty surprise. My well of good humor is just about all run dry."

The previous day had been spent inspecting the apartments assigned the two couples. Jasmyn had almost wept at the sight of hers; when it came to Sally's turn, she could not help but laugh.

Pierre and Jasmyn had been assigned a two-room apartment in a rundown central-city tenement. The French consulate had dumped so much furniture and fittings inside that there was scarcely room for one person to walk about, much less for two people to start a life together. The apartment was on the second floor above a busy street; with the continual din below, they had to shout to hear each other. The single small balcony overlooked a central courtyard of cracked cement and weeds and a dirt-filled fountain. There was no sunlight or sky at all, the view totally blocked by clotheslines strung from higher balconies. Along with the bedlam of crying babies and screaming children and screeching mothers came the continual sound of dripping water. The air stank of starch and cheap detergent.

Sally's apartment was equally ridiculous, but on the opposite end of the scale. The pre-war building occupied an entire city block. She had opened the door to discover a residence spanning the entire floor. The paltry bits of furniture supplied by the consulate had only amplified the cavernous depths. Their exploration had taken on the air of a trek, calling out to each other to find their way back together, their footsteps echoing loudly from wooden floors and distant ceilings. There were six bathrooms and nine fireplaces. Nine. The kitchen was larger than Jasmyn's entire apartment.

Without further ado, they had commandeered two baffled drivers and cars from the French consulate and spent the remainder of the day shifting every stick of furniture from Jasmyn's apartment to Sally's. That evening they had pumped each other up, ready to do battle with both men for the right to live together. To their astonishment, neither had offered any argument whatsoever. Jake had seemed relieved. Pierre had said little, but had given the impression that they would probably not be around long enough to need to worry over accommodations. His entire second day had been spent in further explosive encounters.

Then the note had arrived with Sally's breakfast tray.

Sally was growing restless to move out of the hotel and into something more settled. She had no complaints about the hotel itself, other than the feeling that eyes followed her everywhere and privacy had become a relative term. Even room service was losing its appeal. Sally had slipped open the note, read the brief invitation to morning coffee, then gone to fetch Jasmyn.

*　　*　　*

Together they walked up the long winding drive, past ancient rosebushes trained to climb over a variety of surfaces. Rose-covered fountains sprayed musical water. Heavy stone walls were almost lost beneath their burden of blooming vines. Ancient trees and even older Roman columns were surrounded by trellises, upon which roses had been trained to grow and bloom in profusion.

"Oh, how simply marvelous. You must be Mrs. Burnes."

Sally stopped, searched, could not locate the source of the voice. "That's right."

"And right spot on time." An elderly face lifted above a rose-clad embankment and beamed at them. She wore a wide-brimmed straw hat and a smile as brilliant as the morning sun. "No mean feat, in these uncertain realms."

"Mrs. Hollamby?"

"Call me Phyllis, won't you, my dear? It's so much smaller a mouthful." She rose to her feet with the help of a sturdy cane, stripped off her gardening gloves, tottered over. "And you must be Mrs. Servais."

"Call me Jasmyn, please."

"Such a lovely name, it would be a pleasure." Bright eyes peered from a friendly face. "And the name matches the lady, I must say. Two enchanting guests for coffee, how splendid." She brushed at the dirt staining her simple cotton shift. "Just look at this, would you? Such a mess. I do so apologize, but it is so very difficult to keep track of time when I am out in my garden. You must think me terribly rude."

"I've always felt that was one of the nice things about gardening," Sally replied. "Having a perfect excuse to get good and messy."

"What a charming thought." She peered at Sally a moment longer, then nodded as though having reached a decision. "I have ordered coffee to be served in the garden. It's so pleasant this time of day."

The table was sheltered by a rose-covered trellis and layered in starched linen. It supported a silver coffee service and settings for three. Jasmyn exclaimed, "This is beautiful."

"Thank you, my dear. Yes, mornings are positively delightful out here. By midafternoon, however, I fear the atmosphere can be a bit overpowering. Roses seem to give out more scent with heat, or perhaps it is that so many summer days here are windless." She settled herself like an aging dowager and said to Sally, "Perhaps you would be kind enough to pour."

"I'd be happy to." As she steadied the heavy pot, she said, "Mrs. Fothering told us it was important that we try to meet with you."

"Yes, she has been kind enough to inform me of your little encounter." Sky-blue eyes twinkled merrily. "And of your meeting with our little friends the governess and her Swiss companion."

Sally tried to match the woman's light tone, though it cost her. "She said we were in grave danger."

Phyllis gave a gay peal of laughter, and the years positively melted away. "I would not pay overmuch attention to such blatherings, if I were you, my dear."

Sally felt a rush of relief so strong it left her weak. "But they were so, well, convincing."

"Deadly serious," Jasmyn added.

"Well, they would be, wouldn't they? I mean, that is why our Mrs. Fothering did not inform them of her own purpose on the journey, which was to see if they were worthy of joining our little band. Nor have they been told what role I myself play." She took a delicate sip, went on, "You see, my dear, there are those among us who feel they can give greater merit to their deeds by filling their little worlds with unnecessary drama."

Sally sank back in her seat and glanced at an equally restored Jasmyn. "Then Jake and Pierre aren't in danger after all."

"Why, of course they are, my dear." Phyllis Hollamby smiled brightly. "They are gathering intelligence in Turkey. There could scarcely be a more perilous occupation in all the world."

"But you said—"

Mrs. Hollamby reached over and patted Sally's hand. "I simply said that these women and their melodrama were out of place. Such ladies like to fill their lives with commotion. That is their choice. But to instill unnecessary ferment in the heart of a newcomer is, well, excuse me for saying it, but it really is simply balderdash." She looked from one to the other and aligned her features before saying sternly, "Now, you really cannot allow yourselves to take this so seriously. All the world is full of peril. Both your husbands have lived to wear their well-earned decorations because they are experts at the art of survival. If you wish to assist them with this next challenge, you must begin by being alert and calm and steady."

"That's what we had decided as well," Sally told her.

"Well of course you have. From all reports, you're both cut from proper staunch cloth." She looked from one young woman to the other. "I must tell you, what we have heard of your own war records has impressed our group enormously."

Jasmyn glanced in Sally's direction, then asked, "You know about us?"

"Oh my, yes. Otherwise we would have watched and waited before making contact. We must be extremely careful, you see. As to how, well, let us simply say for the moment that our network has extended at a most remarkable rate. People are relocated, and they take both the work and their desire to participate with them. New connections are made, new little circles started."

"That's what you call yourselves? Circles?"

"That is correct, my dear," she agreed, the humor reforming her two dimples. "Among ourselves, we are known as the Circle of Friends."

"Meester Jake." Ahmet was fairly dancing in place as Jake bounced up the stairs after lunch. "Is unauthorized stranger in your outer office."

"I told you not to call me that," Jake said, brushing by the little man as though he was not there. He had just spent an hour listening to Pierre moan about the barriers being placed in his way and was in no mood to pander to such whinings.

"But this man—"

Jake wheeled about, put on his sharpest parade-ground face. "Did you hear what I just said?"

Ahmet backed up a step and protested, "This most serious matter!"

"So is this," Jake said sharply. "If you want to talk with me, you will learn a proper form of address. Got that?" Before Ahmet could reply, he wheeled about and pushed through the front doors.

Corporal Samuel Bailey snapped to attention when Jake appeared. "Afternoon, Colonel."

"Don't they ever let you sleep?"

"Aye, sir." Being a graduate of Parris Island, the corporal took no notice of Jake's continual steam. "The first Tuesday of every other month."

Jake bit down on the smile as Ahmet scurried up alongside. "My new *assistant* shown up yet?"

"About an hour ago, sir." Just a flicker of a glance Ahmet's way, no more. "Mrs. Ecevit walked him up personally. She's already started the vetting process."

"That's the kind of news I like," Jake declared. "Efficiency and good news in equal measure."

A sudden thought turned him back. Ahmet missed bouncing off him by a hair. "You wouldn't know what Sergeant Adams' first name is, would you, Samuel?"

"Sergeants don't have first names, sir," Bailey replied. "They have them surgically removed when they earn their stripes."

"Morning, Daniel," Jake said, firmly shutting the door in Ahmet's protesting face. He surveyed the pile of boxes fronting the rickety metal desk and demanded, "What's all this?"

"They were here when I arrived, Mr. Burnes." Daniel Levy looked up nervously from the papers in his hand. "I'm sorry. Should it be Colonel Burnes, sir?"

"Skip the sirs for a start. You can call me Jake when we're alone. Mr. Burnes will do when guests are around." He pointed with his chin at the papers. The bearded man was evidently very nervous. Putting their relationship swiftly onto a footing of work and results might steady things down. "Any idea what this stuff is?"

"It appears to be cost estimates from a building project. Actually, several different projects in various locations." He shuffled the papers in his hand. "But they are hopelessly jumbled. It appears that no one has made any effort whatsoever to keep note of the incoming or outgoing flow of money. The reports were simply dumped into these boxes as soon as they arrived."

"Figures." Jake glanced about the bare, seedy office. "This place could sure use some dressing up."

"I am quite comfortable, sir, I mean, Mr. Burnes."

"Mr. Burnes it is," Jake said easily. "Okay. We've got to get a few things straight. Number one, we're probably on our own here, at least in the beginning. Number two, we're going to be facing pressures from all sides. Refer all such prodders to me. Number three, I need you to get this mess straightened out as quickly as possible. Tell me where the projects are located, who the major players are in each case. See if you can get some idea what they're doing. I want to go into my first meetings with at least a basic knowledge of what is going on."

"I understand." Daniel gradually stilled, his nerves easing with the focus of a task at hand.

"Time is crucial here. The faster we can work, the greater chance we have of catching the opposition off guard."

"You can count on me, Mr. Burnes."

"I know I can," Jake said, and meant it. "Notice anything peculiar so far?"

Daniel glanced at the piles he had already sorted. "Only that there are no tender documents among these. None I have found so far, that is."

"I don't understand. My basic instructions were that each project was to be awarded after a minimum of three bids had been received, the project going to the lowest qualified bidder."

"Well, perhaps they are in the two boxes over there," Daniel said doubtfully. "I have not looked in them yet. But I started with the ones dated earliest, and so far there is nothing except requisitions for more funds and receipts for money spent."

"Then something isn't right," Jake said. "Keep digging."

"I will, Mr. Burnes." A moment's hesitation, then more quietly, "You cannot imagine what it means to receive this job."

Jake nodded, crossed his arms, said, "I have to warn you, Daniel, there is a chance that our little party here might end up being short-lived."

"Mrs. Ecevit has warned me of the obstacles we face." A different form of uncertainty surfaced, one more akin to embarrassment. "My wife, you must understand, she was overjoyed to receive this news. She has asked if you might be able to join us tonight."

Jake took in the same shiny suit as yesterday, the evident hunger, said quietly, "I don't think I could make it for dinner. But I would be delighted to stop by after for coffee."

"That would be wonderful. Thank you."

"The thanks are all on my side." Jake turned for the door. "I'm going to see the personnel people, wherever they are. I want to arrange for you to have a bonus for starting early. Say I used it as a kicker, since we needed to get going quickly. Whatever I can arrange for you to receive, I'll have them drop it by this afternoon. Then I'll be up with Mrs. Ecevit."

Jake caught a glimpse of Daniel's face as he closed the door. The look of unmasked gratitude carried him through the aggravating process of wrangling funds from a tight-fisted personnel officer. That done, he traipsed up the stairs and down the long corridor to the political officer's outer office.

He knocked on the open door, watched the sharply chiseled face rise from her papers. He asked Mrs. Ecevit, "Can you spare a few minutes?"

"I suppose so," she said reluctantly.

"Thanks." Jake entered the office, motioned to the single high-backed chair. "Mind if I sit down?"

"Please." There was no warmth to her invitation nor her eyes. She watched him with a blank stare, giving nothing away. "Mr. Edders said you wanted to ask me questions."

"That's right. I was wondering if you could give me some background on the political situation here."

The wariness did not ease. "Why?"

"So I won't have to walk in blind," Jake said simply.

She sighed. "It is not a simple Western sort of situation here, Mr. Burnes."

"Why," Jake said mildly, "does this not come as a surprise?"

She looked at him sharply, found no derision, and after a moment's hesitation said, "In the 1920s, General Ataturk wrested political power from the Ottoman monarchs and introduced a limited democracy. I say limited, because only one political party was permitted. But I must also remind you that this came after more than three thousand years of rule by absolute monarchs. It is only since the late thirties, after the general's death, that opposition parties have come into existence."

Jake leaned back, delighted with the chance to sit and learn from someone willing to teach.

"When the funds arrived from the United States, they came with orders to avoid dealing with former Nazi collaborators at all costs. This was almost impossible. There were many Nazi sympathizers within *both* parties, many of whom never said so outright. The politicians, like people throughout our society, became split, some split even within themselves. One moment they saw the Nazis as examples of the discipline necessary to stop the threat of Russia and the Communists. The next, they were terrified of what a Nazi victory might mean to our country and its future."

"Good to hear."

"You must not leap to swift conclusions, Colonel Burnes. This is not America, with its history of democracy and a foundation built upon human liberty. This is Turkey. We were ancient before your continent was even discovered. We have survived thirty centuries of dictatorship and authoritarian rule. Do you hear what I am saying? Thirty centuries. Such a legacy makes many people wary of democracy. They see it as weak. They fear that the extremists will be granted too much freedom and will use it as an opportunity to wage civil war."

"And it was these same people who backed the Nazis?"

"There you go again," she replied crossly. "Trying to place an American-style analysis upon a truly Turkish problem."

Jake leaned back, crossed his arms. "So straighten me out, why don't you?"

Dark eyes flashed fire. "In ten minutes, you want me to explain thirty centuries of struggle and conflict?"

"You could start," Jake replied, holding to his easy tone, "by explaining why it is that you are so angry with me."

"I am not angry with you," she snapped. "I am angry with the system that has placed someone like you, with no true understanding of the crisis we face, in charge of something as crucial as these building funds."

"You could do worse," Jake responded quietly.

"I don't see how," she snapped back.

"You could be facing someone who refused to listen," Jake answered. "Or was unwilling to put up with your attitude."

Mrs. Ecevit reacted as though slapped. "My what?"

"You heard me." Jake made a message of looking at his watch. "You've used up three minutes with this tirade. That leaves seven minutes for the history lesson, or more anger. Your choice."

She gave him fifteen seconds of a smoldering stare, then, "You probably do not even remember where we were."

"You were about to tell me why it was wrong to assume that the Nazi sympathizers were the ones fearing civil war."

Perhaps it was his quiet tone, perhaps the focused way he repeated the crux of their discussion. Whatever the reason, she was forced to pause for a moment and look at him with a touch more caution, a bit less resentment. "It is wrong," she finally replied, "because there were hundreds of thousands, perhaps even millions of people, who in the moments of greatest fear thought that perhaps the Nazis represented the answer. Not the Nazis themselves, you understand, but the concept of a strong central rule. That perhaps Ataturk was wrong, perhaps the country was not ready for the freedom of democracy."

♦ "Why not?"

"Because, Colonel Burnes, democracy requires a majority consensus. It requires most people to want democracy to *succeed*. They must follow the pattern. They must vote, they must accept the rule of the leaders, they must at least try to follow the laws. If they do not, democracy breaks down. But our own people, many of them, do not *want* democracy. They see it as a Western evil."

"The Communists?"

"They are the largest and most dangerous antidemocratic faction we now face. A few of the extreme Muslim factions feel this way as well. And here is another crucial point missed by your analysts. They hear of a few extremists condemning democracy and the West, and they say this is the opinion of *all* Muslims, of *all* Turks. They arc worse than wrong. They are dangerously blind to the truth."

A knock on the door turned them both around. The adjunct Fernwhistle stuck his head in and smirked at the sight of them sitting there. "Your assistant said you might be here. The consul general wants to see you, Mr. Burnes. Now."

Jake rose to his feet and extended his hand. "I would like to come back if I may."

She inspected the hand suspiciously. "Why?"

"Because I would rather hear these things from someone who is genuinely concerncd," Jake replied, "than from someone who only tells me what they think I want to hear."

Her head cocked to one side, the eyes rose to meet his, and finally she accepted his hand. "Very well, Colonel Burnes. I shall be willing to tell you what I can."

"Ah, Colonel Burnes, they found you, excellent."

"Consul General Knowles," Jake said, entering the room. He stopped short at the sight of Pierre seated beside a skinny, dark-suited stranger. Beside them sat a beaming Dimitri Kolonov. Pierre's expressive face flashed him a warning frown, then settled back into masklike stillness. Jake turned back to the consul general. "Sorry, sir, I didn't know a meeting was scheduled."

"Strictly impromptu. You know Major Servais of the French consulate, I believe. With him is the consul general's adjunct, forgive me, I have not caught your name."

"Corget, m'sieur." The man spoke without moving his lips, his face as stiff as the rest of him. His slender moustache looked painted on.

"Right. And this is Mr. Kolonov from the Russian consular staff."

"We've met."

"Indeed we have, Colonel." The Russian appeared to have an inexhaustible supply of tailored suits and fine silk ties. He exuded an ice-cold cheer as he rose to his feet and shook Jake's hand. "I would have hoped to have heard from you before now."

"Just trying to get on with my job," Jake replied.

"Which brings us to the matter of this little gathering. Sit down, Colonel. I'm afraid I have a meeting scheduled to begin in less than ten minutes, so we will need to come right to the point."

"That should not take long." The Frenchman's moustache writhed like a captured caterpillar as he spoke. "This morning I have received a strongly worded protest from the Turkish government. It appears that funds they have been expecting to receive have not yet arrived."

"I regret to report that just such a protest has arrived at my office as well," Dimitri reported apologetically.

"To my office as well, the third this week," Fernwhistle said smugly. "And the British. Their adjunct was on the phone to me this morning, wondering what the holdup was."

"That is simple enough," Jake replied. "I have not yet authorized payment."

"And why not, pray tell?" the Frenchman demanded.

"Because I need to make sure the money is being spent correctly," Jake replied. "And could somebody tell me why the Turkish government is taking such an interest in payments to local companies?"

"Because companies and the government," Dimitri replied smoothly, "are one and the same."

"Come again?" Jake looked from one face to the next. "You mean we're dealing with government-owned companies?"

"Bravo," Fernwhistle said. "I do believe he is finally catching on."

"That will do," Consul General Knowles interjected. "You see, Colonel, before the war, the Ataturk regime took on the monumental task of propelling this country from what amounted to medieval serfdom into the twentieth century. They did so by using government funds to establish modern companies in a variety of industries."

Jake looked from one man to the next. "So no alternate bidders are available for our projects?"

"None that matter," the Frenchman sniffed.

"My dear Colonel, the other companies are privately owned," Dimitri Kolonov said, false regret oozing from his voice. "And private ownership is being pushed forward by the opposition party."

"Everything is becoming clear," Jake said. "The party preferred by Russia, I take it, is the one in power."

A glint of something beneath the polished surface flashed into Kolonov's gaze. "The party in power is *everyone's* friend."

"Right." Jake turned and spoke to the group as a whole. "My orders are explicit. I am to obtain tenders from three companies for each project, then assign the project to the lowest bidder."

"Preposterous!" Fernwhistle almost bounced from his chair. "This is absolutely outrageous."

"I agree wholeheartedly with my colleague." The Frenchman's moustache threatened to crawl right off his face. "To delay payment any longer would be absurd!"

"I'm afraid our gallant ally has a point, Colonel," Kolonov purred. "There is no time for such a search. Nor would we want to offend our hosts."

"Those are my orders," Jake said, biting down hard on each word.

"Well, not for long," Fernwhistle announced with grim satisfaction. "I have just received word that a dispatch that promises to rectify this ridiculous setup once and for all is due from Washington in three days."

Tom Knowles turned a cold eye onto his assistant. "Why was I not informed of this?"

Fernwhistle gave his bow tie a nervous tug. "It just came over the wire as we were gathering for this meeting, sir."

"Well, that changes matters, then." Tom Knowles showed a weary resignation as he rose to his feet. "I suggest we postpone any further discussion until this dispatch arrives. Good day, gentlemen."

In the corridor outside the consul general's office, Dimitri Kolonov patted Jake on the back. "I would urge you to come to our reception tomorrow night, Colonel. Enjoy the splendor which your position offers you." The steely glint resurfaced. "While there is still time."

Jake walked slowly and watched the others pull away in a tight cluster, leaving him and Pierre momentarily isolated. Pierre murmured, "Three days."

"Not much time." Jake shook his head.

"We must act fast," Pierre said grimly.

"What we need," Jake agreed, "is something that points to genuine wrongdoing. I sense in my gut that corruption is rife. We've got to locate a lever that will pull the lid off this mess and expose the need for something other than political shenanigans to be in control here."

Pierre's face folded into deep furrows. "I did not know you spoke Turkish."

"What?"

"These shenanigans, they are the party in power, yes?"

Jake had to smile. "It's good to have you on my side in this."

"Yes you do indeed need me," Pierre agreed.

"I better get back to digging," Jake said. Three days.

"On that, my hands are tied," Pierre said. "But find something my friend, anything that needs tracking down, and then together we shall spring into action."

Jake nodded, distracted by a tiny thread of thought that came and went so fast he almost lost it. Then it returned, gathering strands.

Pierre saw it happen and declared, "You have a plan."

"Sort of."

"I know that look," Pierre insisted, and clapped his friend on the back. "Suddenly I am eager for the days to come."

Chapter Seven

JAKE BOUNDED DOWN the stairs from the consul general's meeting, and he entered Mrs. Ecevit's office with such force that he almost startled her from her seat.

"Sorry," he said, breathless from the chance that there might truly be something to do. "Can you arrange a meeting with the opposition party?"

She settled back, but the startled expression did not leave her face. Instead, it deepened to outright consternation. "What?"

"The opposition party," Jake said, unable to contain his impatience. Three days. "And fast. I need to talk with them immediately."

"But," she glanced at her watch, "it is after four o'clock."

"Tomorrow morning, then. Early as possible."

Her impeccable English slipped a notch. "This meeting, it is most important?"

Jake let his desperation show through. "If anything has ever been urgent, it is this."

"Very well," she said carefully. As though in his demand he had uncovered something. "I can do this."

"Outstanding." He felt the tension ease a fraction. "And could you come with me as translator? I'd be happy to clear it with your boss."

"The man I have in mind speaks excellent English," she said, finally gathering herself. "But yes, I would like to come."

"I do not like this," Jasmyn declared.

"It's too late in the afternoon to start playing tourist," Sally agreed. "But Phyllis said this tour guide might have something important."

"*Could* have information that *might* be important," Jasmyn repeated. "And we have a thousand things waiting for us to do at our new home."

Sally stopped to smile at her friend, amused but pleased at her transformation from freedom fighter and desert princess to doting bride. "You are happy being married."

Jasmyn nodded shyly. "And Pierre has been so worried. I do not like him coming back to the hotel and finding our room empty."

"He is a very lucky man," Sally said quietly.

"He has made me very happy," Jasmyn replied simply. "I want to do the same for him."

"If there is something truly important here," Sally said, "we should find it out."

Jasmyn hesitated, then decided, "Not a moment longer than necessary."

Beyond the square and the mosques stood the Topkapi Palace. From a distance, the buildings were lost within the surrounding park. Only the corner peaks rose higher than the trees, shadows of the past looming above the leafy green. Jasmyn and Sally followed the throng down the broad passage, slowed with the others at the entrance gates, and searched. Almost all the faces around them were Turkish.

Suddenly a smiling face in a blue tour-guide uniform appeared and announced, "Welcome to Topkapi. I am Jana. Come, we must hurry in order to visit the important chambers before the palace closes for the night."

As she led them through the main gates and down an ancient cobblestone lane, Jana went on, "The Topkapi Palace was home to sultans for more than six hundred years."

"I did not come here for a history lesson," Jasmyn murmured.

The guide gave no sign of hearing. "Come, we must inspect the treasury."

"I have no—"

A hand fastened upon her arm. "Come, I said."

They entered the inner courtyard, passed between the hulking guards, and entered a low-ceilinged dungeon full of museum-style display cases. Despite their impatience, the first case drew an appreciative gasp.

"Yes, there, now this is better," the young woman said quietly. "Just another pair of Western tourists viewing some of Istanbul's many treasures." When a group moved up alongside, the woman's voice became brisk. "This eighty-six carat diamond is the fifth largest in the world. And the gold sheath beyond it contains the Topkapi dagger, handled only by the ruling sultan. The largest of those three emeralds you see there at the crest is hollowed out and opens to reveal a watch inside."

Sally waited until they had moved away from the tourists, then demanded quietly, "Why are we here?"

"Look, see here, one throne after another, all covered with gold and studded with precious stones. There is a saying that here in this one room is enough gold to make copper seem rare."

"If we were not going to be able to talk," Jasmyn insisted, "why did you ask us to come?"

"Because you are being followed and closely watched," the woman said, swinging around. "Now, please, for all our sakes, play the politely interested tourist.

"You have to remember, of course," the woman went on more loudly, "that a fifth of all the spoils of war were the sultans' due. And the Ottomans won many wars. They conquered and ruled all of Greece, much of Eastern Europe, all of North Africa, Egypt, and the Middle East." She pointed toward the stairs rising from the chamber's far end. "Come, we must visit the harem."

They allowed themselves to be led up a winding set of steep stone stairs. Just as Sally's head rose above the treasure vaults, she glanced back to see who if anyone was watching her way.

"Don't turn around, that's a good dear," the woman hummed lightly, her words swiftly lost to tight echoes and the scraping of their shoes.

"I wonder if anyone is actually following us at all," Jasmyn whispered back.

The woman waited until they had reached the rise and entered a grandly decorated chamber to say, "Let us hope you never have to meet them face-to-face." Then, as others crowded in behind them, she steered them over to one corner and continued in a louder voice, "This grand chamber was the central parlor of the harem, the forbidden court of the imperial wives and their children. It was guarded over by eunuchs and elder women, their lives as shrouded in mystery then as now."

Sally glanced about the lofty hall, with its rose marble pillars, its gleaming balustrades and chandeliers and deep covering of carpets. "It looks like a gilded cage."

"And indeed it was. It was often a lonely and degrading existence, especially for those out of favor with the sultan or the senior wives. These rooms harbored intrigue and vicious conflict, the women vying to become the power behind the throne. At the peak of Ottoman rule, these chambers were home to more than a thousand women."

"So sad," Jasmyn murmured.

"Come." The guide led them down a narrow passage, showing the chambers where the women lived their quarantined existence. "The Topkapi is more than just a palace," she told them. "It was known as the Forbidden City of the Sultans, and for many of these women it was the only world they ever saw."

The rooms grew cramped and dingy as they continued down the passage toward the chambers occupied by the most junior of wives. Pressed by passing time and by other, more lustrous sights, the crowds did not follow. Jana stopped and listened for a full minute, one hand upraised to hold them to stillness.

Once she was certain they were truly alone, the professional smile fell away. "We have only a moment," she whispered. "A friend works within the Russian consulate. She has heard them speak of your husbands."

Jasmyn's voice had a catch which even the echoes and the whispers could not erase. "They are in danger?"

"There is great concern that they are going to un-cover something. What, we have not been able to determine. But whatever it is, the Russians are most concerned that it remain a secret."

"That's not much to go on," Sally murmured.

"Listen, then. The Russians have prepared a sub-terfuge. You have heard of the dolls called *matri-oshka*?"

"The painted wooden dolls, one inside the other," Sally said. "I had one when I was a child."

"We use them to describe how the Russian mind attacks a problem," Jana said, her voice a pressing hiss. "Your husbands must not be taken in by what *appears* to be the problem. There is something else. Something deeper. Something the Russians are deter-mined to keep hidden at all cost."

"But how—"

Footsteps scraped along the corridor. Instantly Jana straightened and became the smiling tour guide once more. "Yes, I agree, this is a most fascinating set of chambers. But, please follow me, there is so much more to see, and so little time."

Daniel Levy rushed over as Jake climbed from the taxi. "It is so good of you to come, Mr. Burnes."

"My pleasure." Jake tried to shake off the distrac-tion of having found neither Sally nor a note when he had returned to their hotel. He had shrugged off his disappointment with the thought that she and Jas-myn were probably working at the apartment, where they were scheduled to move in two days. If, Jake amended his thoughts, they were not moved out of Turkey entirely by that time. He glanced up at the crumbling building that fronted the noisy street and asked Daniel Levy, "You live here?"

"No, no, but this is as far as a taxi will bring you, and you could never find your way alone the first time. Please come." He led Jake through what at first appeared to be a side entrance to the half-ruined structure but in fact proved to be a long, narrow passage. "I regret to inform you, Mr. Burnes, that my father has decided to join us tonight."

"It will be nice to meet him."

Daniel Levy cast a doubtful glance back over his shoulder. "I am afraid that might not be true. My father has strong feelings against, well, against foreigners."

"You mean," Jake interpreted, "he doesn't much care for non-Jews. Given what he's recently gone through, I can't say I blame him."

"He is old, and he has been sick. For some time he has lived for little more than the synagogue, the Torah, and we his family." Daniel turned down another lane, the balconies overhead almost touching across the passage. "Age requires that we grant allowances that otherwise would not be permitted."

"He wishes you were working for a Jewish company," Jake guessed. "He wants to size up the opposition, see if he can scare them off."

Daniel sighed to a stop at a tiny intersection. "You are a most observant man, Mr. Burnes."

"Don't worry," Jake assured him. "I've been given lots of practice recently at keeping hold of my temper."

"This is not," Daniel said quietly, "how I had hoped the evening would proceed."

"Then we'll just have to make it the first of many," Jake said, and glanced down the side passages. Both led off in winding mystery. "What is this place?"

"One of the ancient Christian quarters," he explained, glanced at his watch, and hurried on through the winding maze with easy familiarity. "The Muslims did not seek to cast out all their forebears. Quite the contrary. They needed them and invited many to stay. But as second-class citizens, never to rule again."

Jake looked up at the statue of a praying angel guarding a corner, so worn by time and sun and rain that the face was almost gone. This weathering granted the statue an even greater sense of gentle peace, of endless repose. "And the Jews?"

"There were a few here before, of course. The Diaspora sent Jews to settle almost everywhere they were welcome, and some places they were not." He turned into a lane more narrow than the others. None bore markings or street signs or indications of where they might lead. "But a great number fled here from Spain. You have heard of the great battles against the Moors?"

"Yes."

"The Spanish should not be condemned too harshly for their persecutions afterward." He cast a rapid smile over his shoulder. "A strange thing to hear a Jew say, but true nonetheless. The Spanish had fought for two centuries to cast out the Muslim invaders who had swept up from Africa. Many Jews followed along in the Arabs' wake, my family among them. When the Muslims were finally cast out, Spain continued in what they saw as a natural part of this same war and ordered all who remained in the country to either become Christian, or leave, or die."

"And your family came here?"

The dark beard nodded. "Once the Ottomans had conquered Constantinople and changed its name to

Istanbul, the sultans wanted to see it continue as a great trading center. But the Islamic code forbade the charging of interest, which is a necessary part of international trade. The great Ottoman families saw only two professions as fitting and proper, so their offspring either became landowners or members of the royal court. Thus the Jews and those Christians willing to remain and work under Muslim rule were invited to work as traders. More Jews than Christians accepted the invitation, for the simple reason that my ancestors had nowhere else to go."

"Your story is like a bit of living history."

"More than you might imagine. When we are alone, my family still speak the language called Ladino, the Spanish we brought with us four hundred years ago. From what we understand, this is the only place on earth where it is found today. Yet for us it still lives and breathes, a vibrant language. We have numerous books published each year, only available in our Ladino tongue." He pointed through an ancient portico. "Through here, please."

Suddenly they were enveloped by birdsong and the sweet scents of flowers and water and grass. The garden was walled and tiny, not twenty paces to a side, but coming as it did in the middle of the high-walled lanes, it was a delight. "Beautiful."

"This garden is entrance to the Jewish quarter." Daniel pointed to an ancient structure rising from one corner. "This is one of the oldest synagogues in Istanbul. My family has worshiped here for over four hundred years." They slowed their pace to enjoy the garden's radiance. "My family prospered under the Ottomans. Istanbul of the Middle Ages was both bank and warehouse for East-West trade. Letters and goods arrived from all over the world, destined for the merchant families."

He pushed through a heavy wooden gate, walked up a passage lined by a profusion of flowers, and entered an apartment building. The inner corridor was old but spotless, and smelled of cooking and disinfectant. They climbed two floors, past the sounds of children and adults and music and laughter, and stopped before a massive, age-stained door.

Daniel paused to kiss his fingers and press them against a small metal box nailed to the doorpost. He tapped lightly, opened the door, and called, "Miriam?" He then gestured to Jake. "Please, Mr. Burnes, you are welcome."

A dark-haired beauty entered the hallway, wiping her hands upon an apron. Her smile was as warm as her voice. "It is indeed an honor, Mr. Burnes."

Before Jake could respond, Daniel said quietly, "And this is my father."

Miriam's eyes dropped with her smile as an old man shuffled past her, peering at Jake with rheumy eyes. Gray curls poked from about his skullcap. When no hand was offered him, Jake gave a stiff bow and said, "An honor, Mr. Levy."

The man inspected him from head to foot, then turned to his son and demanded, "You are certain this is necessary, permitting entry to a goy?"

"Papa," Miriam said tiredly.

The old man went on to Jake, "I say this in English so that you can hear and understand, *Colonel* Burnes. Yes, yes, I know, you now hold a civilian position, but an officer is an officer is an officer. A goy and an officer of a foreign army. Here. In my house."

"Papa, please," Daniel's voice implored quietly. "You shame me."

"No, it is you who shames this house. Such an invitation, never have I heard of such a thing."

Jake kept his tone as steady as his gaze. "It is true I remain an officer in my country's army," he agreed quietly. "This is something I remain very proud of. I was called, and I served."

"America has long been friend to the Jews," Miriam said, her tone downcast.

"Yes, yes, I know of your family's sentiments," the old man snapped. "And how even now they wish for this man to come and visit them, so that they might press him for visas." He stared balefully up at Jake. "But my place is here, I tell you. This has been home to my family for almost five hundred years. Twice again as long as America has been a nation."

"He has been ill," Daniel said apologetically.

"I am not ill," the old man retorted. "I am confident in the face of my adversaries."

"Papa, shame. He is a friend."

" 'Though an host should encamp against me,' " Jake quoted, wanting only peace with the old man, admiring him and his stubborn strength, " 'my heart shall not fear: though war should rise against me, in this will I be confident.' "

"What is this?" The old man backed up a pace in astonishment. "You are quoting the Psalms to me?"

"Did I not say?" Daniel spoke quietly. "An exceptional man, Papa."

"Please, please, you must enter," Miriam urged, ushering Jake down the hall and into the living room. "Take this seat here. It is the most comfortable. Daniel, come help me in the kitchen, please. Papa, you must behave, do you hear?"

Jake remained standing, looking around the room. It was cluttered with the possessions of ages—chairs etched with ancient floral patterns, a high-backed wooden bench scrolled with Hebraic writing, a copper-topped central table, aged carpets upon the floor. Jake found himself drawn to a series of framed prints upon the walls. Most were in Hebrew, but one was in a different, almost cuneiform-shaped script.

"My ancestor received that letter some two hundred years ago. It is curious that you would choose it to inspect." The old man watched Jake from his chair. "You see, Colonel, that letter is from a Christian, one you would probably call a soldier, but we would prefer to think of as a pirate. Of course, what are we but ignorant Jews?"

"I would never have thought of you in such a way," Jake said, taking the chair Miriam had shown him.

But the old man did not let up. "That letter, Colonel Burnes, was written by this Christian *pirate*, who had captured an ancestor of mine and was allowing him to send one letter begging for ransom money. The Christian, you see, was willing to sell this innocent trader and his family for the price of one sack of gold per family member. The trader was begging for his life." The old man's gaze was bright and keen and watchful. "My family has kept that letter upon our wall ever since as both reminder and warning to watch out against the treachery of outsiders."

"It was not Christians who imprisoned you and your son in the camp," Jake pointed out.

"No, indeed not." The dark eyes remained steady and accusing. "Not this time."

"Enough of this, enough." Daniel entered the room bearing a platter of sweets. "We did not invite this man into our home to insult him."

But Jake kept his eye upon the old man, held by a sudden thought so strong he knew it was a gift, an invitation. "I wonder," he said calmly, "if there might not be a point where we can know a meeting of the minds."

"Impossible," the old man expostulated.

"Perhaps a meeting of the hearts as well," Jake went on, feeling the gentle guiding force. "Perhaps even, in time, become friends."

The old man's eyes narrowed, but something held him silent. Daniel stood over the pair of them, his questioning gaze shifting back and forth.

Jake leaned forward. "I would consider it an honor," he said quietly, "if you would teach me of the Torah."

Chapter Eight

JAKE SIGHED HIS way into the office building's ancient elevator. He watched as Mrs. Ecevit slid the brass accordion doors shut and pressed the top-floor button. He waited as the floors clanked by, his mind far too slack for what lay ahead. But he could not help it. His world was out of kilter. His heart thudded miserably in his chest. He sighed again.

Mrs. Ecevit glanced his way. "There is something wrong?"

He started to deny it but did not have the strength. "I argued with my wife. Last night. And again this morning."

"Ah." She nodded. "Men are such bad quarrelers."

"I sure am." Jake watched her ratchet the inner door back and push the outer one open, then followed her out. "I can't win a debate. She's much more intelligent than I am. So I lose my temper and end up ordering her to do what I want her to do."

For the very first time a hint of something human, something warm and compassionate, showed through Mrs. Ecevit's brittle shell. She slowed her pace. "I do not know American women, but if they

293

are anything like intelligent Turkish women, they would not like such an order very much."

"No," Jake agreed. "Sally sure doesn't."

He tried to compose himself as they entered a large outer office, but the weight of his heart pulled his face back into the same slack lines. Jake watched from the doorway as she walked over and gave their names to an attractive receptionist.

Mrs. Ecevit returned to where he stood and said, "We are early, and the man we are scheduled to meet has other people with him."

"No problem." Jake sank down into the corner seat, as removed as possible from the cheerful bustle filling the large chamber. Mrs. Ecevit took the seat beside him, her eyes darkly humorous. He said, "I'd give anything never to have to argue with her, not ever again."

The humor broke through then, and Mrs. Ecevit dropped ten years as she flashed white teeth and chuckled. "Ah, Mr. Burnes, you Americans are so wonderful at times."

"Call me Jake. I can't be talking about something this personal and hear you call me by my last name."

"All right." Another flashing smile, and he realized that beneath that diamond-hard exterior dwelled a truly striking woman. "You may call me Anya. There is an expression we use very often, 'Tomorrow, tomorrow the apricots.' It is very Turkish. The story goes, once there was a handsome young man, just like yourself, I imagine. He was pressing his favors upon a lovely young maiden. As he grew more impatient for her answer, she replied, yes, all right, but tomorrow, tomorrow when the apricots appear on that tree. Only the tree she was pointing to was a pear tree."

"Meaning I'm asking for the impossible."

"Yes," she agreed, trying to recover her accustomed solemnness, but the light in her eyes giving her away. "But it is very nice that you would even wish for such a thing. It is very romantic. Would it be impertinent of me to ask what happened?"

Jake sighed his way into the tale, the situation he faced becoming impossibly entangled with his worry—Sally's meeting the two women on the train, the Russian's appearance, the confrontation with Fernwhistle, Sally and Jasmyn's talk with Mrs. Hollamby, his own meeting yesterday afternoon with the consul general and the time limit placed on him. "Then when I came home last night," he went on, "Sally had just arrived back from some clandestine meeting at a place called Topeppy."

"Topkapi," Anya corrected. "The sultans' summer palace."

"Whatever you say. Anyway, she and Jasmyn were led around by a stranger who tells them the Russians have planned some deception to pull us off the track."

"It would not surprise me," Anya said slowly. "That would be very much a Soviet-type strategy."

"This woman also told her we were being followed. All of us. Then they heard something and hightailed it away." Jake grimaced at the thought. "I was furious that she'd taken such a risk."

"And she," Anya finished for him, "was furious that you did not appreciate her efforts."

"Don't tell me you were in the lobby and heard us." He dropped his head. "I can't believe we argued in a hotel. We might as well have been standing in the middle of the street."

"Hotel staffs are paid to be discreet. And no, I was not there, I did not need to be. It is one of the most ancient of disagreements. You want to protect her, she wants to help you."

Jake lifted his head. "So what's the answer?"

"For you to be grateful, and for her to be careful." Again the flashing smile. "And keep hoping that the tree will someday grow apricots."

"Anya, so sorry to have kept you waiting." A young man in a finely cut Western suit rushed over, took both Anya's hands in his, smiled, then turned as Jake rose to his feet and offered his hand. "And you must be Colonel Burnes."

"This is my husband, Turgay Ecevit," Anya said.

"Your husband," Jake said dully.

"Turgay is director of this office, which runs the party's Istanbul-based operations," she said with quiet pride. "He is also personal assistant to Celal Bayar, leader of the Turkish opposition." She looked up at her husband, then back at Jake. "As you can see, I did not need to hear your discussion of last night. I know it all too well."

Her husband looked from one to the other. "What is this?"

"Just finishing a discussion," she said quietly. "Perhaps we should begin another. Colonel Burnes has very little time."

Istanbul was a world of endless contrasts, where modern met the ancient and the timeless held place with the immediate. Handcarts bustled between smoky buses and clanging streetcars. Donkeys brayed as they pulled wooden carts and impossible loads. Women stepped over craters in the sidewalks, one hand gripping eager children while the other fanned the flames of conversation. Great clouds of noise and diesel fumes and fresh energy billowed in the air. Despite the ache she felt over quarreling with Jake, Sally found herself captivated by the excitement and the mystery of it all.

The fish market was on the legendary stretch of water known as the Golden Horn, an inlet of the Bosphorus. The stalls did not line the streets because there was simply no room. The buildings bellied right up to the street, and the lane dropped directly into the rocklined water. Enterprising fishermen used broad flat-bottomed boats as stalls, standing in one end, calling their endless song of quality and selection and price and barter, one hand slinging water over the stock to keep it shining and fresh. Potential customers walked the crowded lane, leaned over the railing, waved their arms, and argued prices with exuberance. Overhead, gulls echoed their boisterous refrain.

"Ah, there you are, my dear. And on time yet again. How marvelous." Phyllis Hollamby walked up, moving briskly even while leaning heavily on her cane. "And where is your lovely companion?"

"She had to attend another reception with her husband."

"Pity. But it can't be helped, I suppose." A keen ear picked up on the unsaid. "What did your husband think of the information you got from Jana?"

"I'm not sure," Sally said dismally. "We ended up arguing about my taking risks."

Phyllis gave a magnificent sniff. "Men. They are so utterly blind at times, aren't they, my dear?"

"Jake is a wonderful man," Sally said defensively.

"No doubt, no doubt. And he must love you dearly, to have such concern for your well-being. Yet one would think that, given the critical nature of his affairs, he would welcome a bit of help."

"Not to mention the time pressure," Sally added, and related the three-day ultimatum.

"Well, there you are." The dimples appeared in age-spotted cheeks. "Still, I suppose if men did ever reach perfection, life would become an utter bore. Don't you agree?"

Despite the weight of her heart, Sally could not help but smile in reply. "I don't think there's much chance of that."

"That's my girl." Mrs. Hollamby reached over and patted Sally's cheek. "Your husband is a most fortunate gentleman. I hope he realizes that."

"He does," she said, then amended, "most of the time."

"Well, we shall just have to remind him, then, won't we?" She spun about. "Come along, my dear. I smell adventure on the wind."

Sally hung back. "Jake doesn't want me taking any more risks."

"Who said anything about risks?" Phyllis sniffed. "From now on, we shall limit ourselves strictly to a bit of sightseeing. Not even your gallant but somewhat overprotective husband can object to that."

"Have you heard, Colonel, of *yagli güres*?"

Jake accepted a tulip-shaped tea glass from the attendant, holding it gingerly by the rim. "I don't even know if it's animal, vegetable, or mineral."

"None of them." Turgay accepted his glass, thanked the young man, sipped noisily. "It is a distinctly Turkish form of wrestling in which men oil down their bodies, then grapple for a hold to throw their opponent off his feet. It is a dance of conflict and balance and opposing powers, and it says much about my land. We grapple with ourselves, Colonel. The modern with the ancient, the Muslim with the secular, the democratic with the authoritarian, the internal with the great powers to every side. To govern Turkey is a constant struggle in which one slip spells disaster."

Jake lifted his glass, felt the liquid's near-boiling heat before his lips touched the rim, lowered it without tasting. Drinking such tea had to be an acquired trait. "Sounds like a risky business to be in."

"To understand just how risky, Colonel, it is necessary to explain a bit of our history." A more thoughtful sip, then, "In 1453, after a bombardment lasting fifty days, the city fell to the Ottoman Turks. It is said that the paintings and mosaics upon the church walls sweated from fear. The pope himself offered daily prayers for deliverance from what he saw as two equally great evils, a large comet and the Ottoman ruler, Sultan Mehmet. But the city did fall to the sultan. The city of Constantinople was renamed Istanbul, and a period of Ottoman domination began which lasted almost exactly five hundred years. The domination was absolute. Opposition to the ruling sultan and his court was strictly forbidden. There was only one voice, one law. And with time, this law became increasingly corrupt. By the time World War One broke out and the sultan decided to side with the Germans, Turkey was trapped within the nightmare of a hopelessly backward, hopelessly corrupt regime. Time and the rest of the world had passed us by."

Turgay had more the air of a passionate professor than a politician. He was tall and striking, with chiseled olive features and intelligent eyes. He carried his authority with the ease of one for whom such trappings mattered little. The fire of conviction ignited both his gaze and his words. "After the debacle of World War One, a general called Mustafa Kemal, later renamed Ataturk, which means Father of the Turks, led a war of insurrection against corrupt Ottoman rule. The struggle ended in 1923. In the eyes of the common man, Ataturk had won a victory on par with Mehmet's original taking of Constantinople. This gave him the power to sweep aside Ottoman history and declare Turkey a republic.

"Ataturk was determined to drag Turkey out of the Middle Ages and into the twentieth century. To him, this meant a complete break with Ottoman religious past. So Turkey became not only a republic, but also secular, meaning that religion and state were separated once and for all. Ataturk also embarked on a rapid expansion of state enterprise, education, and health care. The Latin alphabet replaced the Arabic, and the entire nation, literally, went to school. For the first time in its history, the common man was given the opportunity to read and write. And women were freed from imprisonment behind the *sharia*, or Islamic code of law."

Anya Ecevit sat listening to the history lesson with a patience that surprised Jake, seemingly content to set aside her normal drive and energy and share in her husband's interest. Jake found himself watching her as much as Turgay. "Yet there was a downside, as you Americans say, to this reform," Turgay went on. "A very great one. All these new laws were strictly enforced. No opposition, or even opposing thought, was permitted. Anyone who voiced an opinion contrary to the new, modern, secular state was considered a traitor."

"Sounds familiar."

"Indeed, yes. Fortunately for Turkey, Ataturk was both a charismatic leader and a statesman, a figure greater than life, one determined to lead Turkey not toward aggression, but rather toward a new future."

"You sound almost awed when you talk of him," Jake said. "Strange to hear, coming from an opposition politician."

"In your country, perhaps. But in my country, Ataturk was in truth the *only* politician. It is because of him that we are free to be politicians at all. So you see, Mr. Burnes, although I disagree with where the country has arrived, I do not disagree with the path upon which it trod nor the leader who brought us here."

"This Ataturk must have been quite a man."

"Indeed he was." He grimaced apologetically. "But Turkish politics remain treacherous, Colonel, with intrigue and corruption practiced with a skill learned over hundreds of years. That is what we the opposition are up against when we begin speaking of much needed change."

Jake decided his tea had cooled enough to risk a sip. "So what is the answer?"

"We of the Democratic Party do not condemn Ataturk's policies. Our leader was himself once a prime minister under Ataturk. But we feel that if progress is going to continue, private enterprise must be given a chance to succeed. We are worried that if both political power and business remain within the hands of central government, the old problems of corruption and intrigue will resurface."

"And strangle you all over again," Jake agreed. "I don't see why there hasn't been American support for this."

The couple exchanged glances before Turgay responded quietly, "Nor do we, Colonel. Especially after we won almost a third of the parliamentary seats in the last election. But your government persists in seeing any opposition as a threat to stability and an entry point for the Communists. We have been trying to tell them that unless we are given an equal chance to express our views, in other words, be the opposition in the truest sense of the word, the risk of Communist revolt is even stronger. But it has been hard to find someone willing to hear us out. So very hard."

"I have been trying to set up a meeting like this one," Anya added, "for almost a year."

"People are to busy, there is too much going on, they are worried about rocking the boat," Turgay said. "We understand some of the reasons. But we disagree as well."

"So do I," Jake agreed. "I don't know if I can help, especially as I might be replaced in a matter of days. But maybe, just maybe, we can set some wheels in motion."

"This is the chance I have been searching for," Turgay exclaimed, leaning forward in his seat. "Tell us what we need to do."

The ferry from Istanbul to the Asian shore was a welcome release from the city's fierce grip. "Istanbul is one of the most marvelous cities in the world," Phyllis declared fondly. "It straddles Europe and Asia and joins the cultures of East and West. Not to mention the wealth of its past. So much history, so many civilizations, that time blurs, and the city comes to count the years as mortal man does minutes."

She pointed toward the approaching shore. "The lands that lie in Asia are known as Anatolia. Some of the local villagers declare themselves citizens of Anatolia, not Turkey. They are a fiercely patriotic lot."

Sally gazed across the azure waters to the gently sloping hills. "This is beautiful."

"There is talk of a bridge, but many are against it. I most certainly count myself among them. It would only mean more hurry and rush, and the city already has far too much of both." She took a deeply satisfied breath of the sea breeze. "Crossing the Bosphorus by bridge would be like holding hands with gloves on. The thrill would simply be lost."

The city rising from the opposite shore had the look and feel of a sprawling village. The pace was slower, the air stiller, the buildings seedier, the people from a different age. Sally walked alongside the older woman and relished the delight of discovery.

They passed a shop filled with vast piles of clutter. Outside, two men sat at a rickety table, the younger man listening eagerly to the elder's lecture. Despite the heat, the old man wore a blue knit skullcap in the manner of one who seldom if ever took it off. Sprouting from either side was a flowing white beard that fell broad and square to cover the top three buttons of his tattered shirt. One hand curled around his cane, while the other directed the flow of conversation in the air between him and his younger companion.

"My husband operated one of the largest foreign-owned companies in Turkey," Phyllis said as they walked, her tone as casual as though she were discussing the weather. "In a land such as this, it is utterly impossible to disengage something of that size from the realm of politics and intrigue, so he

inevitably found himself in the midst of things. He
was as adamantly opposed to my own involvement
as your husband is to yours. But in time he came to
see me as an invaluable asset, able to hear things and
visit places utterly closed to him." She gave Sally a
reassuring smile. "You must give him time, my dear.
It is not true that men don't change. They do, but
ever so slowly."

A hint of the previous evening's frustration resurfaced. "I'd rather watch a glacier melt."

The dimples reappeared. "You do my heart such
good, my dear. If you will permit an ancient woman's
advice, perhaps you need to learn patience to match
your own husband's need for greater open-minded-
ness."

They stopped to permit passage to a young man in
khaki overalls carrying a stack of empty oil cans. His
load rose up to a level twice his height. A coiled blanket draped over his shoulders granted some padding
to his back. The ropes that tied his load were tangled
into one great knot, which he gripped with both
hands. He huffed noisily with each step.

The sight of the young man laboring like a pack
horse sobered Phyllis. When he had passed, she said,
"This is a country where the present is tangled with
the past. For the rich, there are the pleasures of living
where the cultures of Arabia are married to the life-
style of the Mediterranean. For the poor, I am sorry
to say, the life of serfdom still remains."

They took a cobblestone lane up between two
buildings that appeared to be carved from the hillside. Despite her age, Phyllis maintained a brisk
pace. Finally they stopped before an ancient house of
wood and brick. It leaned tiredly upon its neighbor,
the windows and doors and floors reset to remain

more or less level. Phyllis raised her cane and rapped sharply on the doorframe. An older woman appeared in the entrance, as broad as she was tall, her head covered in a white scarf as translucent as a veil. She beamed toothlessly at the sight of Phyllis, backed up with as much a bow as she could manage, and invited them in.

"It is polite to take off your shoes here," Phyllis said quietly. The woman offered them pairs of house slippers decorated with brightly colored beads and handsewn designs, then led them through the foyer and into her home.

The floors were of broad wooden planking, darkened with centuries of oil and polish. The carpets were gay, even those so worn that the designs had become mere grayish shadows. The living room table was broad and low and circular, and carved from a single sheet of bronze. An old man rose from a low divan and tottered over, hand outstretched. Phyllis greeted him with a genuine smile and words in Turkish. Sally allowed herself to be directed toward a padded couch standing barely a foot above the floor. She followed Phyllis's example and half sat, half knelt with her skirt tucked tightly around her knees.

Phyllis turned to her and said, "This gentleman used to be employed by my husband's company. You will find that in these lands, such employment creates the sense of an extended family, with all the obligations and duties of a patriarch."

The old woman returned with a copper tray bearing four ceramic cups, each nestled within its own copper shell, and an oddly shaped long-handled vase. Instantly the room was filled with the fragrance of coriander and coffee. Sally said to Phyllis, "I didn't know you spoke Turkish."

"Only a few words," she replied modestly before returning to an animated discussion with the old man. The woman left once more and returned with a second tray, which she set down between Phyllis and Sally. It appeared to be filled with unbaked dumplings, each rolled in finely sifted flour. She then lifted the bronze pitcher and poured what to Sally looked like steaming black mud into each little cup. Sally accepted her cup with murmured thanks and looked doubtfully into the tarry depths. "I'm supposed to drink this?"

"Let the sediment settle a little first," Phyllis replied brightly. "And you must take one of these Turkish delights. They are homemade."

Sally looked at the tray again and realized, "They are coated with pure sugar."

Phyllis selected one, took a bite, hummed her appreciation to the beaming old couple. "Be sure and smile when you swallow."

Sally chose the smallest and forced herself to ignore the sugar dust that filtered into her mouth and nose as she raised it and bit. The glutinous mass melted to release the highest concentration of oversweetness she had ever experienced. She swallowed it as she would medicine, forced down the choking sensation, managed, "Absolutely amazing."

"That's a dear," Phyllis said, her eyes sparkling. "I do wish you could see your face just now."

Sally held grimly to her smile, lifted the cup, swallowed a mixture of fiery pungent coffee and grit. After the sweet, the coffee was not half bad.

"Now finish the sweet," Phyllis instructed.

Sally switched her forced smile toward the Englishwoman. "You've got to be joking."

"Eyes are upon you, my dear." Phyllis finished her own, then licked her fingers in an ecstasy of appreciation. Sally watched her with astonishment, then without thinking what she was actually doing to her stomach, placed the remaining candy in her mouth and took it like an oversized pill. Phyllis smiled in approval. "Oh, well done."

"I am about to keel over with sugar shock," Sally said brightly to the old couple.

Phyllis laughed gaily and said something in Turkish. The couple beamed with delight and responded animatedly. Phyllis bowed her thanks and said, "They have just made to you a gift of all the remaining candies."

"I am absolutely speechless," Sally said, bowing in turn.

The discussion then took a somber turn, and the elderly couple spoke at length before permitting Phyllis time to turn and translate, "They have a son who is now working on a construction project some eighty miles from here." She glanced at the couple, murmured, "It is most curious."

"What is?"

"Well, they say that all the men there know that the project is funded by the Americans. But what they would want with a cultural center built miles from anywhere is baffling."

"Maybe they have it wrong."

"They positively insist that these two items are correct, that it is to be a cultural center, and that it is being financed by the Americans." Phyllis's normally cheerful demeanor was sobered by what she had heard. "But there is more. They say their son and all the other men are receiving two weekly payments. One is to do the construction, the other is to do it as slowly as possible."

"That," Sally decided, "makes no sense at all."

"Quite. And yet they insist it is true. And they insist there is a rumor, well, actually more than a rumor, that this second payment is quietly coming from the Russians."

Chapter Nine

"*H*E WANTS TO KNOW," Daniel Levy translated for Jake, "when the next installment is going to arrive."

"Tell him the same thing I said when he asked me five minutes ago," Jake replied stubbornly. "When I've been satisfied that the first funds have been well spent."

They were seated in a tumbledown shanty propped next to a rubble-strewn pit on the outskirts of Istanbul. The documentation in Jake's file had proclaimed that this was to become part of a new factory for the production of electronic components. All Jake could see for the money spent so far was a huge hole in the ground. He turned to Daniel. "Show them the bill for the steel."

Two men sat on the other side of the desk. One was dark and short and angry, his round face covered with stubble and sweat, his hands grimy and strong. The other was slender and nervous and a talker, filling the air with words that Daniel translated in swatches of nonsense. The young man accepted the sheet only reluctantly, barely glanced at the figures to which Daniel pointed, then continued with his

309

dialogue: They had assumed there was an understanding with the American authorities. These delays in receiving payment were slowing down the construction process. Over and over, the same words, leaving nothing answered or resolved.

Jake pointed at the bill which the man now held and said through Daniel, "That says my government has paid for seventeen tons of support girders. Where are they?"

The man's voice was a constant irritating drone. They are ordered, they are ordered, they are coming, it is all according to plan, yes, it is most unfortunate that the American gentleman does not have experience with Turkish building methods, but we are a poor country and payments must be made in advance. On and on and on the words poured from the nervous man, politely pressing for the release of funds, promising that everything was moving according to a schedule neither man could produce. All the while, his companion sat and smoldered and glared at Jake. Jake returned the stare as calmly as he could manage, feeling as though his brain were being turned to oatmeal by the endless verbiage, knowing they were intent on wearing him down. Jake rose, knowing this was the only way to stop the noise. "I will release more funds when the girders have been delivered and when the concrete foundation, which my records show we have also already paid for, has been laid."

The burly man spoke for the first time, his words gnashed between grinding teeth. Daniel translated quietly, his calm murmur untouched by neither fatigue nor the others' rising unease. "Delay any further, and all work will stop."

"I don't see work being done anyway," Jake retorted, not fazed in the least by the man's ire. He would far prefer a battle with the builder than this endless tirade from the bureaucrat. A sudden thought caused him to ask the suited gentleman, "Are you from the government or from the construction company?"

The nervousness increased, the stream of words quickened. Before Daniel could translate, Jake held up his hand. "One word will do. We're going to start getting some straight answers around here, or I am pulling out of this mess entirely." When Daniel hesitated before translating, Jake glanced his way and said, "Tell them that word for word."

The atmosphere within the shanty instantly electrified when the words had been said. The burly man rose to his feet, shouting and gesticulating. The nervous man poured out a continual battering of words. Jake motioned with his chin for Daniel to stand. "I've had my fill. We're going to see some real work done, and we're going to start getting straight answers, or we're shutting you down." Daniel had to raise his voice to be heard. When the translation was completed, Jake ignored the response. He finished, "And that is final."

When they were back in the consular car, Jake said, "You can't tell me that what we saw there is normal progress, even for here."

"Construction materials are in short supply, so partial payment in advance could be argued for." Daniel mulled it over, then decided, "But no, what they have done so far does not explain the urgent need for more funds. And their attitude is a mystery."

"Totally baffling," Jake agreed.

"It is as if they were intentionally trying to slow us down."

Jake stared at the bearded man. "What makes you say that?"

"One would expect those who are faced with having their funds discontinued at least to offer something definite to ease the tension. A written time plan, a bit of progress, a willingness to meet you halfway." Daniel added apologetically, "Perhaps they know of your own dilemma and think they can outlast you. But if so, why did they not simply refuse to meet with you? I have the feeling that something else is at work here."

"As though they wanted to tie us up in knots," Jake suggested, "so we wouldn't look anywhere else."

Daniel considered this, his eyes never leaving Jake's face. "You have heard something?"

"My wife did." Swiftly he related what Sally had told him about the matrioshka dolls and the tour guide's warning.

"Perhaps this is indeed confirmation of her rumor." Daniel stroked his beard, said distractedly, "Your wife must be a remarkable woman."

"Yes, she is," Jake said, and felt a renewed pang over their argument. He changed the subject with, "If anyone asks, I want you to appear to be working strictly on this one project. But in truth I want you to set this aside and look for something else." Jake ran back over the discussion and shook his head. "That project was a mess, but it's not enough to keep the ax from falling on my assignment."

"You think there are watchers within the consulate?"

"Watchers, definitely. Whether or not they're actually working for the other side, I can't say. But with the pressure we're under, it's a risk we can't afford to take."

"Let me see if I understand this correctly," Pierre said, picking his way over the uneven cobblestones. "We are going to spend our evening with a man who does not like us, studying a religion that is not ours, learning from someone who does not want to teach."

Jake stopped to face his friend. "Are you about finished?"

"Forgive me, my friend. I am French. You must use your more sensible American mind to explain how I have this wrong."

"In the first place, how can he dislike you if he's never met you?"

"An excellent question," Pierre replied somberly. "I must ask him that myself."

"In the second, the Torah is the Jewish term for the Books of Moses, the first five Books of the Bible. *Our* Bible. Theirs and ours."

"I am beginning to see the light."

"Ever since I started studying the Old Testament," Jake went on, "I've wondered how the Jews see this book, which was given to them by God. Given to *them*. They had the Old Testament Scriptures in their possession for over a thousand years before Christ brought the answer to the entire world. They were the first crucible, Pierre. They were the ones who showed that the law alone was not enough."

"I believe I know you as well as anyone, save your wonderful wife," Pierre murmured. "Yet still you manage to surprise me at the unseen turn."

"This is a great opportunity," Jake persisted.

Pierre grasped Jake's arm and turned them about. "Then come, my friend. Let us go and continue with the adventure of learning."

Jake had returned from work to find Sally still out, her succinct note saying only that she had gone for some sightseeing and shopping. He had pushed aside his disappointment at not being able to apologize in person and tried as best he could to do it in a note. He had then found Pierre in the lobby, sulking over the continued frustration of being trapped within a meaningless cycle of functions and events. Jasmyn, he had reported dejectedly, was at a tea party given by the consul general's wife. Jake had taken pity on his friend and invited him along to his study time with Daniel Levy's father.

After making their way down a confusing maze of lanes, Jake was enormously pleased when the familiar little gate came into view. They crossed the synagogue's tiny garden, entered the apartment building, and climbed to the floor above Daniel's.

They were met at the top of the stairs by a suspicious gaze and a pair of skullcaps. The hand thrust forward, and the querulous voice demanded, "You must both wear the yarmulke to study Torah."

"Fine," Jake said, accepting them both. "This is my friend Pierre Servais. Pierre, this is Joseph Levy."

"I am charmed, m'sieur."

The gaze squinted down further, and the old man demanded something in French.

"I do indeed have the honor of being French," Pierre replied in English.

Again there was the rapid thrust of snappish French.

"I am here because this gentleman has brought me," Pierre replied, persisting with his English. "I am with this gentleman because he is both my friend and my teacher. That I have found to be the rarest of combinations."

The old man turned to Jake. "You speak no French?"

"Unfortunately not."

He sniffed and turned his attention back to Pierre. "Teacher of what?"

"Of all that is most important," Pierre replied solemnly. "Of all that would have remained invisible and unseen, were it not for Jake."

The response unsettled the old man. He opened the door, stepped back, and motioned for them to enter. They followed him down the entrance hall to a study filled with overstuffed horsehair furniture. "Sit, sit. I shall fetch tea."

"That is not necessary," Jake said, choosing a chair as large as a throne and slipping on the silk cap.

"Sit, I said. The water is already boiled."

Soon enough he returned, bearing a large silver tray with three glasses and a vast, ancient tome. Only after he had set down the tray did he happen to notice the books in their laps. "What are those?"

"Bibles."

"*Christian* Bibles," he said, with a great sigh and a shake of his head. Still, he handed out the glasses, then seated himself across the low table from them. He sipped his glass, making the inblown breath to cool as he drank, again, his eyes casting back and forth from one man to the other. "You have heard of the *Me Am Lo'ez*? No, of course not. How could you?"

Another sip, then he set his tea aside, and with it his indecision. Jake actually saw it happen. As though the argument that had clouded his voice and his gaze since the earlier meeting was now over. A decision had been reached.

"Some call this the greatest work of Ladino literature ever written," Joseph Levy said, looking down upon the leather-bound volume. "Its history is the history of my people, the Jews of the Mediterranean." He swiveled that great book around so that it faced his visitors. "My grandfather learned his first Torah lessons from this very book, taught to him by his father. It has been in my family for over two hundred years."

"I thank you for sharing it with us," Pierre said quietly, speaking for them both.

Joseph Levy opened the book from what appeared to be the back cover, then Jake realized the writing was in the Hebrew script and thus printed from right to left. Joseph Levy showed them an opening page decorated to appear as a great medieval door. The sides were colonnaded and dressed with flowering vines, the base carved from stone, the roof crowned with light. The door was open, to reveal rows of Hebrew words. The bottom corner of the page was darkened and worn.

The old man turned the book back toward him, ran his forefinger across the top lines, and murmured the singsong cadence of something long memorized. He looked up and intoned, *"Barukh atah adonoy, lamdeni chukekha,"* and then in English, "Blessed be thou, O Lord; teach me thy statutes." He looked from one to the other and asked, "Can you tell me the source of these words?"

"The hundred and nineteenth Psalm," Jake said quietly.

Both men stared at him for a moment. Then Joseph Levy gave a fraction of a nod. He placed his thumb upon the page's well-worn groove, and in a delicate practiced motion pushed the page up and over. The next page was entirely different, written in letters so small that from where Jake sat they appeared to be an almost solid block. Along the left-hand edge was a second, smaller column, almost like an afterthought. Joseph Levy reached to the tray and came up with something Jake had missed, a silver rod perhaps half again as long as his hand, so old and used that the scrollwork on the handle had been worn smooth. "One of you shall perhaps read for us the opening passage of the Book of Genesis. You may read from your Christian Bible."

Jake nodded to Pierre's silent enquiry. The Frenchman picked up his Bible and read, "In the beginning God created the heaven and the earth. And the earth was without form, and—"

"Stop, stop, the first passage only, I said." The old man's crossness had a different quality now, that of habit passed down over generations, a means of teaching with verve, with character. "It is just like the young of this day, wanting to take in all the Torah in one gulp. Hurry, hurry, hurry, a headlong rush to nowhere." He examined Pierre with frosty contempt. "Well, my young man in a hurry, those first ten words alone contain enough thought and mystery to occupy you for an entire lifetime."

Jake leaned back, thoroughly satisfied. This was going to be good. He just knew it.

"Listen and I will tell you. There was once a great king. His name was Talmi, you goyim knew him as Ptolemy. He inherited the crown of Egypt from Alexander the Great. In the year 3500, or 260 B.C. according to your count, Ptolemy discovered that none of the books in his vast library were able to satisfy his

hunger for truth. He sent word to Jerusalem, requesting that people come to translate the Torah into
Greek so that he could read it for himself. Seventy-
two sages, six from each of the twelve tribes, made
the journey. They carried with them the Books of
Moses, written upon scrolls in gold ink. Real gold.
The king thought this was done to honor him, but in
truth it was because the sacred text was normally
written and studied in black ink, and in this way
they were handing over to a nonbeliever that which
did not have the sanctity of the true Torah.

"The king received the wise men with all honors
and great gifts. He set an entire island at their disposal and asked that they set about immediately
translating the five Books of Moses into Greek. And
here is where the hand of God showed itself. The
king had made arrangements so that once upon the
island, the wise men would not be able to converse
either with each other or with the outside world.
Ptolemy, you see, wanted *each* sage to translate the
entire Torah."

It was only when the thumb lowered to the page
corner and lifted and turned that Jake realized he was
hearing a teaching from the inscribed text. Not once
had the old man even glanced at the page before him,
so well did he know the story.

"In this way, the king felt he would be able to tell
the difference between what was human and what
was divine within the sages' scrolls. The human
would vary from person to person, and the divine
would remain the same. And here is the first way we
know that the great Lord intended this as a miracu-
lous sign. Although the sages had no contact with
each other, all seventy-two of them completed their
work upon the same day. What is more, all five

Books—the Books you call Genesis, Exodus, Leviticus, Numbers, and Deuteronomy—all were translated in just seventy days. And that is where the name for this translation comes, the Septuagint, the Seventy."

"We use that term as well," Jake offered.

"Of course you do. All the world, Christian and Jew alike, refer to this great work, yet who takes time to remember the miracle of its making? And the miracle does not end there. Oh no. It continues with what was written in those seventy-two translations.

"How do we know the Lord's hand was at work? Look at the words of the passage again. 'In the beginning God created the heavens.' But this is not how the Hebrew is written. Oh no. The original says, *Bereshith bara elohim*, which means literally, 'In the beginning created God.' But these sages, all working separately, decided that this would be misleading to someone who was not aware of the Hebrew tongue. They might think that someone or something called beginning had created the divine.

"And yet why did the Torah not simply say 'God created in the beginning'? Why was this so? Listen, and I will explain. It is because God is not like an earthly king, who wishes to be first and ahead of all others. No, God is in the middle of things. He is here with us, wherever we are, and the placing of His name was intended to show this."

The old man looked from one to the other, then said in quiet triumph, "And so it was that when the sages were brought back to the court of King Ptolemy, not only did they present him with *all* the books completed by *all* the sages upon the same day, but *every word of every translation was identical.*

Not a difference was to be found, down to the smallest item. Thus did Ptolemy and all his court come to accept that the *entire* Torah was truly divine."

Again the unseen page shift, a pause for a sip from his glass, time enough for Pierre to cast an astonished glance in Jake's direction. Jake nodded his agreement. This was incredible.

"One more point, and then we in our modern hurry shall move on. Notice the word *beginning*. Now turn to the Book of Jeremiah, the second chapter, the third verse. Read this, one of you."

Jake found his place and read, "Israel was holiness unto the Lord, and the firstfruits of his increase."

"That is enough. Observe the word *firstfruits*. This in Hebrew is another word for beginnings. And so we see that Israel, the chosen people, were alluded to in the very first words of the Book of Genesis. The gracious Lord set them there at the onset of His divine teachings, reminding us for whom the words were spoken."

Another sip, then the dark eyes glanced from one man to the other and Joseph Levy asked, "Shall we continue?"

The knock, when it came, was so unexpected that all three men jumped. The door opened, and a worried Daniel Levy called from down the hall. "Papa? Miriam noticed your light was still on. Are you all right?"

"Of course I'm all right. Why shouldn't I be?"

Daniel Levy stepped into the room wearing a dark overcoat buttoned up over what appeared to be pajamas and slippers. "It's almost two o'clock in the morning. What are you doing?"

"Two o'clock? It can't be. We have not even finished the first chapter."

"First chapter of what?" He walked over, looked down at the book, and his eyes widened. *"Bereshith?* You are teaching them *Bereshith?"*

"Genesis," Joseph Levy corrected, rising slowly to his feet, testing each joint in turn. "They do not speak Hebrew, remember."

Jake tried to follow him up and realized only then that his back had locked into place. Pierre rose at an equally gradual pace. Jake said, "I guess we better be going."

"Yes you should," the son agreed, still scolding the father. "Miriam and I worry over you constantly, but when our backs are turned, look at what you do."

"There is nothing wrong with the teaching of Torah. A man does not grow ill studying the holy word."

"No," Daniel countered, supporting the old man with one hand on his arm. "A man becomes ill by staying up all hours of the night and not taking care of himself."

"This has been a great honor, Monsieur Levy," Pierre said gravely.

"I'd sure like to do this again," Jake said, then added for Daniel, "and I promise to watch the time."

Joseph brushed off his son's hands, turned to the pair, inspected the two faces. "Look at them, would you? Where have I seen that expression before?"

"Papa, it's late, and we must all—"

"I remember another face that shone after six and seven hours of study," the old man persisted. "A young boy who ate the words, who could not learn fast enough, who cried when it was time to halt."

Daniel's hand dropped back to his side. His beard moved up and down, but no word came.

"I remember," the old man continued, "a boy who would never leave me alone, who met me at the end of my most tiring day with pleas to open the sacred book, to teach him more of the stories and the mysteries of the words." Joseph pointed with one ancient, crooked finger at Jake. "Why do I remember? Because here before me are faces shining with that same hungry light. Minds and hearts so open to the words that the eyes illuminate the room."

Daniel glanced uncertainly toward Jake, his mouth opened slightly, the dark eyes questioning and vulnerable.

"Perhaps you should join us, my son," Joseph Levy said quietly. "Perhaps it would do you good to come and see these two eat the words as you once did, to join with us in the miracle of Scripture."

"With our wives," Jake said quietly, "if that would be all right."

"Of course with your wives," Joseph Levy agreed, yet kept his eyes upon his son. "For what is a family without the Holy Scripture to bond them?"

"It is late, Papa," Daniel Levy said weakly.

Jake and Pierre shook hands with the pair, then let themselves out. Silently they walked down the stairs, passed through the outer portal, and stepped out into the night. Only when they were back upon the lane, beneath the stars of another Istanbul night, did Pierre sigh and glance down at his feet. "How is it, my friend," he said to Jake, "that I can walk upon this tired and wounded earth while my mind and heart soar through the heavens above?"

Chapter Ten

JAKE AWOKE TO the smell of coffee and the sound of rustling papers.

He rolled over, sat up, and watched as Sally poured a cup and walked to the bedside. "You were so late coming in last night, I decided to let you sleep."

He nodded thanks, took a long sip, sighed at the pleasure of that first swallow. "I was at Daniel's. Pierre went with me."

"I saw your note." Her gaze was calm, resolute. "Jake, we have to talk."

The set of her chin and the sound of her voice called his fuzzy mind to attention. "Can I finish this first cup?"

"Just sit and listen." She took a breath, went on, "I know you said what you did because you love me and because you were worried. But you have to understand, I am who I am, just like you. I want you to live the life of adventure that you crave, but I have to be a part of it. Not waiting at home for you to return when it's over. I want to be there taking part *with* you."

Jake finished his cup and watched as she took it from him, walked back and refilled it, then returned to sit and hand it over and say, "This is the only way it is going to work."

"I know," he said quietly. "I knew it before I opened my mouth two nights ago."

"Let me finish. I have lived through too much and been on my own too long to ever be happy just sitting around, waiting for my man to come home."

"I wouldn't ever want you to be that way," he said, loving her.

She gave the mattress between them a muffled slap. "How am I supposed to argue with you if you keep agreeing with everything I say?"

"I don't want to argue with you," Jake replied. "Not ever again."

The resolute squaring of her chin softened a little, despite her best effort to keep it set. "You need me, Jake."

"More than anything," he agreed.

"I can be a big help to you."

"I could not get through a single day without you," he agreed.

The chin quivered, but this time with suppressed laughter. "And you love me. A lot."

"More than life itself," he agreed happily.

"So there won't be any more of this nonsense over where I go and what I do?"

"All the time," Jake countered. "I can't love you like I do and stop worrying. I just have to squelch my desire to give orders."

She flowed into him then, her arms welcoming, her gaze loving, her lips warm and tender. She kissed him, leaned back far enough to stroke his face, smile, and whisper, "Apology accepted," before embracing him again.

*   *   *

Sally watched him dress from her place on the bed, a habit of old which had somehow been misplaced during the clamor of their new assignment. Jake raised his collar, slid the tie into place, repeated the thought: *Their* new assignment. He turned toward her and reveled in the half-smile which played over her lips. Such an incredible lady.

He pointed down at the scroll of maps strewn over their table. "What's all this?"

"Oh, something I heard yesterday." She related her trip with Phyllis and the old couple's tale. "I had a lot of trouble even finding the place."

"What's it called?"

"Kumdare." She slid from the bed and walked over, her robe billowing about her. Jake straightened enough to watch as she leaned down, her reddish-gold hair spilling upon the page. She set a finger down, said, "Here it is."

He squinted to see an alien name perched upon a narrow spit of land. "Doesn't sound familiar."

"They said it was a tiny village, just one road in and out."

Jake knotted his tie, leaned over and tried to concentrate, but found it difficult with the closeness of her. He gave up, turned, and kissed her neck.

"Pay attention," she ordered, but hugged his arm to keep him close.

"Doesn't ring any bells."

"I know. But they were so insistent that the Americans were paying for this construction project."

"Kumdare," he repeated, committing the name to memory. He studied the map again. The tiny village rested upon an empty elbow of land. The place appeared utterly isolated, situated at the other end of the Bosphorus, at the point where the strait opened into the Black Sea. "It's miles from anywhere."

"I know." She straightened and wrapped her arms around him. "There's not much time left, is there?"

"Less than two days," he said as lightly as he could manage, not wanting the moment to end just yet. "According to what Fernwhistle said in the meeting, the dispatch should arrive sometime tomorrow."

"I'm supposed to meet with Phyllis this morning. She's trying to set something up, I don't know what."

"So it's Phyllis now, is it."

Sally nodded, still distracted. "Jasmyn's already left for someplace called the Sophia Mosque, I think I've got that right. She's meeting the woman who took us through the palace." She looked up at him. "If we find out anything, should we come by the consulate?"

Jake sighed and gave in as the pressures rose to surround him. "You can try. I don't know where I'll be." He sketched out what he had learned yesterday, including his meetings at the construction site and opposition headquarters.

Sally listened with increasing seriousness. "You have to watch out as well, Jake."

"I know."

"These people aren't going to just let you walk off with their fat little contracts."

"I'll be careful, Sally."

"Especially if they're pocketing part of the proceeds." She started to wring her hands, looked down and saw what she was doing, searched for the pockets to her robe. "Promise me you won't do anything rash."

"I've already arranged for backup," he said, and explained about the Marine guards.

"Well, they won't do any good unless you take them along." She reached for him again, a grip intensified with fear and love. "Go," she whispered, "and come back safe."

Jake entered his office and said to Daniel in greeting, "Ever heard of a place called Kumdare?"

Daniel froze, one hand deep inside the last of the unsorted boxes. "How did you know?"

The stance and the tone were all the warning Jake needed. Quietly he shut the outer door, walked over, spoke more quietly, "Know what?"

"One bill I have found, just one. And just this morning." Daniel eased himself upright. "But already you have heard of it."

"A rumor," Jake said, and told him what Sally had learned.

Long wax-colored fingers rose to stroke his beard. "You think maybe this is the project our opponents wish to keep hidden?"

"I don't know. Maybe. You say there's a bill?"

"Just one. But the largest so far. A requisition, really, simply confirming that payment was required for work done up to . . ." Daniel searched through the clutter on his desk, came up with a single handwritten invoice, finished, ". . . the beginning of last week. For a cultural center, or so it says here."

"Have you ever heard of this place?"

"Never." Daniel shook his head, his eyes not leaving Jake's face. "All my life I have lived and worked in Istanbul, and this village is unknown to me."

"How are the roads outside Istanbul?"

"Very bad," Daniel replied without hesitation.
"And to the smaller villages, even worse."

"Strange place to set up a center for anything,"
Jake mused, then decided, "Go downstairs and see if
you can set up a priority call to London. It's time I
had another chat with Harry Grisholm."

"Once, this great city was called Byzantium, a
small Greek fishing village on a naturally protected
outcrop of land. Then it became Constantinople,
home to the last Roman emperors and center of the
civilized world. Later came the Islamic invasion and
the Ottoman Empire. Now it is a city clinging to the
edge of Western civilization, an uneasy mix of cultures and histories."

Jasmyn nodded and kept her face politely alert as
they walked at a measured pace through the rubble-
strewn parkland. Jana played the cheerful tour guide,
one of many leading groups or individuals along the
crowded lanes. "At its height, the palace begun by
Constantine had five hundred public halls and thirty
chapels. All that is left now is this ragged garden,
these crumbling walls and pillars, and these fading
mosaics set in what is now a field of rubble."

They crossed the grand square and walked toward
the Sophia Mosque, joining a throng of chattering pil-
grims. As they climbed the stairs, Jasmyn followed
Jana's example and tied a kerchief about her head.
Inside, the great dome seemed almost translucent,
with decorations as delicate as a painting upon porcelain. The grand expanse of floor was cushioned by
multiple layers of carpets. The light was filtered and
gentle and as still as the dust which drifted in the air.

"The Church of Aga Sophia was originally built
fifteen hundred years ago by the Emperor Justinian."

Jana examined the younger woman and asked, "You are Christian, yes?"

"I am."

"Does it trouble you to see that such ancient churches are now mosques?"

"A little." Jasmyn reined in her impatience and looked to where a giant mosaic of Mary and the Christ child decorated one wall of the upper balcony. The walls around it were scarred by what appeared from that distance to be sword thrusts, as though ancient warriors had scraped off all but that one lonely mosaic. To either side, towering pillars supported great black shields twice the height of a man, upon which were emblazoned Arabic script in fiery gold. Directly overhead, the great dome seemed to hover in space. "At least the structure is still here."

"Indeed so. This mighty building has survived lootings, wars, and earthquakes. In fact, it is built upon the foundations of a church erected two hundred years earlier by Constantine himself. That church was destroyed by a fire." Jana pointed about at other mosaics, half-figures whose faces had been left while their bodies were destroyed, prophets reaching out across the centuries, and scarred images of the risen Christ. "There were great arguments about these, as Islam forbids the making of images. But any which were somewhat hidden, like those in the upper balconies, and all that depicted prophets shared by both Islam and Christianity were permitted to remain."

Jana led Jasmyn toward the front, saying, "When the church was converted to a mosque, fragments of the Byzantine furnishings were kept and used." She pointed to the pulpit, the entrance adorned with a velvet drape embossed with Arabic script. "That pulpit, for example, is twelve hundred years old. And these carpets cover a vast array of Byzantine mosaics."

Jasmyn took a deep breath of air laden with dusty age and asked quietly, "Are we being followed?"

"I cannot say for certain," Jana said, and smiled brightly as she pointed out one of the great black shields. "But I fear so."

Jasmyn nodded and tried to hold her attention where the tour guide directed. "Why are we here?"

"Are you aware of a village called Kumdare?"

Jasmyn started at the word, recalling her conversation with Sally the night before. "Why do you ask?"

Jana threw her a shrewd glance before returning her attention to the gold-encrusted dome. "It is good to be cautious with strangers such as myself. Kumdare is the name of a village on the Asiatic coast. The Americans are supposed to be building there. For some reason, the Russians have taken great interest in this project." She dropped her arm, turned, and smiled with false animation. "Whatever it is that you seek, it appears that you may find the answer there. Only take care. The Russians will do anything to protect their secrets."

"Jake!" Harry Grisholm's cheery tone rose above the telephone's crackling static. "How nice to hear from you. How are you, my boy?"

"Well as can be expected," Jake shouted back. "When are you arriving?"

"I still cannot say for certain, but I am pushing hard as possible for sometime early next week."

"No good." Jake gave a succinct version of the pressures he faced, then stopped and listened to the static. "Harry?"

"I'm still here, my boy." For once the almost constant cheeriness had failed him. "It sounds as though they have us both over the diplomatic barrel."

"Sure looks that way to me," Jake agreed. "Have you ever heard of some project we're supposed to be financing at Kumdare?"

A second silence ensued, cut off by Harry saying, "Now that you mention it, something about a cultural center. Do I recall correctly?"

"That's what I have here," Jake called back. "But why—"

"Absolutely unimportant," Harry cut him off. "What is *extremely vital* is that you keep a *watchful eye*. Are you reading me, Jake?"

"I'm not sure," he said, scrambling to locate a pen and paper. "You're saying this center at Kumdare—"

"Is totally insignificant." Even the crackling line could not disguise the sudden tension in Harry's voice. "You recall our previous conversation, my boy?"

"About listening in."

"Precisely. I *command* you to *watch* carefully and use your *post* to *observe*. Then, whatever happens, you can return from this with useful lessons. Are you following me?"

"Trying hard," he said, writing out those words to which Harry had given special emphasis.

"Very good. There is little time left, Jake. I am counting on you to hold to what is of the *utmost importance*."

"You can count on me," Jake said, inserting a confidence he did not feel.

"I have no choice, so long as my hands remain tied here. Take care, my gallant friend, and remember me to your charming wife."

Jake looked down at the words he had scribbled and shouted, "Daniel!"

The bearded face appeared in the doorway, inspected him, declared, "You have learned something."

"Maybe." Jake reread the words on his paper. "If I understood him correctly, it's not going to be a cultural center at all. It's a command post. For observation."

Daniel stared at him. "Observation of what?"

"That's what I intend to find out." Jake sprang for the door. "I've got to run for that meeting with Turgay. You try and contact Pierre Servais at the French embassy. Go over there in person, don't trust the phones. Tell him we leave in two hours." Jake was halfway through the outer office before turning back around and saying to the utterly baffled young man, "And if you can get either Adams or Bailey of the Marine detachment alone, tell them the exact same thing."

Chapter Eleven

$\mathcal{S}$ALLY RUSHED DOWN one cobblestone lane after another. With each step she grew more certain that she had gone astray from Phyllis Hollamby's directions. Domes and minarets poked through Istanbul's perpetual cover of dust and noise. The city wore a scruffy look, as though the builders were in such a hurry to move on that nothing was ever quite finished and no one had time to clean up afterward. But the vibrancy was stronger than anywhere Sally had ever been, an electric quality that caught her early in the morning and held her tight in its excited grip all day.

Faces in the crowd were dark and Oriental and extremely friendly. Sally finally stopped an old man and asked for directions. He rewarded her with a great beam of welcome and a stream of Turkish. He then proceeded to halt a well-heeled woman carrying a shopping bag. She too gave a smile in Sally's direction. That proved to be not enough, so she walked over and gave Sally's hand an energetic pumping, then offered another stream of unintelligible words, followed by a great hoot of laughter shared with the old man. They then stopped a third person, and then a fourth, until within five minutes Sally was surrounded by a crowd of some fifteen people, all smiling and kindly chattering away to her and pointing in fifteen different directions.

Eventually one elderly woman took her hand, and with a gap-toothed smile gently led her down the street in the same direction from which she had come.

"Spice market," Sally insisted.

The woman responded with a great smile and more Turkish, tugging her cheerfully along the crowded lane.

Five minutes later Sally was rewarded with a cheery, "Ah, there you are, my dear. How utterly splendid." Phyllis smiled at the old woman still holding to Sally's hand. "Busy making friends, are we?"

"I got lost, and she adopted me."

Phyllis exchanged a stream of conversation with the delighted old woman, who would only go after having given Sally's hand yet another shake, then kissing her on the cheek. Phyllis waved as she walked off, and said to Sally, "This ability of yours to make friends will serve you well, my dear. Is the delightful Jasmyn still with Jana?"

"I guess so. She is supposed to meet us here when she is done."

"Splendid." Phyllis turned toward the entrance of what appeared to be a stubby brick warehouse with three central domes. "Well, then, perhaps we should begin."

The extended roofline cut a dark swathe through the gathering heat. Phyllis led her into the welcoming shade and told her, "When Egypt fell to the Ottomans, suddenly a flood of exotic roots, seeds, fruits, and spices appeared along the docks of Istanbul. That gave rise to the Egyptian Market, or Spice Market as it is also known today."

Sally allowed herself to be led inside, and discovered that the warehouse was neither square nor short, as the exterior suggested. Instead, the grand colonnaded hall extended in three vast lanes, the vaulted ceiling rising forty feet above her head. Crowded around the ancient columns were shops selling everything from oranges to ground cumin. The air was heavy with the fragrance of cinnamon, coriander, bay leaf, and lavender.

"The building was originally made of wood," Phyllis continued merrily. "But gunpowder was sold here as a cure for hemorrhoids, and too many of the stalls kept blowing holes in the old roof. So three hundred years ago the sultan had it rebuilt in stone. They did a lovely job, don't you agree?"

"You make it sound like it all happened yesterday," Sally replied.

"If you wish to make Istanbul a part of yourself, you must treat time as the city does. Days and weeks and months and years and even centuries will gradually begin to melt together before your very eyes."

Sally examined the older woman. "Why are you helping us out so much?"

"Because I have absolutely nothing else to fill my days."

"I find that hard to believe."

"It is true nonetheless." Phyllis raised her free hand to the side of her face. In that simple motion, all her years lay exposed. The hand was age-spotted, the fingers shook gently, and they missed the first time they wiped at the damp that gathered at the corner of her mouth. "My George perished seven years ago. I started to return to England, but my goodness, since I have lived all my adult life out here, what on earth was I to return to?"

"You don't have any children?"

"One daughter. She lives in Portsmouth and complains of how her dear mama refuses to simply lie down and give up the ghost, as she feels all elderly old windbags should do upon demand."

"You are not that elderly," Sally replied, liking her tremendously. "And most certainly not a windbag."

"Thank you, my dear. But I do confess, were it not for my inner source of strength and the occasional opportunity to make a difference in this way, life and this burden of years would simply be too much for me to bear. I have always been active, you see. It is this feeling that I still have something worthy to contribute that keeps me going."

Sally waved as Jasmyn came into view and said to Phyllis, "You have certainly contributed to making things better for us since we came. We can't thank you enough."

"I have done it as much for myself as for you," Phyllis replied, smiling a welcome to Jasmyn. "By giving, I am rewarded beyond measure. Freely I have received, freely will I give on to others."

Sally stared at the older woman. "You are a believer?"

"I try my best to follow the Lord's call." She turned to Jasmyn, asked, "How are you, my dear?"

"Troubled," she replied, her beautiful face clouded.

"Yes, that I can most certainly see. Alas, that is the problem of dealing with anything tainted by the Russians these days. They do so love to stir the waters with trouble and intrigue."

"But I did not mention the Russians."

"You did not need to." Phyllis Hollamby turned both women around by starting down the central hall herself. "Unfortunately, their interest in Turkey has become almost suffocating. Identify any distressing crisis, and you will most likely find the Soviets at work."

"And this Jana," Jasmyn demanded. "You are sure we can trust her?"

"Ah, she had information for you, did she? Excellent. Yes, Jana is a remarkable young woman. Her father worked as office assistant to my husband, and we have helped with the cost of her education. She is doing further work in political science and will someday be a force to be reckoned with, mark my words. She is fiercely patriotic and sees the Soviets as the greatest single threat to her country's future. Yes indeed, you may certainly trust her and any information she manages to gather on your behalf."

As they walked by one brilliant display after another, Jasmyn outlined what she had heard from the young woman. Phyllis heard her out, then pointed them toward a stall with the words, "Let us hear what this friend has to say, shall we?"

Sally followed her over, asked doubtfully, "And then?"

"And then, my dear, we shall find it time to make a decision." Phyllis beamed as the wizened stallholder doffed his cap and bowed at their approach. He stood among wicker baskets piled high with ground spices, their odors a pungent perfume. There were clove and coriander, cumin and curry, pepper and basil and bay, all the colors and smells of the Orient. The man was as timeless as the market, aged somewhere between forty and eighty, his grin almost toothless and his eyes almost lost in leathery folds.

Phyllis pointed toward several piles, and the man used a small scoop to fill one bag after another, weighing each on an ancient scale using tiny copper weights, arguing politely with her over prices. He filled the intervals with murmured snatches of conversation, a flurry of words that gradually tightened both their faces, until Phyllis finally pressed money into his hand and turned from his final bow with a taut smile.

Sally waited until they had moved away before demanding quietly, "What is the matter?"

"Smile, my dear, and look interested in the displays," Phyllis said, her voice overly bright. "He says there are eyes upon us."

"Jana said the same thing," Jasmyn said.

"Don't look so worried, dear. We are just a trio of foreigners enjoying a day of sightseeing and shopping." Phyllis nodded approval as Jasmyn released a blithe little laugh. "Excellent. In anticipation of this, and from what we learned yesterday, I took my car across on the first ferry this morning. I also took the liberty of packing a lunch for us."

She smiled and pointed toward a display that none of them saw. "This way I hope we shall be off and away while our footsore followers are still searching for a vehicle."

"You are truly amazing," Sally said quietly.

"Thank you, my dear. Now, you must hurry back to the hotel and leave a note for your husbands. Say simply that we have gone for a drive down the coast."

Sally resisted the urge to search the surrounding crowds. "Where are we going?"

"It is time," Phyllis replied, "for us to see what lies within this village called Kumdare."

* * *

The Flower Market was a vast domed building that resembled the inside of a palace, all ornate porticoes and grand mirrors and chandeliers and windows taller than Jake. The building stood upon a steep-sided hill looking down over the glistening waters of the Golden Horn. Beyond its waters rose the thrilling prospect of the old city and all its mysteries.

A chamber opening to one side had been turned into an eating hall. There, fragrances of well-spiced food mingled with those of the flowers to create an intoxicating bouquet.

Jake walked over to where Turgay Ecevit was seated and shook the proffered hand. "Sorry I'm late."

"Do not bother to apologize, Mr. Burnes. Diplomats are always expected to be delayed. It adds importance to their posts, being able to claim some grave diplomatic crisis."

Jake seated himself and replied, "In this case, it's the truth."

"No doubt, no doubt." He showed jolly disbelief. "I have taken the liberty of ordering a small meal for us. I hope that is acceptable."

"Great. I missed breakfast and I'm starved." The waiter appeared, clad in a ballooning white shirt and a multicolored vest. He set down plate after miniature plate until their table was crowded with a dozen small dishes.

"Mezze," Turgay explained. "It means a thousand dishes."

There were two different kinds of lamb, on skewers and grilled with peppers and pine nuts. There was salad of diced fennel and basil, beans both cold and hot and all heavily spiced, yogurt mixed with a variety of ingredients, and triangular pastries filled with cheese or spinach or meat. Fish and shrimp and shellfish made up the remaining portions, all swimming in spiced garlic oil. Jake surveyed the feast. "A small meal?"

"Wait, there is more," Turgay said, and suddenly the air grew pungent with woodsmoke and roasting lamb. A chef and his assistant rolled over a great wooden trolley with a revolving vertical spit. The lamb was layered thick as a man's reach, and the charcoal banked in an upright grill. The spit was turned slowly, the outer blackened layer stripped off with a knife longer than Jake's arm, then caught in a frying pan with a wedge cut out so that it fit up snug to the spit. Jake watched as the meat was set upon an oval platter and covered in a layer of spicy tomato sauce, then with another layer of meat, a layer of yogurt, and a final layer of meat, and the entire dish topped with diced onions and fragrant herbs. The mustachioed chef set down the plate with a flourish, then added two platter-sized loaves of fresh unleavened bread.

"Bursa kebab," Turgay announced proudly. "A favorite of mine."

Jake allowed his plate to be heaped high, tasted, pronounced it all delicious.

While they ate, a troupe of musicians wandered through the hall. To Jake's mind, Turkish music was the most thoroughly Oriental part of the culture. A half-dozen drums and tambourines kept up a complex beat while the remaining instruments joined in constant discord and the singing rose strident above it all. The overall effect was as exotic and flavorful as the food.

Over cups of treacly thick coffee, Turgay produced a sheaf of papers from his coat pocket. "I have prepared the list as you ordered."

"I do not," Jake responded, "make it a habit to order around a foreign government—or even members of the opposition party."

"You hold the purse strings," Turgay reminded him. "That adds great power to any request." He unfolded the sheets. "There are five companies which we could identify in the time you gave us."

Jake peered over the list. "All are large enough to handle construction projects of this size?"

"All have already done so," Turgay answered. "When will you have the bidding documents ready?"

"Maybe never," Jake said, and decided the least he could do was explain the time pressure he faced. As he described the recent developments, he refolded the documents and tried to settle them into his jacket pocket. "Having a list of companies that could have been sent tenders will make good ammunition, but I've still got to find something big enough to blow a breach in their defenses. And fast."

Turgay nodded his understanding, pointed at what Jake held, asked, "What is that?"

Jake looked down and realized he had pulled out his New Testament to make room for the papers. "I like to carry a Bible with me."

"Ah, a Christian." Turgay smiled approval. "I have often wanted to argue the points of this religion."

It hit him then, a sudden sense of the answer prepared and waiting. "I will not argue with anyone," Jake replied quietly yet firmly. "Not over this."

Turgay shrugged his disregard. "Discuss, then."

"Not that, either." Jake pressed the documents flatter, fitted his New Testament back out of sight.

The outright rejection confused the handsome young man. "This is a most curious matter, Mr. Burnes. If it is so important that you carry this book with you always, why will you not discuss religion with me?"

"Because it is not just a religion to me," Jake replied. "It is my *faith*. It is the bedrock of my life. Faith is not something that can be shared through intellectual debate. You can't hold it out at arm's length and analyze it and come away understanding anything."

"Most remarkable," Turgay murmured.

"If you want to hear the message of salvation, I would be happy to share my experience. If you wish to speak of the ache of an empty heart, I would be privileged to listen and share with you what faith has done in my own life. If you would like to pray with me, I would be honored to bow my head with yours."

Turgay drummed his fingers on the table, clearly ill at ease with the direction the discussion had taken. "Perhaps we should return to the matter at hand."

"Fine with me." Jake settled back, content. He had made the offer, planted the seed. It was up to the Lord now to perform His miracle.

Chapter Twelve

"ARE YOU A BELIEVER as well, my dear?" Phyllis directed the question into her rearview mirror without slowing a fraction.

"I have witnessed far too many miracles," Jasmyn replied faintly, her face blanched, her eyes pinned to the vista sweeping by outside her window, "not to believe in God."

"So very glad to hear it," Phyllis said gaily. "So very glad."

The road, such as it was, wound its way higher and higher up a cliffside flanking the Bosphorus. Sally tried as hard as she could not to look to their left. Blue sky swooped down a terrifying distance to sparkling blue waters below. Occasionally the road leveled and curved away from the sea, entering one hard-scrabble village after another. Phyllis did not slow a fraction from her headlong rush, but scattered chickens and goats and donkey carts and villagers with true British aplomb.

"Faith is a marvelous addition to one's life," Phyllis said, utterly blind to the effect her driving was having on her two passengers. "I simply cannot

imagine what I would have done after George's un-
timely demise had I not had my faith to shelter me."

The car was a truly enormous Citroen, the long
snout a perfect wedge for Phyllis's form of driving,
which consisted primarily of setting the course and
allowing everyone else to simply get out of her way.
In place of turn signals, two great flaps extended
alongside the doors. When Phyllis wished to turn,
she pushed one of two levers on her sculpted chrome
dash, and the metal flag flapped out and down with a
bong from the signal bell. The problem was, Phyllis
neglected to bother with the flags until she was already spinning her wheel. And she used her rearview
mirror only for talking with the passenger in the
backseat. Their journey was therefore punctuated by
horns and screeching brakes and shouts fading into
the distance. Sally had long since given up turning
around to survey the chaos. All she could see in their
wake was a great, billowing dust cloud.

Phyllis came within inches of jamming a donkey
cart over the cliff, spun the wheel, and blithely
slipped into the path of an oncoming truck, then just
as swiftly slid back in front of the cart. As the bray-
ing donkey, shouting driver, and honking truck faded
into the distance, Phyllis declared proudly, "Almost
there, ladies. You can see the village on that next
crest up ahead."

"Praise be to the Lord above," Jasmyn said faintly
from the backseat.

"Now, then." Spurred by the sight of their destina-
tion, Phyllis pressed down upon the accelerator, and
the great motor beneath the long black hood roared
in delight. Sally slid another notch down in the
overpadded seat as Phyllis continued briskly, "You

must recall that we are here as tourists, simply visiting a quaint little fishing village."

Sally closed her eyes as the far wheels skidded around a curve, sending a spray of rocks cascading down to distant waters. "You're sure this speed is necessary?"

"Why of course, my dear," Phyllis replied, misunderstanding her totally. "You yourself have said that the letter dismissing your husband will arrive sometime tomorrow."

"She meant," Jasmyn tried feebly, "must we drive so fast?"

"Always best to outrun trouble, I say." Phyllis spun the wheel with the ease of one raised on hairpin turns. "You will both be happy to know I have never had an accident."

"And never will have but one," Sally replied, but her words were lost in yet another truck's blaring horn.

"We must follow up any lead we have," Phyllis said, returning to the matter at hand. "The spice trader's story was the third bit of evidence pointing toward Kumdare. Where there's smoke there's fire, I say, especially when the Russians are fanning the flames."

The spice trader bought from several local markets in the region around Kumdare, and twice he had heard of foreigners buying provisions. Pale-skin foreigners who spoke smatterings of Turkish with a distinctly Russian accent, and who never returned to the same market twice. Their presence was remarkable enough to cause talk.

Phyllis rounded the final bend, swooped down and into the unsuspecting village, halted in a paved courtyard, and cut the engine. Then she turned and beamed at her two passengers. "Now, that wasn't so bad, was it?"

The cicadas hummed a constant refrain to the heat and the sun. Their buzz seemed to make the air even hotter. The road they walked was little more than a narrow gravel path between crumbling stone walls, with the sun and twin minarets for direction markers.

"This village was a way station for travelers two thousand years ago," Phyllis told them as they walked. "Traders would harness their pack animals in a circle around their goods, then sleep outside them in double rows for security."

Old men sat and stared at their passage, fingering amber worry beads. Children scampered and giggled and pointed at the oddity of foreign women in their midst. The village girls were quick and as pretty as tiny porcelain dolls, dressed in brightly colored dresses and miniature headkerchiefs.

They entered the central square, where a local market attracted a crowd of chattering, haggling locals. Squinting against the fierce sun, Sally ignored the glances tossed their way and inspected her surroundings. The village had been constructed to endure the heat in comfort. Verandas were broad and built around great sheltering trees, the multitude of branches offering far more protection than mere roofs. Outer walls more than three feet thick offered substantial barriers to the heat. Restaurants and teahouses were open affairs, tables spread out on the verandas, beckoning diners into their shadowy cool depths.

Sally turned to Jasmyn and observed, "You look a little queasy."

"So do you." She tried for a smile. "I do not look forward to the trip back."

"Me, neither," Sally agreed. "Now that we're here, I wonder what we're supposed to do."

"Whatever it is," Jasmyn said, "it is bound to attract attention. I feel eyes upon us everywhere."

"Yoo-hoo, ladies," Phyllis called and waved. "Over here, if you please."

Sally started to complain that her feet were already begging loudly for a rest and the sun was sweltering, but Phyllis beckoned impatiently. She sighed and gave Jasmyn a minute shrug. Together they walked over to where a man was poking a metal rod down the mouth of a broad wooden cylinder. Phyllis smiled at her approach and announced, "I have just what you need."

"What I need," Sally said, "is a nice, cool bath."

"And some shade," Jasmyn added.

"I believe you might like this even better." Phyllis turned to the man, who despite the heat wore a voluminous shirt, a vest sewn with bits of reflecting glass, and a tall fez. She said to them, "Step closer, if you will."

"What for?" But Sally did as she was told and instantly was consumed by a wave of coolness. She gaped, bringing a delighted laugh from both Phyllis and the throng of children who now surrounded them. The man grinned but did not stop with his energetic stirring. Sally leaned over the cylinder to gaze down the narrow opening and saw a white, doughy ball at the base. She felt the coolness even more strongly. Sally stepped aside so that Jasmyn could take a look and demanded. "What on earth?"

"You will see." Phyllis chattered to the man, who gave a mock half-bow, reached for a small metal plate, raised his long rod, and scraped off some of the dough. Instantly the surrounding children were clamoring for attention, their faces and voices a mixture of pleading and laughter.

Phyllis plucked a spoon from a glass on the ledge, then handed the serving to Sally. "Taste."

Gingerly she touched a tiny portion to her tongue and exclaimed, "Ice cream!"

The children squealed with delight and absolutely butchered the words in an attempt to imitate Sally's surprise. Phyllis handed Jasmyn a plate, accepted her own portion, and said, "This gentleman travels from village to village all summer long. You can hear the bells on his little truck a mile or so off. Nowadays this cylinder is packed with dry ice, but when my children were young he came in a cart with straw packed around great bales of ice. The day he visited our area was something they looked forward to all year long."

Sally took another tiny scoop and watched as Phyllis gave the man a handful of coins and began doling out ice cream to all the surrounding children. Their excitement was so great they could scarcely stand still long enough to accept the little metal platters. Phyllis calmed them with a gentle tone, her face suddenly unlined, her eyes as bright as the children's. When the last child had been fed and the last whimpering plea stilled, Sally asked, "You mentioned having children, but I thought you told me that you only have one daughter."

"That's right, dear." She smiled in reply to the chorus of delighted giggles. "My son was killed in the war. That was the George I referred to earlier, when I said faith had proven so important to me. My husband, God rest his soul, had endured two years of a lingering illness before he was taken, and the dear man was ready to go. George was another matter entirely." Her tone was bright, her voice matter of fact, but the pain formed two deep holes at the center of her gaze. "George was a pilot. We lost him in the Battle of Britain."

"I'm so very sorry," Jasmyn said for them both.

"Thank you. You are both such dears." She looked back down to the eager little faces, gained strength from their joy. The gaze tightened, focused. "George gave his life so that we might enjoy this wonderful gift of freedom. I feel it is my duty as his mother to continue where he left off. Which brings us to the matter of our journey today."

Phyllis leaned upon her cane and lowered her head close to the children. She asked them a question. A chorus of little voices piped up in reply. The ice cream vendor added his own basso agreement, nodding vigorously and pointing off in the same direction as the multitude of smaller hands. Phyllis half spoke, half sung another query, and instantly the children were on their feet, licking the metal platters shiny-clean, handing them and the spoons back to the vendor, all of them grasping now for a hand of Sally or Jasmyn or Phyllis.

Surrounded by eagerly chattering children, the women were led out of the square, down a side street, and beyond the tight cluster of central buildings. The farther they walked, the more dispersed grew the dwellings, with farm animals bleating over the children's animated chatter. Above and to the right, away from the water's glittering surface, rose a rocky hillside. The ridgeline bore an ancient stone city wall, the parapets rising like uneven teeth. The women were led through a tumbledown opening, the flanking pillars all that was left of what once had been a mighty city gate. Beyond that point, the way became little more than a cattle track. Sally forced her way through the eager children to take Phyllis's free hand and help her over the rougher patches.

By the time they made it over the second hill, all three women were breathing hard. The children gathered about them at the crest, pointed forward, and competed loudly for the privilege of telling the story.

Sally looked down the swooping distance to where the hill joined the cliffside and fell in rocky jagged-ness to the sea. They were at the highest point within sight, and the view was awesome. The Bos-phorus shimmered like a brilliant blue mirror more than a thousand feet below. In the distance, the nar-row strait's opposite shore rose like pale, frozen waves.

Phyllis shushed the clamoring children, turned her attention back to the vista, said, "I believe we have found our answer, ladies."

Sally nodded agreement. The hilltop was marked by a series of small surveyor flags, and three piles of earth and stone marked the beginning of squared-off cellar pits, but otherwise nothing had been done. Yet the structure's intended purpose was alarmingly clear.

Jasmyn pointed toward the horizon. "Look, there!"

Sally squinted against the harsh sunlight, felt her chest fill with a sharply indrawn breath. Steaming toward both them and the Bosphorus's narrow en-trance passage were seven enormous ships. Each sil-houette sprouted over two dozen menacing gun barrels. And streaming out behind every central smokestack flew a flag.

"The hammer and sickle," Jasmyn breathed.

"Soviet battleships," Sally agreed.

"Come, ladies," Phyllis said, returning to brisk urgency. "We have news to convey."

Chapter Thirteen

"*W*ATCH OUT!"

Pierre drove wide around the horse-drawn hay wagon, sliding back into place before the oncoming truck could do more than clip his front fender. He sounded genuinely affronted as he said, "You are feeling more nervous than usual, perhaps?"

"The idea," Jake replied, "is to arrive there in one piece."

"First you tell me to hurry, and now you want me to slow down?" Pierre shook his head. "Perhaps you would be more comfortable in the backseat."

Jake jammed both feet down on an imaginary brake pedal as Pierre swung the heavy consular vehicle around a ninety-degree bend, spewing gravel off the road and over the cliff and down the several hundred feet to the sea far below. "Maybe we should have taken the consulate's driver after all."

"I thought the idea was to go in secrecy," Pierre replied, not slowing even a little. "And to do so with all possible haste."

"We won't be able to give them much help lying at the bottom of the sea."

"Let us hope," Pierre replied, accelerating to an even faster pace, "that they do not need our help at all."

Jake had returned to the consulate from his meeting with Turgay to find both Pierre and the two Marines ready and chomping at the bit. At Jake's insistence, they took two cars minus drivers. The Marines were ordered to follow a few cars back and see if anyone tried to follow. Any move toward them, and the Marines were ordered to take what Jake called extreme evasive tactics. At the words, grins sprouted from both soldiers.

It was not until they stopped by the hotel on their way out of town that panic set in. Jake came racing out of his room and almost collided with an equally frantic Pierre. Jake looked at the sheet of paper his friend was waving. "I don't believe this is happening."

"Kumdare," Pierre groaned. "By themselves."

"Did they leave a time of departure?"

"It does not matter," Pierre said, too impatient to wait for the clanking elevator, taking the stairs in three-step leaps. "They are ahead of us and without protection. That is all we need to know."

Pierre glanced over to where Jake kept a death's grip on both the side armrest and dash. "You are beginning to make me tense."

Jake shot an exasperated look at his friend. "I can't tell you how sorry I am to hear it."

"Blinders," Pierre said, taking a curve wide and fast, sweeping back just in time to avoid attaching them to an ancient bus which itself took the swerve like a boat on high seas. "I knew I had forgotten something."

Jake forced himself to turn away from the precipice, tried not to think how naked it looked without a guardrail—just an empty void dropping out and down to distant rocks and glittering sea. He watched through his side window as the Turkish afternoon blurred past. Dark mustachioed men and kerchiefed women driving donkey carts piled like miniature mountains. Villages anchored by needle-slim minarets. Mud-brick walls, dusty children, bleating animals, metal roofs. Then rows and rows of carefully cultivated crops, distinguished at their speed more by smell than sight. Vineyards, olive groves, herb gardens, vegetable patches, all tilled in the timeless manner by human labor and wooden implements.

"Car wrecks," Jake observed. "There's one at almost every curve."

Pierre jammed on the brakes, swerved, slowed long enough to trade compliments with a Turkish driver, then sped on. "I agree. These people know nothing of proper driving." He plowed through a flock of sheep, carefully avoided the shepherd's flaying staff, finished, "Which is another reason why one must drive quickly. Any slower and trouble would have time to catch up with us."

Jake sighed his way deeper into the seat, decided if he watched much more, he would not survive long enough to live through an accident. He crossed his arms, closed his eyes, and gave his fate grimly over to God.

Jake awoke with a start to the sound of screeching tires and blaring horns. To his vast relief, his eyes focused in time to tell him that all the noise belonged to other vehicles. He rubbed his face. "I fell asleep."

"For almost an hour," Pierre crowed triumphantly. "A grand testimony to my perfect driving."

"That's impossible," Jake said, trying to shake the remnants of sleep from his brain. "It can't have happened."

"While you rested in my watchful care, I have discovered the secret of driving in Turkey," Pierre declared.

Jake searched through his window, observed dismally, "We're not there yet?"

"It is quite simple," Pierre continued. "The most important rule is, there are no rules!"

"I suppose that makes sense," Jake said, "to a Frenchman."

"Exactly!" Pierre blithely ignored a truck that was trying to cut into the stream of traffic from a side road by jamming its snout far into the road. Pierre simply swerved into the face of an oncoming vehicle, then swept back and continued smugly, "Once you understand this, the rest is quite simple."

Jake raised himself up, suddenly more awake than he had ever been in his life. "Any sign of the Marines?"

"One car back," Pierre said, risking a glance in the rearview mirror. "I must say, that corporal certainly does know how to drive."

For once, Jake was not sorry when traffic suddenly snarled, leaving them crawling forward through an overheated cloud of diesel fumes. They entered yet another village, one removed from time, sheltered in groves of hazelnut and beech. To one side, men turned an ancient concrete mixer and piled bricks beside an unfinished house, all by hand. To the other, tobacco leaves hung on a clothesline to dry. Underneath scrabbled a flock of scrawny chickens.

Pierre smiled at nothing, asked, "Do you remember Vera Lynn?"

Jake turned away from the window. "What?"

" 'We'll meet again, don't know where, don't know when,' " Pierre sang in a truly atrocious voice. "Do you not remember that, my friend?"

"I can't believe I'm hearing a Frenchman ask me that."

"Vera Lynn," Pierre sighed. "She sang for the heart of every Frenchman as we fled the German invasion of Paris."

"I hate to spoil a good memory," Jake told him. "But Vera wasn't singing for the French."

"No?" Pierre mulled that one over for a moment, then shrugged. "Well, she should have been."

"I'll be sure to pass that along the next time I see her," Jake assured him.

"And Doolcy Wilson. What was that wonderful song of his, 'As Time Goes By'?"

"No more singing," Jake begged. "And it was originally Satchmo's song."

Pierre gave him an astonished glance. "You do not care for my voice?"

"Let's just say it runs a close second to your driving," Jake said.

"And 'Moonlight Serenade,' ah, that was a lovely one."

"What's gotten you taking this walk down memory lane?"

Pierre shrugged easily. "Me, I am thinking how the war is behind us and yet the danger is with us still."

"You don't seem very troubled by the thought."

"Ever since the Bible lesson with M'sieur Levy, I have been thinking," Pierre said. "My life is good these past weeks. Very good. I am married to a wonderful woman. I have work that could be worthwhile if only the politicians would let me get on with it. My country is at peace once more. And I have friends. Good friends."

"Thanks," Jake said. "And likewise."

"And," Pierre continued determinedly, "I am thinking that I have begun to let my faith slip. I realized that last night. I have started to take my prayers and my studies more lightly. I do not seek to learn so swiftly now, because life is good." Pierre glanced toward him, somber now. "But life moves in circles, does it not? Just as with politics and diplomacy and the currents of conflict that surround us."

"Just who," Jake asked quietly, "is the teacher, and who the student?"

"It is my responsibility to use these good times to prepare for the bad," Pierre went on. "It is an opportunity I cannot afford to pass up. I can only remain strong and steadfast if I see these quieter times as opportunities to grow."

"To prepare," Jake added, admiring him.

"The Bible teaches me that with my faith I am building my life upon a strong foundation," Pierre agreed. "But still it is *I* who must *build*."

They passed the village's outskirts, and gradually the congestive grip on their speed was loosened. Jake said with a smile, " 'The Boogie Woogie Bugle Boy of Company B.' You remember that one?"

"The Andrews Sisters." Pierre laughed. "Oh yes. He made the company jump when he played reveille, blowing eight to the bar. I loved that song."

"And Benny Goodman," Jake recalled, grinning. "I remember when he came out with that new girl singer, Peggy—"

Then they were hit. And hit hard.

*　　*　　*

"Sir? Can you hear me in there?"

Jake stirred, groaned, shifted, and felt the glass around him tinkle and settle. He came fully alert, swung his head, felt a swooping panic when he saw that the driver's seat was empty. "Pierre!"

"Over here, my friend," he said through Jake's shattered window. "Can you move?"

Jake winced at the lance of pain caused by the nodding of his head. Pierre was bleeding from a gash in his forehead, but otherwise he seemed all right. "I think so."

"Easy, sir," Samuel Bailey said. "You took quite a hit."

Jake reached for the door handle, realized it was not where it was supposed to be. Gradually the idea worked through his fuzzy brain that neither was his seat. Jake struggled to orient himself and realized his entire side of the car had been shifted over a full foot, sitting now where the gearshift had formerly been, resting up alongside Pierre's seat. His side of the car was concave, and he was jammed in so tight his legs could not even move.

"You will have to slide up and out of my side," Pierre said.

Jake nodded, fought down a moment's panic when his feet did not respond to instructions, breathed more easily when he finally managed to extricate one leg. Sergeant Adams stuck his buzz-cut and shoulders through what remained of Pierre's door and said, "Here, sir, let me help."

Limply Jake allowed himself to be gripped and tugged and pulled free. He half scrambled, half slid across and out of the door, then had to be helped to stand upright. He looked over to Pierre. "Are you all right?"

"It was your side that took the hit," Pierre pointed out.

Jake examined his friend. "Then why are you holding your ribs?"

"Colonel Burnes!" A familiar voice with its coldly polished tones called out. "I thank the heavens you are all right!"

"Back off," snarled a furious Sergeant Adams.

"Get out of my way, you oaf." An immaculate Dimitri Kolonov tried futilely to brush by the leatherneck. "Call off your dogs, Colonel, I beseech you."

But Adams was having none of it. He blocked the Russian's advance, then rounded on a second man, a heavyset fellow with the slanted features of a Mongolian. "Either of you try to take another step, and I'll make me a Russian sandwich."

"Really, Colonel, I must protest. This really does go beyond the bounds of decency."

Jake did his best to ignore the Russian, looked around, saw that their car had been pushed to one side of the road. The traffic roared by, unimpressed with just another roadside tangle of metal and broken glass. "What happened?"

"You got blindsided, sir." Samuel Bailey did not try to keep his words from traveling over to where the Russians stood. "We had these two in our sights, stayed between them and you the whole way, but just after we got through the village, this truck appeared out of nowhere and did its best to take you out."

Jake examined the wreckage, saw how his side had been bent to an almost horseshoe shape, gave silent thanks for the gift of coming out alive. "Where's the truck?"

"It backed out and took off," Bailey said.

"Not before the driver waved over at your little friend here," Adams added.

"This is preposterous," Kolonov snapped. "Such wild accusations are beneath men of our stature, Colonel."

Jake ignored the Russian. "Can we take your car?"

"We could have," Adams rapped out, remaining a one-man barrier against Kolonov's advance. "But our Russkie friends here managed to plow us into a wall."

"Outrageous. Colonel, I must protest. We were simply trying to avoid striking your unfortunate vehicle."

"You can go sell that one to the navy," Adams snarled, and shoved the burly guard hard when he took another step toward the group. "Back off, I said!"

"And now you resort to violence. Tch, tch, what a pity it had to come to this." Dimitri Kolonov gave a regretful smile and motioned toward a gap in the wall. Instantly two additional men appeared. "I regret to inform you, Colonel, that your man has provoked an international incident. These men are empowered by the Turkish Security Force and are here to place you all under arrest."

"They are as Russian as you are," Jake said.

"Acting as instructors to the local police, all official and aboveboard, I assure you." Dimitri showed a smooth palm. "I do hope you intend to come along without causing further embarrassment, Colonel."

"We've been set up," Adams snarled, trying to cover three directions at once.

"I thought there were more than two of them in that car," Bailey muttered.

"We are protected by diplomatic immunity," Pierre protested.

"Naturally, this must be checked out thoroughly," Kolonov purred as the two guards, joined by Kolonov's burly companion, began a flanking action. "But until such time as your consulates can confirm your official status, I fear that you must be treated as common criminals."

"It won't work," Jake said.

"Ah, but, Colonel, this is why your country fails so miserably at the great game. A delay here, another postponement there, and suddenly a new policy appears, making all your efforts futile."

Jake played for time, willing strength back into his legs, knowing he was not up to this. Not yet. He sensed more than saw both Bailey and Pierre begin sidling away from the confines of wall and car. "What is it that is so important about Kumdare?"

Kolonov gave the smile of a hungry cat. "A pity you shall never have the chance to find out, Colonel. I must warn you, my men are armed and prepared—"

A squeal of rubber, the blare of a horn, and a familiar voice shrieked, *"Jake!"*

"Now!" shouted Pierre, already airborne and spinning before the single word was out, slamming into one guard before the man had time to recover and go for his weapon. Adams and Bailey moved like a well-trained team, making short order of the other two. In the space of two breaths, the roadside was littered with three crumpled forms.

Pierre bounded to the waiting Citroen, pulled open the door, called back to Jake, "Anytime will do, my friend."

Jake refused either to limp or to wince. He moved stiffly but steadily for the car.

"I formally protest," Kolonov started. "This is a most—"

Jake looked through the open window as the Citroen rolled away and said, "Why don't you just blow it out the old kazoo."

"We are not out of the thicket, I fear," Phyllis declared above the sound of wind and roaring engine and squealing tires and a chorus of protesting horns. "Not yet."

"Their car wasn't in much better shape than ours, ma'am," Samuel Bailey pointed out.

"Unfortunately, most of their vehicles carry portable short-wave radios," Phyllis replied.

Pierre continued to look from Phyllis to Jasmyn and back as though to say, Look, see, this is how a woman should drive. "It is doubtful that a portable voice set would be able to reach Istanbul."

"They are highly amplified," Phyllis replied. "The most modern available."

Jake slid down another notch, so that the wildly swinging scene in front was more fully blocked by Bailey's shoulders. "How do you know all this?"

"I told you about the Circle of Friends," Sally said. She was wedged so tightly into the backseat that even turning toward him was an effort. She asked for the tenth time, "Are you sure you're all right?"

"Fine, just a little bruised."

"You look so pale."

Jake winced as the great black Citroen hurtled around a slow-moving cart, into the flow of incoming traffic and back again so fast it was hard to believe it actually happened. He held grimly to his thought rather than give in to the rising terror. This woman was worse than Pierre. "No amateur organization would make it a practice of knowing the type of equipment carried by Soviet spies."

"Speaking of amateurs," Pierre murmured from the other side of the backseat, "my hat goes off to you, madame. I would be most grateful for the chance to take driving lessons from you someday."

Corporal Bailey swung around to nod agreement in Pierre's direction. "I gotta agree with you, Major. Up to this point, I would have said you were the cat's meow. But this dame, I mean, Mrs. Hollamby here, she's in a class of her own."

"Nonsense," the old lady demurred, as a faint flush of pleasure crept up her neck. "I have simply adapted to the world in which I live."

The two Marines sat up front with Phyllis; Pierre and Jake manned the two backseat windows with their wives in between. Jasmyn had hardly breathed, much less spoken, since the journey began. The one advantage to their cramped backseat was that it kept Jake from bouncing about. Every inch of his frame seemed to be bruised and complaining.

From his corner position, Jake watched Sergeant Adams grimace and shut his eyes as they came within a hairsbreadth of plunging over yet another cliffside curve. It gave him a sliver of comfort to know the leatherneck found this journey as nerve-grinding as he did. "I still want to know—"

"You are quite right, Colonel," Phyllis calmly acknowledged. "It is both a relief and a pleasure to know that we have allies of such caliber. You see, my husband was more than simply the head of a British company's local subsidiary."

"A spy," Jake said, the pieces falling into place. "He worked for the British Secret Service."

A flicker of approval passed through the rearview mirror. "Just so. He was a remarkable man, my husband, and it was a pleasure to work alongside him. As his health deteriorated, he increasingly came to rely on me. His decline began at the onset of war, you see, and he felt it would be an absolute crime to let our side down. Then, within a ten-month period, I suffered the double loss of both my husband and my son. Despite all my prayers, the resulting void threatened to consume me. Thankfully, by then Whitehall knew of my own efforts and began to treat me as an agent in my own right. The pressure of supplying them with information helped enormously to see me through that critical period." Another glance in the mirror, this one directed toward Sally. "It was a true godsend, the fact of being not only needed, but actually important in such a crucial period."

Sally asked, "And the Circle of Friends?"

"All true," Phyllis replied. "And all amateurs. Which is one reason they have continued to remain such a valuable asset."

"And you are their conduit."

"Quite so, Colonel." Phyllis entered and departed from a village so fast that all they saw of it was dust and blur and a few scattered feathers. "And their filter. I fear the dear ladies in their unbridled enthusiasm pass on a great deal of chaff with the grain."

"I would be honored if you would call me Jake."

"Why, how very gallant. It would be an honor."

Pierre cleared his throat. "I still fail to see the need for concern over what the Russians will be able to pass back to Istanbul."

"As to the exact range of their radios," Phyllis said, "I am not certain. But I do know they would have been able to pass on the information through a more powerful channel."

"Of course," Sally cried. "The ships!"

Jake winced at the sudden pain of trying to swivel and look down at Sally. "What ships?"

"This way, hurry!" Despite the need for her cane, Phyllis set a pace down the boarding ramp that had them all trotting to keep up. The next departure was a passenger ferry, so she had blithely swung into a space far too small for her enormous vehicle, and led off on foot. She had timed their rush for the boat perfectly, for as the last of them scampered on board the ropes were cast, the whistle blown, then the ferry shuddered and started off. Jake leaned heavily against a metal pillar and searched the docks, but could see no sign of pursuit.

"Maybe she gave them the slip," Bailey offered hopefully.

"More likely," Pierre replied, moving up alongside, "they have decided to concentrate their forces closer to the lair."

"I fear the major is correct," Phyllis said.

Sally slipped her arm around Jake and asked yet again, "Are you sure you're all right?"

"How could he be? He has survived an attack from the Russians that clearly has rattled his bones." Phyllis pointed her cane toward a set of empty deck chairs. "Really, Colonel, I must insist that you sit down. Your day is far from finished."

Jake sighed his way over and down, as tired and battered as he had felt in his entire life. The group moved with him, settling into nearby benches, pulling over available chairs. "I do not see," Pierre said, "how you can be so sure this Kumdare site is truly intended as an observation post."

"Harry told me the same thing on the phone," Jake said. "Or tried to."

"It is the perfect location," Phyllis replied. For all her years, the day appeared to have left no mark on her at all. If anything, she seemed to have taken nourishment from the excitement. Her voice remained fresh, her eyes sparkling and alive. "This stretch of water is like the narrow neck of a bottle. Any ship wishing to enter the Mediterranean Sea from either the Caspian or the Black Sea has to pass through the Bosphorus."

"And those two seas," Pierre murmured, "are the locations of the Soviet Union's only warm-water ports. The only ones not shrouded in ice for several months a year."

"Precisely," Phyllis said approvingly. "Russia has sought to conquer Istanbul for centuries, back even when it still was known as Constantinople. Czar Ivan the Great went so far as to call it the key to world dominion. Capturing it would open the vast wealth of all southern Europe and northern Africa to direct attack. Britain has gone to war with Russia over this narrow passage no fewer than four times. After the last battle, a pact was finally signed that permitted Russian vessels free passage through the strait, but only so long as they carried neither weapons nor munitions."

Jake struggled to cast aside the rising wave of fatigue and demanded, "Then why all this subterfuge about a cultural center? Why not simply open up a watch station and be done with it?"

"Two reasons. First, because Turkey stands at the edge of a political precipice. And second, because too many of our politicians stubbornly insist on seeing Russia as our gallant ally. They have too much invested in this friendship to accept that Stalin and his minions are as power mad as the worst of the old czars. What they fail to accept is that the Soviets are seeking to gain through subversion and deception what they could not obtain through force of arms."

"They are trying to install a Communist government here," Sally offered.

"Not only Communist," Phyllis said, casting her an approving glance. "They want a puppet regime under Moscow's direct control. Even as we speak, we are witnessing the same tragedy happening throughout all of Eastern Europe. That is why this station is so vital to all our interests."

Despite his best efforts, Jake found it impossible to keep his eyes open any longer. The lids fell as though louvered down, the voices mingled with the rumbling motor and the wind and the cry of gulls, and he was gone.

Chapter Fourteen

"*J*AKE?" SALLY'S GENTLE hand rocked his shoulder once more. "We're there."

He groaned his way to wakefulness, feeling he had been asleep for less than five minutes, then groaned a second time when his muscles complained stiffly. He let Pierre and Samuel Bailey help him to his feet because he had to. Phyllis watched sympathetically as he tried to unleash his complaining limbs with a few simple stretches. "If it is any consolation, Colonel, the fact that the Russians went to all this trouble is a clear indication that they consider you a grave threat to their plans."

"I guess I should be grateful," Jake said, wincing as the boat jammed the dock and knocked them about.

"Be glad you are alive," Pierre said, offering Jake his arm. "When that truck appeared from nowhere, I thought we were both leaving this earth for good."

"Don't talk like that," Jasmyn said sharply. "Not ever."

"Come," Phyllis said, starting for the lowered docking platform. "Those waiting taxis will soon be taken."

By the time they made it to the rank of antiquated vehicles, Jake's legs and his mind were moving a bit more comfortably. He said to the two Marines, "I want you to take a second cab."

"Good, a plan," Pierre said, his mobile features rising in a vast smile. "I find great relief in the news, my friend, that your head is working once more."

Jake ignored him. "They'll probably be watching the consulate entrances."

"Most certainly," Phyllis interjected.

"We'll take one taxi and work up a diversion. See if we can get them to follow us. Then you two scramble over the side wall and make like greased lightning for the consul general's office."

"You can count on us, sir," Bailey said.

"An excellent plan," Phyllis said. "I remain most impressed with you, Colonel."

"If for any reason Knowles isn't available, head for Barry Edders. Tell him we have concrete proof that the Russians are sabotaging the construction of our observation post in Kumdare. Inform him also of the reason behind it, this sighting of Soviet warships making way for the Bosphorous, and through that into the Mediterranean, in direct breech of international treaty."

"Consider it done," Sergeant Adams assured him.

Jake turned to Phyllis. "I can't thank you enough for everything, ma'am."

The old lady raised herself to full height. "And just what do you intend to do," she demanded imperiously, "once you have managed to draw attention your way?"

"Run," Jake said, turning back to the Marines. "Everything depends on you getting through."

"Like the corporal says," Adams replied, his chin as aggressive as a battleship's prow. "We won't let you down."

Jake nodded, turned to Sally. "I want you to go with Phyllis."

"There is absolutely no way I am letting you go off on your own, the state you're in," she said, her eyes flashing fire. "So you can just put it out of your tiny little mind."

"And you, don't even start," Jasmyn warned Pierre before he could even get out the first word.

"Quite right," Phyllis said crisply. "I shall not be brushed off so lightly either, young man."

Jake looked from one stubborn woman to the other. "Listen—"

"You're wasting valuable time, Jake," Sally snapped.

"Indeed so," Phyllis added primly. "And just where on earth did you intend to run?"

"Heads up, everybody," Jake said, as their taxi rounded the final corner and the consulate gates came into view. "Here we go."

Their vehicle had the single grace of being large; the ancient Packard had no doubt once been a proud touring car, but time and neglect and countless miles of bad roads had reduced it to a creaking, amiable wreck. The driver was as friendly and elderly as the car and as tiny as it was huge. He was almost lost behind the massive steering wheel. A change of gears meant lunging to one side and ducking his head beneath the dash, momentarily losing sight of their direction, so he drove almost entirely in second. Jake felt his hackles rise at the thought of trying to lose a pursuit in this rocking bucket of bolts.

The simple fact of being the only person who could communicate with the driver had granted Phyllis pride of place. She sat erect in the middle of the front seat, with Jasmyn beside her. Sally sat in the back-seat between Jake and Pierre.

When the consulate came into view, Jake tensed at the sight of three cars and a dozen stern-faced men blocking their entry. A pair of Marine guards were arguing and gesticulating for the men to move their vehicles. They refused to budge.

Sally abruptly leaned across Jake and shouted through the open window, "Oh no, it's them! Quick, quick, let's get out of here!"

The angry arguing cut off as though a switch had been hit, and the men watched open-mouthed as the car ambled good-naturedly past their station. "Hurry, hurry, they'll see us!" Sally added for good measure. Then she leaned back and accepted the men's astonished gazes with a satisfied smile. "I think that probably lit a fire under them, don't you?"

Phyllis directed the driver down a narrow side street. He cackled delightedly and did as he was told. Jake shot a glance through the back window and caught sight of a Keystone Cops maneuver, a dozen men colliding with one another in a mad scramble for their cars. When an ancient building blocked them from view, he turned back and asked, "Any chance of going a little faster?"

"This appears to be the best he can manage," Phyllis said, pointing him down another lane more narrow than the last. "Besides, our best hope rests not in speed, but in subterfuge."

The old city's lanes were a maze of contradicting directions. Jake soon lost all track of where he was or where they were headed. Phyllis, however, did not waver for an instant. The driver followed her directions with affable chatter, clearly enjoying himself immensely.

They entered a small square and stopped before a cavernous opening. "This is it," Phyllis said. "Everyone out."

The driver clutched his pay in one hand and waved them away with a final cackle and a grin of dark-stained teeth. Jake eased the ache in his back and legs, asked, "Where are we?"

"The Grand Bazaar," Phyllis said, stumping ahead at a rapid pace. "And now I really must ask that we make haste."

Cool shade swiftly replaced the sun's blazing heat as they walked down the gently sloping avenue and entered the bazaar. Within the winding lanes, walking vendors sold sticky sweets from great wooden trays, while others advertised water and tea with creaking cries, dispensing their wares from huge copper urns carried on their shoulders. Shop displays spilled out into the lanes, colorful pageants of carpets or spices or bronze tables or gold jewelry, stacked far above Jake's height. Old men sat outside shops now run by a younger generation, playing backgammon on boards so battered the triangular patterns were mere shadows on the wood. Their fingers picked and tossed the dice and slapped the pieces with such rapidity that from a distance the games sounded like a continual drumroll. Occasionally a youngster would come and whisper in an elder's ear; replies and advice were granted without a moment's pause in the game.

"Under the Christian emperors, traders from, Amalfi, Genova, Pisa, and Venice were all granted commercial rights on the boundary between Europe and Asia." Despite her rapid pace, Phyllis still found

both breath and interest to tell them of their surroundings. "The Grand Bazaar is the largest commercial site of its kind in the world and was established
and built for these traders, largely in the form you
find it today. Just as then, its sixty streets are divided
up among various crafts. There are more than four
thousand shops, backed by small factories and countless warehouses. Come."

She led them into a tiny store selling bright multicolored cloth for drapery and upholstery. She
stopped and shook hands with the stallholder, turning to introduce her gathering. The slender merchant
bowed his welcome and made a gesture for them to
be seated. Politely Phyllis spoke a few words, and
instantly his demeanor changed. He gave a second
bow, this one of hurried respect, then walked to the
back of his little shop. He glanced to ensure that the
front entrance remained empty, then swept back one
broad Venetian cloth to reveal a small door. Jake
ducked his head and followed the others through.

Behind was a narrow series of chambers, one after
the other, each occupied by a hand-operated loom.
The men worked in undershirts—not against the
heat, for the rooms were almost chilly in the en-
closed gloom, but rather against the closeness of the
air. As Phyllis led the others unerringly down the
constricted passage, the workers observed their progress without pausing in their work.

Phyllis stopped within an end chamber that obviously served as storeroom, empty and dark save for
the light from the previous chamber. She pointed at a
ring set within the floor. "I must ask the major to
kindly assist me."

"Most certainly, madame," Pierre said, and bent to
the task. The thick-planked door creaked and

groaned and reluctantly opened. Jake peered through, saw only blackness.

Phyllis lifted a battered lantern from its nail and carefully lit it. "There is a compass in the base. Be careful that you do not spill fuel when you take it out, for this is your only light."

Sally peered into the gloom and asked, "What is it?"

"The reservoir. Take care. The steps have not been used in years."

Even Pierre showed doubt over the sheer blackness beneath them. Phyllis gestured impatiently. "You must hurry. A boat waits at the base of the stairs. And be most careful." She jammed the lantern into Jake's hand. "Go directly north. About a kilometer away there will be a series of slits making a circular pattern of illumination. It is an ancient water tower. There are stairs leading up to a street-level door. I will be waiting for you there with a car."

Jake fingered under the lantern, undid rusty catches, pulled out an ancient compass in a cracked leather case. "You're sending us down into the sewers?"

"Listen to what I am saying," she said impatiently. "This was the city's water supply, built by the Romans. It is vast. A hundred years ago, two British explorers set out by boat to find the other side. They were never heard from again." She gestured toward the black hole. "Remember, go directly north. Do not stray at all from the course."

Jake watched Pierre gingerly feel his way down, bent over, and handed his friend the lantern. In the ruddy glow he glimpsed a small concrete station with dark waters lapping on all sides. He helped Sally and Jasmyn down, then looked at Phyllis. "What about you?"

Despite the gloomy shadows, her smile showed clear. "Who on earth would dream of making trouble for a harmless old woman? Now go. I will meet you at the water tower."

Jake was greeted underground by a sleeping head.

The stone guardian had long since fallen over on its side, the face now resting half submerged. Even so, it was broader than Jake was tall. He stepped onto the nose, grasped the ear, and swung himself up and over the chin. He stood and saw that attached to the back was a small rowboat. "It's here."

"So are they," Pierre hissed. "I can hear them talking above us."

Sally hesitated and demanded, "What about Phyllis?"

"We won't do her any good in jail," Jasmyn pointed out.

"Or wherever else it is they plan to keep us," Jake agreed, and eased himself down by a series of pitted footholds. He helped Sally and Jasmyn down to Pierre's waiting arms, watched them settle in the stern, then stepped into the unstable boat and centered himself with one hand on each gunnel. Once in the bow, he accepted the lantern from Pierre and watched as his friend stripped off his shirt and draped it over the light. Instantly they were enveloped in impenetrable gloom.

Sally started, "What—"

Pierre hissed for silence just as the darkness was illuminated again, this time by a flashlight beam from above. Not trusting the oars to move silently, Pierre lifted one out of the oarlock and gingerly steered them away. Voices called back and forth, the noise echoing through vast distances. Jake craned, searched, saw no end or wall or marking. Just a forest of huge pillars rising from the black waters, stretching out in every direction as far as he could see.

Quietly Pierre paddled on one side, then the other, steering them from one great pillar to the next, placing ever more distance between them and the searching light.

"We might as well admit it," Pierre said, not bothering to whisper any longer, and uncovering the lantern to reveal worried faces.

Jake leaned back from his turn upon the oars, agreed wearily, "We've gone a lot farther than a kilometer."

"We are well and truly lost." Reluctantly Pierre turned to where voices bounced and echoed behind them.

"I guess you know what that means." Jake massaged his back with both hands, searched the great vaulted ceiling overhead.

"It is our only hope of ever finding our way out again," Pierre agreed resignedly. "Here, my friend, let me take up the oars again."

Carefully Jake traded places, then tried to give Sally a reassuring smile as Pierre steered them around and back toward the echoing voices. She did her best to reply in kind, despite the worried light to her eyes.

It had proved far harder than they had expected to maintain a steady northward course. The vast reservoir was actually split into a myriad of chambers by pillars that grew into long sweeping walls. Earthen embankments rose like shallow shorelines, looming suddenly upward to connect with the ceiling high overhead. Jake held his lantern up high, recalled Phyllis's warning about the two British explorers, and hoped desperately they would at least be caught in time.

Time passed in agonizing dips of Pierre's oars until a flashlight beam split the darkness and a great shout of triumph sounded from close at hand. Soon a pair of boats were winging toward them, hemming them in, as more shouts and calls bounded back and forth around them. They were swiftly ringed by boats. Turks rowed toward them, under the careful supervision of lighter-skinned silent men. A rope was tossed and made fast to their bow. They were all too tired and dejected to protest as they were rowed back in the direction from which they had fled.

Wearily Jake assisted the ladies up and back over the great leaning face. He ignored the proddings and shouted orders, and climbed up the rusting ladder into the little storeroom. It was almost without surprise that the first words of English he heard came with the polished accent of a victorious Dimitri Kolonov. "You have given us quite a mad chase, Colonel. A pity that it must now end with you and your associates occupying a pair of rather dank and musty cells."

"I think not," another voice said, startling them all.

Jake raised his exhausted head, squinted through the gloom, and saw Consul General Tom Knowles stride into the crowded room. He was flanked by a grim-faced contingent of Marines. Knowles marched straight up to the dumbfounded Russian and said, "I am formally taking charge of these people."

Phyllis Hollamby's gray head appeared behind Tom Knowles. She smiled at Sally and explained, "When you failed to arrive, I decided, as they say, to call out the Marines."

Sally beamed back in undisguised relief. "I'll find the words to thank you someday, I'm sure."

Dimitri Kolonov's mouth worked several times before he managed, "Really, I must protest. These people have violated numerous statutes and must be held—"

"In protective custody under my personal supervision," Knowles snapped back. "I remind you that they are all holders of diplomatic immunity."

The Russian's eyes scampered frantically for another ploy, but he could manage only, "I must warn you, my superiors will raise serious protest at this affair."

"On the contrary, it is *I* who must warn *you*," Knowles replied, his eyes hard as bullets, "that you are on the precipice of creating a major international incident."

Impatient at this palaver in a tongue he clearly could not understand, one of the Turkish police grabbed Jake's arm and roughly pulled him to his feet. Before he could protest, a shrill lash of Turkish froze the room. Anya Ecevit stepped from behind the consul general to unleash a full barrage upon the Turks. They stepped back, clearly cowed by the onslaught. Only when there was a circle cleared about the four did she pause, turn to Jake, and say, "Are you all right, Colonel?"

"Fine," he said quietly. His head felt ready to burst from the aching fatigue.

"You don't look fine," Anya said. "You look beyond exhausted."

"Enough of this malarkey." Knowles dismissed the Russian and his minions by simply turning his back on them. "Sergeant, you and your men help these people along."

"Right you are, sir." The sergeant glided over and offered Jake a supporting arm and a grin. "It'll be a pleasure."

Chapter Fifteen

"*A*H, COLONEL, COME IN, come in." Tom Knowles was already on his feet as Jake pushed the door open. "Hope you're feeling better."

"Fine, sir." Two days' rest had restored Jake in both mind and body. Not to mention the lift he had just received when Anya Ecevit had greeted him with the news that Charles Fernwhistle had been recalled to Washington. Jake took the offered seat and nodded in reply to Barry Edders' broad smile. "Ready to get back to work."

"Glad to hear it. A great deal has been happening, and even more is left to do." Knowles nodded toward his political officer.

"Right." Edders made a futile gesture to straighten the folds of his rumpled suit. "As you have no doubt gathered, Europe finds itself facing more than simply the peril of war's aftermath."

"Soviet aggression," Jake offered.

"Exactly," Knowles agreed, too animated to release the topic to Edders' care. "One by one, the nations of Eastern Europe have begun falling like dominoes, entering into the nightmare of total Soviet Communist domination."

"There was a hurried conference in Washington the day before yesterday," Edders continued, "followed by an emergency meeting of both houses of Congress yesterday. Your findings were included in the President's address."

Jake sat up straighter. "What?"

"This is of the utmost importance," Knowles assured him. "President Truman has informed Congress that unless vital emergency aid is sent immediately to the prodemocratic governments of Greece and Turkey, within months they could both fall to the Soviets."

"Maybe even weeks," Edders added gravely. "We're talking right down to the wire here."

"In the face of this potential disaster," Knowles went on, "the President requested that a special aid package be offered to these nations, so long as they are willing to fight openly against Communist aggression."

"They're already calling it the Truman Doctrine," Edders said. "I saw it on the wire this morning."

"The aid you have been sent to handle is merely the first trickle of a growing flood," Knowles told him. "It is vital that two things happen, and happen immediately. First, that people such as yourself are chosen to handle the funds in a manner which remains totally removed from bureaucratic battles. And secondly, we must ensure that the disbursement of these funds fosters this country's democratic process and the growth of their private sector." Knowles eyed him gravely. "With your agreement I will offer my strongest recommendation that this task be kept in your most capable hands. It will be an enormous and largely thankless undertaking. But I could think of no one more suited to the challenge."

*   *   *

Jake glanced at his watch—a half hour yet before Sally was to join him for lunch. Sally and Jasmyn were like two excited children, full of plans to turn their vast apartment into a joint home. This ability of hers to go from sharing his work and his life to delighting in being a housewife amazed him.

Yet in his impatience to share the news of his appointment with her, time seemed to hang as still as the dust-laden heat. He looked out his window, where through the trees' leafy green towered ancient domes and minarets. Numerous mosques rose and fell like man-made hills.

Directly below him, the streets were a constant, tumultuous theater. Young men pushed great hand-carts bearing everything from logs to spices to carpets to bronze. A boy walked by balancing a folded cloth on his head, upon which was balanced a broad metal platter; on the platter was a pile of soft pretzels as tall as the boy. Jake watched him saunter down the slippery cobblestone lane, calling out to each passerby and doorway, accepting coins and pulling out wares, all without losing his balance.

In the far distance, Jake could catch a glimpse of boats nestled up to ancient docks or resting gently at anchor in the protected waters of the Golden Horn. There was a stillness to the noonday air, a vibrant sense of timeless energy so magnificent it made mockery of all human noise and strife and ambitions.

Jake swung about at the sound of a quiet knock at his door. "Come in."

Daniel Levy entered. "I hope I am not disturbing you."

"Not at all. Have a seat." Jake unleashed his grin. "It looks like your job is going to be more permanent than either of us had dared hope."

"You are staying on, then." The bearded man sighed his relief. "That is wonderful." A nervous tug at his beard, then he added, "My father will be pleased as well. He has asked when you will be returning for another lesson."

"Tell him," Jake replied, "I'd like to make it a regular event, if it's all right with him."

Daniel hesitated, his eyes downcast, then said quietly, "There is another side to the book you saw, the *Me Am Lo'ez*. I did not discover it until our lives were disrupted by the war, when we were settled in the camp. But it was there all along." He raised his head, asked Jake, "Have you ever heard the word *pilpul*?"

Jake resisted the urge to steer the conversation forward, much as his mind wanted to return to the gladness that the day contained. There was something here, some opening that his mind did not recognize, yet was clear to his heart. He could sense an opportunity, a purpose to the moment. So even though his head and his world clamored to race on and leave the opportunity and the quietness behind, he settled back and said as calmly as he could muster, "I don't think so, no."

"It is a Yiddish word, and means a meandering argument with no real purpose or direction. Like many such expressions, it has a meaning that can only be understood through example." The dark gaze turned away and inward, not seeing the room and the brilliant sunlight filtering through the window. "I must speak again about our internment during the last stages of the war. Conditions inside the camp were not too bad. Oh, the food was awful, of course. The barracks were overcrowded and always either too hot or too cold. The camp itself was utterly bare."

"I could never imagine," Jake said quietly, "being falsely imprisoned behind barbed wire and then talking about it as calmly as you do."

"My people have learned to endure much," he replied, his eyes distant and sad. "But that is not what I wished to discuss. I mentioned it only for you to understand that it was not as the camps which you have seen. It was a camp, yes, and it was very difficult, but our greatest battles were against boredom and uncertainty. We did not know anything, you see, not what was going on outside the wire, nor what was to become of us. The soldiers themselves had been ordered to discuss neither with us. Any wisp of rumor swept through the camp like wildfire, and as usually is the case with such, almost all the rumors were bad. Worse than bad. Horrible. A mysterious truck with no markings was either delivering poison for our food, or cement to begin building the gas chambers. Dreadful rumors. In many respects, they were worse than the camp itself."

He lapsed into silence then, his face drawn, his expression brooding. Jake watched him for a moment, then granted him privacy by turning his attention to the street below his window. A pair of youngsters struggled by, one pushing and the other pulling at a spindly wooden cart piled with a mountain of turnips. The boys could not have been ten years old, yet they looked born to the task of toiling down the sweltering street, almost as ready to collapse as the overburdened cart. A very harsh land.

Daniel drew himself back with a sigh. "Where was I?"

"I'm not sure," Jake said slowly, turning back around. "You were going to describe for me the meaning of a word."

"*Pilpul*, yes, of course. Thank you. The imprisoned young men were truly beside themselves, as you can well imagine. Most were married. They only took those over eighteen years of age, you see, and it is our tradition to marry young. Many had families, babies, and no news. No word of how those families were keeping, where money and food were coming from, whether they too were perhaps being herded into camps."

Daniel shook his head slowly. "It was an awful time for many. They turned to talk of violence, some against the regime here in Turkey, which was ludicrous, of course, a paltry handful of Jews plotting the downfall of a regime governing a Muslim country of some fifty million. What did they expect, that suddenly the impossible would happen and a Jewish leader would be elected? But they were young, and they were frightened, and logic played little part in their discussions. The majority began making plans to emigrate. To leave their home of centuries and begin anew in Palestine. The thought of a free Israel gave many the focus they required, you see, to believe that there truly would be a tomorrow."

Daniel paused a moment, deep in memories, then continued, "A few of the elders gathered with the ones planning to emigrate. But most realized that they could not pull up the roots of centuries and move to a country that did not in truth exist. The uncertainty of such a journey was, at their age, beyond their ability to imagine. So they retreated into Torah.

"Night and day they gathered, little groups banded together around this vast camp, growing in numbers until some contained as many as a hundred or more graybeards. They would sit, and they would argue. Not discuss. Not debate. Argue.

"Did they offer answers to the young men who drifted listlessly about the camp? Did they lead them in prayers for their release? No. They sought escape into the minute. They argued over things of no value. Items so intricately complex that none but their inner circle could follow, much less care about."

He picked up a pen, studied it, set it down, all without realizing what he had done. "I will give you one example. In the first volume of *Me Am Lo'ez*, there is instruction given over the prayers that one should say before opening the holy Scriptures, and again when completing one's study. The reason for this is clear. Reciting these blessings shows that a person considers the holy words to be precious and that the act of study is an act of worship."

Daniel shook his head at the memory. "But the camp elders, they took this simple instruction, and they elaborated on it. They tore it apart with their endless questions and arguments."

"I think I see," Jake said, recalling another passage, one from the New Testament.

"They spent weeks arguing over points of no importance. If a person is up all the night and begins the day with a Torah reading, should he first say the morning prayers or the Torah blessing? If a person is reading the Torah and finds an error—remember, all our Torah scrolls are written down by hand—does he say the final blessing when he stops? Should he first take another scroll and repeat the segment as it is correctly written? If another scroll is opened, should the first prayer be repeated?"

Daniel tugged angrily at his beard. "On and on it went, with the arguments raging back and forth, day after day after day. At a time when unity among the Jewish community was most critical, these elders, these leaders of our people, would gather in groups and declare that other bands of elders were heretics. Worse than the nonbelievers, for they desecrated the name of Torah with their wild opinions. Such comments incited rages which shamed us all. And over what? Details which meant nothing to us, to our plight, to those among us who were racked with fear and worry and pain."

Daniel shook his head again bitterly. "That is why I have resisted returning to my studies of the Scriptures since we were freed from the camp. I cannot help but remember where such studies led us in our hour of greatest need."

When he was sure Daniel was finished, Jake said carefully, "There was another Jew who condemned the elders of His time for just such a waste."

Daniel looked at him, his focus slowly tightening. "This is Jesus, yes? You are speaking of the Christian *messach*?"

"I mean no offense," Jake said quietly. "But I thought I should at least tell you that He too spoke against the leaders who did not see to their people's dire needs."

Jake waited, knowing that to press would be to drive the moment away, possibly close the door for good. Either Daniel wished to hear or he did not, but it had to be his choice.

Daniel sensed the patience as an invitation, and the hand working his beard calmed to thoughtful stroking. After a long moment he said, as much to himself as to Jake, "I have spoken to you of what has remained most troubling to my heart. You have listened as a friend. How could I do less?"

A friend. "Thank you," Jake said. "Can I read you something?"

"Of course." Daniel watched with widening eyes as Jake unbuttoned his shirt pocket and drew out his New Testament. "You carry your Bible with you?"

"I like to have it," Jake explained, hoping he could find the passage, "in case I have a free moment and want to stop and have a time of quiet."

"A time of quiet," Daniel repeated softly. "Such words from a man of such action."

"Here it is," Jake said. "Matthew 23:23. 'Woe unto you, scribes and Pharisees, hypocrites! For ye pay tithe of mint and anise and cumin, and have omitted the weightier matters of the law, justice, mercy, and faith; these ought ye to have done, and not to leave the other undone. Ye blind guides, which strain at a gnat, and swallow a camel!' "

Daniel eyed him gravely. "This Jesus of Nazareth said that?"

"He did indeed," Jake affirmed. "That and much, much more."

T. DAVIS BUNN, originally of North Carolina, spent many years in Europe as an international business executive. Fluent in several languages, his successful career took him to over 40 countries of the world. But in recent years his faith and his love of writing have come together for a new direction in his life. This extraordinarily gifted novelist is able to craft high-powered political and historical fiction, as well as simple yet compelling stories like *The Quilt* and *The Gift*. Davis's aim is to entertain and inspire. He and his wife, Isabella, currently make their home in Henley-on-Thames, England.